Praise for the Historical Novels
of Diane Haeger

❖

"In Haeger's impressive Restoration romance, King Charles II and his mistress . . . leap off the page. . . . Charles and Nell are marvelously complex—jealous and petty, devoted yet fallible. Haeger perfectly balances the history with the trystery." —*Publishers Weekly*

"Engagingly deep romantic historical fiction." —*Midwest Book Review*

"Romantic . . . filled with intrigue and danger." —*The Indianapolis Star*

"Set against the vivid descriptive detail of Rome and Trastevere, Haeger's tale of how the ring came to be obscured in the Raphael masterpiece resonates with the grandeur and intimacy of epic love stories. . . . This romance is first to be savored as the wonderful historical tale that it is."
—*BookPage*

"Lush . . . [a] rich yet fast-paced story." —*Historical Novels Review*

"Spectacular. . . . Haeger explores the fascinating, rich, exciting, and tragic life of Henry II's beloved. . . . Lush in characterization and rich in historical detail, *Courtesan* will sweep readers up into its pages and carry them away." —*Romantic Times*

"With her wealth of detail cleverly interwoven into a fabulous plot, Diane Haeger has written a triumphant tale that will provide much delight to fans of historical fiction and Regency romance." —*Affaire de Coeu*

NEW AMERICAN LIBRARY NOVELS
BY DIANE HAEGER

The Secret Bride

The Queen's Mistake

IN THE COURT OF HENRY VIII

DIANE HAEGER

NEW AMERICAN LIBRARY

NEW AMERICAN LIBRARY
Published by New American Library, a division of
Penguin Group (USA) Inc., 375 Hudson Street,
New York, New York 10014, USA
Penguin Group (Canada), 90 Eglinton Avenue East, Suite 700, Toronto,
Ontario M4P 2Y3, Canada (a division of Pearson Penguin Canada Inc.)
Penguin Books Ltd., 80 Strand, London WC2R 0RL, England
Penguin Ireland, 25 St. Stephen's Green, Dublin 2,
Ireland (a division of Penguin Books Ltd.)
Penguin Group (Australia), 250 Camberwell Road, Camberwell, Victoria 3124,
Australia (a division of Pearson Australia Group Pty. Ltd.)
Penguin Books India Pvt. Ltd., 11 Community Centre, Panchsheel Park,
New Delhi - 110 017, India
Penguin Group (NZ), 67 Apollo Drive, Rosedale, North Shore 0632,
New Zealand (a division of Pearson New Zealand Ltd.)
Penguin Books (South Africa) (Pty.) Ltd., 24 Sturdee Avenue,
Rosebank, Johannesburg 2196, South Africa

Penguin Books Ltd., Registered Offices:
80 Strand, London WC2R 0RL, England

First published by New American Library,
a division of Penguin Group (USA) Inc.

First Printing, October 2009

1   3   5   7   9   10   8   6   4   2

LIBRARY OF CONGRESS CATALOGING-IN-PUBLICATION DATA:

Haeger, Diane.
The queen's mistake/Diane Haeger.
p. cm.
ISBN 978-0-451-22800-0
1. Catharine Howard, Queen, consort of Henry VIII, King of England, d. 1542—Fiction.
2. Great Britain—History—Henry VIII, 1509–1547—Fiction. I. Title.
PS3558.A32125Q44 2009
813'.54—dc22   2009021043

Set in Simoncini Garamond
Designed by Elke Sigal

Printed in the United States of America

For my children, Elizabeth and Alex,
who make me incredibly happy.

The Queen's Mistake

February 12, 1542
The Tower, London

"I swear by God, I have *never* abused my sovereign's bed!"

Wept pleadingly, the words were lost on the wind, one that blew over a nation that cared nothing for the young queen, nor the grim fate she steadily neared. Yet, horror-stricken, she spoke them still, a silent testimony to the truth no one wished to hear. "In the name of God and all his holy angels, and on the salvation of my soul, I am innocent of the crimes for which I am condemned!"

Pale and weakened by her three-month ordeal, Catherine Howard leaned for support against the railing as the barge swayed and bobbed on the water of the Thames, returning her to London. It slowly approached the forbidding Tower, the very place where six years earlier her cousin Anne Boleyn had lost her head over the very same accusation: infidelity against the king. Oh, how little she had dreamed in those long-ago days that she would follow in her cousin's footsteps and also marry King Henry VIII . . . and be condemned by him.

Surrounded by stone-faced Yeomen of the Guard, their swords drawn to keep her from bolting, Catherine gazed out across the thick, green tide of the Thames to the shoreline. She felt the breeze on her face. *Alive . . .* she was still alive. She was still free from the Tower, if only for a few moments more.

She had cried and pleaded for all of the days she had been locked away by her own husband, the king. She had confessed to the things she had done, and in the end she had even begged Archbishop Cranmer for mercy.

But there had been one final thing she could not do, and that was to lie about Thomas. No, she could never agree to that.

A moment later, the barge was moored at the Tower dock and a trembling Catherine, in a dress of stark black velvet and an unadorned French hood, was swept up the frost-covered steps. Only her sister Margaret, Lady Arundel, and her chamberlain's wife, Isabel, Lady Baynton, remained with her now. She and her companions were quickly escorted into the compound past the Tower Green. There, she would die the next day in the cold, gray February air.

If she had been given only a moment to face Henry she knew she could have changed his mind. But she had no access to the king and previously he had refused to see her. She believed she was being kept from him now because he would be able to see the honesty in her eyes, and her devotion to him, and Archbishop Cranmer would not tolerate that—not when he was so close to achieving his goal.

She knew her greatest crime was not a supposed infidelity, but rather that she did not believe as they believed. She was a Catholic in a Protestant country, and in a time of great religious tumult, Catherine Howard was too great a risk to leave as queen. Her destruction had been complex and utterly thorough. She had been young, naive, and entirely outmatched. She had just turned nineteen. The only weapon she possessed—the king's love for her—had been no help to her, because after her arrest and banishment to Syon Abbey, she was as far from King Henry as Cranmer could send her.

Now she had returned to London for but one day more. No one was to be executed on a Sunday. Her angry husband would show her some ironic modicum of respect, at least in that.

She was led to the Tower apartments, and after the heavy rounded doors were closed and bolted behind her, she saw the room was lined with rich tapestries and heavy oak furnishings. The cavernous, vaulted ceiling was ornamented with an intricate Byzantine fresco. But all the rest, wrought of old gray stone, was cold and Spartan. Catherine moved on trembling legs to the stone window embrasure and sank upon it, curling her arms around her knees.

"I should like to go bravely." Her voice shook as she spoke, and she gazed in terror through the small oriel window down onto the green.

As it had for Anne Boleyn, once again the scaffold had been hung with black cloth and strewn with straw. *Blood.* There would be so much blood that would flow into the hay and stain the block when they severed her head. Her mind filled with the terrifying image. Her heart throbbed, full of horror, fear pulsing with each heartbeat. She longed to cry out, *Cease this! Cease the madness!* Yet that would be pointless. Instead, she tried to calm herself with her own words.

"If I am to lose my head after all, I should very much like to make a good impression."

Both her sister Margaret and Isabel had been faithful to her since the beginning. Now they exchanged a glance, their faces pale.

"Your Grace shall do your duty bravely—if it comes to that," Margaret said haltingly.

"I think there is no other possibility now but for it to come to that. He will not see me, nor answer my letters. . . . He will not hear me at all."

Catherine drew in a ragged breath. Tears fell in glittering ribbons down her cheeks. *Henry . . . my Henry. How gentle, how loving you could be. . . . How have they made you believe the worst of me?* She pressed the unbidden thoughts from her mind. She had not wanted to believe he could ever do anything so barbarous as execute another wife. Especially her. She had been different, devoted, when he was no longer young or strong or healthy. She was the fifth wife, but she had been meant to be the last. Now she would die the same shameful death as Anne Boleyn. She too would soon be replaced.

She had been only twelve when Anne had died, but the horror of it had haunted her sleep for years. How could anyone butcher his own wife? Cut off her head so savagely? As a child, sometimes in the dark of night in the grim old stone manor of Horsham, she thought she could hear Anne screaming right before the ax fell. She would never forget the day it had happened.

Catherine had been with her mother in their manor house on the edge of London, not far from the Tower. They heard a shot, and Catherine felt it down to her depths. It cut across the crystal cloudless sky, called out, then echoed as a hollow, deathly sound.

Catherine glanced up and watched her mother's face. Her mother took her hand, her grip viselike.

"What does it mean?" the little girl asked, feeling the cold of her mother's hand.

"It means that your cousin is dead."

"The queen?"

"Cousin Anne has lost her head. And that is what the shot is telling the king, who has not the courage to witness the fate he ordered for his own wife."

Catherine remembered her petite, beautiful cousin, married to the King of England. Anne had been so kind to her when Catherine had been received at court last year. Catherine glanced up at her mother's face, not so pretty any longer. Continual illness made her appear far older than her twenty-seven years. It had bleached the girlish loveliness from her smile. Lines and parchment-thin skin now defined Jocasta Howard as a frail woman, as did her cold and brittle hands and fingers. Catherine would always remember the icy press of her mother's grip, as if she were not as full of life's blood as other women.

"What will happen now?"

"He will take another queen," said her mother.

"Will the next one lose her head as well?"

"I would not say it is impossible."

They walked on through the feathery emerald copse on the manor grounds.

"Mother?"

"Yes, my love?"

"What did Cousin Anne do to cause her to lose her head?"

"She was not wise with men, especially with her king."

Catherine could almost feel the descending ax, feel the column of her own slim neck in the wooden groove of the block on Tower Green. She shivered and squeezed her eyes shut. She knew her mother would not want her to cry for Cousin Anne. It was not safe now for any Howard to show sympathy for the executed queen. "Well, I am never going to trust a man. Then I shall never need to be wise."

"One day you must, my love. You are a Howard."

"Then will you help me, if I must? Choose for me? I trust no one above you."

"Darling girl, if you are very fortunate, the Duke of Norfolk himself shall choose your husband, and you shall need that, since your poor father is the youngest son and there is nothing left to him or us but his Howard name. You are already beautiful enough for me to believe the duke will one day extend that honor, though, and if he does you must trust him."

"But Uncle hated Cousin Anne," she cried, losing the calm she *had tried to maintain. "I heard Father say so! He worked for her death to save himself! Is Uncle not the reason she is dead?"*

"That came much later, when the duke lost faith in her. In the beginning, it was he who helped her to become queen."

Then, as if on second thought, the mother with the shadow of death upon herself tried to soothe her young daughter. "In the beginning, Anne was perfect for the king . . . and, my darling girl, you do so resemble her that it sometimes frightens me."

Now her mother's words from long ago echoed like ghosts in the room.

So much of what her mother had foretold that day had come true. Certainly she was correct in predicting that Catherine's future would ultimately be decided by the Duke of Norfolk. There was no one else who cared for or about her after her mother's death. Catherine's father, Lord Edmund, had remarried the moment her poor mother was dead, as his genteel poverty forced him to seek his way among wealthy women. Eventually he went on to find two more wives, one after another. His search gave him no time for Catherine, who was left alone with her Howard grandmother, who did not love her or want her. When Edmund died, Catherine did not shed a tear, because she had barely known him. Yet she knew she would carry the impact of his abandonment of her for the rest of her life.

To distract herself from these memories, Catherine turned to her two companions in the bare Tower room. "I wonder, my ladies, could you ask that the executioner's block be brought here to my chamber tonight?" she said haltingly, tears glittering on her smooth young face.

Surprised, the two women exchanged a glance. "Your Grace?" her sister asked.

"I should like to learn how to place myself upon it before tomorrow."

For a moment, her sister's quiet weeping was the only sound.

Then Lady Baynton said, "If it would be a comfort, indeed I shall ask."

Catherine did not respond, but drew back the brass latch and opened the window to gaze again upon the scaffold—stark and looming beneath the drab, gray sky. The terror built in her chest and ebbed again. She knew it would return. How could it not? From it, there was no escape. There had never been any escape for her from anything.

❖

The executioner's block arrived after dark and instantly dominated the room. In the flickering candlelight it loomed, square, low and heavy, its deeply carved groove—the place for her neck—in ominous shadows. As she willed herself to face the block straight on, Catherine's trembling began again. She drew in a shuddering breath, trying to force herself to move toward it. She wrapped her arms around herself and tried to still the fear. Yet the terror crept forward again, taking her over.

She would do this; she must do this now. It would make it easier in the morning. Slowly then, and with the greatest determination, Catherine took three small steps and sank onto her knees before the block. Her mouth was bone-dry, and there were no more tears in her eyes. She held her own hands out behind her back, then leaned forward and pressed her neck into the groove. She shifted lightly as her heart slammed into her ribs so violently that she could hear nothing at all, feel nothing but the flesh of her little neck against the groove. Behind her, Margaret gasped, then renewed her weeping.

This was the end, then. The end of nearly two years of caring for Henry . . . and yet desperately loving Thomas. The six particular seasons, where she saw now that her life had been forever changed.

They were seasons of being loved by them both, of making choices she did not wish to make, and the sacrifices—the unending heartbreak of never fully having the man she truly desired. Yet all of it felt now like just a moment in time. Together, the three of them had been shooting stars across the night sky, but one that had burned brightly was now meant to just die away.

Before Henry, she had been a simple girl with beauty and promise, harbored in a world of seclusion at Horsham. She had given Henry everything—given him her future and her fidelity. Yes, God . . . she had denied herself and Thomas what they desired most to give Henry that.

The one thing she had neglected to give him was the truth.

If I had known the cost of those early days in my sheltered country world . . . If I could change it all . . . If I could but return to the beginning . . .

SPRING

The First Season

"The best days are the first to flee."

—VIRGIL

Chapter One

April 12, 1540
Horsham House, Norfolk

*T*hey bade her to follow with their soft, lewd chuckles and their beckoning hands. Then they both disappeared in a swirl of skirts and linen petticoats as they raced around the carved landing post up ahead of her.

The stairs narrowed with each turn as Catherine followed, each landing darker than the one before. She gripped the banister, her heart racing. Joan Acworth and Katherine Tilney laughed at her and whispered behind their raised hands. They were mischievous fools, ladies-in-waiting and servants in the house and companions to the motherless noble girl of seventeen with no other friends, no allies but them. But they were also wild young women, and they put pleasure above all else.

"Hurry, or we shall be discovered," Joan said with a giggle, her red hair like a flame as she disappeared around the next corner, where Catherine was meant to follow.

"She shall join in again once she has seen him," she heard Katherine Tilney whisper of her with a muffled laugh. "She has the same Howard blood as the rest of that lot. She'll not be able to help herself."

They were waiting as she rounded the corner, just as she knew they would be, two young men from the village, standing with their hands on their hips. Both were wearing black hose, tunics, and white shirts beneath. Both were broad shouldered and, to Catherine, looked slightly foolish. One of the men, with a flat, freckled face and green eyes, took Joan and led her first through an arched doorway into an attic room. They went to a low table that dominated the room and was covered in draperies and dust-caked linen, and there they began to fumble with hose, petticoats and shoes.

"Watch and learn, Cat!" taunted the remaining boy as if she were one of them. "It is what your cousin knew well!"

"Pray, do not encourage her." The freckle-faced boy chuckled. His expression was piqued with a disturbing combination of lust and concern as he drew off a painted leather belt at his waist. "This is the very thing that killed poor Mistress Boleyn!"

Catherine hung back for a moment, but she was still unable to turn away. What was it that made something so foul, yet so powerfully alluring? Groans and laughter cut through the silence and passed across the heavy thud of her heart. Desire topped the sounds like foam on warm ale. The freckle-faced boy drew Joan over to a corner of the room and pressed her down onto the floor, onto a pile of folded draperies, his honeyed phrases whispered desperately in the shadowy, paneled attic room. Catherine gripped the doorjamb, feeling her own excitement rise. She closed her eyes but they snapped open again. *Mother, what would you do if it were you? There is no one to tell me that now. . . .*

"Shh!" bade the boy when Joan began to laugh too loudly.

She responded by playfully slapping his cheek. "Now, where is your spirit of adventure?" she teased.

"Consigned to hell with the rest of me, if the old crone catches us!"

But now the other couple had joined them, and Catherine stood silently watching. A pale shaft of moonlight through the row of attic windows cast the four of them in deeper shadows. Bending, moving, clutching . . . flesh against flesh . . . legs entwined.

And then, from the darkness and shadows, he emerged. He had been waiting for Cathcrine, as she knew he would be. It was not the first time any of them had played this game.

Francis Dereham moved toward her, tall and lean, his smile, as always, a slight sneer. Coils of honey-colored hair lay loose on his forehead. Even this part, the illicit nature of it, drew Catherine. There was something so dangerously appealing about being bad in such an otherwise dull existence. His lips brushed the nape of her neck. She felt her slender body tremble and a wild sensation rush through her. She had not liked him so much at first, as she had been overpowered by his self-confidence, and his always appraising eyes.

Then she had fallen in love with him.

Or so for a while she had believed.

He took her in his arms now and pulled her close. His sensual touch was a world apart from the awkward groping of Henry Manox and his fumbling, spindly fingers as they sat together practicing her lute, he pretending to teach her music. But those lessons were long over. That was before Francis had come to work at Horsham and everything had changed.

It was not long before Francis had her skirts raised and her embroidered linen drawers cast aside. It was not their first time. But the act seemed mechanical now that her love for him had begun to fade. Mechanical . . . and yet still there was a dark pleasure for Catherine in the act. It came from the knowledge that she had power over someone, or at least his lust, for a little while, if not over her own life.

She skillfully drew Francis to her, tightly wrapping her arms around his neck as his mouth came down on hers. His bare flesh was warm and oddly reassuring. *Do not tell me you love me anymore,* she thought. Lust was one thing, and she found her ability to command his desire an irresistible pleasure. But love was something else. She did not want that complication any longer.

When it was over, he began to laugh. Catherine pushed him away in response, drew her drawers back on and smoothed down her plain green dress with a flourish of indignation. It might all be a game, but she still had a romantic heart.

"You *are* going to marry me, you know," Francis declared, drawing up his own hose before he turned and stretched out beside her, his head balanced on his hand.

His laughter faded to the same sly smile that had won her so swiftly away from Henry Manox. Francis was arrogant and condescending, yet boldly sensual.

"You know that I cannot."

"Do you not love me any longer?"

"Of course I do," she lied.

"Then we are still troth-plighted, just as always."

Catherine felt a smile curve her own lips. It was good to have someone love her. Even if she did not return the emotion any longer, it gave her the feeling that she had a life apart from the dowager duchess, her grandmother, who tolerated her here at Horsham only out of duty.

"So we are betrothed." His smile grew. "But for now it must be a secret."

"Bit too late for that!" The boy with the flat, freckled face laughed as he stood across the room to adjust his own hose.

"Don't mind him, Cat," Katherine Tilney soothed. "He is only jealous that it was Francis and not he who captured a Howard prize."

The conversation was interrupted by a sudden thud, followed by the stamp of small feet on the ancient plank floor. Then they all heard the jangling of the old dowager's heavy keys.

"Catherine Howard!"

The voice was cold, clipped and full of reproach. How well Catherine knew the sound of it! The six of them scrambled to their feet, all in fear of its forbidding tone. More footfalls, heavy, angry— and more keys jangling. She was checking every door below, and she was too near!

"Pray, Cat, go, or she shall discover us all!"

Dutifully, Catherine went to the door, not thinking, only acting. Self-preservation—that key trait of all Howards, ingrained in their souls—took over. Out the door, wide skirts flying, heart hammering, she fled down the hall.

"Catherine Howard, present yourself at once!"

"Coming, my lady grandmother!"

The dowager was waiting on the landing below, her spine stiff and her face all sharp angles and hollows in the candlelight. But there was not a hint of color on her gaunt cheeks to bespeak her anger. She stood waiting in her widow's black dress, square-cut neckline hung with a chain of gold and pearls, her veined hand curled over the top of a carved ebony cane. Deep and heavy, the scent of ambergris swirled around the old woman in her gabled headdress bordered with pearls.

"I knew I should find you here. Were you not told to stay away from the attic rooms after dark?"

"I was, Grandmother."

"Were you alone in your defiance?"

The truth was a hollow thing. It bore no protection. Her grandmother's piercing black eyes sunken into hollows rattled Catherine as they bore down on her. *Confess the truth and save yourself . . . yet, reveal it and there would be no one for me in all the world.* There was nowhere to run, nowhere to hide. There was no choice.

"Alone, Grandmother."

"And those girls, they did not lead you to something up there?"

"No, Grandmother."

Black lace spilled back from her spindly wrist and wide bell sleeve as she pelted Catherine full-force across the shoulder, careful to avoid her pretty face. The blow from her hand sent Catherine tumbling back onto the steps, legs slipping out from beneath her. The back of her head hit the banister. Pain rocked her. She clamped her lips shut, refusing to make a sound. Her face blanched but otherwise there was no sign of the pain. Acknowledging weakness would only make things worse.

"Defiance shall *never* be tolerated in a Howard girl."

"Yes, Grandmother."

"You honor this family and at all times you do as you are bidden!"

Agnes Howard, Dowager Duchess of Norfolk, widow of the family patriarch, did not actually care where her niece had been. Catherine knew that well enough. The gaunt old woman's sole concern was the maintenance of order in the grim and sprawling household. An orphaned daughter of her husband's fifth son, Catherine received a minimal education in court manners, etiquette, dancing and music, out of obligation to the noble family name. She had not, however, received any inheritance from her impoverished father, who was too far down the line of Howard sons to have any property to leave his children. Other than the few mandatory skills she was perfunctorily given, Catherine was left quite unkindly on her own. In her loneliness, the only freedom, the only happiness she enjoyed was in memories of her mother—and in promiscuity.

Catherine faltered, yet only slightly. No one would have noticed it. No one except, perhaps, her mother . . . Ghosts . . . they were still and always would be everywhere. As if she heard a voice, she turned to look down the hall behind her. And she saw her mother before she'd died . . . and herself.

"How much do you love me, Mother?"

"As much as the moon and the stars, and to the disturbing exclusion of all else," Jocasta replied with devoted sincerity.

"But Margaret was your first, and Edward after that. Should you not love them just a little bit more?"

"You are special beyond words, Catherine. We are so alike, you and I. To me, you are the greatest joy in all the world, because in you I see all of the things I shall never be but shall watch in you with great pride."

The vision of her mother vanished with those words, but she did not dare to stand until the dowager had gone and she was alone again. Submission was part of the respect the old woman demanded. She had not earned respect, but she demanded it nonetheless. As she stared at the now empty hallway, memories of her mother flared and slipped away again. They disappeared into the pain and the unbearable ache of being absolutely alone in the world.

❖

The next morning, as the sky darkened for rain, Catherine escaped the drafty corridors and the cold, grand chambers, going alone outside and down the long flagstone path from the dining hall terrace. It led to the ordered parterre, with its rows of clipped yew trees fashioned into sentinel cones. From there, she began to run, going as fast as her legs could take her through the gardens and beyond. As she glanced back, she saw the manor become slowly smaller in the vista behind her against a broad expanse of gray sky. It sprawled on a hilltop, its many additions and infinite windows capturing and reflecting back the emerald green of the vast wooded area and undulating hills of Norfolk.

Once she had reached the apple orchard on an opposite hill, Catherine sank against the trunk of a tree heavy with bobs of bright red fruit, then drew her knees to her chest. Her full auburn hair had fallen free from its twist with the running. Curls tumbled down her back and shoulders, an unruly red-gold wave. Her skirts pooled on the ground around her, part of a slightly worn dress of plum-colored linen, with large puffed sleeves edged in old ivory lace. It had been pretty enough once, when the style of it had been in fashion, back when it had belonged to her second sister. Her clothes were never new, and yet no matter what she wore, Catherine was still utterly beautiful. Her skin was smooth, her eyes large and pale gray, and her shape small and slim. There was more than a hint in her of the captivating beauty her cousin Anne had been.

"I thought I might find you here."

She had heard no one approach. Catherine glanced up, feeling herself a million miles from the house, and even farther from the magnificent girl her mother had meant her to become. She looked up, shielding her eyes from a sudden steely shaft of sunlight that had broken through the clouds. Before her, Dorothy Barwick stood, stout and full cheeked. A Horsham servant, she was the only woman with even a modicum of tenderness for Catherine, and even that came in measured doses.

"Mistress Acworth told me what happened last night."

"Mistress Acworth is a wretched fool, and I am even worse for protecting her and the rest of them."

A glimmer of a smile crossed Dorothy's face, and, at seeing it, Catherine felt tears press against her eyes again. She hated feeling foolish, but she hated feeling weak even more. "I could not think how to tell her no."

"But of course *she* was not the only one you could not think how to refuse, was she?"

"Francis means nothing to me."

"Dear girl, take great care with that." The woman with warm, brown eyes, a full, fleshy face, and thick fingers knelt and touched Catherine's chin, her expression turning to one of empathy. "You certainly mean a great deal to Master Dereham. Anyone with eyes can see that."

"What else am I to do in this dull old place? All of the others do it and laugh about it afterward. Mistress Acworth says we are all just having a bit of harmless fun to pass the days."

"Did your mother not tell you that you would be chosen by the duke for something far greater than that? Did she not say that you were to keep yourself apart?"

"I told you that in confidence, Dorothy! You are not to go tossing it up in my face now. Besides, you know perfectly well my mother is long dead."

"Yet her dreams for you did not die with her, my girl. They live on as brightly as that charming light in your eyes, so very like hers."

Catherine shook her head and refused to feel the emotion that any mention of her mother always brought. That would come later, when she was alone in her bed to remember all that she had once had, and lost, in the woman who had always believed in her. "The duke cares nothing for me," she said angrily. "He never leaves the king's side anyway, especially now that His Majesty has taken another wife and needs to ingratiate himself to her."

"The princess from Cleves, they say, will not long remain number four."

Catherine felt petulant and not a little foolish for what she continued to do with Francis, no longer for love, but simply out of boredom and for the thrill of getting away with it. "Well, no matter my mother's dreams for me, *I* shall become nothing more than a country wife one day, just like all of the rest of you. I am practically a servant in this house as it is. I might as well enjoy your country ways."

"Oh, there is far more in store for you than that." Dorothy chuckled indulgently. "And sooner, perhaps, than you think. The Duke of Norfolk and his son have just arrived from court, and His Grace seeks to reunite with *you*."

It had been two years since she had seen her father's eldest brother, a man with thick silver hair and hard, marble black eyes, a man she had instinctively disliked since early childhood. He was loud and brash and easily unkind. But he was Lord High Treasurer of England and, along with Thomas Cromwell, second in power only to the king himself. Through sheer cunning, he had managed to escape the specter of his own niece Anne Boleyn's fall from grace, and to remain at Henry's side to counsel and advise him. Whatever Norfolk did in his life was for self-preservation and advancement, to the exclusion of all else. If he wished to reunite with Catherine, it was not out of any warm family feelings or nostalgia.

"Why should he wish to speak with me?"

"You shall discover that for yourself soon enough. I do wish I were you, though. It is all rather exciting."

"Do not ever wish that, Dorothy. No one in the world should ever wish to be me," Catherine said, sensing an encounter ahead, one that would determine her future and one that she would not like.

❖

In a straight-backed chair in the vast library, its walls hung with ancient portraits in heavy gold frames and massive bookshelves that smelled of beeswax, Thomas Howard, Duke of Norfolk, sighed impatiently and crossed his long legs. Knobby knees dominated scarlet velvet trunk hose with silver slashes. He wore a soft, tilted hat and a velvet doublet slashed to match his trunk hose and trimmed with costly silver braid. His eldest son, Henry, Earl of Surrey, stood beside him. More slightly built than the duke, and not yet silver-haired, Surrey had the same swarthy countenance, dark eyes, and tight mouth that commanded respect as his father.

The girl was taking far too long, thought the duke, and he was in no mood to indulge the poor relation that she was. He had surveyed all of the other Howard daughters, and there was no promise in any of them or he would not have come at all. Catherine's elder sister, Margaret, the only one with any beauty about her at all, was already at court and of no carnal interest to Henry. Norfolk had seen that for himself. Already a wife, she had no innocence clinging to her now—certainly nothing of a challenge for the old dog. King Henry was forty-nine, overweight, and not easily aroused.

But Henry's new fourth wife was just now selecting the members of her household. The time was right at last—old wounds well enough healed—to bring another relation forward. *If* he could find the right relation, it just might remove the dark stain of Anne, and the specter of his own involvement in that nasty affair.

The poor, graceless Cleves mare—how different and unappealing the reality was from the portrait that had preceded her! If she had but seen Anne Boleyn's mysterious beauty or Jane Seymour's gentle, seductive allure before agreeing to come to England, the German princess, with the square face and pockmarked skin, would have known she was not long for her place beside a king—or a man—like Henry VIII. In this game, one must consider all of one's moves, just as much as one must in war. One must plan and arrange. He had not survived so long by allowing events alone to dictate his destiny.

As always, *he* would dictate events and, thus, continue to thrive at a vicious court.

He glanced up to see Catherine sweep into the room, all unkempt and out of breath. Seeing her caught him off guard. Was it possible to change that much in two years' time? The echo of Anne Boleyn was strong upon her: The way she stood, the turn of her neck—even the color of her eyes; they were the same startling shade as Anne's.

"Your Grace." She curtsied properly.

There was a silence.

The Duke of Norfolk stood, cold and formal. But his gaze was upon her. Apparently his useless brother Edmund had actually been good for something after all.

"Come here, girl," he said more stiffly than he meant to.

Catherine's simple dress whispered across the polished plank floor. She lowered her head, but only slightly, then met his gaze again.

She was not afraid of him. *Good. Very good.*

"Have you no proper headdress?" he asked sourly.

"I do not like to wear it. I have only one, but it is old and it makes my head itch."

So she had something of a haughty spirit hidden beneath that simple, hand-me-down dress. Father and son exchanged a glance.

"Then you shall have a new one, and you shall learn to tolerate it. As you shall learn to tolerate much."

He was honestly stunned by her. It was not just her startling, youthful beauty, but it was the fact that she was here, locked away like some untapped treasure, and he was the first to discover her.

Suddenly, he was aware of his stepmother's steely, contemptuous stare as she sat across the room behind her embroidery stand. Norfolk did not like Agnes. In marrying her, his father had shown his weakness. He tolerated her only for the gossip it would cause at court if he did not. And also because she might prove useful. In her care of Catherine, his hunch apparently had been correct.

The girl was exquisite, and so perfectly virginal, so far out here where no one could touch her before the right time. She had passed those tests. But to keep Henry's interest beyond a bedding, there must be more. There must be something at least moderately clever about her that would resonate with a jaded, articulate and demanding king.

"Sit down with me, Catherine," he instructed. "Are you still called Cat?"

She sank properly into the high-backed chair opposite his, still looking directly into his eyes.

"That was a child's name, and I am no longer a child, Your Grace."

"How well I see that." He watched her face. There was something behind the innocence that assessed him critically. "How are your dancing lessons progressing?"

"I do respectably with the galliard, Your Grace, but only tolerably with the pavane."

"Easily enough remedied." A glimmer of a smile warmed his bony face before it disappeared. "And your mastery of the lute?"

"I have not had instruction for a month's time. But before that, I could play without anyone flinching awfully much."

He saw a hint of her father then in the way Edmund's slim mouth had fought a bolder smile, and Norfolk cleared his throat to vanquish it completely. That was what his father had done when he was trying very hard to appear stern before his children.

"I have Master Manox returning this very afternoon," the dowager interrupted, and Norfolk only then remembered the old woman was there. He thought of the carefully worded tale she had written to him. He doubted Agnes had told the entire truth about why the music instructor had been relieved of his duty. Indeed, there was an entirely different story he had heard. His son had offered a bit of money to a servant in his stepmother's house. Mistress Lassells was Catherine's bitter rival for the music teacher's affection, and she had revealed to his son that Henry Manox had fallen in love with Catherine and not her. Their frequent lessons and his roaming hands had been all the gossip in the old manor house until the dowager had sent him away.

Clearly the old woman had her fill already of inappropriate suitors, drawn like bees to honey by the ripeness of this pretty and potentially useful tool before them. But the duchess had confessed none of this to the duke. Instead, she had written only to inquire whether someone might be brought from London to fill the role of music tutor. The letter had arrived just as Thomas had observed the king tiring already of his Cleves queen, and so he had remembered that young Catherine well might be of age for his consideration. All other matters had been dropped, and there had been no time to find a proper instructor who could come out to the country.

"Wise of you to return her at least to her former instructor, Agnes," the duke finally said. "In spite of a bit of adolescent folly, she is a maiden still, I trust?"

"Maiden enough for King Henry's court," the dowager replied, smiling her dispassionate, thin-lipped smile. "So will she suit then?"

He stood formally, becoming fully the imposing figure he was to the rest of the world. "I shall let you know my decision."

"When? For pity's sake, Thomas, instruction is not without its cost. And if I were being asked to go on tolerating it all and arranging it for—"

"I shall send word to you from court by month's end. See that her dancing skills are brightened and that she can play 'My Own Heart's Desire' on the lute without mucking it up. His Majesty enjoys that tune above all others and despises when someone cannot see it through. Just in case, do remind the girl frequently that His Majesty is how he currently prefers being addressed. Now, we shall have a hot meal and a rest before we set off again."

"You will not remain the night?" the dowager asked in apparent shock as Catherine critically watched their interplay.

"In this old crypt? Goodness, no. I much prefer the comforts of civilization."

As he moved to leave the room with a sweep of his great black cloak, Catherine stood. "And the new headdress, Your Grace?" she called after him.

He paused and glanced at her again, this time with far more appreciation than he'd shown in the beginning. "You shall have a new French hood by tomorrow. And do learn to wear it with style while I am away," he said crisply. "They are all the fashion at court these days."

❖

"So how do you find our young Catherine? Shall we send her to be a lady of honor to the queen?" the duke asked his son as they galloped over the golden bracken back toward the palace in London. "Shall we not send her to London and see how she fares in his company?"

"Father, she is an innocent to the complexities of court."

"Ripe as a new spring plum, I say. Perfect for the old hound."

"But perfect for what?"

"For anything the king desires. Whore or queen, either choice would help our standing. For however long it lasts, she seems quite malleable and virginal enough—and the Cleves mare is certainly not long for the position. I am told His Majesty seeks to divorce her already, and she has been his bride for but a few months."

"Would we consign our own Cat to a fate like the Spanish queen,

or my poor cousin Anne after her? Even his wife Jane Seymour enjoyed no greater fate than death in childbirth."

"If Catherine can be useful to the family, by all means. At the
very least, we can present her as one, and hope for the other whilst
we wait."

"Father, you are a ruthless man."

"No doubt one of the qualities you most admire in me," quipped
the Duke of Norfolk to his son.

Chapter Two

April 13, 1540
Horsham House, Norfolk

or two young men who had grown up in the same village and struck an interest in the same girl, Henry Manox and Francis Dereham could not have been more different. Catherine was reminded strongly of that fact yet again the moment she stepped into the music room and saw Manox standing beside the virginals. His slim, slightly pasty face was, as always, alive with the same kind of worshipful devotion that had earned her disdain months ago when she had begun to notice Francis.

Henry sat dressed in unadorned beige velvet with an ivory collar, his slightly trembling fingertips moving onto the instrument as a blind man would touch things. When their eyes met, she knew that he knew what was about to happen.

"It is good to see you again, Catherine," he said, his thin voice holding a slight quaver.

There was a moment of strained silence between them. His fingers left the virginal and his hand dropped limply back to his side. At the age of fourteen, Catherine had been fond of him and she had waited for their lessons with girlish anticipation. She had even enjoyed the moments of their nearness as they had sat in intimate

27

proximity to each other, two stools side by side before the keys. Even now she could remember first becoming aware of the fragrance of him, not musky like her uncle, and not even largely male, but slightly sweet and vaguely seductive.

"It was you, was it not?" she said, still looking into his glassy eyes above a small, weak mouth. "Spiteful little thing that she is, Mistress Lassells told you, and you, hoping to gain favor, told Grandmother where I was last night, didn't you?"

He tipped his head, not denying the accusation, still gazing at her with the adoration that had begun to make her feel slightly ill.

"Shall we begin our lesson?"

Catherine moved nearer, glancing back at the open door to make certain no servant was listening this time.

"How could you do that to me? You knew she would flog me for it."

"Sadly, the path of last resort is sometimes the only means of making youth see the error of their ways."

Her eyes narrowed. "It was not an error of my ways when it was you touching me, was it, Master Manox?"

"Dereham is beneath you, Catherine," he declared in a pleading whisper as his eyes narrowed slightly. "He is just like all of the others. I am different."

Light footfalls beyond the open door silenced them both for a moment until they passed. Catherine drew nearer, sank onto a stool and took up her lute. The pleading never left his dark eyes.

"How could you have done that to me?" she asked again as she began to strum, entirely unable to play an actual tune for her anger at how she had been betrayed by a man she had trusted.

"Do you not realize how unfavorably you are being used by nearly everyone? How you are bound to be hurt by their ambitions?"

She stopped and really looked at him for the first time since she had come into the music room. "Not if it is by my choice, Master Manox."

"I am told you are troth-plighted now with Dereham."

Again there were footfalls beyond the open door outside in the corridor. It was now clear that someone meant to listen to their exchange. In this place she had grown accustomed to the notion of having no privacy, only judgment and punishment.

"Is it the truth then?"

Catherine felt herself tense even more, plucking at random strings only to make a bit of noise and maintain the impression of a true lesson between them. The nearness of Manox was almost repugnant to her now. He did not understand her need for adventure and excitement, here where there was nothing other than monotony and loneliness. He certainly did not understand *her*. Catherine had been a young girl of fourteen with Henry Manox, one with a girl's longing and a naive perspective. But that was her no longer.

There was no one here she could trust. She was glad to be leaving. Glad the decision about her betrothal to Francis had been made for her as well and she had not needed to break his heart.

It came to her then, as Manox sat beside her, piqued with expectation, that he was a man whom she had once believed for a moment in time she might love, just as she had later believed she might love Francis. But now he was a man who could ruin things for her out of jealousy, as pious Mary Lassells was trying to do out of envy. Mary may have seemed like an innocent servant, but she could not have been more different from the others.

"Mary is an evil, envious girl," she blurted out.

"Take care, Cat. That is all I am saying. I have tried only to protect you."

"I wish you would not be angry with me," she replied sheepishly, honing her skills at manipulating men for the pleasure she found in it. Henry was taken aback by her sudden shift in tone.

"I wish more things than you could ever count," he said, softly, walking toward her. "I still have the cap with our initials that you made for me." He reached for her hand.

Catherine took it, forcing a strained smile. "I'm glad. I would not want you ever to forget me completely," she said, knowing he'd hear more in her words than she intended. Yet she enjoyed watching him believe her. It was part of the game she was learning, and it was good practice.

After he had gone, Catherine felt herself smile. To someone so young, the feeling of total power over another person, like the power Manox's lust for her gave her over him, was utterly seductive. If there was a chance that she might go to court, that she might begin her life in truth, Catherine wanted more than anything to take it. Certainly more than she wanted either young man with whom she had so foolishly tarried for lack of anything better to do at the time.

❖

Mary Lassells was waiting for Catherine in the dormitory. It was late afternoon and everything in the long, vacant hall was gray with shadows and filtered light. The other girls were serving the duchess downstairs, so the two girls were alone when Catherine came into the room.

"How do you manipulate men like that and sleep peacefully at night?"

Catherine spun around. "So it was you listening. I am beginning to know the players at last, it seems, even though I am about to change theaters."

"It must be nice to know your future," Mary said coolly.

"None of us knows that. But I do know I am going to court, so you needn't concern yourself any longer with how I sleep, or do not."

They faced each other like two cats. "Henry deserves better. For that matter, so does Master Dereham," Mary said.

Catherine arched a brow contemptuously as she sank onto her small bed, slipped off her shoes and began to put on her other, softer slippers meant for dancing.

"Henry, is it? Does he call you Mary as well?"

"His affection for me is far from the foul things you have with men. We pray together and study, which is well beyond what a Catholic hypocrite like you would do. One who is bent on whoring herself for the family name at court. Although if you ever accuse me of speaking this way to you I shall deny it."

"We pray to the same God as reformers, Mary, just perhaps less critically. And you may wish to watch your tongue. I might be in a position one day to help you instead of being the rival you see me as."

"Help me off a bridge, no doubt. You fought me for Henry's heart, then Francis's, and won them both with your body, without truly wanting either. I would not trust you with anything I valued."

Catherine lifted her chin. "As you like. But never say I did not offer a truce."

"Oh, I shall never forget any of the words you have spoken to me—and others. You can be quite certain of that. Your face, your voice, and your choices are all etched into my mind forever."

Catherine looked at the plain-faced servant appraisingly then. "Apparently you do not read your Bible so well as you claim or you would know the Lord's commandment against envy."

"Trust me, Mistress Howard, you would be the last person I would envy."

She stood and brushed past Mary on her way to the door. "I wonder if Henry Manox would say the same thing once he knew you were in love with him and working against me while he was in love with me. Perhaps you should tell him the truth of your mortal affection for him the next time you are praying together, since that is all you have managed to get him to do with you?" Catherine said.

She paused for only a moment, then went out into the corridor without looking back. Just as she was with Henry Manox and Francis Dereham, she was relieved to be leaving Mary Lassells, who knew all of the things Catherine had done with men in the darkness of the dormitory and the music room—stories that could quite easily ruin Catherine's life.

❖

As promised, a beautiful and very fashionable French hood arrived two days after the Duke of Norfolk's visit to Horsham. It was delivered along with a summons. Catherine was requested at court to attend the new queen in her household as one of the noble maids of honor. Immediately, everyone at Horsham began to look at the young girl who had slept with the servants with different eyes.

With Katherine Tilney, Mary Lassells and Joan Acworth attending her, Catherine sat on the edge of her bed with nothing to do for the first time in her life. She was not allowed to help her old friends pack her own trunks. Silently, she gazed at the clothing and belongings strewn around the dormitory. These things before her were the sum total of her life so far. There were two dresses once belonging to her elder sister, Margaret, who was Lady Arundel; a chemise and stockings of her own; the pair of shoes for dancing, worn through at the toes; and in the center of things, like a crown, the new French hood.

It was blue velvet lined with silk and dotted with real pearls.

The absurdity of its elegance amid her worn things was bittersweet, she thought on a sigh.

But Catherine knew perfectly well why she was being spirited away to court: She would be trotted out like a fat, delectable Christmas goose, to be given over to whomever her family chose for her. She had heard how every worthy courtier patterned his behavior on the king's own. Having had four wives, and a string of mistresses, King Henry had a reputation that escaped no one in England or beyond. In spite of his middle age and how stout he had become at forty-nine, she had heard that he was still athletic, and still a powerful magnet for every girl who met him. At least, that was what she had been told.

She had personally been in his presence three years earlier, when he and Queen Jane had made their progress toward Richmond. They had stopped for the night at Horsham and been entertained by the dowager duchess.

As a girl of fourteen, Catherine had been surprised by how plain the queen was, her face pale, her features simple. Her voice was thin. She was the complete opposite of her cousin Anne Boleyn, and Catherine now realized that had likely been the point.

The king had not even noticed Catherine for the presence of his newly pregnant bride. Catherine had stood in the entrance hall amid a collection of others. Having dropped into a deep curtsy as the royal couple entered, she was singled out by her grandmother in no way, and not noticed by anyone except the young, unassuming queen herself. As Catherine had risen, she remembered now how their eyes had met, each holding the other's in an odd way, as if each knew the other. Catherine shivered now with the memory. She was thinking how that poor girl was dead nearly three years already, and that the child that had swelled her body that day had become the tragic cause of her premature death, as well as the king's heir.

The child was Prince Edward, the king's only legitimate son.

Perhaps it was that she was going to court now, to live in the household of the queen who had replaced Jane Seymour, that made the memory of that single meeting between them come alive for her again.

"Your Grace," Catherine had said softly.

Jane Seymour's smile in return had been small and yet regal. "You look very like her."

Catherine knew she had meant Anne Boleyn, and there was just a hint of spite in her words. The Seymour family ambition was nearly as strong as the Howards'.

"I do not remember her well, even though she was my cousin. I was too young when she . . ." Catherine thought whether to say "died" or "lost her head." She chose neither.

"I have seen the portrait at Windsor Castle, although it hangs in an alcove near the back stairs now." Jane Seymour had met her gaze then. "Walk with me, will you?"

Coming from the queen it was more a command than a request.

Catherine was full of fear that she would say the wrong thing and face the wrath of a spiteful grandmother absolutely bent on improving the Howard place with the king. The four ladies who accompanied her and Jane were more fashionably dressed than the startlingly plain queen, Catherine thought. Each was draped in velvet, sleeves slashed with gossamer silk, their gowns adorned with ribbons or pearls. Jane herself had begun as a maid of honor to Anne Boleyn when it was the Howard family in favor, not the Seymours. Things at court kept shifting.

"Do you find pleasure here?" she had boldly asked the queen as they strolled together beneath an arbor with pale pink roses tumbling over the sides of a painted lattice.

"I find I miss the peace of a simple life. Especially now," she *added, folding her hands over the large swell of a royal child beneath her breasts.*

"*In truth, Your Grace, I think a country life is overrated.*"

"*As court life most definitely is as well, believe me.*"

Again they exchanged a glance as they walked, each biting back a slight smile.

"*Seymours are not to find pleasure in the company of Howards, you know,*" *Jane said so softly that no one but Catherine could have heard her for the sound of the birds trilling from the lacy canvas of trees around them, and the brush of a delicate spring breeze over the gently rolling emerald landscape beyond.*

"*Nor are Howards to find friends among Seymours.*"

"*Doubtless you are told that, and wisely so. There is something unique about you, though, Cat. May I call you Cat?*"

"*Your Grace may speak to me as you wish in all things.*"

Jane smiled again as she turned to look straight ahead. "*I would enjoy having you about me to speak of the country idylls, which you know so well, and to remind me from time to time of them. I will speak to the king on the matter.*"

"*Respectfully, Your Grace, a Howard girl come to court, one who looks so much like Queen Anne as they tell me I do? The king would not want me in your company, I should not think.*"

"*She was never the queen; remember that, Cat,*" *Jane replied with a surprisingly firm tone.* "*The marriage was never truly valid, the courts found. His Majesty came to see that after the bloom of his passion for Mistress Boleyn had faded.*"

After my cousin could not give him a living son, was more to the point, Catherine thought.

"*I shall speak of you to him presently, though.*"

Again, Jane Seymour pressed her hands to her rounded belly—the pride in that gesture nearly as obvious as the pregnancy. "*Just now I do believe the king would give me the moon and the stars if I asked them of him. What is a simple duke's niece compared with that?" She softly chuckled. "He shall grow fond of you once he knows you, as he is fond of all my ladies, Cat. I know he will see you are nothing like Mistress Boleyn once he knows you."*

But Queen Jane's desire was never fulfilled. The child, Edward, had brought about his mother's death within three months of her offer to bring Catherine to court.

Catherine had never seen Jane Seymour again. Nor had she ever forgotten her.

"You've still not told him you are to leave, have you?"

Mary Lassells's question brought Catherine back to the present, and she again looked around the room strewn with her belongings. It was a moment before she realized the stout, malcontent girl had meant Francis Dereham. In a place like Horsham, with little to do but trifle, then gossip about it later, Catherine was surprised he did not know already. It seemed nearly impossible that he would not.

"I imagine he knows."

"The only person who might have dared to tell him, out of spite, is Master Manox, and your music instructor seems quite mute on the subject."

There was judgment in her voice, something Catherine had heard before, but never so fervently.

"You've taken his heart and used it, Catherine. A most unchari-table thing to do before God."

"Francis took other parts of me, Mary, so I trust before God it shall be viewed as an even exchange."

Mary looked away. "I shall pray for you in it."

"Your prayers sound like pity, and I do not need that, since I am going to court."

Catherine glanced over at the new headpiece, symbolic of so

much promise and duty, and the next moment she noticed the hem of Mary's dress, which was frayed and worn. The disparity seemed glaring in this odd moment when the stout, homely girl had revealed more of her envy than ever before. Catherine watched Katherine Tilney place two folded nightdresses into one of the open chests. The more blithe of her companions was unaware of the rivalry stirring only a few feet away. Catherine had never felt uncomfortable with any of the Horsham women, because she had believed herself one of them, and learned to behave so. Now, in an instant, everything had changed.

"Pray for me then, if you like," Catherine finally amended. "Only make certain He is the Catholic God of the true and proper church that you know I follow."

"I shall keep that in mind as with the many things I know about you already, Mistress Howard," said Mary Lassells.

❈

In a plain thatch-roofed cottage down a dirt road from Horsham, John Lassells, a little pig-faced, freckle-cheeked young man, pushed a gray, lukewarm leg of mutton around on his dish at the table. His sister, Mary, sat across from him, eating as well, and beyond her through the open window a bee droned, then disappeared.

They were not far from the manor house, yet they might as well have been a million miles for the difference between the dowager's residence and the cottage where Mary Lassells had spent her own childhood.

"She has not told Dereham yet, has she?"

"Nor has anyone else."

"Surely he has been told of the packing. Yet the poor fool goes around the estate like a lovesick pup, still bringing her tokens of devotion."

"As he should have done for me, if he'd had any sense."

Mary turned to gaze out the open window through which the fresh spring breeze gently blew. Everyone knew about the tokens Francis Dereham had given Catherine, as well as the scarf she had given him in return, embroidered inside with their initials. But with Dereham's tokens had come the understanding that they would one day marry. Catherine owed him the truth of the real destiny that lay before her now—even if he should have known it himself all along.

"Mistress Howard would say it began as a lark to them both, something to pass the time," Mary murmured flatly. "Yet it became much more to Master Dereham along the way. Because of the troth-plight he actually speaks of her as his wife to any of us who will listen."

Mary took a sip of ale and let out a sigh. "And yet it is a question whether that should be made her fault when he knew perfectly well she was a Howard. Her own uncle is the most notorious person in England for his ruthless ambition."

"Surely his reputation does not exceed the Seymours'."

"They are the same, I think," Mary answered.

"I tried to reason with her myself, but she is still such a frivolous girl," said the older Dorothy Barwick as she sat down beside Mary on the rough-hewn bench, and lowered a dish of mutton onto the table with theirs. "She seems completely incapable of understanding the consequences of her actions. For all of the education you girls seem to have foisted upon her, Catherine remains dangerously naive."

"The 'poor girl,' as you call her, has traded on her ability to seduce every man within a day's ride of Horsham to a future of luxury living beside the queen," Mary said bitterly, her own envy overtaking her.

"I don't suppose it is the queen with whom she is actually being taken to live. Not if the old duke has anything to say in the matter," Dorothy answered.

"You don't honestly feel pity for her, do you?" John asked Dorothy, his lips parted in an expression of pure incredulity, a spoon poised at his mouth.

"I pity anyone being tossed to the wolves. Especially a girl who goes to her fate with a smile because she has absolutely no idea what truly lies before her. You all bear a responsibility for the wanton girl Catherine has become. It was love she was searching for while the lot of you were purely pleasuring yourselves."

"You know not what you are saying," Mary snapped irritably. "I have changed, and I have tried to bring the others away from that pagan world. My brother and I have prayed for our sins and begged God's forgiveness for what was youthful folly."

Dorothy leaned back, gazing critically at the brother and sister at the table. "There is a price to be paid for all folly; make no mistake about that. It is only a pity that the poor dear who is about to meet that debt at court is poor Cat Howard. She has been trained here like a whore, while the old duchess turned a blind eye in case there would be some benefit. Catherine has absolutely no idea at all what is in store for her or what to do with it. You would both be wise, before God, to pity and not envy that."

❖

In a rich yet outdated riding costume of dun velvet, one she had borrowed from her grandmother, Catherine glanced around a final time at the dormitory as she waited for the horses to be brought to the front of the manor. She had lived much of her life here like a servant, and yet her heart was racing now at the thought of the great unknown that lay ahead. And, while she no longer loved him, and perhaps she never truly had, she realized as she was preparing to leave without even seeing him to say good-bye that a part of her would actually miss Francis.

Somewhere along the way, while learning how to play the game and to toy with men, Catherine had for a while actually cared for him. She felt a little pull of guilt upon remembering that. She did not love him any longer. She was uncertain whether she could ever truly love anyone, for the urge to survive overpowered her desire for anything else. But he had most definitely made an impact on her life.

"So then it is true?"

The sound of his voice, uncharacteristically reedy and trembling, startled her. He was so close behind her that Catherine could feel his breath on the back of her neck. But she did not turn to face him.

"How can you go when you are my wife?"

"Surely you realize we are not really married, Francis. Our troth-plighting was a game only."

"Not to me."

She turned around slowly to see him standing there, entirely bereft. His eyes, which were normally so brightly blue and full of mischievous pleasure, were bloodshot and misted with tears. His hands hung limply at his sides, as if all the life had gone out of him. His desperation brought a sensation of revulsion from Catherine rather than compassion. It made her think too much of Henry Manox, who had pleaded tearfully when she had ended things with him.

"I haven't any choice, Francis," she said in a low voice. "It is the will of my uncle, the Duke of Norfolk. You have always known who I am, not just who my grandmother treated me as."

"Ah, but *you* haven't known it." He shrugged his shoulders slightly. "And it was that part of you I foolishly allowed myself to love."

"You should not have loved me. It was folly. They were games we played, all of us."

"It would have been easier to cut out my own heart than not to fall in love with you. You have become a great beauty, Cat, full of promise. The Duke of Norfolk sees that as clearly as any of us. But he alone has the power to take full advantage of it."

"They say I look too much like my cousin Anne Boleyn to find any real favor at court. Her memory still looms large with the king. I suspect my uncle plans to use me rather as a set of eyes and ears to spy for him in the queen's household."

"And to make a good match with someone of his choosing."

"Yes, likely that."

Catherine glanced back at Dereham. "I'm sorry I did not tell you myself. I just really did not know how. Forgive me?"

"One last embrace in the bargain?" he asked, his charming grin for the moment returned.

Catherine laughed blithely for the first time in days, and let him fold her into his arms. She would miss that—the challenge and the little victories of seducing a handsome, sensual young man like Francis. She could only guess at the complications of the royal court before her.

"My lady grandmother and the Duke of Norfolk both believe I am still an innocent, you know."

Francis held her away with mock incredulity. "Do they truly?"

"Of course."

"And yet sending a kinswoman into the very seat of all power without the armor to do battle and triumph seems unwise." He lowered his gaze. "You are, after all, of an age, Cat, a babe in arms no longer."

"You are saying the Duke of Norfolk knows what I, what we—"

"Your grandmother does, at the very least, I should think."

"But she beat me for any sort of defiance or, worse, for any interest in men."

"To maintain her hold, quite likely, not halt your education. Did you not ever wonder why the keys to your dormitory were so easy for me to obtain?"

Catherine felt faint. "You are saying she has raised me up like a trained whore?"

"Perhaps she allowed things for the greater good. You said it yourself: You are a Howard, and one to whom much is given and from whom much is expected."

"And what do *you* expect of me, Francis? Is that not far more to the point?"

"What I expect is for you never to forget who your friends are, Cat."

As Catherine gazed into his crystal blue eyes for the last time, she could not help thinking that there was far more to his words than what he said. Thank the Lord she would be getting away from her past, for good. A new life, no matter what surprises it held, seemed better to her in light of what would be here for her if she stayed.

Chapter Three

April 1540
Whitehall Palace, London

*S*omething grand must be done before Catherine's arrival, and it must go with the precision of clockwork, Norfolk decided. There could be no error if this was to succeed as he intended. His son Henry was only one of two people whom he dared trust with his ambitious plan, the other man being Stephen Gardiner, Bishop of Winchester. He was a man who despised the enemy Cromwell almost more than Norfolk did himself. They were a triumvirate in his plan to bring the true Catholic Church back to prominence, to unseat Thomas Cromwell as King Henry's chief minister, and return the Howard family to ultimate favor with an increasingly volatile monarch.

The risks in it were nearly as great as the potential reward.

Norfolk sat in his apartments in the east wing of Whitehall Palace at his ornate writing table, with a crystal pot of ink and a box of sand before him. Wearing elegant gray velvet, with black slashings in his wide sleeves and a heavy silver chain across his chest, he was a formidable figure as he paused to consider the next sentence in the directive he was writing to his son, who was at their family home at Lambeth.

Until the moment was absolutely perfect, until he was satisfied that the groundwork was meticulously laid, they must bide their time. The marriage to the German Anne of Cleves was unraveling, as he had expected.

But could Catherine be clever enough to take advantage when the moment came?

The marriage between Henry and the princess of Cleves had been a disaster of epic proportions from the first moment the king had set eyes upon her. Seeing them together had been the single thing that had sent Norfolk to Horsham after the debacle of his other niece. Ah, no matter now. But Anne was four years ago, and his own standing at court had been renewed, if not quite yet his place in the king's trust. Those foolish snakes the Seymour brothers had seen to that, slithering in and taking prominence of place with their weak little sister Jane before Anne's blood had even dried on the block.

"Pardon me, but it is time, Your Grace."

Norfolk turned with a start. He dropped his ink-dipped pen, spraying the parchment black. He had been so deep in thought he had not even heard the door open to admit a portly and balding servant.

"Already?" he asked the servant, disregarding the onyx pool before him.

"The music has begun, Your Grace, and His Majesty has danced a tourdion. I thought you should not wish to miss another."

His dark marble eyes narrowed as he tossed sand on the wet ink before him. "Why did you not come for me sooner?"

"Your Grace did not answer the door, and when I called out to you some moments ago, you were most firm that I should go away."

"Yet you are here now?"

The servant inclined his head. "This time His Majesty the king sent me for you, so I let myself in."

Norfolk jumped to his feet and hurried, nearly at a run, down a staircase and across a covered bridge lined with oriel windows, then down the paneled corridor, shoe heels clicking across the intricate tile floor in the vast echoing silence. The lime-washed walls he passed were lined with massive tapestries and torchlight that flickered in the dim light of early evening as he neared the great hall and the sound of the music.

The banquet in honor of the new queen and her German emissaries had already begun when he arrived in a sweep of fur-lined black velvet. But there was an empty seat beside the king usually reserved for Cromwell. Since it was Cromwell who had orchestrated, then pushed for this already disastrous union, it came as no surprise that he was nowhere in sight.

Norfolk had been given a chance with Anne. Now he had a second chance.

Catherine must not disappoint him.

Her future and his own depended upon all she had learned at Horsham.

❖

Catherine stood in the courtyard of Horsham, putting on her riding gloves and gazing into the dry-lipped, scowling expression of her grandmother, who had come out grudgingly to bid her farewell. A cool breeze blew across the gently rolling terrain as Catherine curtsied properly to the woman who had been more keeper than relation.

"Remember," the dour old woman finally said, "you're going to court with nothing beyond your passable looks and your Howard name. If you are very, very fortunate, you may become a maid of honor, but your personal state of poverty keeps you no better than the girls with whom you shared that dormitory, unless you do something bold about it. Never forget that."

Catherine had an overwhelming urge to make a face just then, or to say something spiteful in response. She had been aching to do that for years, and yet she had always been forced into compliance.

"I understand, my lady grandmother."

Agnes arched a silver brow. "Do you? Are you certain?"

It would be impossible not to understand your contempt of me, she thought. "I do," she said instead.

"Do you also understand, somewhere in that empty head of yours, how that lark to seduce not one but two of my servants could put you in jeopardy of never making any sort of important match at court?"

"How would anyone discover such a thing, and why would anyone care about the indiscretions of a country girl from Sussex?"

The retort came tumbling out like marbles rolling across her tongue before she even knew what was happening. She stood stone still, but refused to drop her gaze from the dowager duchess's cold stare. But this time Agnes would not dare to hit her, not when her soft skin and smooth face were the only chance in the world to regain the Howard standing. Catherine knew it and belligerently took full advantage. The silence stretched on. Catherine still did not break her gaze.

"So you do have something of your cousin Anne in you, after all."

"Thank you, Grandmother."

"Pray only hope it is not the part that landed her on Tower Green, separated from her head."

Catherine felt a shiver deep in her chest, but she would not show it. "Everyone wishes me well, as I do them. They will speak against me to no one."

"A spurned heart is a dangerous thing."

She was not certain whether her grandmother meant Henry Manox or Francis Dereham.

"They shall marry one day and forget the past, just as I plan to do."

"And for your sake, and for the family's, I shall pray for that, since the alternative could be ghastly."

Suddenly, before she could say anything more, the old woman drew something from a pocket in her blue slashed bell sleeve. A ruby suspended from a silver chain glittered in the sunlight through the clouds as she held it out to Catherine.

"My husband, the duke, gave this to your mother on her wedding day. He thought it might bring her luck. It quite obviously brought her no benefit. So, since I have no use for it . . ."

Her words fell away as she awkwardly offered the chain to Catherine. She reached out her hand and took the precious piece of the past her grandmother offered. She had so few things by which to remember her mother. There was no painted likeness, no letter. Only one linen-and-lace chemise had been left to her, one Catherine greedily guarded. Now there was this personal offering from a woman with whom she had felt no personal connection at all before now. As they stood near the entrance to the manor, a breeze whistled softly through the bough of evergreen trees above them.

"Did she wear it?" Catherine's voice was shallow, and she could barely force herself to speak.

"Out of duty to him, whenever she visited my husband, yes, Jocasta wore it prominently."

So at least it had touched her skin. It had been a part of her, Catherine thought. Now it offered a connection to the only time in her life when she had been the recipient of real affection.

Catherine placed the necklace at her own throat and clasped

it behind her neck without breaking her grandmother's gaze. She vowed she would always wear it to remind herself of what she had lost upon her mother's death, when she was forced to this sheltered, verdant countryside. There had been no love or affection for her here, but she would try to find that again at court . . . if some courtier, suitable to her uncle's purposes, might actually come to love her. She had been training herself for a long time to find just that.

❈

Dorothy Barwick had been personally chosen by the dowager duchess as companion and chaperone on the journey to court. But Catherine entirely disregarded the stout older woman and rode silently a pace ahead of her and the rest of their retinue of escorts and luggage, still feeling the sting of betrayal at how judgmental the servant had been. How like Mary Lassells Dorothy had become, she thought. At court, things would likely be no safer for Catherine, so she was determined to be even more careful about whom she trusted now.

As they rode across broad lands, meadows and marshy fields, then through rich woodlands, Catherine fingered the silver chain and the small ruby suspended from it. Her anger at Dorothy and memories of her grandmother helped her keep from longing for the comfort of the only world she knew. She must accept once and for all that she was only a poor relation in a slightly shabby hand-me-down riding costume, with nothing but a pretty face and an infamous pedigree to smooth a path. She would have to call upon her own wits and resources to make her way at court.

By the time they reached a monotonous forest filled with birds trilling and harnesses jangling, Catherine's mind flashed with fleeting images of the king she remembered, and the two of his four queens she had known, her cousin Anne and Jane Seymour. It made perfect sense to Catherine that her cousin Anne had fought for King

Henry, even at the moment of her death. For a king as tall, athletic and handsome as Henry had been in his youth, attracting the attention of any and all females had obviously been a matter of course.

From a distance, to Catherine, King Henry had seemed frightening, enigmatic and incredibly grand. What would he be like now?

Catherine glanced up at the lacy bough of trees above her as she rode and felt herself smile. Despite her modest beginnings, now that she was away from Horsham, the possibilities of her future truly seemed boundless. For the first time in her life she was free . . . free of the constraints of a strict grandmother and the general bonds of youth. She had resented life at Horsham, but she saw a purpose now, because all of that had brought her here and was moving her toward an adventurous life with the new queen. Perhaps there was even some noble courtier who could give her the life to which her name if not her experience entitled her. As she rode closer to London throughout the day, the excitement of it was a palpable thing.

"Cast off the old for the new without regret," she remembered her mother saying. She thought not of Horsham but of Francis Dereham. He would heal and find a proper wife. She glanced over at Dorothy, who was nodding off, chin to chest, eyes closed as her horse created a dozing rhythm beneath her. This really was all for the best. Catherine looked straight ahead and lifted her chin proudly. For the first time in her life she actually felt like a Howard.

Chapter Four

*T*he banquet hall at the king's palace in London was vast, with a soaring buttressed ceiling and paneled walls warmed by a series of grand tapestries depicting scenes from Ovid's *Metamorphoses*. The hall was lit by dozens of shimmering white tapers flaring in silver wall braziers and chandeliers above, and the floor was strewn with sweet green rushes. In spite of the massive space, the room was filled with the scent of food and unwashed flesh. The music, a volte, was upbeat, played by musicians placed above them in the gallery. But the sound did not suit the king's mood.

Norfolk sat beside him, Henry in his massive carved throne beneath the canopy of state, the collection of silver plates before them catching the lamplight. The duke watched from the corner of his eye as the king swallowed goblet upon goblet full of wine, never once turning to his other side to acknowledge his queen. Henry was in a particularly foul mood, and he had been since the morning, when he had relented to his wife's request to attend Mass with the German ambassador and her brother, the Duke of Cleves.

Norfolk watched Henry chew with the intensity of a goat. How forty-nine years, and the death of three wives, had aged him, the duke thought callously, taking a swallow of Rhenish wine. He barely touched his own food, but glanced out at the colorful collection of court ladies and gentlemen dancing in a swirl of fabric before him.

Where he had once been slim and athletic, then strong and burly, Henry now was rotund and slow, a great bulk of a man whose still-slim legs recalled a hint of what he once was. Yet even that was deceiving. One of his legs was infected with an abscess the physicians could never quite heal for him. Not even his purple velvet coat embroidered with pearls, gold cap studded with diamonds or the chains of silver that glittered near his throat could hide the loss of his vigor. His receding copper gray hairline, bloated face and ambling gait confirmed his age almost as much as the appearance of his body did. Where, as husband to Anne Boleyn, he had had hunting, hawking and jousts to keep him trim, now they were rare at best, and his most vigorous exercise was eating—and that he did in great volume.

Fearing reprisal for seeing the truth that His Majesty wished to hide, courtiers wisely averted their eyes and chatted amongst themselves as the king ate, but everyone was all too aware of the array of platters piled with venison, ginger goose and huge meat pies set before him. In a single day, the massive English court consumed together more than a dozen sheep, nearly twenty pigs, one hundred chickens, and well over a thousand loaves of bread.

Finally, as Norfolk had known he would, Henry wiped the grease from his mouth with a white silk cloth, handed it to the steward behind him, then leaned toward the duke.

"Have you yet thought of a way to terminate this marriage without my risking England's alliances?" he bluntly asked.

Norfolk had waited four years to be needed again. That seemingly simple request, which the king had made for the first time a fortnight ago, had begun the wheels turning on many things.

Henry had married Anne of Cleves to maintain the delicate alliances between England, France and Germany, and as king, he knew he could not disturb that balance now. Norfolk knew he must be mindful of everything he did, as his actions affected far more than the royal marriage bed. There was no room for error in his advice to the king. Cromwell was about to discover that well enough himself. Norfolk had battled the cleric and the Seymour brothers quite long enough.

"I do believe there is a way, yes, Your Majesty."

"Well, tell me, man! No time like the present."

But just as he was about to speak, the queen interrupted them.

"English is not simple, but I keep trying to speak it." The queen chuckled, her guttural Teutonic tone sounding almost like grunting.

Norfolk glanced past the king to the place on his left where the new queen sat happily chattering away in her achingly clotted and awkward English with her adviser, Earl of Waldeck. The music changed to a slower branle. It would have been easy to be overheard now. Her laughter in the relative quiet was a grating sound. Henry rolled his eyes and drained his goblet yet again.

"That is still the lady's constant refrain to one who attempts to address her in English." Henry groaned.

"Has the English tutor not met with the queen's satisfaction?" Norfolk dared.

Henry slammed the jewel-encrusted cup onto the table, and for a moment all eyes were upon him until he waved his fat, freckled hand, and the silk of his cuff spilled back beneath his sleeve. "Everyone meets with her satisfaction, because she is dumb as a post!"

"Forgive me." Norfolk wisely inclined his head.

"Yes, yes, well. But can I be rid of her then without seeming a tyrant to the world?"

"I am advised by the Bishop of Winchester that the marriage remains unlawful so long as it continues unconsummated. If we take that tack, then indeed Your Majesty is still actually unwed."

Norfolk watched as the king considered this possibility. He dared not speak further. Not yet. They both surveyed the dancing for a time, lovely court ladies in fashionable French dresses, slashed sleeves, long, tight stomachers, chains and smart new hoods of velvet and silk adorned with ribbon or pearls. Norfolk watched the king stir.

Henry was most vulnerable when he was in love or in want of love.

Either would do.

"My Lord Bishop of Winchester has met with Your Majesty's ministers and has posited that, as a first step, Your Majesty provide a personal deposition of the facts."

"And the political risk if I am seen to be insulting my wife, Norfolk? What of that?"

"It is a fine and delicate road to walk, to be certain, Your Majesty. Forgive my saying so, but what Cromwell has gotten you so hastily into may take great patience and skill to extract you from."

"Damn Cromwell to hell for his meddling, and for his eyesight!" He growled. "I believed the old bear. He assured me the queen was a beauty and I trusted him."

"As Your Majesty should be able to do," Norfolk replied calmly, driving the first nail into Cromwell's newly constructed coffin.

The queen turned to Henry then, as if she sensed she was being spoken about. Yet still her smile was wide, her nature enduringly sweet. Norfolk saw the effort she took to find a few words that would be intelligible to the king. Despite her attempts to be pleasing to Henry, when he thought about how many times the king had tried to bed her, even Norfolk grimaced. Her face was square and masculine, her skin was pockmarked, and her body was overly plump. Even when she was garbed in fine embroidered silk, the reality of how unattractive she was could not be masked any more than it could with Henry.

What made it worse was that Norfolk genuinely liked her. Anne was jovial, kind and compliant. If only she did not look so much like a horse. But it was precisely this that gave him the chance to elevate his own standing. Come to think of it, he really should be thanking Thomas Cromwell for his gaffe. *Ah, well,* he sighed to himself.

All truly was fair in love and war . . . and ambition.

❖

To Catherine, London was a dirty, dizzying tangle of horses, carts, stray animals and shabby beggars. They came at her and passed her, nearly knocking her from her own horse on narrow muddy lanes and twisted, cobbled causeways amid refuse-scented air. As she and Dorothy rode among a contingent of her uncle's guard into this new, foreign world, women hung from windows in timbered old buildings that sagged like tired old men unable to stand. Pigs and sheep moved randomly about, taunted by mangy barking dogs, all of whom left their pungent feces in the road. It was not long before Catherine could barely think or breathe through the noxious mix of dung and refuse. She was not certain what she had expected of the city, but it was certainly not this.

Even the briny scent of the Thames as they neared it was a welcome relief from the other odors. Catherine felt revived as she glanced at the wide waterway filled with barges and smaller bobbing vessels, banners and brightly colored pennons fluttering in the cool spring breeze. Then suddenly she saw, on the other side of the river, a vast maze of buildings, towers and gardens, all fronting the snaking, glittering Thames like a jewel in a crown. Whitehall Palace.

Once they crossed the river and reached the palace, she stopped her horse behind her grandmother's two groomsmen and waited while they addressed the Tudor guard standing at the massive redbrick gatehouse. A moment later the great iron gate, emblazoned with a huge gold letter H, was drawn back and their retinue proceeded through a stone archway that held a gallery. As they passed beneath it, Catherine could hear music and laughter coming from the rooms above, and she wondered if the king himself was there.

That single memory that she had of him flashed across her mind again; he was handsome, full of humor and so sophisticated. She could not quite imagine what she would do the next time she was shown into his presence. This time, they would not meet in the modest surroundings of Horsham, but at his own magnificent royal court. She only prayed she would not prattle on like a silly child, as she had done the last time when she was a child and he had visited their home with Queen Jane.

Finally, the party dismounted in the gravel-covered courtyard near a large door in a three-story stone building dominated by large mullioned windows. She glanced up and yet tried not to stare. She must try at least to look as if she belonged in a place like this. A moment later, two young women came through the door together and approached her. They were older than she was, yet sumptuously and fashionably dressed—one in a scarlet-colored silk dress with a square neckline, the other in green damask with great bell sleeves. Both of them wore chains of gold and pearls at their slim waists.

Catherine twisted her riding gloves nervously at the sight of them approaching.

"I am Lady Douglas," said the woman in scarlet.

"And I am the Marchioness of Dorset, but you may call me Frances."

Catherine curtsied to them, knowing exactly who they were. Both were the king's nieces, Frances being the daughter of the king's beloved sister, Mary, who had died seven years earlier, and Charles Brandon. Their love story from a quarter century earlier had become legend already.

Margaret, Lady Douglas, was the daughter of Henry's other sister, who had gone away to become Queen of Scotland. Henry VIII was well known for keeping those most dear to him nearby . . . unless they betrayed him.

"You're to follow us. We shall get you settled while the queen is at dinner with His Majesty," said Lady Douglas with a kind though slight smile.

Catherine turned back to Dorothy Barwick. For the first time in days, she felt a twinge of regret that Dorothy's journey was to end here, as this older woman was her last connection to the safety and predictability of Horsham. Once Dorothy left, she would be entirely on her own.

"Can you not come with me for just a little while?"

"They will feed us and give us time to rest. Then the dowager duchess made us promise to be on our way back to Horsham directly," she said in a kind, understanding tone. "This is something you must do on your own, child. Your uncle would not want me with you. I certainly do not present the right image."

Catherine felt the sting of tears in her eyes. "Forgive me for being angry these past few days. I know you have only ever tried to help me."

Dorothy moved nearer and pressed a gentle kiss onto Catherine's forehead. "You have been like a daughter to me, Cat, and I sometimes have behaved too much like a mother for my own good. Take care, dear girl. Watch yourself here. Behind all of the elegance are ruthless people, many of whom will see you as a threat to their own plans."

"How could I be a threat? I am here hopefully as a maid of honor to the queen."

"Never forget who your cousin was, or how she met her death."

With that, Lady Douglas interrupted them. "Follow us, if you please, Mistress Howard."

Catherine turned back one final time, unable to see Dorothy for the tears that now clouded her eyes. "I shall write to you."

"No, you won't, child." Dorothy smiled. "But I understand."

Catherine followed the two noble nieces compliantly then, without looking back again. She could not at that moment bear to see the familiar face a final time. They went through the open door and into the vast, cold north wing of the palace, then quickly climbed a wide stone staircase brightened by stained-glass windows bearing images of crosses and shields in red, green and blue. In the silence, with only the sound of shoe heels and the swish of skirts, her heart began to pound.

I really am on my own now, Catherine thought.

There would be no turning back.

The queen's apartments were a crowded, jumbled mix of German and English voices, which Catherine heard as she was shown into the stately presence chamber. The room itself was large and cold, with rich, intricate paneling on the walls and ceiling, and two great leaded glass windows curtained in sapphire blue velvet bearing the king's coat of arms woven onto the fabric in gold thread. The furnishings, however, were clearly German pieces that Anne must have brought to comfort her. They were heavy and ornate in style, darker wood than anything English, and adorned with brightly painted flowers and words Catherine did not recognize. Two women sat in a corner near the fire in high-backed chairs before a small table, silently sewing. They did not look up as she and the king's nieces passed them.

"Now then, you will attend Her Grace here along with us. She takes dinner every day at this hour, often with the king, and if you are not one who is chosen to accompany her to her meal you will remain here to dine with the rest of us. Then you are free to read, play cards or sew, as we all do, until she returns. Queen Anne is a fair and generous woman who likes her ladies happy, so I trust you shall not find your role among us too taxing," said Lady Douglas.

"Have I particular duties for the queen?"

For the first time, Margaret's rosy Tudor smile bore a spark of arrogance. "Maids of honor are companions to the queen, Mistress Howard. We are here for her pleasure, to accompany Her Grace in prayer, on walks, or to dinner, if it pleases her. Surely your uncle explained all of that to you."

"Or perhaps your cousin before her death?" chimed Frances with surprising condescension.

"I did not know the previous Queen Anne," Catherine replied, struggling to keep the tone of self-defense from her voice. Showing fear with sophisticated women like this could do her no good.

"We sleep with Her Grace in shifts, at her pleasure as well, one beside her, another on the small bed opposite her own. For those who do not sleep with Her Grace, there are other rooms attached to the household where you will be able to rest alone."

"And if the king desires to visit his wife for an evening?" Catherine could not resist asking, genuinely surprised that a woman so freshly wed would have a well-established system of sleeping companions with her ladies, and not her husband. But then she saw Frances and Margaret exchange another of their small, furtive glances.

"You really do not know?" Frances asked.

"Your uncle did not tell you *that* either?" Margaret Douglas chimed in.

"The king does not find that sort of pleasure in his wife's company." A third voice came from behind her. The tone was sweet and young but as firm as the other two had been. Catherine pivoted around to see another woman of her approximate age in a compelling green satin dress, with a heart-shaped face. Catherine could see beneath the crown of her hood that her hair was pale yellow.

"But they were married not even four months ago."

"Yes, and gossip is that Master Cromwell is about to pay for that particular mistake, in all likelihood rather dearly, if your uncle and my lord the Bishop of Winchester have anything to say about it."

"Then why am I here to be added to her household if Anne of Cleves is not to have a household at all for much longer?"

"You really *have* been out in the country too long, haven't you? Good luck at this court, with your lack of sophistication." Frances chuckled before turning away and walking over to another table that held wine ewers and goblets.

"Oh, Frances, you needn't be so harsh about it," the third girl said. "I am Jane, Lady Rochford," she continued, turning to Catherine. "And I do agree that you would do well to be cautious here."

"I am discovering that rather swiftly."

Viscountess Rochford. She knew the name. Of course, yes. Jane had been married to Anne Boleyn's brother, George. Jane's testimony against her own husband had helped send him to the block right beside Queen Anne. Catherine felt a shiver as she looked into the pretty, gentle face before her. These were not the simple girls of Horsham—that was for certain. She would need to be very cautious with everything she did and said from now on—most especially about whom she eventually chose to trust.

After the long trip and the trauma of being thrust into overwhelming opulence and a network of complicated relationships, that night Catherine found the solitude of her small antechamber bedroom jarring. She longed for the sound of laughter, the reassuring movements in the dormitory of other women around her, and the comfort of predictability that was no longer a part of her life. Catherine sat alone on the small bed in a room no larger than her grandmother's wardrobe. It was a drafty little space with a bed, a side table, a wardrobe closet, and walls unadorned but for the single oriel window. She drew her knees to her chest and wrapped her arms tightly around them. At the foot of the bed her trunk lay open. She caught sight of her mother's chemise and the new blue French hood. She would wear them both tomorrow for her introduction, along with her mother's silver chain and ruby.

And something else that had just arrived.

At the foot of the bed lay a suitably fashionable blue velvet gown to match the hood. The duke had made her wait for that. Another symbol of his total dominance over her, not only as the head of her family but also as the person who could tell her what to say, with whom to speak, and even what to wear.

Catherine laid her head on her knees and her loose auburn curls tumbled forward, hiding her tear-brightened eyes like a veil. She was meant to be here. It was the life her resourceful mother had hoped she would have. The life she might have had all along had she not been orphaned. Those days were gone, she told herself. And she tried not to think too much about what would happen tomorrow with these women of the court, and with a new queen who apparently was not in any more favor than she.

❖

Agnes held on to the polished oak rail of her staircase at Horsham as she climbed it with slow, labored steps. She was feeling drunk and, surprisingly, more than a bit sad at the absence of the little mischief maker. Catherine had been gone for only a single day, yet Agnes had actually begun to miss her, although she had trouble admitting that to herself. What would the excitement around here be now?

Yes, at least she would miss that. And having to pretend to dislike her.

The truth was that Catherine had always reminded her of herself as a girl, far too much for the good of either of them. Agnes did not want to revisit the past through one so young and beautiful with a promising life ahead of her; it only made her more aware of the fact that she was now nothing but an aging dowager.

The foolish child had no idea that Manox and Dereham had both been planned so that Catherine could hone her skills in the time-honored art of seduction. What courtier or king, after all, would ever desire a clueless country beauty for more than a meaningless tumble without the talents to capture, then keep him?

What Agnes had not anticipated was both boys falling in love with her.

Beyond that, Anne Boleyn had been a teacher in terms of what would be required of a new Howard girl. Just because Anne had lost control in the end, there was no reason to doubt the formula: Beauty. Resolve. Seduction.

Howards were not born and raised up to be anyone's fool. In that respect Catherine would be more than a small challenge, since she still had no idea of the full effect she had on men. But at court she would learn that soon enough.

He was waiting when Agnes came into her bedchamber, when she was weary and far from interested in seeing him. But it was their dance, as it had been all of these months as he rose up from village boy to page in the opulent house of a duchess. He was magnificent in his simple brown jerkin and nether hose, his coils of honey blond hair loose on his forehead.

Francis Dereham came to her as she paused near the door and

placed his hands on her shoulders in the precise way that she had taught him months ago.

"Did I invite you here?" she asked coldly, moving away from him and into the room, pausing only to slip off her shoes.

"You rarely do. Experience has been my teacher."

"As you sought to teach my granddaughter?"

"At Your Grace's request, as always."

What a mature woman of her sixty-three years had longed to believe, what memories of youth had forced upon her, had driven Agnes to more regrets than she could ever count. Years made women pathetic and desperate to rekindle their youth, and she was no exception, no matter what excuses she gave herself for beginning this dance.

She sank heavily into a carved chair beside the hearth, and he came to her just like always. She was angry that he was here, but she would have been angrier if he had not come at all.

Ah, the discontent of age, when mirrors and memories were the enemies almost as much as time . . .

As Francis knelt before her, she held out her bare left foot. He pressed back the hem of her dress in the way that months ago had become their custom and their prelude. It was the one thing he could do for her that she actually missed from a man. *Ah, Thomas,* she thought. *Look what has become of me with you gone. Once I was the social center of court. Entertaining all, confidante to the queen . . . Now I am reduced to seducing a lowly page boy.*

He was plying her toes with deft fingers, and her eyes rolled to a close with the pleasure of the sensation. As Catherine's life was beginning, her own felt nearly at an end, and the constant realization of that—along with the reason such a young man was truly here—made her angry all over again. Aging was repulsive. *At least that is over for you, my love,* her mind said silently to her husband, dead sixteen years already. He had been more of a companion in battle than a lover, but she missed his reassuring counsel most now. Yet she resented him nearly as much as she did her stepson, the current Duke of Norfolk, for making her a dowager. For making her feel so old.

For making her vulnerable to young men like this.

Francis pressed himself fully onto her, touching featherlight kisses onto her neck as though she were a mistress he actually desired. As though she were Catherine. Agnes pressed away her own sense of disgust, knowing what he likely felt by touching a woman of her years when there were so many willing girls upstairs in the dormitory. But age had its privileges. So did money and power.

After he had pleasured her and she had done the same for him, he stood to refasten his codpiece and Agnes yawned. It was an audible sound.

"You do not wish me to stay the night?" he asked, feigning a note of hurt.

"I have never wished it."

"I only thought that perhaps now, with your granddaughter gone, a woman like you might be lonely."

"A woman like me?" she repeated, angry anew for putting herself in this position.

She was useless here and slightly more than pathetic. Manipulating was the only aphrodisiac left in the world to a widowed woman of a certain age, and it had begun to occur to her only after Catherine's departure that even that paltry joy was now escaping her.

My house in London, she thought as Dereham smoothed back his hair, so predictable in his speed, so disappointingly like a colt rather than a stallion. He was more a bother now than the game piece he was when she knew she was sharing him with her own granddaughter behind the clueless chit's back. Youth really was such a predictable bore. As she watched him straighten his jerkin, Agnes realized, for the first time in years, that she missed court. She missed the danger. But most of all, she missed the sight of a man, his passion newly spent, gazing down on her with adoration rather than duty.

London. Yes. To the city. To the activity.

To the power.

She would leave this boy behind because she could.

Unlike Francis, her only duty was to herself. *Pitiful fool,* she thought.

Chapter Five

*C*atherine woke to a shaft of sunlight in her eyes.

As they fluttered open, she saw Lady Rochford looming over her, hands on her hips, gown in hand. Clearly, Jane was in no mood to tarry.

"Well, come on then. We haven't got all day. The queen is an early riser."

"Won't the king be—"

"I thought we made that situation clear to you yesterday." Jane gave a small chuckle, then pulled back Catherine's bedcovers. Catherine's skin turned to gooseflesh as she lay in a plain cambric shift and no cap. "Bets are being placed as to how long the Cleves woman will remain queen. Other wagers have gone out as to whether she will actually keep her head if she objects to a divorce. And Boleyns do know a little something about that."

Catherine struggled to sit up, sunlight shining in her eyes. That seemed an oddly callous remark from someone capable of such kindness. Boleyns and Howards were indelibly joined by divorce and death.

"They are married barely four months' time."

"I am told the king calls that a *lifetime*."

Then I am here for nothing, Catherine thought, feeling a little shiver of panic. Now that she had at last broken free, she dreaded an expedited return to Horsham, Manox, Dereham and the sour dowager duchess, which would certainly happen if there were no queen to serve.

Jane helped her into her shift, stockings, underskirt and the new blue gown from the duke, cinching the pearl-studded bodice tightly. Catherine smoothed out the long, wide sleeves and skirts, thinking the silver thread–lined blue velvet was the most elegant thing she had ever touched. She tried not to think about the hard boning of the stomacher, which prevented her from breathing. She stood before the mirror as Jane bound her hair tightly, drawing tears. A moment later, Jane placed the hood onto Catherine's head as Catherine watched her own reflection in the mirror before her.

"Perfect," Jane proclaimed. "Now a bit of alum. Your cheeks are pale as flour."

"I've not yet worn color," Catherine said hesitantly.

"There are a great many things at court you have not yet done, my pretty little cousin," Jane replied with a cryptic little half smile that faded quickly. "But Howards do them all sooner or later."

Jane went to the dressing table and selected a small silver pot from among the vials and bottles. Swiftly, she spun Catherine toward her, tapped a small bit of the contents onto each of her cheekbones, and rubbed it in roughly with each of her thumbs. "There now. You are presentable. We must go. We're late as it is."

Catherine followed close at Jane's heels, like a little dog, through the maze of rooms comprising the queen's apartments. They passed meticulously dressed ladies lounging, laughing and chatting in low tones, all of them glancing up at her appraisingly without missing a beat. Clearly she was nothing to any of them.

Finally they arrived before two liveried guards who still wore the black lion of Cleves as they stood ready. Jane nodded to them and, magically, the tall, carved oak doors were parted.

Catherine noticed the aroma of the queen's bedchamber before anything else. It was pungent, foreign. The grand room had few furnishings, save the massive oak bed, with the royal arms embroidered in silver onto its tester, and a row of chairs along the walls beneath huge, dark tapestries on heavy rods. As they crossed the carpeted floor and neared the bed, they passed by a large coterie of women and two men speaking in a clipped, guttural, foreign tongue. She felt her heart begin to race, and she wondered if she would understand them if they spoke to her, and if the new queen would be displeased that Catherine could not address her in her native tongue.

There was a duo of ladies at the foot of the queen's bed as she neared. The headboard bore the initials H and A above the year 1540 and was adorned with carvings of cherubs, one of them clearly pregnant. Catherine glanced over at the two women. She recognized them as her own half sister Isabel, Lady Baynton, with whom she was not close, and the fair-skinned, doe-eyed Anne, Countess of Hertford. As Catherine and Jane neared, the others instantly fell silent, glancing up guiltily, as if they had been speaking of her. Catherine felt her knees weaken further still.

She was quite terrified.

At the foot of the queen's heavily carved bed, where the embroidered drapes parted, Catherine and Jane each made a deep curtsy.

"This is her then?"

The queen's English was clotted, as if she had stones caught in her throat. Catherine realized that the aroma she had noticed upon entering the room was coming directly from the bed. A musky, odd perfume swirled around Henry VIII's fourth wife. Although she was propped up against a row of overstuffed pillows, Anne of

Cleves appeared to be drowning beneath embroidered bedcovers and a heavy fustian nightdress and cap. Her corn-colored hair beneath the cap was straight and matted, like a cobweb, but after the memorable beauty of Anne Boleyn and the quiet elegance of Jane Seymour, it was her face, more than anything, that surprised Catherine. Although she did not want to have an unkind thought about the queen, she could not deny that the woman was ugly.

She sat with a little pet marmoset on her lap, both of them eating apples and nuts from the same silver dish.

When nothing but silence followed the queen's question, Catherine dared to answer herself. "Your Grace, I am Mistress Howard," she said in her sweetest and most dutiful tone.

The queen looked up at her appraisingly in the awkward silence, as did the other women. A door clicked to a close behind her. There was the echo of shoe heels. A small half cough. Someone whispered.

"Approach," the queen directed. It was a single, taut word.

More unintelligible words followed as an older woman standing beside the queen, dressed in a gown of German design, leaned in to converse with her.

Catherine held her breath.

"Her Highness desires that the rest of you leave us," the woman instructed. Her accent was thick, but her words were articulate and understandable. The maids of honor quickly complied. Jane touched Catherine lightly on the arm, as if giving her a spark of courage, then vanished along with the others. Again, the sound of a door closing cut through the awkward silence.

"It was your cousin who was my husband's second wife," the queen sputtered out in words so awkwardly articulated that it took a moment for Catherine to understand them. "It was Mistress Boleyn who stole the king from his true wife. Pray tell me that ambition does not run in families."

The older woman who stood beside the bed, with her hands linked before her, rephrased the queen's comments until Catherine understood her entirely. Despite the challenge in her words, Anne of Cleves wore a gentle expression, and there was great kindness in her wide brown eyes. She, too, was a stranger at court, trying to find her way through an already tumultuous history of wives and mistresses. Doubtless the queen herself knew the rumors of her husband's disfavor and wondered what was to become of her.

"I am to tell you, on Her Grace's behalf, that I am called Mother Lowe. I translate for her and protect her interests."

"I am at court only by Her Grace's leave. My goal is only to serve her," Catherine replied.

The queen spoke in German in reply to that, and Mother Lowe translated: "'And to help me play the lute,' she says. She was told that you are tolerably skilled, and the king favors a woman who can play."

Catherine inclined her head. "It would be my great honor to try."

"See that you do more than try," Mother Lowe replied in warning. "Her Highness needs to depend upon those around her to help her standing with her husband, not hinder it."

"It will be my honor to do what I can," Catherine amended, unsure of what she could teach anyone on the lute that might impress the very discerning King of England. The queen recommended feeding pieces of apple to her pet marmoset. Catherine knew this meant the conversation was over. She was led to the door without ceremony by the short, silver-haired Earl of Waldeck.

"You did well, Mistress Howard," he said in a lowered voice, thick with the same accent as the queen and Mother Lowe. "Her Grace is pleased."

"May I ask how you can tell?"

"She invited you to help her, of course. That is a rare thing in a place where none of us are yet free to trust anyone." He leveled his eyes at her, which were nearly as gray as his hair. "See that you do not disappoint her. Everything is at stake for her right now."

She curtsied clumsily to him as he motioned for the guard to open the door. The meeting was over. In less than three minutes, Catherine had met the queen.

And she felt as if she had taken on the weight of the world for all of the expectations surrounding their new relationship.

❖

Outside in the privy chamber, the king's two nieces, Lady Douglas and the Marchioness of Dorset, stood with their ears pressed against the door. The royal guards stood at attention, ignoring their eavesdropping. The women were too highly placed by king and queen to bar them.

"Well?" said Frances to her cousin. "What do you think? Is she a threat?"

"That depends," Margaret answered with caution. "For whom do you fear the threat?"

"For the poor queen, who is foolish enough to befriend her. Catherine Howard is a threat beyond measure. She is everything Henry always craves. The precise type for which he gives up everything. Surely you can see that. She is rather like a cat alone with an unsuspecting little mouse. A fat German mouse without the sense to see that her greatest rival is staring her in the face."

❖

Later that afternoon, Catherine watched silently as the queen was dressed in a costume different from the one she wore to matins. It was not the intricate, somber ritual she had been educated to anticipate. There was much low laughter and chatter in German between Anne, Mother Lowe and the queen's stout personal maid, Gertrude.

The rest of the day was straightforward enough. The women attended matins in the king's chapel and walked the gardens with the clumsily moving queen in her square, heavy dress. In both situations, Catherine walked behind the others, and the only words spoken between the queen and her ladies, or the Earl of Waldeck, were ones she did not understand.

Her disappointment was immediate. She was not liked, understood or utilized. She was like a painted fixture, an ornament. She was up at dawn, dressed, bejeweled and perfumed, then bored beyond belief by the monotony of her day. At least Queen Anne laughed frequently, Catherine thought, as they strolled amid the trellised walks, fountains and marble pillars of the royal gardens. The only thing she had decided for certain since coming to court was that Anne of Cleves seemed a happy woman in less than happy circumstances. Her husband was displeased with her, and she could not even make her case in a language that would win him.

Three days passed and Catherine still had not been presented to the king; although in that time not even his wife had been granted the courtesy of being admitted to his presence. There was such monotony in waiting. In sewing. In listening to music. In reading. In the endless walks. In her self-enforced silence as the hours stretched on. She realized that life at court was not much different from at Horsham. His Majesty was either dining, resting or praying, according to the reports.

Each night, Catherine slept alone in the little anteroom above

the queen's apartments, and early each morning, as a show of friendship, Jane Boleyn herself came to talk with her and help her into a
new dress and stylish hood, like those of the other women. Yet she
was not one of them. Jane seemed the only one willing to speak with
her as the long, idle days passed. There was an ongoing competition
for the queen's favor, as well as the king's, among the ladies of the
queen's world, she quickly realized, but she was not considered a
player in the game at hand.

On her fourth day at court, when she had begun to regret yearn-
ing to leave Horsham, she met her uncle, the Duke of Norfolk, on
his way back from vespers on a stone path beneath a heavy gray sky.
He matched her stride easily as they walked behind the queen's attendants near the sundial and a little garden of primrose shaped into
a heart and a star. He held his hands behind his back and did not
look at her as he spoke. As always, he was dressed forbiddingly, in a
coat of black velvet with a collar of rare lynx.

"So you have found your place easily, I see."

"As easily as a lamb lives among lions."

Catherine had never seen the duke smile, but a slight expression
of amusement turned up the corners of his mouth now. "Much is
changing, child. You are where you are meant to be."

"I suppose it matters not that I do not wish to be here."

"You are in the household of the Queen of England. Be patient
for your turn."

"I am ignored in her household, my lord."

"These days are difficult ones for the queen. When you are
called upon, take solace in knowing that you will be ready," he said
encouragingly.

"But exactly who is it you expect to call upon me?" she asked
petulantly, and loudly enough that the Marchioness of Dorset
glanced back and gave a little scowl.

Catherine lowered her head.

"I do not yet know the path. Only the destination."

"How could you possibly know the future?"

She was angry, tired and suddenly more homesick than she had ever thought possible, and she really did not care what he had meant by his comment.

"I have asked the queen's leave to allow you to dine in my apartments this evening. It will do you good to reunite with your cousin, who has just returned to London."

Catherine did not like her cousin Henry, Earl of Surrey, any more than she liked the duke. She thought of him standing there at Horsham, leering at her. Like his father, he was the sort of pompous lout who was too interested in himself to be manipulated by a pretty girl or to actually care about her either. She trusted neither father nor son. But under the circumstances, an evening with family was difficult to refuse.

"Thank you, Uncle, for the invitation."

"There now." He smiled, looking more like a cat stalking its prey than an uncle concerned with his niece's future. That, of course, did not surprise her. "See how much nicer it is when you are accommodating? Even your color changes to that very pale pink that is so comely."

At the place on the grounds where two stone urns met the knot garden planted long ago by Henry's first queen, Catherine of Aragon, Norfolk stopped suddenly. Catherine glanced at the ladies as they continued on ahead of her, but remained with Norfolk. Control of her was his in all things. "I am told the queen desires that you help her improve her skill with the lute. I spoke highly of your ability, so the request comes as little surprise."

"She did mention it at my introduction. But I am no music instructor, Your Grace."

He chuckled at her, and the sound was condescending. "You will learn quickly enough here, Cat, that you shall be anything you are asked to be, so long as it helps you get ahead. I shall send an escort for you at two. See that you are ready," Norfolk said as he turned to leave.

Catherine had to run to catch up with the queen's other ladies.

✤

She wore the blue velvet to supper, her first gift from the duke, in hopes that it would please him. Jane had ornamented Catherine's hair with a circlet of pearls, much as a mother might have, but she did not wear her mother's necklace. Catherine did not wish to make herself vulnerable to a man who had so much power over her, especially a man she did not trust.

She and her escort were silent as they left their horses in the courtyard of Lambeth House, an imposing brick-and-ivy gated manor that lay across the river from Whitehall. In London, the duke stayed in accommodations at court, but he had been left this estate upon his father's death, which he shared with Agnes when she chose to come to the city. Catherine had heard the story many times. Since the duke was in the city most often, the house was done to his own taste, all of Agnes's things placed there during her marriage now removed. In their place were dark, masculine furnishings, walls covered by tapestries and heavy silver torches. Little of the duke's father's imprint or his wife's remained on the house. The slight to his stepmother, whom he had always only tolerated, was intentional.

"Welcome," said a young nobleman who greeted her nonchalantly at the door with an unexpected, easy smile. Catherine raised her guard against it. No one here seemed to show kindness without a purpose. "Please follow me. His Grace and the Earl of Surrey await you inside."

Catherine noticed that the well-dressed young man was handsome, near her own age, with rich, dark eyes. Perhaps the evening would not be a total loss if he was kept nearby, she silently mused. She could hear muted conversation as she neared the sealed, carved oak doors. But silence fell sharply when a liveried page opened the door with gloved hands to formally admit her. She found her uncle and cousin much as she had at Horsham—the duke in a high-backed leather chair near the fire and Henry Howard standing beside his father. Yet there were others present. A small, stout man with thinning white hair sat in the chair opposite the duke, and two servants stood beside him. To her greatest surprise, Jane Boleyn stood with them, along with Catherine's own elder sister, Margaret, Lady Arundel, whom she had not seen in over a year. By their expressions, it was more than obvious that they knew something Catherine did not. Jane was the first to step forward. She held out her hands in welcome.

"We were speaking of the queen," she said with a smile.

Kindness and sincerity. It made her wary. "That concerns me how, precisely?"

Jane's expression was alive. "Only that Her Grace, the queen, expects you to work with her tomorrow and the day after in preparation for a banquet where she hopes to play the lute well enough to impress the king."

"Your appearance is much improved since I last saw you, cousin," Henry said kindly, yet his tone sounded stiff and insincere. "You do surprising justice to costly clothing."

She thought better of the sarcastic reply she longed to deliver, waiting until she could fully determine what this evening was about and what they expected of her beneath what seemed like their wafer-thin cordiality.

A liveried servant announced supper, and Catherine walked beside Jane down the long corridor behind the duke and his son. She longed to ask Jane for the truth. She longed for a friend in this new and complicated world. Yet she had sworn at Horsham not to trust anyone until she knew the game players well enough. Out of habit, she nervously reached for her mother's silver chain, remembering only then that she had chosen not to wear it. As the party moved into the hall, with the aroma of cooked meats strong and inviting, she regretted its absence. She thought of the necklace as an amulet that could fend off harm, as her mother had once done for her.

At her uncle's long and polished trestle table covered with glittering silver, Catherine was seated between Jane and the pleasant-looking young man with the dark tousled hair who had first greeted her. As they dined on the first course of sturgeon, he affably introduced himself as Gregory Cromwell, son of the king's powerful minister Thomas Cromwell.

On her other side sat another distractingly handsome young man. He was taut and muscular, like Cromwell, with brown, slightly shaggy hair over his forehead, vivid blue eyes, and the trim whisper of a beard along the square line of his jaw. It struck Catherine, as the next course was served on silver trays, that he seemed as wholly inattentive as young Cromwell was attentive.

Something about the young man's eyes made her chest palpably ache. He was that attractive, near to physical perfection. Yet his cool demeanor put her off, and Catherine resolved to speak to Gregory Cromwell instead.

"Are you at court in my uncle's service then?" she asked, taking a swallow of wine from a gilt cup emblazoned with the Howard family crest.

"I always serve myself first." He smiled slyly. "But, in truth, I accepted a position in your uncle's household as a favor to my father, who wanted me to keep an eye on the duke on his behalf. But, of course, your uncle invited me to join his household only so he could keep an eye on my father through me. That's simply the way court works."

"And your friend, who is it that employs him?"

He glanced over with an expression of surprise, as if he had forgotten anyone was there. "Master Culpeper?" He chuckled almost too affably. "Oh, he is not my friend. A man with any true sense of our king's court cannot afford friends among rivals."

"Unless they are women," Culpeper suddenly replied. He revealed he'd been eavesdropping, but did so in a tone that so bordered on arrogance that Catherine took offense.

He was gorgeous, all right, and he knew it.

"I am certain you have your share of friends and rivals, Master Culpeper," she replied.

Catherine tipped her chin up in irritation and looked away. She suddenly realized what was disconcerting her so. It was not simply his good looks and cool demeanor. It was the fact that Culpeper was the first man she had ever met who seemed utterly indifferent to her beauty.

She was driven to spite him because of it.

Some of her emotion must have shown on her face, since he studied her for a moment, then exchanged an interested glance with Cromwell. The rest of the meal passed uneventfully, as Catherine found she did not know how to deal with a man like Culpeper, and she watched Cromwell turn his attention to speak with Jane.

As soon as the meal was over, Culpeper rose and went across the room, where the evening's musical entertainment would be performed. Catherine watched him for a moment, then turned away.

She found herself turning directly to Gregory Cromwell. Clearly he was keeping a sharp eye on her and her reaction to Culpeper. Now, as they rose together from the dining table, he took her aside.

"Take care with that one," he said with a slightly twisted smile. "He's one of the king's favorite young gentlemen of his privy chamber, and he well knows his power."

"And you, Master Cromwell? Are you anyone's favorite?" she asked, trying to flirt enough to show she didn't need a distraction from Culpeper.

"Not the way Thomas Culpeper is," he quipped.

"He seems arrogant and far too vain."

Gregory chuckled. "You would likely be the first young woman to believe you could not tame him."

"I did not say I could not. I simply would not wish to."

"There is nothing quite so appealing as a beautiful woman who knows what she wants—and what she does not," he mused.

They both smiled in a sudden show of camaraderie. If she could not befriend any of the women at court, the men would do nicely instead. Men were less complicated and far more predictable, as far as she was concerned.

They had crossed the large room to the other side, where a musician was now seated and was softly strumming a tune on the lute to entertain them. It was a pretty, distracting melody that Catherine knew she could play much better.

"Tell me, Master Cromwell, would you like to show me around my uncle's grounds? I could do with a bit of air."

She glanced over at Thomas Culpeper to see if he was watching her, which he was. She felt that was a victory of sorts. Meanwhile, Gregory had missed her prior glance to his rival, and was now beaming with pleasure at her suggestion.

"I would be honored, Mistress Howard," he replied, smiling as the song came to an end.

She decided she needed to do something to take her mind off everything in the world that was worrying her. She wished to forget, if only for a little while. At least, that was the excuse for her flirtation, and it was as good as any, Catherine thought, feeling the desire for a new bit of mischief. A little extra attention from a young man, at least, would restore her pride.

The gated grounds of Lambeth were predictably laid out in a forbiddingly formal pattern beneath the clear night sky. It was so like her uncle to have approved its design. Catherine linked her slim arm with Gregory's taut, muscular one as they passed two stone urns on pedestals flanking a separate path. He led her along the path, and Catherine did not object. He was handsome enough, and she needed reassurance that she had not lost all of her charms.

There was the rich scent of flowers and still, mossy water as they sank onto a stone bench, well hidden from the rest of the garden. As the crickets chirped in the cool evening, he drew her into his arms and kissed her. Catherine felt her body reawaken under his skilled touch. Her mind spun away from her worries as it always did in a man's arms, away from conflict and uncertainty and toward pure pleasure.

She was not shy with him, nor was he with her. They embraced and kissed deeply. A moment later, he grasped her hand and drew it down forcefully, onto himself. She did not object. She knew her behavior had long been considered promiscuous, but seducing men was the one thing in the world she knew how to do well. Besides, she thought as she kissed him again, there really was no reason not to while she waited for something else more important to happen.

❖

Norfolk watched her go.

The duke had made it his life's work to see everything—and to know even more.

Just as well the girl had lured young Cromwell out to the garden, he thought, fingering his goblet he had brought from the supper table while feigning absolute attention to the performance, even nodding in time to the music. Catherine could use a bit of practice on these more sophisticated court gentlemen. Clearly she had grown accustomed to having her way with gentlemen in the dowager's house, but honing one's skills never hurt anyone. These well-dressed, educated men were a different breed from the country bumpkins who dotted the estate at Horsham as plentifully as hunting dogs.

At least, he thought with a little smile, she had chosen to dally with the married and harmless Gregory Cromwell, and not Culpeper, who had clearly caught her eye. Culpeper was nothing, after all, but trouble. He was handsome, unmarried and dear to the king, but he went through well-placed women like water. And Catherine was a stunning but very silly little chit, too useful to waste on someone as dangerous as that. He would have to keep a sharp eye on her from now on.

Norfolk noticed a great commotion among his servants, which suddenly disrupted the musical performance. Servants were flying in and out of the paneled dining hall at Lambeth in a panic. His servants were like bees, or children—neither of which he favored. Norfolk watched disdainfully as three of his pages dashed to a window and peered down at the entrance courtyard below. But the duke was seasoned enough to understand the only thing it could mean.

"Your Grace, the king comes!" one of the young pages leaning out the window announced to him in a tone of hushed panic.

Norfolk groaned heavily, then heaved himself from his high, straight-backed chair. Flattering though it was to be called on like this by the sovereign, he felt a little as if he were being hunted, he thought. If he wished to host His Majesty at a moment's notice he would have stayed in his apartments at Whitehall.

An instant later, everyone sank into varying versions of their deepest bows and curtsies as Henry stalked into the room in a rich crimson cloak lined with ermine. His French hat was tipped to a fashionable angle, and the jewels at his chest nearly concealed his great girth, fleshy face and bearded jowls.

"Am I too late for supper, Norfolk?" Henry asked with a bemused smile turning up the corners of his wet little bud of a mouth.

"Your Majesty's presence is an honor, always," Norfolk flattered him as he went to greet the king with a wide smile trained into believability.

A place was quickly set at the banquet table, and the most elegantly upholstered chair was positioned beside Norfolk's own. With the king's arrival the music had abruptly stopped, and in the silence there was only the clink of dishes and silver as servants worked quickly to accommodate the unexpected royal guest, even though the meal was over.

"Sit," Henry directed the others standing about with a swat at the air. Everyone returned to the dining table. His bold signet ring glittered in the firelight as he moved toward the chair. He paused one final moment as a large silver goblet of wine was poured from a jewel-encrusted ewer for him.

"I am told your young niece is here dining with you. Where is the girl? I've not seen her since she was a child, but I hear she has inherited the Howard beauty without the Boleyn curse."

For an instant, Norfolk was surprised. The king had not made any reference even casually to Anne for four years. Norfolk was on guard now, wary of what Henry might say next, and how he should respond when it came to so volatile a subject. The king enjoyed toying with people—Norfolk knew that well enough from personal experience. But this seemingly spontaneous visit was the key to setting his plans in motion. One look at Catherine from the always-amorous monarch, and Norfolk could initiate the next phase of his plan.

Glancing around, Norfolk saw that Catherine had not yet returned from her stroll with Cromwell. He felt irritation begin to creep up beneath his elegant doublet and the heavy, glittering chain across his broad chest.

He turned to the page beside him and said, "Find her." In an instant, the young man slipped from the room and was gone.

Norfolk directed his attention once again to the king.

"Your niece is installed now in my wife's household, is she not?"

"Newly so, yes, Your Majesty."

"And how has she found it so far?"

"It is early yet, to be honest. Few of the women know her."

"Or accept her," the king replied with a little chuckle, taking a large bite of the lamb that had been served. He seemed not to notice or care that no one else at the table was eating. As he began rather sloppily and loudly to chew, his knobby chin bobbing, a bit of sauce dribbled onto his copper beard. "They are like cats, those women, sleek, beautiful, but capable of scratching your eyes out the moment they feel threatened."

"Eloquently put, Your Majesty."

"Is your Mistress Howard a threat then, Norfolk?"

Norfolk caught himself before he showed the surprise he felt at the blunt question. Was he asking if she was another Anne Boleyn? Norfolk decided to keep his tone and response light. "If you will permit a doting uncle, she is a beauty, certainly. But only the ladies themselves could say the rest for certain."

"I am told the queen has kept her at a distance since she arrived."

"I think perhaps that might have been the ladies' doing more than the queen's."

Henry arched a ginger eyebrow. "Any difficult lady in particular I should know about?"

"I am told of no particular lady, sire. It is only experience that is my teacher in this."

"And a wise teacher it is." Henry laughed as he swallowed a large gulp of wine, then belched. "The truth is, I wanted to have a look at your niece for myself. To see without my entire court looking on if there is a resemblance."

The resemblance he meant, of course, was to Anne Boleyn. No one dared speak of it, but Norfolk knew everyone saw it. There was no reason Henry would not also.

Henry sighed beneath his breath, shivered, then stiffened. "If only she had not argued with me so much at the end, Norfolk, especially over Elizabeth's place in things, I might have been able to spare her life."

Henry was more vulnerable to his unhappiness and to these bouts of nostalgia and regret than the duke fully realized. But Norfolk had an uncanny instinct for timing and opportunity. He could not have wished for a better scenario to set the first elements of his plan into motion.

Norfolk glanced back at the door. Where the devil was Catherine?

"Now then, speaking of Boleyn women . . ." said the king, chewing another mouthful of food as he looked across the table at Jane. His gaze settled there, and for an instant he was motionless.

From Henry's expression, it struck Norfolk that this was the first time in four years the two had been in such close proximity since Jane's banishment. She had only just recently been allowed to return to court. Even though she had testified against her own husband, who was Anne's brother, Henry had never seen Jane as an ally, but rather an unpleasant reminder of that dark and desperate period. Since her return, Jane Boleyn had remained in the background of the queen's staff. Until now.

"I wish to meet your little Catherine tonight," Henry said, fingering the goblet before him as he sucked his teeth. "If, that is, you can find her."

Just then, the page charged with finding Catherine approached Norfolk's chair to whisper into his ear. "Forgive me, Your Grace," he said, breathlessly, "but Mistress Howard seems to have gone missing."

❖

The next morning, not in the mood to be seen by anyone but his closest advisers, Henry sat slumped at a long table in his privy chamber back at Whitehall. Sitting with him arrayed around the table were the men who advised him in running the kingdom. Norfolk was there, along with both his rival Thomas Cromwell, and his ally Stephen Gardiner, Bishop of Winchester. Nearby sat Charles Brandon, Duke of Suffolk, who had been Henry's boon companion since childhood as well as his dear departed sister Mary's second husband. They were also joined by Dorset, who was married to Henry's niece; Thomas Wriothesley, one of the king's principal secretaries; and Jane Seymour's brothers, Edward and Thomas. It was not the public presence chamber beyond the double doors where he usually met with his privy counsel, yet this chamber was far from intimate. It was massive in size, and the walls were covered with tapestries, wood panels and tooled plasterwork. In the center was a grand alabaster fountain.

"So how do you advise me now, Cromwell? Do you *still* recommend the queen, even after four months' time? The King of France does not seem any more likely to side with us and against his new friend the emperor on this political issue. He's going to stand with those who stand by the queen. Are you willing to stake your life on her?"

As his question hung ominously in the air, Henry leaned back in his chair, steepled his stubby, freckled fingers, and watched the furtive, worried glances of his counselors. Each was happy, he was sure, not to be the one to whom the sovereign had directed his anger. Like a great wave on a turbulent sea, all eyes in the room shifted to the big man with the small, deep green eyes and the mouth that was turned down somberly at the corners.

The silence was deafening.

Henry waited. Norfolk watched.

A heartbeat later, Cromwell cleared his throat and leaned forward. "A way has opened up that could change the course of things, if Your Majesty desires to pursue the path."

The king arched a brow. His face was mottled red with frustration.

"I desired it the moment I laid my eyes upon my wife! And I ask you, my Lord Chancellor Cromwell, by pointing out this path, do you admit that the course you initially set for me and for England was not a wise one?"

"I act for my country and my king first before all things," Cromwell carefully replied.

"A pity you do not reverse the order," commented Charles Brandon, who sat beside the chancellor.

"They are one and the same, I assure you, Your Majesty."

"Then find me a plausible way out of this sham!" Henry bellowed.

"Can it be done legally?" Stephen Gardiner wondered aloud, hoping to divert any new threat Cromwell was conjuring up to thwart his and Norfolk's plan to depose of the queen.

"Legally, yes, the marriage can be annulled. There is little doubt the queen was betrothed to the Duke of Lorraine before she came here," Norfolk replied, as if he and Stephen were the only ones in the room, but loudly enough for the king to hear. "Can it be done safely is another matter, now that France and the emperor are so closely aligned."

Henry slammed his fist hard onto the table, snorting like a bull as his great jowls flapped beneath his copper beard. "What in God's heaven ever allowed me to trust your vision of beauty, Cromwell? The woman is horrendous; she smells sourly of ale, snores in her sleep, and grunts like a wild boar when she makes those fainthearted attempts to communicate in anything close to the language of English!" Henry bolted from his chair. "Ready my horse! And summon Culpeper. I cannot stand the sight of any of you!"

No one dared make a sound until the king had left the privy chamber in a hobbling gait, the great double doors closing behind him with an ominous thud. The ulcer on Henry's leg had begun again to trouble him, and everyone who had been around His Majesty for any length of time knew that made him as cantankerous as an old goat.

As soon as the door closed behind Henry, the counsel turned from grave silence to fast and furious chatter.

"Well, this indeed is a fine mess," said Edward Seymour, sitting cross-legged in a pumpkin-colored suede jerkin with a heavy gold chain across his slim chest. His impeccably clean fingers played with a slip of parchment that lay on the table before him. He wore a twisted smile as he shot a glance at his younger brother, Thomas.

"The king wants out of this disaster, and there will be spoils for the man with the courage to provide the means," Brandon observed.

"Another divorce would be dangerous," Thomas Seymour dutifully added. "And if the queen contests a divorce, the minister who proposes a battle should expect blood on his hands."

"A wife to follow Anne Boleyn to the block will leave a legacy of blood with the people," Wriothesley said.

The king's privy counsel looked accusingly at Cromwell.

Someone cleared his throat.

Cromwell's guilt over Anne of Cleves was like a poison mist in the room, settling heavily around them.

"If only you had rightly championed Lord and Lady Lisle's comely daughter Anne as queen rather than as a useless mistress," Stephen Gardiner cruelly pointed out, "all of this might have been avoided, and there would likely be an heir inside the queen already."

"He will be rid of the Cleves mare, whatever it takes; that is certain. And doubtless there will be someone to replace her before we see autumn leaves on the trees at Greenwich," observed Brandon. "The only question now is, Who will be unfortunate enough to be next?"

❖

Cromwell was raging with anger by the time his son arrived.

The king's giant, thickly set chancellor lunged forward. He swatted the boy's ears as the great velvet bell sleeve of his coat knocked Gregory in the mouth.

"What the devil were you thinking, Gregory? Do you know what this may well have cost me? You were with her, were you not?"

"With who?"

To Cromwell's surprise, his son appeared genuinely perplexed. His blue eyes were wide and his face was flushed as Cromwell grabbed the side of his smooth, youthful face. Gregory Cromwell was mildly attractive, yet it was his charm and his clever tongue that had always given him an alarming ease with women.

Before and after he had taken a wife.

"Did you honestly have no idea who she was?"

His eyes widened with realization. "Oh, the girl at Lambeth, you mean? How did you know about that?"

"I know everything, you useless lout!" He charged, swatting his son's ear again. The large gold ring on his forefinger clipped the boy's cheek, leaving a mark. "I am Lord Great Chancellor of England! Few know more than me!"

"Except, perhaps, her uncle." Gregory Cromwell bit back a nasty smile. "Look, old man, I did you a favor by taking that position with Norfolk. I thought perhaps I could help you, so I went to his supper last night. I thought it would please you."

"You think with your prick, which has always been your problem—and my own," he growled, and pivoted away, the great velvet cloak swirling between them.

This boy, this upstart, had always been dear to him. He had coddled him, spoiled him and excused him, and the fruits of his indulgence were now his to bear.

"I thought it might help soften the Duke of Norfolk toward you if I showed her some kindness," Gregory said in a tone that bore just a hint of pleading. "Gossip at court is that Norfolk and the Bishop of Winchester are doing all they can to poison your standing with the king. Maybe he would soften toward you if he thought I was helping him out. Clearly the Howard girl has been brought to court to make a decent marriage. But she must be desperate. What is she but a fourth or maybe fifth daughter of a youngest son with a scandalous cousin to darken the path before her?"

Cromwell was speechless at his son's twisted logic. But he recovered soon enough. "And so you thought taking her maidenhead was the way to win her uncle's favor?"

"There was no maidenhead to take, Father." He chuckled dryly.

"Mistress Howard was not a virgin?"

"Would that every courtier like me could couple with a virgin so experienced as that. Now, do you want me to continue seeing her, Father, or would you prefer I leave that pleasure to someone else? Because Catherine Howard most definitely will find the interest of someone more powerful before long."

Chapter Six

*C*atherine stood against the wall, hands behind her back, and silently watched as the king's nieces, Lady Margaret and Lady Frances, prepared the queen's dressing table. Bottles, vials, and jars were lined up in the order of her preference. Tortoiseshell-handled brushes and combs had been meticulously cleaned and lined up neatly beside silver-topped jars of rose-berry water, lavender oil and rare cinnabar. The array was ceremonial, each item's placement full of purpose. Dressed in a rich cambric dressing gown, the queen was accompanied from her bed to the dressing table by Jane Boleyn and Lady Lisle, whose well-placed court connections and relentless ambition had brought her here. Her goal now was to secure a post for her two daughters with the new queen, since her whoring of Anne, the eldest, to the king had not worked. In the corner near a window, a harpist played the queen's favorite morning music to soothe her waking.

Catherine watched the fulfillment of each duty carefully in the event that she should be called upon to perform it herself. She knew her uncle was far too ambitious, and would be unforgiving of the least error she might make. She was here at court because of His

Grace, a butterfly freed from its cocoon that could be captured easily and put away again for any misstep.

To remain, she must find more favor in the queen's household, anger no one who had the power to speak against her, and, on the whole, search for a husband not only wealthy enough to keep her but well placed enough to please her family.

It was startling to see how unattractive the queen truly was without adornments, although she wore her habitual kind smile and aura of serenity. It was strange to Catherine that a woman who more resembled a kitchen maid than royalty was queen. She spoke almost no English among her ladies and her own ambassador, the Earl of Waldeck. She must feel safe to be herself here, Catherine thought, free from the restraints of another culture, another language and the expectations of a husband whom everyone knew disliked her.

A moment later, Jane glanced up at Catherine and held out a wide tortoiseshell-handled hairbrush. Furtive glances were exchanged between the other women, who stood compliantly behind Jane. Clearly, Jane was extending an opportunity, and perhaps a small, public olive branch for the behavior of the others. At least, Catherine would choose to think of it that way for now.

The queen sat on her small embroidered stool and gazed into the gold-framed table mirror before her as Lady Margaret took one of Anne's hands and began to rub it with a lightly scented cream. Jane nodded to Catherine to begin brushing out the queen's long, stick-straight hair. It was coarse, Catherine noticed right away, like a horse's tail, but it was the color of corn.

"How have you found court thus far, Mistress Howard?" the Teutonic queen asked in clotted, sticky words that, even in their proper construction, barely passed for English.

"Frankly, I have found it a challenge, Your Grace," Catherine replied smoothly and honestly as she brushed the queen's hair in long, even strokes. "But my mother always said to be prepared for any challenge."

The queen glanced up at Catherine in the mirror's reflection. "Your mother is . . . ?"

"With God, Your Grace."

Even after all of these years, speaking the words made Catherine sad.

"Mine as well," the queen said, then added something in German.

The stout, silver-haired maid called Gertrude replied. They spoke back and forth twice before the woman translated. "Her Grace says you have much in common. She is pleased to know that."

Catherine nodded courteously, and her eyes met Anne's in the mirror's reflection. A moment later, the queen rose and was directed to her dressing closet by the Marchioness of Dorset and Lady Lisle.

"That went well," Jane said to her in a low, cautious voice as the queen left the room to dress.

"She seems uncommonly kind."

"Her Grace has the heart of a doe. Since she has been here, everyone has remarked upon it. Unfortunately, she has the face of a donkey."

"Will the king divorce her, as they say?"

"I am told he is seeking a way, yet it is difficult, since the marriage was made to cement an alliance that England very much needs. It would be better, perhaps, if he took a good mistress."

As they walked the length of the privy chamber and waited for the other ladies to return with the queen, Catherine considered that. She had been only ten years old when her cousin Anne Boleyn was made queen, but she remembered an animated conversation about the marriage at dinner between her parents and the Duke of Norfolk. The memory took her back to that dinner and the sound of the heavy rain against the long windows in the dining hall at Lambeth and her mother's face in the glow of the fireplace as the three adults spoke.

"Why does the king not simply take our Anne as his mistress and keep his Spanish queen and, thus, the respect of his people?" her mother asked. "He could have it all if he were wiser."

"Even if Anne would allow that, Henry never would. There is no fool like a man in love, and he is in love with our little Anne," the duke replied.

"Besides," Thomas Howard had patiently explained to his wife, "if Anne is a queen and not a whore, every Howard gains favor along with her, even younger Howard men whose elder brothers have inherited all of the family largesse."

"Ah, do be careful; you sound a little pathetic with your envy showing like that," her uncle teased.

There was polite laughter between the brothers. But it was laughter that was bitter, and full of rivalry apparent even to a child.

The memory vanished quickly as Jane Boleyn brought Catherine back to the present by saying, "She was testing you, and by the look of it, you passed with flying colors."

"How could you guess that when she hardly spoke two words to me?"

"She is a bright woman, Catherine, one who will do all she can to survive, even if it means befriending her enemies as well as her allies. After you last spoke, Her Grace was told to take care with you. She wants to please the king by learning to play a song, but before she trusted you to be the one to teach her, she said she wanted to look into your eyes. It appears as though she has decided."

Catherine felt herself falter a little. Trust and risk were so indelibly bound together for everyone at court. "Do you know who here is against me?"

"More to the point, in a group of envious women like this you might well ask who isn't. Who would favor a beautiful young woman, one with everything to gain, when some of them have everything to lose by keeping your company too closely? Chief among them is a wife with a husband who has customarily found his wives' replacements among their own staff."

"The lives of the royals are more complicated than I would have imagined," Catherine said thoughtfully.

Jane chuckled dryly as they walked the length of the next room, which was the queen's presence chamber, then out into the tapestry-lined gallery. "My girl, you do not know the half of it, and you have not yet even managed to meet the king," Jane said.

❖

The music lessons had commenced, but the progress was slow going.

Each afternoon, just like this one, the queen and Catherine sat in the garden near a massive stone fountain. With a lute on each of their laps, Catherine hoped to model the appropriate sound of the tune Henry most favored. Even after eight lessons, however, the queen had not found enough coordination to change a chord with one hand while strumming with the other.

Still, Catherine sat beside her and smiled encouragingly at the discordant sound of each clumsy strum. Catherine had never taught anyone anything, so she found the process tedious and frustrating, particularly the maintenance of a believably encouraging smile while the queen played as if she were using only her thumbs.

In broken English, with the help of the Earl of Waldeck, who felt enormous loyalty to Anne and assisted her in any way he could, Anne explained that at the court where she had been raised, her mother had considered it immodest for a young woman to play an instrument or even to sing.

"Her Grace is most pleased with your efforts and her progress," said the earl, who stood behind the queen. His spine was stiff, his silver beard and mustache clipped. He seemed a proud man, yet there was a surprising gentleness to his sapphire blue eyes ringed with long, dark lashes.

"I want so much to please him," Anne said in broken words, but the sentiment and smile were clear. "He is not happy with me as we are now. . . . You will help."

"I shall try, Your Grace," Catherine replied dutifully.

"*Danke schön.* Walk with me?" Anne asked, the offer sounding almost childlike in its tentative delivery.

Catherine nodded deeply. "I would be honored."

They stood and their chairs were whisked away by two royal pages in gilded livery who had been waiting silently nearby. As the two women strolled into the sunlight, the queen's most trusted German servants, Mother Lowe and the earl, followed at their heels, continuing on as translators when the queen could not find the words in English.

Before they walked down the steps that led to the brick path before them, Catherine saw two young men approach. Both were elegantly dressed, one in a cloak of blue brocade, the other in burgundy velvet, and they were laughing. It took a moment for Catherine to realize that they were the young men who had been guests at the duke's supper the week before. The more handsome of the two, she recalled, was Thomas Culpeper. The other, with whom she had so foolishly tarried, was Cromwell's son. But for her very life, Catherine could not recall his full name, or even what she had found the slightest bit appealing about him only a week before.

Seeing the queen, the young men stopped directly before her on the path, and both made sweeping, solicitous bows as pillowy white clouds moved quickly across the broad canvas of azure sky above them. A soft breeze stirred the ends of their cloaks and tufts of their hair.

The queen nodded politely in response. Catherine could feel Mother Lowe tense behind her. Catherine had not been at court long, but she knew that these two young men had unsavory reputations among the women . . . or at least some of them.

"Your Grace's playing was delightful. We could hear it in the orchard," Gregory Cromwell said, flattering the queen with a smile that Catherine thought slightly devilish.

At that, the queen's normally easy expression darkened. It was a change of temperament Catherine had not yet seen.

"*Danke,*" she said in response to Cromwell. But Anne spoke quickly in German to Mother Lowe and the earl. The tone was low, but it was obvious by the delivery that the words were not complimentary.

Catherine and Culpeper exchanged a little glance and an almost imperceptible shrug, creating an odd spark of camaraderie. She had not expected that. There was a human quality in him that she had not noticed when she had met him before. Could she have misjudged him?

Before she could decide, the queen linked her arm with Catherine's and began to lead her forward past both Culpeper and Cromwell and on down the path.

Mother Lowe approached her from the other side. "Her Grace says to tell you those two are to be avoided," said Mother Lowe in a low, maternal tone.

"But are they not trusted by the king?"

"Trusted only by him," Mother Lowe explained, coming up to them on the other side. "The rest of the court knows them to be pleasure-seeking hounds. Cromwell's son, you know, is married to the sister of Queen Jane, so His Majesty refuses to believe anything untoward of him, giving him something of a free reign."

Catherine was surprised by this news and vexed at herself for not knowing about it earlier. She tried to keep her tone even. "And Master Culpeper?"

"Not married, no, but bearing a reputation with the ladies that exceeds all others. So Her Grace hopes you will take care with him," said Mother Lowe.

"Master Culpeper has never even spoken directly to me, so I am sure I am quite safe."

"For now, perhaps," Mother Lowe replied. "But you must not let down your guard. He is one who could easily break your heart, and smile while doing it."

"Then what is it the king so likes about him if he is dreadful?"

"Nostalgia, mainly." Mother Lowe was frank. "Culpeper reminds His Majesty of the time when he as well could break hearts by his looks alone."

"The king has changed that much?" Catherine was surprised. He had always been the most dashing man in England, and he certainly was handsome the last time she had seen him.

"You have not yet met him at court?" Mother Lowe queried.

"No, I've not seen him here. We met only once, but that was several years ago," Catherine replied as she watched a strange look slip between the queen's two servants. "What is it?"

"About the king? That, my dear, you shall have to see for yourself," Mother Lowe replied.

Catherine stole a small glance back at Culpeper and Cromwell, still standing where they had left them, and wondered just what she should expect.

❖

The queen's household was in an uproar. Her Grace had been invited at the last minute to a banquet and an evening's entertainment that night, so the queen would finally play for the king. Anne of Cleves stood, hands on her broad hips, before a selection of dresses made of sweeping Spanish silks and velvets and adorned with long sleeves and tight bodices, gold chains, pearls and pendants, each creation more elegant than the next. In her attempt to please her husband, all of them were in the latest French designs.

At first she had refused the gowns, yet in the end, all of the German fashions she had clung to so loyally were discarded. Catherine could see the desperation on Anne's full, pockmarked face as she considered the dresses held out before her. She was surprised when the queen glanced up at her, then singled her out from all of the other ladies gathered in the dressing chamber.

"Which one would you select, Mistress Howard?"

Catherine glanced over at a sweep of sky blue fabric with full slashed sleeves, and another of yellow silk with white lace at the square neckline, the bodice sewn heavily with pearls. The fabrics and ornate embellishments were stunning. The pearls and diamonds glittered in the afternoon sunlight through the windows, sending a kaleidoscope against the paneled wall. Yet Catherine knew the queen would look like a mouse in the richly detailed, brightly colored fabric of either dress.

She caught sight of Jane Boleyn's expression. It was filled with alarm. The rest of the ladies fell absolutely still, knowing well the risk any maid of honor took in offering opinions to a queen. But Catherine had no doubt that something classically simple would become Anne far more than these flamboyant dresses, as they would not swallow up the little traditional appeal she possessed. It would take a haughty beauty like Anne Boleyn to carry off either the blue or the yellow dress. If she told Anne that, she risked insulting the fragile queen, but if she declined honesty and the king were displeased, she would pay for that as well. Catherine felt her heart race as Anne looked at her with heartrending expectation.

"My favorite color on Your Grace is most definitely green, as it sets off your lovely eyes. The dress you wore to dinner on Sunday was breathtaking."

Anne smiled in agreement. "I do love that dress," she managed to comment.

"May I ask if His Majesty has yet seen it?"

A small flurry of conversation in German was exchanged between Anne and Mother Lowe. The only other sound was a creaking floorboard near the door as someone moved or shifted. Finally, after what felt like an eternity, it was Mother Lowe who cast an approving smile on Catherine.

"His Majesty has not yet seen the dress, so Her Grace will wear it, as you suggest. And she bids you, Mistress Howard, wear the yellow, in order to properly accompany her this evening to the king's banquet. Her seamstress will take your measurements and alter it to your size."

Catherine felt the blood drain from her face. A sensation of guilt crept through her like a December chill. But she curtsied deeply. "Your Grace, I could not," she wisely demurred for the benefit of the court ladies around her, whose stares could quite easily have melted her.

The queen glanced at Mother Lowe, and again there was a flurry of guttural German. "Her Grace is most nervous to attempt a song in the king's presence for the first time, Mistress Howard. She says your company would be a comfort."

"But the dress . . ."

"She says yellow is your color as green is hers. Please accept it as her gift."

The only genuine smile in the room at that moment came from Anne herself. She radiated a kind of goodness that Catherine found mesmerizing in a world of so much backbiting. In response, Catherine made a deep curtsy once again. She was able to breathe only once the chatter of the group had recommenced and Mother Lowe had gone to supervise the fetching of the green dress from the queen's wardrobe chamber.

Catherine glanced around for a task to occupy her. She wanted to melt into the oak wall paneling at that moment, but finding some way to employ her hands so they would not shake would have to suffice. She went to the dressing table and began to line up the bottles and jars, just as she had seen the Marchioness of Dorset do.

"You had better go and prepare yourself," Jane said in a surprisingly sympathetic tone. "Go to the seamstress to get your measurements taken. I shall send the finished dress and servants along later to help you."

She liked Jane, but Catherine could not afford to trust her any more than any of the other women. She knew they all felt themselves more deserving of favor than she, a girl so new at court. She must never forget that. She was always at risk, no matter who tried to be her friend in the coming days.

❖

Loath as Jane was to admit it, Catherine Howard did look like an actual princess in the queen's elegant and newly altered gown, which now fit her perfectly. It was early evening, and the last of the sunlight streaming through the windows, all crimson and fiery russet, played on the pearls and tiny diamonds of the jeweled bodice on her gown. After two servants in beige dresses and plain white hoods had helped her dress, Catherine stood before a mirror, and Jane saw by her expression that she was daring to admire the reflection gazing back at her. The young woman with full amber hair and stunning pale gray eyes was extraordinary. She reminded Jane of a colt pressing at the gate of its stall, aching to break free, to gallop and show the world all that she could do: no restrictions, no rules, yet stumbling with naive enthusiasm. Jane knew only too well how dangerous that sort of attraction to freedom was. Catherine spun around, laughing. It was so easy to envy Catherine Howard. Yet still, it was nearly impossible not to like her.

She needed protection here, and even a bit of compassion. As one who was seventeen years her senior, with a lifetime more of experience, Jane had assigned herself that task. She had made so many grave and costly mistakes with Anne Boleyn. At first they had been friends, then sisters-in-law after she married Anne's brother, George. They had been thick as thieves when they had plotted to oust Henry's mistress, Bessie Blount, from court. Yet from there, things had turned sour. Jane had been angry with her husband when she had discovered the possibility of his incestuous infidelities with Anne, but she had never planned to be the cause of his beheading. Or Anne's, for that matter. Jealousy and envy were a poison, and four years ago Jane had drunk too deeply from that cup. She felt she had been swept away by the events, and now George and Anne were both dead, her own testimony having expedited, if not caused, their violent ends. Having been given a second chance and a formal written offer to return to court by Henry, Jane felt that befriending Catherine was, in a small way, making amends for her part in that whole grisly affair.

"You are a vision, child," Jane said kindly as Catherine spun around like a little girl, and the yellow silk danced.

"I am, aren't I?" Catherine said, more innocently awestruck than boastful.

"Well, if you are quite finished admiring yourself, you had better dash to the queen's chamber. Her Grace will not want to be late to her reunion with the king, as she is doing everything she can to put her best foot forward. She knows how important this evening is. It may very well be her last occasion to impress him before the forces against her prevail."

Catherine's face suddenly paled. "The stakes are that high tonight?"

"They could not be higher," Jane replied meaningfully.

Catherine held up the skirts of her dress and dashed through the tangle of rooms in the queen's apartments. She could think of only one thing: By Catherine's teaching alone, the queen would need to play well enough to find the favor of the great King of England and remain his wife. By extension, Catherine could remain at court. She did not want to think of all that was riding on this single event, but it was difficult not to. Quite simply, her very life was at stake. She could not return to Horsham now that she had tasted the freedoms and luxuries of the court. Yet there were no marital prospects so far, and she feared the duke would lose faith in her abilities to attract a husband and send her away. Perhaps this afternoon, looking as elegant as she did in the queen's dress, she would catch the eye of someone suitable.

She opened the door to a small, paneled reading closet beside the presence chamber that led to the queen's privy chamber. Only a small sliver of light filtered through the stained-glass window, making it difficult for her to see in the otherwise dark room. As she stepped through the door, she at first did not see the small figure of a boy approaching her, obscuring his eyes with his left hand. When she did finally see him, it was too late. His movements were swift and deliberate as he flung a small silver pot of ink in her direction. The ink flew, spraying out like a black fountain and spattering the bodice of her dress. It was a ghastly onyx stain. Catherine shrieked and looked down in horror. When she looked up again, the boy and the ink pot were both gone.

Her breathing was sharp. Splayed out like a web, her hands flew over the wet bodice, smearing the stain and blackening the tips of her fingers. She sank against the wall, feeling her knees give way beneath her.

She had been boldly sabotaged.

Tears flooded her eyes and ran in ribbons down her cheeks. She could indict no one, because there was no one to accuse. Anyone at court could have compelled the page to do it. The queen would think her clumsy at best and arrogant at worst for having taken so little care of a costly gift, especially when there was so much at stake in her own survival at court.

Worse, there was no time to change dresses now, no time even to fashion a makeshift cover. Catherine Howard would need to lift her chin and banish her pride, as well as her desire to know what cruel person had done this.

She reached up for her mother's necklace, which hung around her neck like an amulet.

"Give me courage," she silently whispered.

She would walk behind the queen and Lady Douglas, trying to blend in like the others, and hope with all of her heart that she would not be called upon. It really was all she could do—that, and pray to a God who might well be angry with her for the commandments she had so boldly broken.

❖

Thomas Culpeper was bored already, and the banquet had not yet begun. Days of endless standing, waiting and smiling took their toll. He stood alone beneath an archway near the door and watched each of the young ladies who filed in. It was the only diversion during the endless months of monotony. There were few he had not had for himself already. Sisters. Daughters. The challenge and fun died for him when the access was so easy.

Everyone knew handsome Thomas was a favorite of the king. He rode with Henry, dressed him, played cards with him, even slept in his bedchamber, as the gentlemen of the king's privy chamber were called upon to do. The honor had secured his place at court and cleared the darker aspects of his reputation.

As he stood with his ankles and arms crossed, leaning against the pillar, Thomas glanced down at his elegant doublet of Italian fawn brown velvet. The cape slung gracefully across his shoulders and was secured by a gold clasp that was a gift from the king. It had been a part of Henry's personal wardrobe but had been worn only once, His Majesty had explained, "When I was a bit younger and a trifle slimmer."

Thomas had greeted the honor with proper enthusiasm and just the right amount of humility, characteristics that pleased a steadily aging and widening sovereign. He nodded to Lady Lisle, smiled, then turned away. Jésu, how she bored him with her voice like a horse's whinny, and that expression of expectation mixed with desperation.

Guests were filing in around him, and the stately pavane began to play from the gallery above, which included the pipe, tabor, harp and trumpet. The king would be near. Thomas heaved a sigh, loathing the predictability of another evening with too much food and never enough wine. He would have to watch as the king pretended to be young and handsome enough again to deserve the favor of the young ladies he conquered. Yet who could blame the poor, sodden old bastard who, after four months' time, had yet to bed his own queen?

Henry did not stride but limped and hobbled into the hall a moment later, surrounded by Cromwell, Thomas Seymour and Charles Brandon, and suitably concealed by a tent's worth of dove gray silk heavily bejeweled with a baldric of rubies and small pearls. Everyone, including Culpeper, whom His Majesty passed near the door, dropped into deep and reverent bows as Henry nodded and smiled. The pavane ceased and a fanfare was blared out on trumpets.

A moment later, entering the room beside the queen, he saw the new Howard girl, her small, slim body poured into a sweep of crisp, sparkling yellow silk.

Perhaps it would be an interesting evening after all.

It was odd how she held herself, though, both arms up at her chest as she walked, hands linked at the fingertips as if trying to . . . Ah, so that was it. He saw the small but prominent ink stain directly over her breast. The odds of her having spilled it on herself were slim, and he knew enough of the queen's ladies to figure out instantly what had happened. They were an envious, petty lot, especially Lady Lisle and the Marchioness of Dorset. Someone had been determined to ruin this first banquet for her by any means necessary. The Howard girl was far too pretty and too much of a threat.

Thomas moved toward the queen's chair beside the king. He watched her curtsy deeply to him and try to smile. The poor, ugly Flanders woman could not help but be likable to everyone but her own husband. Lady Rochford and Mistress Howard stood near the queen, then sat once she was seated.

The king was obviously distracted by Anne Basset, Lady Lisle's pretty daughter. He did not even notice Mistress Howard, and he certainly had not seen the ink stain. Nor had the queen. Yet.

Thomas took the seat beside Mistress Howard. The first thing he noticed was her hair. He could smell its fragrance, freshly washed, not perfumed like all the others'. He bit back a charmed smile. You could take the girl out of the country, yet . . .

The stricken expression that darkened the queen's rosy, pock-marked face interrupted his thought. The Earl of Waldeck was behind her, leaning over, whispering something in her ear. Anne of Cleves leaned toward Mother Lowe and began to speak back and forth with her in quick, staccato fashion. Then she said something to Mistress Howard.

It was all very swift, the words whispered and impossible to make out beneath the din of music and chatter. Yet Thomas was fascinated when he saw one of the court musicians bring the queen a lute. He had heard Mistress Howard had been giving the queen lessons, but he had no idea she was ready to play for the king. Just recently Charles Brandon had joked that the queen played as well as she bedded—miserably, if at all.

Amused, Thomas waited and watched, curious and not quite so bored.

A moment later, the queen rose. Mistress Howard and Lady Rochford rose as well. The queen curtsied once again to the king, although this time her normally sweet expression was filled with dread. The focus in the room shifted completely. All eyes now were on the queen . . . and the newest maid of honor.

❖

Dear, merciful God in His heaven! Could His Majesty possibly have changed that much?

Catherine gazed at Henry with disbelieving eyes, her mouth falling open. Where was the tall, commanding, only slightly portly king of just four years ago who had ridden so magnificently into the courtyard at Horsham, along with his pregnant Queen Jane? Could tragedy change a person that much? Yes, he was wearing enough sparkling jewels to ignite fires all across England, and his doublet glittered like a thousand candles in the firelight, but there was no mistaking the girth. His dark green eyes were tucked into deep sockets above sagging jowls beneath a square copper beard. Poor Anne of Cleves. Had she come to England, Catherine wondered, expecting the legend, the man who had seen himself flatteringly painted in dozens of portraits that now hung everywhere she turned? Catherine marveled that the queen had chosen to win his heart rather than be repulsed by him. Catherine felt even more compassion for her queen, and she thought, *By my Lord, thank God it is not me. . . .*

She watched the poor queen make her way on unsteady legs before the table and wait as a chair and another lute were brought to her from the gallery above. She had requested the one on which she had practiced, so the other was left beside Catherine. A sideways glance showed the king's expression of boredom mixed with curiosity. His arched, pencil-thin copper eyebrows were raised slightly, as if he were challenging poor Anne to actually play a proper tune.

"Can she do it?" Thomas Culpeper suddenly whispered to Catherine.

Catherine looked over at him. Lord, he was as muscular and handsome as the king was aging and stout. There was such a stark contrast between the two men on either side of her, each so richly and elegantly clothed, surrounded by ushers, esquires, pages, musicians, jesters and servants. The world of the Horsham dormitory seemed very far away.

"I doubt it," Catherine answered. "But she is desperate to try. She hopes His Majesty will show her favor for this."

"Take it from me, Mistress Howard, the king does not suffer mediocrity well, especially when it comes in such a package," Thomas replied before turning to the queen.

The queen strummed a note, then looked over to Catherine, her blanched face stricken with desperation.

"She has forgotten already!" Catherine gasped, a hand flying up to her mouth.

"You could rescue her, you know," Thomas calmly suggested. "Save the day and play a duet. You've got an instrument right here."

Catherine glanced down at the ink stain, which would be glaringly apparent to everyone if she joined the queen. Culpeper followed her eyes and, in a single elegant movement, as if in response to her unspoken fear, he removed his own velvet cape, flung it over her shoulders, and leaned over to clasp it. In the swirl of noise, movements and swift decisions, their eyes met for an instant. His were wide and glittering above a calm smile.

Jésu, but he smelled delicious, she thought, like musk with a bit of orange flower.

"Fawn brown velvet is quite favorable next to yellow silk." He smiled charmingly. "And the combination also hides a multitude of sins, or at least a single inky grievance."

Catherine leaped to her feet and picked up the lute as the queen stumbled through a few more discordant notes, trying to pick out the tune with her small, stubby fingers. As Catherine approached her, another chair was brought. Master Culpeper must have seen to that too, she thought. She also realized that she had forgotten to thank him for the cape. Hopefully, there would be time for that later. For now, she must try to help the queen with a husband who looked as though he had swallowed something sour.

Catherine saw the relief in Anne's eyes and a small, cautious smile.

"Remember what we learned," she whispered in sweet encouragement. "You strum the second note twice after the first. . . . Shall we play it together?"

"Ah, yes, *danke, danke.*"

As they played and the jumble of notes became a simple tune, Catherine dared to glance up at the king in his tall, carved chair. His chin was balanced on his bejeweled hand, compressing his jowls, but the sour expression had vanished. In its place was a slight and twisted smile. His other hand, covered in rings, fingered the goblet before him.

When the short tune was at an end, there was a moment of deathly silence across the banquet hall. Then, suddenly, the king began very enthusiastically to applaud and the rest of the court followed suit, smiles and approving nods all around.

"Well-done!" Henry loudly proclaimed as both the queen and Catherine nodded to him with the greatest deference. "You have apparently found the proper teacher. But to be certain, I would have her play something on her own."

Catherine glanced over at the queen. She had meant only to help her, not steal the limelight from a wife trying desperately to find a place in her husband's life. She especially did not want to take anything from a woman who had shown her nothing but kindness. Yet Anne sweetly nodded her approval, and Catherine was forced to comply. Songs ran through her mind. *See that her dancing skills are brightened and that she can play "My Own Heart's Desire" on the lute without mucking it up. His Majesty enjoys that tune above all others and despises when someone cannot see it through.* Her uncle's pronouncement at Horsham returned to her, and when she glanced over at him seated beside the king, he nodded to her, almost as if he knew what she was thinking.

She began to play and lost herself for a moment in the pretty piece, which was sweet and melodic. It was said that Anne Boleyn had played this for him the day he had married her. The irony was not lost on Catherine.

"Well, wife, I approve of your teacher!" Henry pronounced

with a strange chuckle as soon as the song was done, as he lifted his goblet to Catherine and those around him followed suit. "To the queen's instructor!"

"To the queen's instructor!" the others dutifully chimed in.

Catherine stood, curtsied and retreated as quickly as possible to her place at the table. Her hands were trembling as she began to unhook Thomas Culpeper's cape, but he put a hand on her arm to stop her.

"You can return it later," he said, smiling charmingly as servants brought out great, glittering silver platters of marzipan and the consort, a group of royal musicians, began again to perform from the gallery above. "Besides, I find I like thinking of you indebted to me."

In spite of herself, his words and delivery made Catherine laugh. Their eyes met again. "Some debts are too large to pay, Master Culpeper."

"And some are far too pleasurable to be thought of as a true debt."

"Well, either way, you must have your cape returned to you. I do not like the notion of owing a gentleman anything."

"Why not spare yourself the inevitable questions about the stain? Certainly your good sense will triumph over your pride."

"With a man like you, a bit of pride would be good sense," Catherine replied wittily.

He tipped his head, the twisted smile breaking through again. "You have been warned about me, I see."

"Wisely so?"

"But of course. A pretty girl should always know what she is heading into, I say," Thomas Culpeper chuckled. "Even if it does spoil a bit of the adventure."

❖

From his seat nearby, Henry watched her. He had not taken his eyes from her since she sat beside the queen to play. Henry had seen the black stain on her gown and her futile attempts to hide it, as a child hides a mistake. It was amusing, he thought.

"So *that* is your niece, Norfolk?" he asked as nonchalantly as he could while a youthful sensation tingled up his spine. "She has changed a good deal since I was at Horsham with Jane."

"Still pretty, though, if Your Majesty will tolerate my saying so," Norfolk dared.

"Pretty once, perhaps—stunning now," Henry amended.

The Duke of Norfolk knew he was on the right path, but each step must be deliberate. "Agreed, Your Majesty, she is that," he said, biting back his smile with a liberal, congratulatory swallow of rich Malmsey wine.

❖

An hour later, to everyone's surprise, the king asked the queen to accompany him on a stroll, so the ladies and courtiers were free to do as they pleased for a time. Catherine accepted Thomas's invitation to dance. The music from the gallery was spirited, the wine was plentiful and the dance floor was crowded with swirls of velvet, satin, and flashes of silver. The light from the flickering beeswax candles, the aroma of sweat mixed with perfume, and the sound of laughter added to the heady atmosphere.

"So then, you do know of your dreadful reputation, Master Culpeper?" Catherine laughed as he bowed, dipped her into a graceful curtsy and pressed a hand to her own in time with the music.

"Gossip is so overrated, Mistress Howard," he replied with a clever smile that lit his face.

She had never in her life seen anything more beautiful. Catherine tipped her head. "Should I pay it no heed then?"

"Oh, you should pay heed to all gossip. Then toss half out and believe about half of that."

"I shall keep that in mind." She laughed.

They twirled and bowed again. "Your uncle is watching us like one of the king's prized hawks," Thomas remarked, still smiling and not sounding particularly bothered by the revelation.

Catherine glanced back across the hall to where she knew Norfolk was sitting. He would be so pleased, she thought, that she had caught the eye of a gentleman of the king's privy chamber. That could not be unimportant. Thomas was handsome, clever and obviously a bit dangerous—challenge enough to keep her interest, most certainly. "He can see as I do that you dance very well."

"You flatter me, Mistress Howard."

"A first attempt to pay back my debt on the cape."

"As I told you, some obligations are far too pleasurable to be thought of as true debt."

They both laughed, and for Catherine, the connection was instant and powerful. A tremor ran through her, and for the first time in her life with a man, she felt disarmed. It surprised her that she actually liked the uncontrollable sensation.

Well after midnight, Thomas escorted Catherine back to the queen's apartments. Since Whitehall was not a single palace but a massive tangle of buildings, even the shortest route could be made as long as one wished. They passed down a long, paneled gallery and out into a large, brick-paved courtyard beside the knot garden. The moon was full and bright, and since it was a cloudless night, it cast everything around them in a silver glow. As they walked, Catherine tried not to look over at him.

But the attraction was overwhelming.

Instead, she looked down at a small weed growing in the crack between the bricks and tried to concentrate on it. He was nothing like Manox or Dereham. He was in a class even above Cromwell's son, and he knew it.

Even his self-assurance drew her.

She could not escape the attraction, nor did she want to. She finally glanced over and caught his gaze. His eyes actually glittered in the evening light. In spite of his glib manner, there was a strange vulnerability just beneath the surface of his smile. He used the clever manner to conceal it, but she could see it there. Anyone who bothered to look could see it.

"So, who exactly is Thomas Culpeper?" she asked, wanting to know more about him.

"The man walking beside you, of course."

"Yet there is always more to one than what one shows the world."

"Quite true."

"Why did you really help me this evening?"

She could see him hesitate. A small wrinkle furrowed his brow, as though he were considering something very serious. "I have three younger sisters," he finally said, "all of whom were always getting themselves into some sort of predicament. Let us just say that coming to the aid of young women has become something of a habit."

"Have you made a habit of violating them as well?" When she saw the same furrow on his brow deepen to a frown, Catherine instantly regretted the flippant question, yet she could not take it back. She wanted to know if he would disappoint her as well. "I find it difficult not to pay heed to that particular bit of gossip."

"Ah, yes. That."

Thomas gazed up into the broad, black night sky, hands linked behind his back for what felt like an eternity. The gossip about what he had done was horrific, and it was the first thing Catherine heard at court after seeing him that day in Lambeth. Jane had also told her that a year earlier, Thomas Culpeper had raped a park keeper's wife. One of the villagers who tried to accuse him had been found murdered, and Thomas was blamed for the death.

"Is that among the portion of court lore I would be advised to disregard or heed, Master Culpeper?" Catherine rephrased her question.

He did not answer her quickly or glibly this time. When he looked back at her, Catherine saw that Thomas's easygoing expression had changed. He was somber and deadly serious.

"Since you asked, part of you must already believe it."

"I am asking you. I will decide what I believe after you answer."

Thomas leaned in very slowly and leveled his intense gaze at her. Having him so close and entirely focused on her made Catherine forget to breathe. The expression on his face was disarmingly sincere. "Find your own truth, Mistress Howard. It is what my father told my sisters, and what I am telling you now. That is always the best path," he said before he turned and began to walk away from her.

"Wait. You're not going to accompany me the rest of the way?"

Thomas paused and turned back. His eyes still drew her, yet there was something strange about them now. "For the moment, Mistress Howard, I leave you on your own for all things. What you decide to do or believe shall be up to you," Thomas said, before he turned again very abruptly and left her alone near a moss-covered statue of Nero.

❖

"It is the best possible fortune. The king actually noticed Catherine this evening, which is what we have been waiting for," Norfolk mused as he sat beside a roaring, red-gold fire that crackled and popped inside his private drawing room.

Beside him, seated in a matching chair and sipping warm ale

from a silver cup, was Stephen Gardiner, Bishop of Winchester, the slim, pasty-faced cleric who supported Norfolk through the dark days of Anne Boleyn and Cardinal Wolsey. Beyond family, there was no one the duke trusted besides Gardiner. Both were devoted Catholics and longed for a return to the true religion in England. They were also both wildly ambitious, and as a team they were a force to be reckoned with.

Everything depended upon the events of that night. Their most dangerous enemy, the Protestant Chancellor Cromwell, had just been granted the title Earl of Essex by Henry, in spite of his faux pas with Anne of Cleves. So that Cromwell could not act in any way on rumors of Catherine that might affect the Howards, and thus defend himself from upcoming blame over the marriage, he was urged to find a way for the king to dissolve his marriage.

While he did so, Norfolk and Gardiner must find a way to vanquish Cromwell entirely.

"There is not an inch of room for error," Norfolk added, immersed in the details of his rapidly evolving plan. "It is imperative that Henry believe it is his own notion."

"Not terribly difficult, considering the extraordinary beauty of your niece," Gardiner replied.

"Ah, but it will take a great deal more than beauty to capture the King of England, now that he is four times wed with only one bride he does not regret."

"You mean Jane Seymour, of course?"

"Who else, you fool! Which gives the apparently still grieving Seymour brothers a distinct advantage in finding a replacement for the Cleves mare. Nostalgia is a powerful draw, which means we must work twice as hard to put Catherine before him in these next days."

"And if we provide the path His Majesty seeks to divorce the queen . . . ?"

"If we can do so without risking his delicate political alliances, the king should be grateful enough to us to diminish the Seymour advantage."

"Do I guess correctly that we have much work ahead of us tonight?"

A thin smile lengthened Norfolk's mouth. "Planning while the enemy sleeps provides the greatest opportunity for reward. It worked initially with my Anne, and we have learned from our mistakes. It shall work with Catherine."

"I do hope Your Grace has learned a thing or two about controlling your nieces in the interim."

"Catherine Howard is an entirely different breed from Anne Boleyn, and she will be an entirely different queen."

"Queen?" Gardiner's mud brown eyes widened with surprise. "Do you truly believe His Majesty will take another queen and not just a mistress after all of this turmoil, four times over?"

"Our king is many things, Gardiner, but foremost is his devotion to God and what is right. He may not know it now, but when we are finished with him, His Majesty will do whatever it takes to make Catherine not his mistress, but his wife."

"One can only hope it will be your niece's wish as well," Gardiner observed. "I saw the way she looked at Culpeper this evening, not unlike the way a dozen other beauties at court have looked at him before."

"But Catherine's desire in this is entirely unimportant. She shall do as she is told and be glad of it. In the meantime, she can dally with Culpeper if she pleases."

"Is that not a dangerous dalliance to permit?" Gardiner asked.

Norfolk finished his ale, then laid his head back against the chair. He was tired, but contemplation of the greatness at hand was a heady stimulant.

"It is apparent that your commitment to our lord has left you little time to understand the complexities of women, Stephen. My Catherine is like a colt: sleek, beautiful, but largely a wild creature whose drive must not be taken for granted. I saw that in her from the first moment at Horsham, and I nearly declined to bring her to court because of it. The challenge with a girl like Catherine Howard is learning how to rein her in to serve one's purpose and not break her great spirit, which is her key asset."

"Let her feel a bit of freedom, whether real or not?"

"Precisely. It is the perception that she has some control that will bend her ultimately to our will," the Duke of Norfolk said.

Gardiner bit back a smile. "Perhaps taming her is too grand a goal, from what I have seen of the girl," he wisely said. "There is a part of your niece, I fear, that means to do whatever she pleases."

❖

The day had been long and tiring to Catherine, starting with the morning attending the queen and leading up to the banquet, the performance on the lute, and her many hours with Thomas Culpeper. She was exhausted by the time she made it back to the queen's rooms after he had left her.

Catherine went into the queen's presence chamber and quietly closed the door. There were candles lit and a small fire blazing, illuminating the vast Flemish wall tapestry. Everyone else was asleep in their own chambers, and the room was empty. A light rain had begun to hit the windows, and the vast room was filled with a chill. Catherine moved across the wooden floor and began to loosen her French hood, which felt tighter than usual. Everything felt restrictive tonight. The headdress was pinching, the tight boning of her stomacher stopped her from breathing too deeply, and the heavy dress pulled her down. Her clothing seemed to be a great reflection of her life.

Everything was weighing so heavily upon her: rules, expectations . . . *Thomas.*

"High time you returned. The dark circles beneath your eyes tomorrow morning shall reveal what you've been doing. And there is far too much riding on your success for such nonsense."

The icy tone was like a sudden rush of cold water, and Catherine stiffened. Her eyes adjusted to the darkness as a figure shrouded in shadows before her slowly turned around. As the figure stepped into the light, Catherine saw the face of the dowager duchess. In a sweep of forbidding black satin, she approached Catherine, her lined face full of reproach.

"My lady grandmother." Catherine dipped into a deep, respectful curtsy, her heart sinking with disappointment. "I did not know you were coming to court."

"Precisely," Agnes Howard replied. "And by the look of things, I did not arrive a moment too soon, before you and the duke made a mess of all that we have worked toward. But Grandmother is here to see that everything works out exactly as planned. Someone has to do it."

Chapter Seven

"Culpeper!" The king bellowed for his favorite young gentleman of the bedchamber. "Where the devil is Tom?" he mumbled to himself after receiving no reply. He suddenly threw back his bedding in a blaze of fury and swung his bare legs over the side of the massive, carved bed curtained with a heavy, gold-fringed tapestry.

"He has been called for, Your Majesty," Thomas Seymour said after bowing deeply.

A moment later, like an errant child, Thomas Culpeper arrived, pushing past pages, Yeomen of the Guard, esquires and clerics gathered at the foot of the royal bed. He stumbled into the king's presence, hat askew, his sculpted, handsome face unshaven.

Henry studied him through tiny, discerning dark eyes, and as his full red brows merged in a frown, all movement in the room ceased. The others knew the look. Henry had been wounded by the Boleyn years. The death of Jane had only deepened the wound, making him more cantankerous and more wildly unpredictable with age. Jocularity could be replaced easily by rage, and in the blink of an eye it often was.

"Good morning, Your Majesty," Thomas said, conjuring an easy smile. "Have you slept well then?"

At that moment, the room was filled with uneasy silence as the courtiers exchanged worried glances, but the tension was broken when Henry began to laugh.

"Better than you, by all appearances. Is that not the costume you wore last evening?"

"Forgive me. It is, Your Majesty."

"Did you actually sleep at all?" Henry volleyed admiringly.

Thomas bit back a smile and advanced, bowing again. He knew the king enjoyed the thrill of hearing about his exploits, and the things he no longer could do.

"I did manage to nod off for a bit just before dawn."

Henry chuckled again and slapped Thomas approvingly on the back. Meanwhile, Charles Brandon slung a crimson velvet dressing gown piped in silver thread across the king's shoulders, and Edward Seymour artfully pushed Henry's thick arms through the sleeves.

"Who was she this time, Tom? Or do I even want to know?" The king chuckled.

"Did Your Majesty himself not advise me against 'kissing and telling'?"

"I am better off in a blissful state of ignorance? Is that what you mean to say?"

Beneath a gilded ceiling carved with Tudor roses, ushers, stewards, cupbearers, grooms, messengers and pages moved in a flurry of activity, while a groom moistened Henry's face and hands with a cloth perfumed with lavender-scented oil. Afterward, Thomas followed Henry into the grand presence chamber, where his dining table was laid with white silk, covered by a French tapestry, and placed before a painted panel depicting Christ's Passion.

Henry slumped into his chair without acknowledging the large group of nobles and servants attending to and clamoring for His Majesty's favor. Thomas stood behind the table so that he might converse with His Majesty, if he felt so inclined. He watched as Henry ate from gleaming gold dishes heaped with boar paté, stewed quail, figs with clotted cream, and his favorite—quince marmalade.

For Henry, eating was among the few joys left to him, and no one, not even his dear Tom, dared interrupt the ritual. A royal steward leaned in and poured him a gilt goblet of wine.

"You are riding with us in the spring jousting tournament today, are you not?" the king asked.

Thomas inclined his head respectfully. "As Your Majesty wishes."

Henry bit into a fig and the juice dribbled into his red-gold beard at the folds of his chin. "I shall need to ride for the queen to show my favor, although, hopefully, this shall be the last time."

The king had often engaged him in conversation about his sham marriage over the past four months. Thomas leaned forward and, in a low voice, said, "Has there been progress on that front?"

"There is a race to see who can unseat her most gracefully. But until there is a secure plan in place, I cannot afford to anger her brother, the Duke of Cleves, or give France and Spain the least reason to think Cleves, the law and I are not a great triumvirate."

"The players in this race are the same?" Thomas asked, curious to know whether the king was fully aware of the many plots being devised at that very moment.

"The Seymours, Norfolk and Gardiner, and Wriothesley, of course."

"And Archbishop Cromwell?"

"The unholy prig who fashioned this debacle in the first place? I doubt I would listen to a single detail of any plan he proposed! Bastard. Saddling me with a wife like her, one who is quite impossible to hate. It is as if God means to punish me forever for daring to marry my brother's wife all those years ago." Thomas knew that Henry was referring to his first queen, Catherine of Aragon.

"Or God has something more glorious in store. Perhaps he wanted you to take this path because it will lead to her."

"*Her*, Culpeper?" Henry asked, tossing a napkin onto his plate as he stepped down from the dais to be dressed for prayer. "Do you suspect that there is yet another woman in my future?"

"I believe the king's future holds whatever he wishes," Thomas replied carefully.

Henry bit back a pleased smile. "So you are a diplomat now, Tom?"

"I would be blessed to have Your Majesty consider me so," Thomas said, though he had little desire to be one.

"Now that, my boy, is where you are wrong. What I value about you, what has always amused me about you, is your rough simplicity. If I wished for well-schooled replies, I would look to Seymour or Wriothesley. Was that not what I told you after I saw you pardoned for your . . . *folly* last year?" Henry said euphemistically, referring to the park keeper's wife.

Thomas nodded soberly "You did, sire."

"Then pay heed to what I tell you."

"I shall, always."

They walked together, Henry's arm still around Thomas's shoulder as they moved through the anteroom and into the dressing closet.

"Now, about that woman you see ahead for me," began the king. "Do tell me what you see in store for me."

❖

Catherine had been called early that morning to wait upon the queen. After three hours of sleep, she had managed to get herself out of bed, but her body felt like lead as she shuffled toward the maid who was waiting to dress her for prayer in the royal chapel. Some of the events of last night seemed like a blur to her by morning's light, including the mysterious ink saboteur and her lute performance for the king.

But she remembered, with absolute clarity, her evening with Thomas. And her grandmother's sudden appearance.

She hated mixing her past life at Horsham with her new life at court. It was difficult enough to have the Duke of Norfolk here, assessing her every action. The notion that the dowager would be just around the corner, scrutinizing Catherine's every move again, was like being forced back into the cocoon after one had become a butterfly and tasted freedom.

A smartly dressed young woman she did not know helped to dress Catherine's hair as she tried to steel herself for another day. She was a pretty girl with a smattering of freckles across the bridge of her nose and smooth, delicate hands that easily drew back Catherine's hair as a maid pinned it, before placing a new pearl-adorned hood on her head. Although Catherine usually regarded other women as enemies, especially the noble ones here at court, she found herself sympathizing with this strikingly attractive girl.

"What is your name?" Catherine asked.

"Anne, Mistress Howard," the girl replied in a soft, cultured tone.

"And your family name?"

"Basset. I am the daughter of Lady Lisle. My father was Sir John Basset."

Of course. Anne Basset's mother, Honor, was married to Viscount Lisle, the king's uncle. Honor was notorious for her ambition, and was frequently seen in the royal apartments, trying to expose herself and her two daughters to the king's notice, according to Jane. She even had Anne bed the sovereign last year in hopes of elevating her status. Anne Basset certainly was pretty enough for the task, but the entire incident had come to naught, and the gossip had been that Lady Lisle had been furious.

Catherine's mind suddenly flew to the ink incident. Was it possible that Lady Lisle had arranged the entire thing as recompense for Catherine's threatening favor with the queen? Anne was in service at court, but she was not a maid of honor, and her younger sister, Katherine, had been refused a position entirely in the queen's household. This was far from what the ambitious Lady Lisle had in mind for her daughters, and Catherine would not be surprised if she were still angling for a way into royal favor.

Court truly was like a battlefield.

Suddenly, her grandmother's presence seemed something of a comfort.

"What do you know of Master Culpeper?" Catherine asked Anne Basset, surprising herself with the question.

"I know that he is handsome and, according to my mother, quite dangerous," Anne replied carefully.

"Someone told me once to take in half of what you hear and then believe less than half of that."

"That seems about right," Anne said as she hooked a gold chain around Catherine's small waist. It was easy for Catherine to see what the king had found attractive about Anne. But perhaps her lack of confidence and the way she constantly averted her eyes was what had prevented it from becoming more than a dalliance. After all, the sovereign only truly fell in love with bold, challenging women.

"Then I shall never trust anyone and think myself quite wise for my caution," Catherine replied.

Catherine laughed with her and felt free for the first time that day. She should not trust Anne Basset, but she saw a kindred spirit in her. They were two similar girls separated in status by the reed-thin line of a name, one being a bit more important than the other.

But she must not forget in the coming days the power of being a Howard, and the responsibility that was likely to come with it.

Soon after, Catherine was in the chapel for the morning service with the rest of the court. The king and queen knelt together at the altar at the front of the small chapel, while Catherine, Jane, Lady Frances and Lady Margaret were nearer the back. Beside them were Brandon, Wriothesley, Gregory Cromwell and Thomas Culpeper, who spent their time during the somber Mass whispering and casting sideways glances at the queen's ladies. Catherine knew they were not listening to the cleric's murmured words. She saw that Brandon had whispered something to Thomas and now was chuckling. Court was such a different world. She would have faced a flogging if she even thought about laughing during prayer. Afterward, as they walked out into the daylight, Thomas accompanied the king, who limped on his painful leg. Catherine still could not get over how much His Majesty had changed. He was stout and sweaty, which was the complete opposite of Thomas Culpeper's tall, lean form and effortless grace. There was a time when the thought of becoming Henry's queen was all any girl could dream of, but as Catherine walked behind him now, his girthy backside swathed in a tent of silk, that old dream seemed more of a nightmare.

She wondered what he had been like in the prime of his youth, in the tempestuous days of Anne Boleyn. What had it felt like to conquer the king at his youthful best?

Catherine's thoughts were interrupted by a smooth voice at her ear. "We really must stop meeting like this."

The man at her side brought her sharply back to reality. She saw, with a quick sideways glance, that his handsome face was lit with amusement at her faraway expression.

"As if we have a choice, Master Culpeper, since we serve husband and wife," she replied evenly, looking straight ahead to avoid his stunning eyes.

"There is always a choice, Mistress Howard."

"Yes, but one rarely has the power to exercise it," Catherine said wistfully.

"Well said. Particularly here at court, where many find it entertaining to watch others fall from power."

Catherine laughed suddenly as they passed beneath a stone archway flanked by carved pillars. Though she was small, the sound was big enough to stop the king and his party. Henry turned around to gaze at Catherine, as did Jane and the Marchioness of Dorset. Their spines were stiff, their faces full of judgment.

"Tell us, Culpeper, have you a joke to compete with Wil Somers?" the king asked, referring to his court jester and friend. "Will loathes competition, which would amuse me all the more."

Catherine felt her heart seize, then beat very fast. The powerful King of England was looking in her direction, with his bloated face, ruddy skin and little turned-up nose that reminded her of a pig's snout. In the awkwardness of the moment, everyone turned to look at Thomas.

"I remarked only that many find it entertaining to watch others fall, Your Majesty," Thomas said matter-of-factly.

There was a sharp, collective intake of breath as everyone waited a beat for the king's response. Surely he would be angry with Thomas for his blunt observation, which would have been better left unsaid. But, suddenly, the king began to laugh a deep, slightly rheumy laugh ending in a throaty cough. Everyone exhaled in relief and wisely laughed with the king. As she witnessed the effect he had on the king, Catherine could not help but admire Thomas. He seemed so carefree, likable, so valuable to royalty, and handsome. He could not possibly be guilty of the atrocity with the park keeper's wife. No, she knew firsthand what envious people were capable of. After the ink incident, slander seemed not only possible, but plausible. Thomas had told her that she needed to make up her own mind about the rumor, so she did: She would not believe something so horrendous of Thomas Culpeper.

Instead, Catherine decided to like him even more.

That afternoon, with flags and banners fluttering in the breeze, Catherine sat between Jane and the flirtatious, middle-aged Lady Lisle in the stands on the north lawn to watch the spring jousting tournament. Anne Basset's mother, an attractive woman swathed in cherry-colored satin, was an older version of her pretty daughter. She carried herself like a perfectly dignified court lady, until Thomas Culpeper rode onto the field and she waved her scarf at him—a request for him to wear her colors. Thomas cantered toward them on a sleek, grand courser and lifted his visor with a gloved hand, granting her request. Catherine saw Lady Lisle smile stupidly and flush like a girl.

Ah, what games mice did play while their well-placed husbands were away! Lord Lisle was lord deputy of Calais, giving his bored wife free rein to do as she pleased.

Catherine watched Thomas's glance move from Lady Lisle to her, then back again, as he extended the lance to Lady Lisle so she could tie her embroidered scarf onto its tip for good luck. The crowd politely applauded the custom. As he nodded to her, Catherine felt an odd twist deep within her solar plexus. It felt, strangely enough, like jealousy, but she sat up a little straighter and shrugged off the sensation as the king advanced.

The king rode a grand black bay caparisoned in tooled silver, and his new suit of armor flashed in the sunlight. Henry nodded to the queen, but just as he took Anne's scarf, embroidered with the letters H and A, his gaze slid across to Catherine and their eyes met. Henry nodded slightly but clearly to her. The royal acknowledgment felt flattering yet strange at the same time.

She glanced over and noticed that her grandmother had seen it and was smiling approvingly. It was a rare sight, particularly for Catherine, and though she was happy to see it, her only thought was that the king might be more inclined to show favor for her budding friendship with Thomas if he knew who she was. As the sovereign, he could destroy a relationship between his most intimate servants just as easily as he could sanction it.

And Catherine meant for him to sanction it.

Breaking the awkward moment, Henry made a show of nodding to the queen and accepting her colors on the tip of his lance, as Thomas had done with Lady Lisle. The crowd cheered. Everyone wanted to believe the fairy tale—that after three complicated marriages, Henry VIII had at last found happiness.

The contests went on into the late afternoon. Thomas had ridden twice and won both matches. In the third, he had wisely surrendered when his opponent was the king, applauding at his own loss in favor of the sovereign. Now, in his second match with the king, he seemed distracted.

Catherine wondered if this, too, was intentional to flatter the king.

Unexpectedly, Thomas's horse reared up on its powerful hind haunches just as the king launched a blow at him with his long, pointed lance. Thomas held tightly to the reins, but the big warrior bay was too powerful. Thomas tumbled to the ground with a clatter of armor and an audible groan. Lady Lisle lurched forward against the balustrade amid gasps and whispers. Jousting could be a brutal sport.

Catherine felt her heart seize as her fingers splayed across her mouth. She waited for Thomas to move, but he showed no signs of consciousness. After another moment, she saw the field aides and servants dash to Thomas's side as he struggled to sit up in his heavy suit of armor. She was overwhelmed with relief, followed closely by another pang of jealousy as Lady Lisle sent a servant to check on Thomas's injuries. Catherine was not certain of much in life, but she knew that Lady Lisle did not deserve to know anything before anyone else. And she did not deserve Thomas.

"He will be fine. Just a few bruises," Jane informed Catherine an hour later, after she had gone to the king's apartments herself. Culpeper had been examined by the royal physicians by order of His Majesty shortly before her arrival.

"Is he well enough to attend the queen's special masque this evening?" Catherine asked, trying to hide the relief on her face.

"He appeared fine to me," Jane said, casting a sideways glance at Catherine's expression.

"You saw Thomas yourself?"

"Of course. The only visible evidence of his mishap is a small gash on his temple where the visor was hinged." She gave a little smile of amusement. "You really could not be more obvious, you know."

"Obvious?" Catherine said, feigning innocence.

"Neither of you could. Only take care; the people of this court are not always what they seem."

"Is someone a danger to me?" she asked. This time she didn't need to feign anything.

Jane tilted her head and paused. "Just take care. That's all I'm saying." She hesitated before continuing. "I saw the way the king looked at you. So did everyone else."

"The king?" Catherine gasped. "Nothing was meant by that. He is married."

"Unhappily. Why else do you think you were brought here by your uncle?"

"To m-make an important match," Catherine stammered. "A match that will elevate my family's standing once again."

"Precisely," Jane gently said.

"But not with the king!" Catherine could not believe what she was hearing.

"Why not? There is no one more ambitious in this world than your uncle, and now the dowager duchess is here as well. The entire court is abuzz about her arrival."

"She is here because of me?" Catherine asked, the pieces finally falling into place.

"Is not everything about you?" Jane said in a matter-of-fact tone.

Anne Basset and Lady Frances entered the room just then to help Jane and Catherine change for the banquet, and the conversation came to an abrupt end. But not without Catherine's having a vague premonition of something dark and very dangerous working its way into her soul as Anne placed a new pair of dancing slippers before her.

❖

The king's mummers worked hard to entertain the court in the great hall, and the musicians played one lively tune after another from the gallery above. The din was topped by laughter and spirited conversation. Catherine laughed and conversed along with the others as she took small sips of the very strong spiced wine.

She had not met Wil Somers before, but the king's trusted fool was also a guest that evening. The thin little man with wide green eyes and an unruly mop of fawn brown hair sat on one side of the king, while the queen sat on the other. Anne seemed so carefree and unaware of the king's discontent. If he was discontent at all, Catherine thought. Perhaps it was just a rumor. More gossip.

Catherine could not help but look up when Thomas at last strode in.

In spite of Jane's words of warning, she had been hoping to see him. He looked magnificent as ever in dun velvet with gold slashings in his wide, fashionable sleeves. As he neared, she saw that he was with Lady Lisle at the center of a group of courtiers. Jealousy quickly overtook surprise, and Catherine took a larger swallow of wine than she intended, causing her to choke. Thomas was near enough to hear her, and when he turned to see her his bright smile faded to one of curiosity at her reaction. Catherine recovered, averted her own gaze and pretended to say something to Lady Margaret. To her embarrassment, the king's niece was neither looking at nor listening to her, and Thomas laughed, infuriating her. She shot him another glance, this time full of petulant anger.

She stiffened in her chair and looked away. *Lady Lisle indeed!*

Suddenly, Gregory Cromwell was behind her with a hand on her shoulder. "Where have you been hiding yourself?" he asked affably, smelling lightly of perspiration and horseflesh, as if he had been riding. "I haven't seen you since—"

"I serve the queen. I am at Her Grace's disposal at all times," Catherine coolly replied before he could finish. She was completely uninterested in Gregory at that moment.

"But you are here now, which is my great fortune, since my wife is not. Come save a poor old married man and dance with me."

She glanced up almost automatically to where Thomas was standing, hoping he would see Gregory's interest in her. To her surprise, he was watching her. *Good*, she thought.

"I would be delighted to dance with you, Master Cromwell," she said. She wanted Thomas to feel the jealousy that she was feeling as Lady Lisle continued to cling to his side.

"Ah, they are doing a tourdion."

"Your favorite dance?"

"Precisely, because it is the one I am best at."

Catherine could not help but laugh at his comment full of more self-effacement than bragging. She pushed back her chair, stood and haughtily strode to the center of the hall with Gregory.

"I wanted to see you again," he said, as they passed each other, then dipped and twirled in time to the music, their jewels and ornaments glittering in the flaming torchlight.

"I am not surprised."

"Not only because of that," he said with a chuckle, "although I would consider that as an added benefit, most definitely."

"I did not know you were married when we met."

"I did not know *you* were not just beautiful, but clever as well. Yet I refuse to hold *that* against you."

Catherine laughed. She could not help it. She liked men, and she liked the game.

"I *am* surprised by how charmingly you dance." She smiled intentionally when she saw Thomas still watching her.

"I am flattered you would think so," Gregory replied as they moved through another tune. "But I did warn you the tourdion was my best dance. I positively have two left feet when it comes to the volte."

"That's probably a good thing, since it is the volte at which the king excels."

"You have learned quickly for how briefly you have been at court."

"I am a Howard," she declared with a widening, flirtatious smile.

"That you are." They bowed to each other as the music and the dance came to an end. Gregory leaned over and whispered to her, "Let's steal away from this miserably warm corridor and do something wild. Let's go wading in the king's Neptune fountain."

"We would be caught for certain!" Catherine exclaimed.

"Is danger not the true thrill of adventure?"

"I wouldn't know. I didn't have many adventures at Horsham."

"Well, then it's high time you start having them here," Gregory said with a smile.

He led her with his slightly sweaty hand through a crowd of people so thick and drunk that they passed unnoticed beneath the Roman arch and through the open doors, where liveried guardsmen stood as still as toy soldiers. They continued down a long, carpeted corridor, then out into the moonlit night and beneath a sky peppered with brilliant stars. The cool night air came at her swiftly, reviving all of her senses.

The Neptune fountain was a massive stone pond encircled by trimmed plants and five brick pathways that led in five directions. Gregory sank onto the edge of the fountain, removed his shoes, and waited for Catherine to do the same.

"I feel so naughty," she said with a tinkling, girlish laugh.

"Splendid. So shall we have a go?"

"It *was* awfully warm in there just now . . ." Catherine admitted.

As she held up her wide skirts, he helped her step into the ankle-deep fountain, and they both began to laugh again. It was so fun to do something so shocking, and possibly even get caught. The night air was crisp as she moved deeper into the cool water.

"Do you like the feel of the moss between your toes?" he asked. "I find it rather erotic."

"It is," she said, playing willingly into Gregory's little game.

"Then we shall have to think of our next adventure before this one is over."

He pulled her toward him, touching her, running a hand up her arm. It was a familiar game, one she could play easily and well. Just as he pressed his mouth against the column of her throat, she sensed another presence nearby. When she drew away to look, the last person Catherine expected to see was Thomas Culpeper. He stood beside the fountain, hand on the dress scabbard at his side, his expression one of challenge.

"A pleasant evening," he said. His words were cordial, but his tone was not.

"Yes," she replied, feeling strangely embarrassed.

"Cromwell." Thomas nodded.

"Culpeper." Gregory nodded in return.

Catherine glanced from one man to the other. The tension grew in the silence, and the distant strains of music and laughter felt farther and farther away.

"Have you had enough?" Thomas asked her, his expression strained and angry now. "If so, I shall escort you back to the banquet."

"Should you not be escorting Lady Lisle?" Catherine asked in a petulant tone that surprised even her. She had not meant to sound so churlish, but the words escaped her lips before she could take them back.

Catherine watched his eyes narrow slightly. "That would be the portion of gossip that I recommended you disregard."

She tipped up her chin just slightly, challenging him. "I believe what I have seen for myself."

"Your eyes deceive you," he said quietly.

"Do they deceive the rest of us?" Gregory asked.

Catherine watched Thomas's jaw clench. He did not reply. Two heartbeats passed before his eyes cut away from her and settled on Gregory Cromwell. A moment later, Thomas turned to walk away. He took only two long strides on the brick path before Catherine leaped from the fountain and snatched up her shoes. Thomas paused and turned very slowly to meet the sound of wet, padding feet on the bricks. Her choice was implicit as she stood before him and let down the skirts of her dress.

Thomas looked angry, she thought. But there was a flash of vulnerability, as she had seen before, set deeply back in his eyes, and she nearly melted when she realized that she was the cause of it.

Catherine slipped on her shoes and then matched his stride as they walked together down the brick path that led back to the lights and sounds of the palace. She dared not glance back, but she knew Gregory was still standing in the fountain, watching them go. It was not until they went inside, up a wide flight of stairs, past the imposing carved pillars and down a long, paneled corridor, that Thomas said in a low, rasping voice, "It was not rape."

"What?"

There was another silence. She watched a muscle flex in his jaw. "The girl, the accusation, the king's pardon—I did not rape her." He stared straight ahead and kept his stride. "I cared for her. She was my youngest sister's best friend. William, the groundskeeper, was attacking her when I found them. He ran away like a coward, so I searched for him. When I found him, I killed him." His face was covered in shadow, but Catherine could tell from his voice that he was telling the truth.

"Would you have killed Gregory tonight?" she asked, her voice faltering.

"You know he is married," Thomas countered, avoiding the question.

"He neglected to mention that initially, as you omitted details about yourself," she said defensively.

"The two situations are entirely different."

"Then why would people make it into something it was not?"

"Because watching people fall from power is more entertaining than the truth. Have we not been over that before?"

"But you did nothing to defend yourself," Catherine pressed.

"It is complicated." He took a deep breath, then continued. "First of all, what one does not say is almost as important as what one does. Gregory's father, our great Lord High Chancellor, managed to tie him by marriage to the late Queen Jane's sister, Elizabeth Seymour. Your ambitious uncle, the Duke of Norfolk, had hoped to win the girl over for one of your brothers. Their war of advantageous marriages has been going on for years, long before I arrived at court myself."

Thomas heaved a heavy sigh and ran a hand behind his neck. They stopped beneath an archway with a small, shadowy alcove beyond. "The girl, the one whom I supposedly violated, was someone I had known all of my life. In the beginning, she was like one of my own sisters. Her name is Arabella, and she was, and is, married, as I mentioned before."

Catherine studied him. Their eyes met again. "Are you in love with her?" she asked.

"I was."

"What changed?"

"I was supposed to meet her that afternoon, but William found her first."

"Why did you not leave it to her own husband to defend her honor, if that was really how it happened?"

In the protection of the heavy shadows, he moved a step closer. She could hear his unsteady breathing and feel the warmth of it on her throat. She noticed a small sheen of perspiration on his upper lip, and she knew now what it all meant to him.

The gossip. The lie. The girl.

"Because she had risked everything to meet me at a place we had chosen, and her husband would have known that."

"So to spare her, you told the authorities that everything was your fault?"

"In a way, it was. It was my penance to take the blame, because I had loved someone else's wife."

"To look like a rapist so the woman you loved did not look like an adulteress?"

"Something like that . . ." His words trailed off.

"The king knew the whole story then? Is that the real reason he pardoned you, not just because he likes your company at the hunt?"

"Yes, that is the reason." He turned to meet her gaze. "His Majesty may be old and fat now, and at times unbelievably quick to temper, but he is rarely without compassion when faced with the truth. I did love Arabella once, but she realized she was in love with her husband. That changed everything. It is all a long time ago now."

As Catherine looked at Thomas, his eyes told her everything was true. She reached up to touch the line of his jaw in response. A tremor ran through her as she did. "I believe you."

"Thank you," he said.

He cautiously lowered his mouth onto hers.

Their kiss was tender and infinitely gentle in the privacy of the shadow-filled alcove, and the sounds of the banquet seemed very far away. The way he touched her made Catherine want him desperately, no matter the consequences. With Thomas, the rush of sensations she felt was something she had never experienced before, and she realized that she was not only playing a game this time. He took her hand and led her back into the corridor, toward the grand door of a room without a guard standing sentry. He turned the iron handle and they went inside together.

The room was mostly dark except for the light of the moon, which streamed through two grand, leaded oriel windows. The odor was musty, and the room felt as if it had been sealed for a long time. Catherine could see a thin layer of dust on the bed, table and a shelf lined with books. Suddenly she felt dizzy, unable to think as her heart beat rapidly. Thomas pressed her against a cool, smooth paneled wall and leaned heavily against her. He cupped her face in his hands and kissed her again, more urgently now. She moaned and felt a shiver of delight as his tongue moved into her mouth. He was possessing her, commanding her with every touch. And she wanted to be commanded. Catherine had always felt in control of this part of the game, but with Thomas, there was only wild desire. The pounding of her heart roared in her ears as she reached down to his belt and began to unfasten it.

"Are you certain?" he murmured against her throat, kissing her, pushing back her headdress until it tumbled onto the carpeted floor. He let his fingers tangle in her hair. "There will be no going back for us if we do this."

"I have no wish to go back," Catherine declared as his silver belt fell onto her discarded headdress. In pearlescent moonlight, she saw the intensity of his gaze and said, "Only forward with you."

Thomas took her to the downy bed, which smelled of must and like an animal because of the duck feathers. She could feel his fingers trembling as he lifted her skirts up to her waist and began to untie her stomacher. Her anticipation was almost painful, for she had never had to wait before.

His fingers trailed down her bare stomach, turning her skin to gooseflesh. As he looked at her, his gaze was passionate but surprisingly gentle, which rocked Catherine to her core. Thomas rose over her, pressing his mouth onto hers as he pushed full force inside of her. Catherine's mind glazed over until she could not think. There was only her beating heart, the way he tasted, and this.

He moved a hand up the expanse of her dress to where her breasts were still held in by the top of her gown, swelling above the binding and the little strip of lace. She trembled at the pressure of his fingers, taking absolute pleasure in him, and she clutched at his back to bring him even closer.

"Jésu!" he cried out with a groan, as Catherine was overcome by the rich, dark warmth of her own completion.

A moment later, he laid his head on her shoulder, and they held each other as their frenzied passion simmered into sweet contentment. She felt his breath in her hair, and thought there could never be a better feeling. But only a moment later they heard firm footsteps out in the corridor, and Catherine glanced at him in silent panic. She had forgotten that this was but a temporary haven. This was court. Nothing they did or thought or said would ever be without consequence.

They heard the footsteps pass by back and forth in the corridor with slight pauses, as if the person were seeking something. Catherine's heart began to race wildly as Thomas rose, quickly dressed and pressed a silent kiss onto her forehead. He waited until there were no more footsteps, then went toward the door. His silhouette quickly faded into the shadows as she heard the door open, then click to a close. He was gone. Catherine lay there alone without moving, knowing that she must wait so they would not be seen leaving the bedchamber together. He had taken an enormous risk with the Duke of Norfolk's prize niece tonight, as she had with the king's favorite companion.

Even so, Catherine knew that they were meant to be together. She saw that now with dispassionate and intense clarity. It was not just what had happened that night, although the act made it more inevitable. Catherine knew, as she lay in the little bed alone now, that her future would be tied up with Thomas Culpeper's forever.

❖

"It did not quite work out as I had planned," Gregory Cromwell said with a sigh as he thought of his planned seduction of Catherine Howard and his dashed hopes of removing her from consideration as a possible future mate for the king.

"Your infinite charms with the ladies are failing you, my boy?" his father asked glibly as he looked up from a writing table in a room that faced the great tiltyard of Whitehall below.

"Oh, I still have plenty of charm, my lord. That was not the problem with the Howard girl."

"Then what was it? I set such a minor task for you; all you had to do was get the Howard girl out of the king's way. If her reputation is sullied enough the king will never want her for anything meaningful."

Though Cromwell spoke lightly, he was brimming with disappointment that his plan apparently had failed. Gregory heaved a great sigh, not happy to be undone, particularly by something as inconsequential as seducing a girl, no matter what his father's intentions were concerning it. His father, a thickly set, aging man with heavy jowls and a pursed, judgmental mouth, would never understand. The chancellor had never been handsome.

"Culpeper is what happened," Gregory admitted.

"Again?"

"That fool has never bested me at romance before," Gregory said defensively.

"I am certain this has little to do with romance, Gregory. That girl is a mindless twit wrapped up in a pretty package. If her name were not Howard, there would be no need even to have this conversation. On her own, without that name, she could never land a king. But I am desperate here! I cannot have another Howard queen or I will most certainly face complete ruin!"

"Her name might soon be Culpeper, by the look of things tonight," Gregory scoffed.

Cromwell dropped his pen onto the parchment at the declaration. He slowly leaned back in his chair and steepled his fat fingers, tapping them together in thought. "Well, now, that *is* an interesting possibility."

"That Culpeper should triumph over your own son is interesting?"

"On the contrary." The king's chief minister let a smile turn up the corners of his little mouth, which was wedged into ruddy, doughlike cheeks. "It is interesting that I might not have to congratulate my greatest enemy's niece on becoming the next queen. Thus, I might not have to witness my own destruction."

Gregory eyes widened at his father's last words, aware for the first time how dire the situation was. "Do you really think she could become queen?"

"You fool, she is every bit the king's sort of girl: beautiful, petite, accomplished at playing the music that he loves. But above all, she reminds him of the single greatest passion of his youth. That is exactly the sort he would marry."

"But he cut off Anne Boleyn's head," Gregory pointed out.

Cromwell rolled his eyes, unwilling to suffer fools gladly, even if the fool was his own son. "Not before he spent a decade absolutely bewitched by her, body and soul. This country was rocked by Henry's passion, and Catholics like Norfolk would do anything to have the country as it once was, including using his niece to gain the upper hand to persuade the king to return to Catholicism. But I swear that shall not happen."

"Do you trust that Culpeper is man enough to woo and marry Catherine Howard right under the king's nose? No one has forgotten what it cost men like George Boleyn, Mark Smeaton and Henry Norris, who were all caught dallying with Mistress Boleyn."

"It will be a race to the finish if we do this," Cromwell warned, heaving himself out of the chair with a grunt. He turned from his son, went to the window and opened the latch, ushering in the cool night air and the sound of crickets from the hedgerow below.

"If we do what, Father?" Gregory asked, not fully comprehending the plan.

"Help Culpeper win Catherine Howard," Cromwell explained, trying not to show the desperation that he felt.

"We are going to work against the king? Is it worth a dangerous gamble like that?" Gregory asked in astonishment.

"We have no other choice, boy. If the king wins her first, the Howards' rise back to highest prominence will be complete. Norfolk would like nothing more than to take away my influence with the king and see to my total destruction. You have been raised your entire life knowing the stakes. Now is the flashpoint. One error and it will be the end of us all."

"How could it have come to this? How could you ever have risked championing that horrendous princess of Cleves?" Gregory asked furiously as Cromwell spun around, his red face burning with anger.

"Do not dare to speak to me with such contempt!" Cromwell flared. "You have no idea what is at stake here! You are a boy, new to a man's world, and I will not have your judgment upon me. I gave you everything you have! Everything in this court, every movement, every word, every breath has always been a gamble, and I do it all for you—for this family!"

"Yet a woman like the queen was too great a gamble to champion. I may be untested, Father, but I would never have put my family at risk in such a way."

The vein in Cromwell's bald temple flared. "You are where you are, with your rich costumes, your costly education, your fancy wife and your place at court, because of me, you ungrateful little bastard! Precisely because I took risks like those!"

Father and son glared at each other for a moment, contempt glittering on both of their faces in a flare of firelight.

Gregory was the first to break the silence. "Do not be a hypocrite, Father. I am too much of a Cromwell not to know that you did everything you did, first and foremost, for yourself. If there was any benefit for your son, it was incidental only."

The king's most powerful minister stepped nearer the boy he had sired but never fathered, despising at that moment how easily he had gotten the one thing that had eluded the king for so long. "Well, my boy, you had better hope and pray, for both of our sakes, that you learned enough from your wretched old father to ensure that Master Culpeper and Mistress Howard come together, or you may find that empty head of yours on the pike next to mine on Tower Bridge."

❖

In the shadowy room where Thomas had just left her, Catherine straightened her heavy gown and adjusted her headdress with trembling hands. As she did, she said a silent prayer that she would not look too disheveled as she walked into the corridor. She was frightened, confused and wildly exhilarated all at once, but she could not tell if it was her tryst with Thomas or the danger of being caught. Catherine tipped up her head, drew in a last breath, and opened the door. To her great surprise, a figure was standing outside of the door, and Catherine let out a little gasp. It was the dowager duchess. Her grandmother had been waiting.

Chapter Eight

May 1540
Whitehall Palace, London

"*G*et on with it, Norfolk," the king grumbled, flipping a bejeweled hand in the air as he lay on his grand black oak bed heavy with fringed curtains. "Let us hear your plan to extricate me from this sham marriage. And be forewarned, I am in no mood for a long explanation."

Norfolk and Gardiner, who stood together at the foot of the bed, where the royal crest was stamped in gold, exchanged a glance as the royal physician treated the open ulcer on Henry's leg with leeches from a glass jar. The putrid odor emanating from the wound caused Norfolk to struggle not to insult the sovereign and openly gag.

The war with Cromwell was on. Norfolk and Gardiner had already informed the king of the changing political landscape. The balance of power between King Francis I of France, the Holy Roman Emperor Charles V and Henry had once again shifted. His two most powerful rivals were not as tightly allied as before, and they did not pose a strong threat to England at the moment. At the same time, his ties to Germany had weakened, making his marriage to the Cleves woman, and the alliance both, unnecessary. Still, to divorce his wife

144

on illegitimate legal grounds could risk his standing on the world stage and his potential political alliances. But Norfolk and Gardiner claimed that they had found legitimate legal grounds.

Carefully, Gardiner handed a document to the king, whose legs were spread wide as the physicians applied feverfew and marigold around the wound. Norfolk drew in a breath and exhaled to ensure that his nerves were steady. There was no room for error in this.

The moment for the Howard family had arrived.

"It is the proof we believed existed, Your Majesty."

Henry's thin copper brows merged as his gaze slid from Gardiner to Norfolk. Finally, he looked down and began to read, his labored breathing the only sound between them.

Norfolk dared to venture, "It was not just a promise between the queen and the Duke of Lorraine. Clearly, Your Majesty, this document shows that the queen's brother had engaged her in an actual contract to wed, binding by any standard."

Henry winced, feeling the pull of one of the leeches. He closed his eyes for a moment, then opened them again, leveling his gaze exclusively on Norfolk. "Then I was never truly married to her?"

"Not in the sight of God, sire, no."

"So it is the Lord's blessing that I did not consummate the marriage, since it is not a true marriage at all?"

"What it means, sire, is that your tie with Cleves—"

"I know what the devil it means, Gardiner!" he snarled, and grimaced as two more leeches were placed into the open wound and quickly took hold.

"It is regrettable that Cromwell sought to engage you in such an alliance without being absolutely certain of the queen's availability," said Norfolk. "No leader in the world will fault you for extricating yourself from an illegal union."

Again, Henry studied each of their faces with angry eyes narrowed in calculation. In the silence, Norfolk repressed his sense of panic at the expression on the king's fleshy face.

"We had hoped the news would be pleasing to Your Majesty," Norfolk said.

"I am pleased. I just . . ." The king sighed and laid his head back against the spray of pillows. "I have no wish to insult Anne or her brother. The queen is a good enough woman. None of this is her fault."

"Of course not, sire. But the facts remain the same either way."

"Would then Your Majesty desire that we take the next step?" Gardiner asked. "We can cautiously craft a suit and—"

"No. This is Cromwell's mess. He led me into it and I fully expect him to extricate me."

"But, Your Majesty," Norfolk intervened with as much caution as he could. "This is a matter requiring the utmost care. Cromwell proved himself inept in the construction of the marriage. Why would we assume his further intervention would bring anything but more complications?"

Henry's face was mottled red with frustration. "He has been my friend, and my adviser, for a decade. He supported Wolsey during my divorce from Anne Boleyn, just as you two sycophants support each other now. For the love of God, when this is over, I will never trust any adviser again the way I trusted all of you!" He paused, drew in a breath, then sank back into the bed pillows as his physician backed away from the bed. "Be that as it may, I still require an annulment, and the man who dug his own grave may as well bury himself in it."

Norfolk struggled not to smile, remembering, understanding and feeling the little chill of recognition that followed. This tactic was classic Henry, and it would work out perfectly for Norfolk and Gardiner. In other words, forcing Cromwell to pursue the nullity suit would be forcing him to admit his failure with Cleves. Once he discovered the challenge before him, Cromwell would be so busy trying to save his own life that he would offer no real opposition to Norfolk's plan.

Yes, Henry was angry with everyone right now, and he would not be eager to trust again. Norfolk knew he would have to be that much more clever in paving the king's path toward his beautiful Catholic niece. It was his duty, after all, not just to the king, but to England and to God.

❖

As Catherine sat in the queen's apartments that afternoon, sewing with Anne and the other ladies, she could not help but let her mind wander to her grandmother's speech from the night before. At Horsham, the dowager duchess had been a harsh, judgmental crone, unbending in all things. But now Agnes Howard was being oddly kind to her.

After Catherine had left her private little sanctuary, her grandmother had walked with her back to the queen's apartments, obviously knowing what had just occurred with Culpeper.

"Are you happy here at court?" she had asked in a strangely maternal tone.

"I am trying to adjust, my lady grandmother," Catherine said, her face still burning with embarrassment.

"And you are taking care? Horsham was a very different place, you know. You were very sheltered there."

"You said I was very silly there."

"You were."

"And petulant."

"You can be."

"And too pretty for my own good."

"It shall be your greatest asset or the quickest way to your downfall."

Catherine looked at her as they walked down a long, paneled corridor, and to her surprise Agnes almost smiled. Or at least, Catherine thought, it was an expression approximating one.

"I have come here to protect your interests," the dowager said, surprising Catherine.

"And my uncle's?"

The dowager's slim smile stretched. "Now, that sounds like a true Howard. Yes, of course, all of ours. Court is not a place where the weak survive. I am here to see that you, however, do."

"Because I am weak?"

"Because there is more than you could ever imagine depending on your success."

When they reached Catherine's room, there was a new dress laid out carefully on her bedcover. It was green silk trimmed with ivory-colored Burgundian lace and a row of emeralds at the bodice.

"I don't need another dress from my uncle," Catherine said, no longer enamored of his expensive gifts now that she knew of his plan to make her queen.

"This one is from me. Child, you are competing with countesses, duchesses and other titled women now, and their ambitions surround you."

"What am I competing for, exactly?"

The doors to the queen's apartments opened suddenly, startling Catherine out of the remembered conversation and returning her swiftly to the moment. She perked up, surrendering her needlework to her lap, as the king, Thomas Culpeper, Charles Brandon, Edward Seymour and Thomas Wriothesley were announced into the room.

Again Catherine noticed that the king walked with more of an effort-filled hobble than the manly stride of his companions. But though he was surrounded by youth, glittering jewels, masculine laughter and yards of velvet and silver thread, the grandeur of his own entrance was not diminished. Catherine was secretly awed to be in the presence of such a man. Swiftly, each of the ladies stood and fell into deep curtsies. The queen's was the deepest gesture and, in her voluminous dress, the most clumsily executed of all.

"Your Majesty comes unannounced," Anne of Cleves sputtered in her Teutonic accent. Catherine felt pained for her.

"Yes, well, spontaneity is, by design, unexpected. Everyone knows that," the king said gruffly.

Anne's square, ruddy face flushed with embarrassment, but she ignored the slight. Catherine watched as a troupe of court musicians followed the king. They settled themselves into a corner and, on Henry's nod, began to play a tune. A velvet-covered chair fringed with gold was swiftly brought forward and the king sank wide-legged onto it. He flicked his wrist as an afterthought, instructing the ladies to be seated around him.

"So what brings you here, sire?" Anne asked awkwardly, clearly uncertain of what she should be doing.

The king's companions chuckled unkindly in response.

"No! Great God, not for *that*!" Henry's sudden smile was mischievous. Apparently, he had guessed his companions' thoughts from their expressions. Sensitive though he could be, Henry still could never quite let a clever quip escape him in the moment, no matter whom it might hurt. "We've just come from a game of shuttlecock out in the yard, and Tom here made a bet, knowing the ladies would be at their sewing. Seymour had called needlework too trivial and easy for men, so Tom wagered that Seymour could not sew a straight line in under a minute's time without pricking a finger and drawing his own blood."

Catherine bit back a smile. She wanted to laugh, but wisely she did not. The king, though physically unappealing, could be surprisingly amusing, she thought, looking at the glitter in his small, dark eyes. They were eyes that held the weight of the world, the reflection of unspeakable horrors and monumental, historical events. Yet here he was, indulging in an afternoon's amusement, smelling of camphor and musk.

"What is his punishment if he fails?" the king's niece Frances asked with amusement.

"Humiliation before you fine ladies seems like punishment enough," Thomas responded with an easygoing smile.

The musicians began to play something soft and lovely as Edward Seymour sat down and Catherine offered the needlework in her lap. Seymour picked up the piece of fabric and needle as if to begin sewing. Everyone laughed as he made a face of mock fright. Catherine felt herself free to laugh, too.

"Very well, then. Off you go," commanded the king.

Everyone began to count and laugh above the music. Even the queen, with her normally dismayed and slightly confused expression, was enjoying the game.

"Bollocks!" Edward Seymour groaned suddenly, sending the fabric and needle clattering to the tile floor as a stream of blood dripped from his finger.

Henry threw back his head, laughing in delight at the outcome. "I knew it could not be done. Now you must apologize to these fine ladies for assuming that their needlework was not a worthy and dangerous business."

Catherine stood and drew a small handkerchief from her pocket as the king's companions good-naturedly heckled Seymour. She pressed it onto his finger, provoking whistles, laughter and moans of envy from the other men.

"There," said Catherine. "That should stop the blood flow in a moment. Apparently your friends told you nothing of the need for a thimble."

"Now, what fun would that have been for him, Mistress Howard?" the king asked.

Catherine glanced up and met the king's admiring gaze. "I find that a level playing field offers the more rewarding outcome, Your Majesty."

I should not have said that, she thought. It sounded as if she had challenged the king, which she had not intended. But the unexpected ensuing laughter from the group assuaged her fears. Henry's smile was even more unexpected. "And yet a wise competitor seizes his advantages if his ultimate goal is victory," he cleverly replied.

Catherine nodded, feeling another quip rising on her tongue, yet she wisely chose to hold it back. Henry signaled to a musician with a nod, and a lute was brought to him.

"I have heard you play, and you are a worthy enough competitor to make it a level playing field," he said.

"Ah, yes, but who could judge fairly when the sovereign is my challenger?" she asked.

Catherine could feel the glances and smiles exchanged around her. She was in the middle of the lion's den, but for the moment, she was amused to be there. Henry handed Catherine his lute with an affable smile as he said, "Then Master Culpeper shall decide. He is my trusted aide, honest with his sovereign in all things. He shall not choose my playing out of loyalty alone." Henry signaled to Thomas. "Come forward and be our judge."

Thomas came forward with a confident stride, his smile as charming as always above that square jaw and adorable cleft chin. Dutifully, Thomas nodded to the king, then turned to Catherine to greet her, though she noticed that he avoided her eyes.

"You may play us something first, Mistress Howard," the king deigned.

She held the lute on her lap, intent on meeting the challenge. For a moment she closed her eyes, thinking of the many songs Henry Manox had taught her and what confidence he had given her to play them. Catherine opened her eyes then and began to strum the notes to the most complicated piece she knew.

Even before the last chord, the king began applauding so enthusiastically that the others followed, all cheering her skill.

"A lovely tune, Mistress Howard," Charles Brandon remarked.

"A pity the king can so easily best you," Seymour said with a laugh.

"I am not so certain now," Henry countered, smiling.

He took the lute onto his thick thigh in challenge. With his other leg extended, Catherine could see a wide bandage below his nether hose. It was common knowledge that he had been battling an infection for several years, and she could only imagine how frustrating it would be to a robust man who had once been a legendary competitor in all activities. As he began to play Catherine carefully watched how his fingers gently plucked the strings, drawing out the most tender sounds. She saw how his expression changed, the melody taking him to another place.

"That was lovely," she said when he had finished. "Your Majesty must definitely take the prize."

"Like any man, in some things I can only hope," he replied vaguely, with a sly smile that widened his pink, moist little bud of a mouth.

"What tune was that? It was so . . . haunting," she marveled.

A silence fell upon the room. Catherine glanced at the faces around her, each one more piqued by surprise than the next. Someone cleared his throat, although she could not tell who it was.

"I call it 'Greensleeves.'"

"You wrote it yourself?"

"I did, indeed, many years ago. For your cousin, actually. It has been a long time since I felt like playing it."

The silence dragged on. Catherine felt a strange twist in the pit of her stomach. *My cousin Anne Boleyn, whom you had executed.*

"So, Tom, tell us," Henry said, changing the subject, "who shall you say is the victor?"

Thomas stood between them with an odd expression on his face. "True talent always trumps carefully studied playing," he decreed, not looking at her. "I say that while Mistress Howard's playing was lovely, Your Majesty is the victor handily."

The group broke out in applause over the foregone conclusion. "Mistress Howard was a worthy competitor, and I should like a rematch very soon, if you would grant me one," the king said, turning to Catherine.

"It would be my honor." Catherine nodded respectfully, trying not to notice the odd glint in the king's eye and the completely altered expression on Thomas's face.

❖

An hour later, Catherine and Thomas walked out into the wet, gray day, down the privy stairs, through the river gate and past the palace wall.

They strolled silently along the banks of the river Thames, watching painted barges bobbing on the water, their flags and banners fluttering in the breeze. They were just beyond the castle grounds, free from the eyes of the court.

They had stolen away from their duties, and each knew their time alone was limited, but it was worth the risk. Catherine was irrevocably in love. She had known that for days. Thomas Culpeper was everything she hoped for in a husband, lover, and friend, and she wanted to spend as much time with him as possible.

As he held her hand tightly, leading her among the boatmen and children running along the shore, Catherine clung to him and thought of her past feelings for Francis Dereham. A year ago, there had been a time, amid all of the dormitory fun and silliness, when she had convinced herself she was in love with him. But those childish feelings paled in comparison to her all-consuming love for Thomas. She would marry Thomas Culpeper tomorrow if he asked her. And he must ask her. Of that much she was absolutely certain.

As if he could sense her thoughts, Thomas stopped and turned to her and very gently touched her face.

"Do you know how incredibly beautiful you are in this pale light?" he whispered.

"I was going to say the very same to you." Catherine smiled.

"We are heading toward a predicament, you know."

"A predicament?" she asked with a faintly arched brow.

"Perhaps I should say 'triangle' instead of 'predicament.' Surely you can see that His Majesty fancies you." Thomas's expression betrayed a hint of pain.

"Then I thank God Almighty that he has a queen."

"That has rarely stopped him before."

"I'll not be a royal mistress, Thomas, even for my family's sake."

"Now, now," he said, chuckling. "I wager you are far more clever than in the beginning the queen was. You should look to Bessie Blount as your example. She died a wealthy woman, and her son became the most powerful duke in England."

"Her bastard son," Catherine said, unconvinced.

Catherine had met Mistress Blount only once, after she had settled into the queen's household, where, strangely enough, Bessie had been named a lady in waiting to Anne of Cleves. Though she was forty years old, a shadow of her beauty was still evident, as well as her sweet temper. It was a pity, Catherine thought, when not long after she arrived at court Mistress Blount fell ill and was forced to leave.

Catherine suddenly processed Thomas's words. "I had not heard that she died."

"Sadly, yes. It was only a few days ago. Word was sent to the king from Surrey, but Bessie herself told me, the day she left court, that she had lived her life well and had no regrets. That is what I choose to remember of her."

They walked past the entrance to a bridge.

"That is how I would like to live my life: absolutely no regrets."

"Too late for me, I'm afraid," Thomas said.

Catherine glanced at him. "And what do you regret, Master Culpeper?"

"For one thing, I regret not meeting you sooner, Mistress Howard." He smiled his dazzling smile.

Thomas led her onto a small covered barge while a dozen others bobbed in the light spring breeze. Beneath a canopy of green silk fringed in gold, they slipped onto a cushioned bench before a table covered in crisp white linen and set with trays of figs, marzipan and apples, and decanters of wine. In private at last, Thomas kissed her passionately, not waiting for her invitation.

"Did you arrange this?" she asked, as her arms slid around his neck in silent compliance.

"Of course." He smiled.

"How brilliant of you."

"I am pleased that you think so."

They spoke of many things in the small jewel of time that Thomas had carved for them on the barge. Catherine had never felt freer or happier. For nearly an hour they ate, drank wine and held each other as lovers until Catherine pressed her fingers into his thick, gorgeous hair.

"My sweet fool, I do so love you," she said, smiling.

In response, Thomas pulled her against him, clamping his arms tightly around her and drawing her into a powerful kiss. She sank deeply into it, enveloped by his body, knowing there would never be anyone else in the world who could make her feel like this. She slipped a hand between his thighs and reveled in his deep groans. She wanted him to love her as much as she loved him.

But he never spoke the words. Afterward, as he led her back to the palace, a strained silence fell between them. She understood that Thomas was a man of few words, which helped him maintain his position at Henry's court. But she had given him her heart and soul, and he had given her only a few moments of passion in return. She wanted to build a future with him and gain the duke's approval, but she was afraid that she was running out of time. She knew the duke was formulating his own plans for her—ones that did not include Thomas—and it would be a challenge to convince him that her plan was better.

Thomas walked back with Catherine to the courtyard. They were alone in the shadow of a pillar when he took her hands and pressed a single, gentle kiss onto her cheek.

"You are the most amazing woman I have ever met," he whispered softly before turning away and walking back to the king's apartments.

It was as close to a declaration of love as she would get for now, yet she still longed for the day when he would let down his guard completely with her. As she watched him go, Catherine decided that convincing the duke to let her be with Thomas Culpeper was worth the risk, especially if Thomas should say that he loved her, too.

❖

For the nearly five months' duration of his disastrous political marriage, Henry had felt frustrated, old and defeated. He was tangled for the fourth time within a matrimonial net. But Norfolk had presented him with a path to freedom, and the duke's pretty, young niece had given him the impetus to wade through yet another complex divorce.

Thinking of Catherine Howard's slim body—and not of his four-year-old son upon his knee—Henry sat patiently on a velvet-covered stool for his court painter, Hans Holbein. Henry's full face was flushed with desire for Catherine and from the noxious odor of paint fumes.

There was a time when he craved nothing more than a son. He had divorced Catherine of Aragon when she could not provide that, and beheaded Anne when she produced only their daughter, Elizabeth. But now that he had a son who had reached the reassuring age of four, when illness took so many infants, Henry felt free to trust, and to desire something more. His heir, this gentle boy as fragile as Jane Seymour, had given him the immortality he craved. Now a young and beautiful wife might give him back his all but dissipated youth as well.

"Tip your head toward His Grace just slightly, Your Majesty," Holbein directed the boy, Edward. "There. Perfect."

"When can we go outside, Father? How much longer will he be?" the boy asked, straining not to move lest he be scolded again by Holbein or his father.

"Patience, my boy. You shall be king one day, and learning to wait for what you desire shall be as important as finding a way to achieve it."

"But I want to play," Edward pressed, his little lower lip turning out in a pout, and tears of frustration pooling in his wide blue-green eyes. His eyes were the exact shape of his mother's, and when Henry looked into them, he could deny the boy nothing.

"Very well, Hans, that's enough for today."

As he lifted Edward from his knee, he saw her. Fresh. Lovely. Full of promise.

"Ah, there you are." The king smiled at Catherine as Edward stood next to his father, tugging on the diamonds and rubies of his doublet.

"You called for me, sire?" she asked.

Catherine was slightly frazzled but looked stunning in a gown of blue embroidered velvet. Agnes and Norfolk were doing a splendid job with her, he thought appreciatively. Trotting her out for sale to the highest bidder.

Good. He could afford to pay any price.

She stood with Lady Rochford, whom he had finally forgiven for her connection to the Anne Boleyn chapter of his life, one that still brought him torment to recall. Henry still could not fathom how he had moved from intense passion to complete hatred for Anne. His transformation during that period still frightened him, and he still could not bear to look upon their child, Elizabeth, who was born of such dark passion.

Sometimes at night, in the solitude of sleep, Anne came to him in a dream, at times as a beguiling, ghostly image at the foot of his bed. He would try to cry out, to call her a witch, to accuse her of robbing him of his heart. But the words never came, and in a frustrating repetition of the dream, her image always snapped away, leaving everything unresolved between them.

He could not believe how much this Howard girl reminded him of the young Anne. The one who had led him into emotional ruin.

He believed Catherine would be different, and just might ease the dark torment of his memories. In truth, he was counting on it.

"My lady Rochford," he said, acknowledging Jane Boleyn with a nod.

"Your Majesty. I have seen little of you since my return to court," said Jane.

"Certainly we must remedy that, but I trust you have been made welcome in the meantime."

"Greatly. The queen is generous and kind."

"Splendid," Henry replied, as Edward fidgeted beside him like a little colt longing to break free. He glanced down at the thin, pale boy, who was not unlike Henry's elder brother, Arthur, at a young age. Apparently, this was a day for memories, Henry thought, willing the image away like all of the others that plagued him.

He glanced at Catherine and noticed how uncomfortable she had become during his exchange with Jane. But he had brought them together intentionally. Each connected him to the darkest part of his past, and facing the two of them together was like facing that phantom image at the foot of his bed. He wanted to deal with it once and for all.

"My lady Rochford, you know the prince."

"Your Highness." Jane curtsied to the little boy in his opulent velvet doublet, jewels and hat, but Edward seemed not to notice her.

"Mistress Howard, I should like to introduce you to my son," Henry said, watching keenly for what would happen next. As Jane had done, Catherine dropped into a deep curtsy, but then moved nearer, as if he were any other little boy.

"That is a fine top, Your Highness," she said of the small red toy he had drawn from a pocket and was trying, unsuccessfully, to spin on the surface of the polished table beside them. "I had one of those when I was your age. It was my favorite thing in all the world, and I was always scolded for having it with me. Would you like to know a little trick I devised for spinning it?"

The child looked surprised to be spoken to with such familiarity when everyone else spoke to him formally, as one would expect of England's only male heir. Henry was equally surprised, but also amused. A moment later, meeting her gaze fully, the child handed her the toy. Catherine took it and, with a sharp, deft twist, spun it onto the table. Henry watched the boy's eyes light with delight.

"Show me," Edward said in a tone of command for such a little voice.

"It is in your wrist. You must snap it like this," Catherine replied, showing him.

In three attempts, Edward was able to spin the little toy. Henry felt as much joy as his son at his success, and he could feel himself smiling.

"Teach me something else?" Edward bade her with wide, hopeful eyes. Henry felt his heart seize. The boy had no mother; he did not even have a strong connection to a particular nurse-maid or servant, so it was a unique moment for the doting father to witness.

Henry placed a hand gently atop the boy's head. "Mistress Howard can return later if you practice your Latin without complaint."

Edward's governess, an older woman with steel gray hair peeking out from her hood, advanced and curtsied. "I will inform you of his performance, Your Majesty."

"Can she truly?" Edward asked.

"It is a promise." Henry smiled tenderly at the boy as he followed his governess and Jane from the room.

"Come look at something." Henry motioned for Catherine to follow him.

Holbein, a squat little man with stick-straight bangs over a sweaty forehead, was cleaning his paintbrushes.

"That shall be all for now, Hans," Henry dismissed the painter, as he approached the still-wet painting with Catherine.

The painting was a slightly stylized image of the king, although his voluminous size showed through. To the left of Henry was a pencil outline of Edward's face, with his exquisite doublet and hat already painted in. To the right of Henry was the shadow of a girl, not yet a full outline. This was meant to be Elizabeth. Regretfully, Henry had not seen the child in nearly a year. Six-year-old Elizabeth was kept at Hatfield, out of his sight but never fully out of his conscience.

Which was precisely why he was inviting her to Greenwich in the summer, one of several stops on the royal progress.

Seeing his other daughter, Mary, was more difficult, and Henry did not like to do it unless it was absolutely necessary. The poor girl had been through too much, and her allegiance was to the memory of her dead mother, Catherine of Aragon. In spite of the bitter end of their marriage, Henry knew in his heart that Catherine had truly loved him, which made the guilt of looking upon their only child's face intolerable.

"What do you think of the painting so far?" he asked the new girl, Catherine Howard, pushing aside his guilty feelings about his daughters.

"I think it is a fine likeness, Your Majesty."

"And what of me?"

"I meant of you, sire."

He smiled like a boy, relishing her flattery.

"There is to be another image in the painting," Henry said, gesturing to the shaded figure. "It will be of your cousin's daughter, Elizabeth."

"She is a fortunate girl to be painted beside so grand a king," Catherine said.

"I struggle to remember that she is still my daughter."

"Children are the innocent ones."

"Indeed. I know your own childhood at Horsham was a difficult one. I am sorry about your parents. I did not know your father, but Norfolk spoke favorably of him."

Catherine was touched by his sympathy. "Many thanks, Your Majesty."

"I am bringing the child to Greenwich. It has been too long since my son had the benefit of youthful companionship. It will do him good to reunite with his sister. The court leaves on progress tomorrow. The queen is fond of you, so you shall stay on in her household while we are away. She could surely use more lessons with the lute." He smiled.

Catherine demurred, and he could see her blush. *Charming*, he thought.

"Her Grace really does need a more advanced tutor than I, though."

"Nonsense. She has improved much since you came to court," said Henry. "I would not change a thing . . . for now."

❦

Jane frowned as she looked at Catherine later that afternoon.

She was exquisite in yet another new dress provided by the dowager duchess. This one was of olive green brocade with large, turned-back cuffs and silk-lined sleeves. Her hair was dressed in a gold net, and she wore a ruby at her throat.

"Staring at yourself in the mirror is not going to make you any lovelier than you are now," said Jane, with a hint of irritation.

"I was just thinking, actually."

"Oh?"

"I *can* do that, despite what people may think of me, you know." Catherine turned away from her reflection. "I was thinking about Master Holbein's painting and wondering why the king did not include Princess Mary. It seems like such a slight."

Jane sighed. "Mary was very devoted to her mother, and it is difficult for the king to look upon her without being reminded of the scandal of his divorce from Catherine of Aragon."

Catherine thought about Jane's words, then asked, "Did Princess Mary look favorably upon my cousin?"

"Not at all. As for our current queen, Mary is not acquainted with her, since she lives mainly at New Hall in Essex and spends her time in constant prayer."

"Sad for a young woman of only twenty-four," Catherine said.

"True, but there was little of the girl left in her when I was last at court. They say, though, that she and the king have made peace. Pulling Elizabeth from the line of succession was a balm to her wounds. It is more Elizabeth and what to do with her that haunts His Majesty now." Jane paused, then added, "But you cannot be bothered with these complications if you mean to survive here. You must worry only about yourself."

"I mean to," Catherine said with a smile, taking one last glance at herself in the mirror.

That night, at supper, Catherine watched the king whispering in the queen's ear as they sat beneath a canopy on a raised dais, flaming torches lighting the walls around them with a flickering glow. They seemed happy enough. Apparently, whatever differences existed between them had been worked out. Catherine was relieved. Now that the king seemed occupied with the queen, perhaps she would be free to pursue a life with Thomas.

But before the dinner was over, the king nodded to Catherine as she sat between Jane and his niece Margaret. A moment later, a page came to her and whispered in her ear, "The king desires that you join him in a dance, Mistress Howard."

"But the queen—"

"Her Grace does not fancy dancing, since she cannot keep up with the king," the page replied simply.

Catherine was afraid to look at poor Anne, knowing that the page's words were untrue. The queen had only ever been good to her, but she could not reject the sovereign's invitation.

Catherine rose from her seat as the king left the queen's side. He took her hand and led her to the dance floor. All eyes were upon them.

"Your Majesty dances very well," Catherine remarked with an easy smile, knowing well that this was how her uncle and her grandmother expected her to behave with the king, as they moved through a tourdion.

"I used to be magnificent."

"Oh, but you still are, sire," she replied quickly, lying poorly. She saw instantly that he knew it.

She was afraid that he would be angry, but the king tipped back his head and let loose a great barrel of a laugh. "Would that it were still true!"

"In my own experience, youth is as overrated as flattery, Your Majesty."

"Beauty and a sense of wit? I had not expected that," the king volleyed.

"I am happy to surprise you, so long as the combination is a pleasing one."

"How could it not be?" He bowed to her, and she curtsied deeply in return just as the tune came to an end.

As he returned to the queen and Catherine walked back to her place beside Jane, she saw him. Thomas was standing beneath a massive tapestry, and he most certainly was not smiling. *Splendid*, she thought, acknowledging him with a happy little nod, much as the king had done to her. She still intended to get what she desired.

And what she still desired was Thomas Culpeper.

❖

Just after midnight, a rap sounded on her chamber door. Catherine knew who it would be. As she pulled the door open, Thomas slipped in, quickly closed it, and wrapped her in a desperate embrace. Catherine knew he was familiar enough with the halls and passageways of the palace to have reached her room unobserved. He tilted her face up and kissed her feverishly, holding her so tightly against him that she could not breathe. But she did not care about breathing at the moment.

Thomas drew her forcefully toward her small bed, unlacing her cambric nightdress and his own nether hose. He did not speak. There would be neither words nor gentleness this time. Only intoxicating passion.

He forced her down onto the bed and rose above her like a powerful warrior above the vanquished, but she did not struggle. She was wild with happiness at his show of passion, his desire to possess her. She had never felt more alive, and she knew that Thomas could not avoid his true feelings for her during moments like this.

Afterward, as she lay sated in his arms, happier than she had ever imagined she could be, Thomas gave her an amused smile and kissed her forehead tenderly. "You certainly are a clever one, aren't you? Is there anything you cannot make a man do?"

"That remains to be seen," Catherine replied, smiling innocently at him. "I shall certainly let you know if I think of something."

As they lay together, Catherine waited again for him to say that he loved her, but her hopes were met with silence. She tried to be content with the fact that he was there with her, and they had all the time in the world. But she could not help but feel disappointed.

❖

Cromwell fell silent in the glow of the firelight that evening as Norfolk sank into a chair near the massive carved hearth. On the table beside Cromwell was an open volume of Cicero, bound in exquisite red Spanish leather, and a nearly empty cup of spiced Gascony wine.

"You poor fool bastard." Norfolk sighed as he shook his head. "I do loathe you. But the bishop has convinced me to extend a bit of courtesy to you. Is that not correct, Stephen?"

Stephen Gardiner stood like a sentry near the closed door, his hands behind his back, his outfit an ominous black. He nodded in agreement, but the expression in his deep brown eyes was blank.

"The court moves to Greenwich in the morning," Norfolk said, as Gardiner walked toward two carved, painted traveling chests that lay open and half packed on a table. He touched a neatly folded silk bedcover.

"You need not have brought out your luggage," the bishop said to Cromwell with a smirk on his face. "You are to remain in London."

Norfolk bit back a triumphant smile, pleased that the king had entrusted him and the bishop to bear the news to Cromwell. He felt like the lead hound on a hunt, privileged to make the first cut on a cornered stag.

Cromwell was taken aback. "Of course I will attend the king in Greenwich."

"No," Norfolk coldly corrected him. "It seems you have a problem that requires your presence here. The king demands a divorce from Anne of Cleves based on proof of nullity, which we recently presented to His Majesty. As you are the one who pressed him into this sour union, His Majesty commands you to extricate him while he is away."

The bishop picked up where Norfolk left off, barely acknowledging the stunned expression on Cromwell's fat face. "We know what you must be thinking. It shall be a difficult situation to navigate while you struggle to maintain his trust. But you cannot possibly deny the king now that the duke has found a legal basis for divorce, which you rashly overlooked in your zeal to choose a wife."

Gardiner walked around the room with an air of authority as he spoke. It was as if he were giving a prepared speech, which he was, unbeknownst to Cromwell. Each word had been planned for maximum effect before they had arrived at Cromwell's door.

Norfolk's expression was one of amusement as Cromwell's fell in devastation.

"So we understand you are wondering how you could engineer a divorce with the least number of harmful repercussions to yourself," Gardiner continued. "Let us consider your options. If you do comply with the king's wishes, you would have to admit that your counsel to His Majesty was faulty and useless from the start, and you would certainly lose your title and reputation, if not more. If you do not, you would be acting in defiance of the king, and you would most certainly lose your life."

"Indeed a dilemma." Norfolk nodded. "So you see, joining the court's progress tomorrow and enjoying the hunt, the banquets and the women would be most unwise, particularly when your head is on the chopping block, so to speak," he added with obvious cruel pleasure.

"To the devil with both of you!" Cromwell shouted furiously, his full cheeks flushing with anger.

"The devil might be the only one who takes you after all the damage you've done," Gardiner observed, shaking his head and making a little *tsk* sound. "Think on it. First there was your support of Wolsey as he rid England of Catherine of Aragon, the only true queen. . . ."

"Thereby ridding England of the true Catholic faith . . ." Norfolk added in a tone of delight.

"And seeing our great king excommunicated by the Holy Father in Rome . . ." Gardiner pitched in.

"Ah, yes, Gardiner, that might well be the worst part," Norfolk replied in mock contemplation.

"The mounting offenses really are almost too numerous to mention," Gardiner added.

Cromwell was overcome with anger, but a hint of fear had crept into his eyes. "I am Earl of Essex, as well as Lord Great Chamberlain—two of the most powerful titles in all of England. You know not of what you speak!"

"Those *were* powerful titles, my lord. But circumstances change," Norfolk said, no longer hiding the smile on his face. He stood and looked around the large room at the trappings of a lifetime of work, scheming and success. Cromwell's apartments were not dissimilar from his own grand rooms down the vast corridor, but Cromwell's had a better view.

That alone was enough to make Norfolk despise him.

"You sought to trap me from the very beginning," Cromwell said accusingly.

"Of course," the duke coldly replied.

"But we all knew that you encouraged the alliance with Cleves, just as I did! Surely the king remembers that!"

"Ah, but that is where you are wrong. I told you what you wished to hear as you schemed. I wisely told the king nothing of the sort."

Cromwell was desperate now, and full of panic. His expression reminded Norfolk even more of a hunted stag. "And you, Gardiner, a man of God—did you forsake me as well?"

"I followed my conscience and God, as I do in all things, my lord chamberlain," the bishop piously replied.

"I am Henry's most trusted minister! You shall not get away with this!" Cromwell bellowed.

"Ah, but I believe we already have," Norfolk replied in satisfaction. "I only hope you live long enough to see what I have in mind for my encore."

❖

A letter, propped neatly on a polished trestle table near her bed, was waiting for Agnes Howard when she returned from the banquet.

"That will be all for now," she dismissed the young girl who waited to help her out of her heavy, tight dress.

The dowager did not recognize the handwriting, which she took as an ominous sign. It was late, and her bones ached from far too much wine and dancing. For a moment, she considered not opening it at all, but the pull of the unknown was seductive for one of an age when life contained few surprises.

She sank onto the edge of her bed and placed the missive in her lap. There were many things it could be, only one of which she feared. With trepidation, Agnes broke the heavy wax seal with her thumb and opened the letter.

If I could wish unto you all the honor, wealth and good fortune you could desire, you would lack neither health, wealth, long life, nor prosperity. Nevertheless, seeing as I cannot . . .

Words and phrases leaped out at the dowager.

There will be a lawful divorce between them; and as it is widely believed that the king, in his goodness, will bestow the honor on you next . . .

Agnes scanned the rest of the letter until she saw the final line:

I trust the queen will not forget her secretary and favor you will show . . .

It was signed by Mary Lassells.

The dowager knew that Mary knew about Catherine's indiscretions with Henry Manox and Francis Dereham at Horsham, and she also realized the Lassells girl could ruin everything for the Howard family if she passed that information on to the king. Someone had placed it here for an unknown reason. It was clear as well that Mary Lassells wanted something, and quite likely it only began with a place at court. The dowager knew she was taking an enormous risk, since if she granted Mary's request, she was also personally placing her right where she could do the most damage. . . .

SUMMER

The Second Season

"Yours as long as life endures."
—Catherine Howard

Chapter Nine

June 1540
Greenwich Palace, Greenwich

While Cromwell remained in London to deal with Parliament on the question of the king's divorce, the court left the city. The huge progress included over two thousand courtiers and ladies on horses, as well as countless carts and wagons. They passed through the vast meadow behind the city, up the hill to the cooler, cleaner air of Greenwich, and ended at the king's vast brick Greenwich Palace amid turrets, towers, pathways and lush privy gardens.

From the time of their arrival, Catherine's presence was constantly requested by the king. Along with Jane, the king's two nieces, Lady Margaret and Lady Frances, and Anne Basset, Catherine spent her days with Henry and his closest friends, singing, dancing, masquerading and hunting. Always, Henry made an excuse for the queen's absence. "She is at prayer," the king would say blithely. "She is writing letters. . . . She is resting with a headache."

But the truth behind her absence was known to everyone, particularly Catherine. She had begun to feel guilty for the attention she received from the queen's husband, despite the fact that she liked the feeling of power that it gave her.

Catherine was so in demand by the king in those first two

days at Greenwich that it was difficult to steal away with Thomas. But Catherine consoled herself by exchanging flirtatious glances and smiles with Thomas when they were in the company of the king.

One late afternoon, as the sun was setting, the king's coterie, consistently comprised of the same courtiers and ladies, sat beneath a fluttering blue canopy, playing cards and laughing. Catherine sat between the king and Lady Lisle's daughter Anne Basset as a singer from France crooned out a soft French tune to the accompaniment of a lute.

Catherine and Henry were engaged in a heated game of primero, which Catherine was quickly losing. "Perhaps, if you allow me, I could help you." The king winked at Catherine.

"But then Your Majesty would more easily win."

"I always win, Mistress Howard." He chuckled, as everyone else laughed with him.

"Very well, I will show you everything," Catherine relented.

Henry tipped back his head and laughed more deeply. "Now, that is a promising response."

"I meant the cards, sire." She fought a little shiver of revulsion as she watched his bearded jowls shake with delight as he laughed.

When his laughter subsided, their eyes met. Catherine touched his shoulder playfully, trying to make light of the connection as she looked away.

"Of course that was your meaning, Mistress Howard. For now, anyway," he said as they returned to their game.

When Catherine glanced up again, she saw Thomas's eyes hard upon her. Her own smile fell until she remembered her duty. Always duty. She quickly caught herself and forced another smile. It was a game, all of it. She had learned it at Horsham, and now she was a master player at court. In spite of the risk that the king might come to think of her as more than simply entertaining, Catherine had no choice but to succeed. She was not about to let any of it go to waste when she was trying to win Thomas's declaration of love and her uncle's approval. After all, with no real money of her own, and an uncle who was a rather frightening enigma with his own agenda, she and her husband would need to remain firmly established in the king's good graces to succeed. Now that she had tasted the finer things in life, keeping Henry VIII's favor was the only path she could clearly see before her.

To win the king's friendship and his approval of her relationship with Thomas was the ultimate prize, and her experiences at Horsham had hardened her enough, she believed, to accomplish that.

Wisely, risking everything, even Thomas, she caught the king's eye again and smiled her sweetest smile.

❖

"Mistress Lassells desires a place at court," the dowager said with a sniff later that day, "and there was most definitely an implied threat in her request."

Norfolk sat back, stunned by the revelation. "Do I even know a Mistress Lassells? Who is she?"

"She was one of the girls at Horsham with Catherine. She knows things about your niece that could ruin us," Agnes explained. Norfolk had been so busy engineering his niece's and the Howard family's rise to power that he had not considered any potential threats to his plans, other than Cromwell.

"How did you reply?" Norfolk queried.

"I have not replied to her yet."

"You must." He rubbed a hand over his craggy face, uncharacteristically unnerved for such a steel-tempered man. "With the king about to divorce the queen, he is at his most vulnerable, and we shall never again have such a keen advantage. We cannot let a country girl ruin our prospects."

The dowager hesitated before her reply. "He came to me. He asked me if she was still a virgin."

"Dear God." Norfolk drew in a breath and exhaled slowly. "What did you tell him?"

"Well, he did not ask in so many words, so my response was equally vague. But His Majesty interpreted my words to both of our liking."

"You told him she was an innocent?" Norfolk was stunned. Now that Catherine's "innocence" had been established with the king, Mary posed a real threat.

Agnes arched her silvery brows. "Would you have wished me to tell him otherwise?"

"Of course not. But truth has a way of coming to the fore with the king. Our family barely survived the Anne Boleyn debacle. Neither you nor I would be able to live with ourselves if something like that happened again."

"That is impossible," Agnes scoffed, frustrated at the duke's lack of will to do what they must. "Henry is irascible, but even he would not behead a second wife."

Norfolk was uncertain. "Who knows what a man is capable of when he is determined? Take me, for example."

"Nonsense." She was firm but her tone was more motherly now. Agnes knew how high the stakes were; they could not allow their resolve to weaken. "Thomas, my dear, do not ever show your doubts when it comes to this family, or you will end up out of favor and at risk, just like Cromwell is for his own particular weaknesses in judgment. It is not the way to win. Do you understand me?"

"Henry can be a vindictive king when he is angry."

"Then keep his anger aimed elsewhere," the dowager replied simply.

"It is aimed at Cromwell right now," the duke said, glad for that stroke of good fortune.

"Splendid," Agnes said. "We shall use Cromwell as a diversion, which will give us time enough to move Catherine in while Anne of Cleves is moving out. If we keep our wits about us, it shall occur before anyone, even the king, realizes what has happened."

But Norfolk remained skeptical. "I am told she grows closer to Thomas Culpeper."

The dowager breezed past this information. "Unfortunately for her, Culpeper is not part of the grand plan. Their feelings in this matter are unimportant. Catherine knows what it means to be a Howard. We never entertained any illusions. Our plan to make her queen will not come as a complete surprise when she is informed."

Norfolk ran his hand through the silver sweep of hair over his forehead in frustration. "But will she comply, Agnes? Or will she fight us? We must not forget that the girl has a strong will of her own."

The dowager laughed. "Queen of England? Think on that. Is there any girl in the world who could resist the lure of such power for love alone?"

❖

The next day, in the late-morning sun, Thomas sat alone on a stone bench by a wide and murky pond with green lily pads floating on its surface. Beneath a broad azure sky, he watched the swans cut across the still surface as he tried to think of the next line of the song he was writing for Catherine. But the words would not come. Strumming the small lute, he played what he had so far.

My love shall always conquer my fear, as your beauty conquers my soul. . . .

He liked that line, but it was all he had so far and he was stymied. Thomas usually maintained an emotional distance between himself and the women he pursued. But Catherine Howard affected him. She unnerved him, and now he was vulnerable and in love. God's blood, he was undeniably in love. That had not been part of the plan when he met her, but Catherine was a rare and brilliant jewel.

He knew that men in love were a careless lot and made too many concessions. He was afraid that his love for Catherine would interfere with his ambition to secure a title and estate from the sovereign. But it seemed that she loved him in return. She had said so. Certainly she cared enough to make him jealous, which she accomplished brilliantly. Perhaps her love was worth the risk.

He could not think of anything else. He was overcome with desire to the point of obsession, but their stolen moments, secret smiles and occasional touches were harder to pull off these days. Though they feared getting caught, Catherine had agreed to meet him that night.

Thomas sang the words again, strumming softly on an old battered lute that had once belonged to his father. His drunkard father, God rest his soul, had sold it for a cup of ale. His distant relationship to the Howard family, through Catherine's mother, Jocasta Culpeper Howard, had earned him little but a place at court. He had used his looks and wit from there. With the first money he earned, Thomas had sent a lad into London to buy the instrument back. It was the only tie he retained to his life before court.

He was startled by a single round of applause behind him. Thomas turned around, bolted to his feet, and swept into a deep bow.

"Lovely, Culpeper," the king announced. "I had no idea you were composing a new song."

Henry, dressed in a costume of hunter green silk sewn with gold beads and diamonds, stood between Charles Brandon and Thomas Seymour, both of whom studied Thomas with discerning, slightly jealous eyes as he bowed to the sovereign.

"It is nothing, Your Majesty. Just a bit of foolishness with chords and words."

"Nonsense. I know a lovely piece of music when I hear it. I may have to honor you by borrowing the tune to sing to a certain lady tonight."

"There could be no greater honor, sire," he lied as he bowed, feeling sick at the thought that a song meant for Catherine would be sung to someone else, probably pretty Anne Basset, whom the king increasingly fancied.

"I shall need to say I wrote it myself, of course."

"An even higher honor, Your Majesty," Thomas replied, feeling even sicker.

The king smiled slyly, looking like the wild young prince he had once been. "I knew I was right to keep you near me, Culpeper. Now, come teach me how to sing your tune, and we shall add a few more lines to it when you are done."

Henry had unwittingly taken his rival's love song as his own.

❈

The queen's apartments were humming with quiet activity. The queen was absorbed in a conversation with the Earl of Waldeck, which no one understood, while Jane and Catherine sat together sewing, as they did with mind-numbing frequency. The leaded windows were open and the warm spring air wafted in, filled with the scent of lavender and gillyflowers. A small boy played a tune on his pipe to which no one listened.

Jane spoke to Catherine in a hushed whisper. "His Majesty has invited you to join him for dinner at the home of Bishop Gardiner in the city."

"Only me?" Catherine asked. She felt an odd welling of panic as she considered the invitation.

"There will be others present, of course, but it is a tremendous honor. It means that His Majesty has taken great notice of you," Jane replied, aware of her understatement.

"I believe he noticed me some time ago," Catherine said as she glanced at the queen, trying to quell her growing sense of guilt from playing such a dangerous game, even for Thomas's sake.

"Your uncle will be pleased, no doubt," Jane pointed out.

"And *I* will be misunderstood by everyone else." Thomas was not likely to forgive her if she did not come to him that night, as she had promised. But all that she did, she did for them.

"You must do me a favor, Jane." She leaned nearer. "Can I trust you?"

Both of them glanced guiltily at the queen before Jane replied, "Of course."

"Do you promise?"

"I promise."

"Then you must tell Thomas Culpeper for me that plans have changed, and I shall not be able to meet him tonight after all."

"Culpeper?" Jane asked, confused.

They leaned closer toward each other. "You promised, and I have to trust someone," Catherine said desperately. "There really is no one else I can tell."

"Have you been . . . meeting with Culpeper for some time now?" Jane ventured to ask.

"Yes, we have been meeting in secret."

"Do you actually . . . love him?"

"With all my heart." Catherine was happy to finally confess her feelings to a friend.

Mother Lowe appeared next to them. "Her Grace wishes to know if you two have heard the rumors that grow daily."

Jane and Catherine exchanged glances, but they knew what Mother Lowe meant. Everyone did.

"I'm sorry, which rumors?" Jane asked, feigning ignorance.

The gruff older woman stiffened at the question as the queen walked up behind her to hear the answer for herself. "It is said that His Majesty is, as we speak, attempting to divorce her."

"I have not been at court long enough to know," Catherine responded, avoiding Anne's kind eyes. "But I have already seen enough to know that rumors fly about these rooms like flies. You could just wave it away and ignore it."

There was a small, uncomfortable silence. Catherine could not imagine what it would feel like to be publicly humiliated by one's husband. Mother Lowe whispered in German into the queen's ear, drawing the attention of all the ladies in the room. The queen replied.

The Earl of Waldeck said something else, then turned to Catherine. "Her Grace wishes you to join her at prayer. Your company would be a comfort to her, she says."

Understanding the translation, the queen nodded in agreement beneath her heavy gabled hood and offered a weak smile.

Catherine's glance slid to Jane. She wondered how long she would have to dress after prayers before she was whisked to dinner with the husband of the poor woman who stood before her. Catherine felt another stab of guilt for Anne and an ache of longing for Thomas. She had never felt an ounce of remorse when she had seduced Henry Manox and Francis Dereham away from Mary Lassells at Horsham. But everything was different here. She cared for the queen, and Catherine did not wish to steal her husband, especially since she had found a potential husband of her own.

Later that evening, Catherine entered the grand house of the Bishop of Winchester, her head held up bravely and her heart racing. She wore a new dress of cranberry-colored silk piped in white lace, another gift from the dowager duchess. She had never felt more beautiful. She heard laughter ahead of her where the torchlights flickered. She breathed a small sigh of relief. Jane was right—she would not be alone that evening.

She walked across the floor, which was covered in rich Turkish carpets. The whole house smelled of cooked meats and savory pies. As she entered the banquet hall, she saw that the king had arrived already. He sat at the table with Bishop Gardiner, Norfolk and Charles Brandon in an understated costume of plum-colored velvet and gold braid. He looked up as she entered the room.

"Ah, the guest of honor," Henry said with a sweeping hand as he stood, making a grand show of her entrance.

Catherine dipped into a deep curtsy as her dress, underskirts and chemise made a crinkling sound. "Forgive me for being late. My driver took roads that were poor at best."

"Death to him then," the king announced.

Catherine looked stricken. He broke into laughter and sank back into his chair with a little grunt of effort. "It was only a jest. A little royal humor, my dear, nothing more. Come, sit beside me."

They feasted on boar paté, fresh sturgeon and pheasant. Catherine had not realized that she was hungry, but the summer air, laughter and ease of the group made her surprisingly ravenous. She had never eaten or spoken so boldly in the company of strangers, but after two hours' time, they were all laughing, joking and singing childhood songs. Catherine glanced at her uncle now and then. She still thought of him as a pompous old man, but she could tell he seemed pleased by her progress with the sovereign.

"I wager Your Majesty cannot sing the words to that last one from memory." She giggled.

"And what are the terms if I do?" he asked, ready to accept her challenge.

"Your Majesty is the only one who can name that," Catherine said boldly.

"Very well. If I am the victor, I receive a kiss from the challenger," he proclaimed with a ribald chuckle. Laughter erupted as everyone awaited Catherine's response.

"I accept, but you must get the words *and* the tune correct."

Henry smiled at their repartee, reveling in the youthful challenge as he placed a lute on his knee and began to play. Catherine perked up a little. Despite his weight and age, she saw how attractive he must have been in his youth. She could also see in him a spark of danger mixed with overwhelming power, which drew her. She found herself looking at him for the first time not as a king, but as a man. He made her smile. He was fun. He was powerful.

As Henry hit the final note, Catherine felt a strange spark of anticipation.

"Very well then, Mistress Howard. You accepted the wager, and I won it fairly."

"Indeed, you did."

Again, laughter rose up as Catherine smiled and approached the king. In response, Henry turned his head to offer his cheek for initial payment. She dutifully bent down and pressed a small kiss where his smooth skin met his neat, amber-colored beard. His skin was surprisingly soft, she thought, and perfumed heavily with musk. Henry turned the other cheek as the bishop's guests began to taunt them playfully, laughing and tapping their cups on the table.

Catherine considered the other cheek with a charmingly confident smile and placed her hands on her hips. "Well, I would not dream of going back on a bet."

"That is splendid to hear, Mistress Howard." Henry laughed.

She leaned over again dramatically for comic effect and kissed his other cheek, which brought a thunder of applause from the guests.

Across the room, Stephen Gardiner, robed in black velvet and crisp white surplice, stood with a goblet of wine in hand, chatting in low tones with Lady Lisle.

"I do believe we are looking at number five," she quipped.

"By God's grace, I hope you are right. This sweet little scene before us could bring England back to its former glory."

"Who would have thought such a silly girl could be responsible for that," Lady Lisle said with a hint of jealousy in her voice.

"A *beautiful* silly girl could," the bishop replied. "Especially if Norfolk gets his way."

"He is a crafty old buzzard masquerading as a phoenix emerging from the ashes. I can only marvel at his ability to rescue his family from complete disgrace."

"The duke is my dearest friend, and I shall not have you speak of him like that, especially when my livelihood depends on the success of his plans," the bishop reminded her. "Besides, there is enough largesse to go around. Your own daughters shall not be forgotten by the duke. I know you shall see to that."

✦

Thomas had asked for and been granted the evening off from service. He had expected to see Catherine when he heard the knock at the door, but was disappointed to see Jane. His eyes narrowed and his jaw tightened at the sight of her apologetic expression. He knew why she was there.

"Where is she, my Lady Rochford?" When she did not respond, he pressed on. "I know she is not with the queen, because I just saw Her Grace in the courtyard below taking the night air."

He could feel his face growing hot with anger as Jane averted her gaze. He had written Catherine a song and mustered the conviction to put away his own ambition and tell her that she was the first woman he truly loved. But it was all for naught.

Thomas clamped his hands onto Jane's arms and squeezed them desperately. "I have a right to know!"

"It was not her choice, Master Culpeper. You cannot be too hard on her."

His brows furrowed as he frowned. "She is with the king?"

"We all serve the same master. P-please try to understand."

"Serve, perhaps, but need she be his whore?"

Jane glanced down at her arms, and Thomas only then realized that he was hurting her. He instantly loosened his grip and his hands fell to his sides.

"I do not believe he would use her so, especially if he has a greater goal in mind for her in the future," Jane said.

He rubbed a hand across his face, trying to collect his emotions. "I have feared this moment. If he wants her, he *will* have her. His marital history proves that."

Jane could not disagree.

Thomas glanced at the bed behind him, strewn with rose petals he had plucked earlier that day. He felt like a fool for a woman, and he did not like this new sensation at all. He shoved past Jane and stormed down the musty paneled corridor full of evening shadows and the scent of beeswax from a fresh polishing. But he did not notice that. He was on a mission.

He knew exactly where to find his friends, other carefree courtiers like him who knew how to help him forget. He strode purposefully to the royal stables, selected a sleek, saddled Spanish jennet and set out through the woods behind the palace. Angry and hurt, he tried to expel the words to the song he had written for Catherine from his mind. King or not, Catherine had made a choice tonight, and it did not include him.

Thoughts of Arabella, the park keeper's wife, suddenly returned to him, though he tried to suppress them. He could see her face in his mind as if she were before him. He had not told Catherine the entire truth about her. While Thomas knew that rumors still circulated about the incident, they were mostly false. But things had not played out entirely the way he had explained them to Catherine either. He was no hero. He had been violently angry that night. He had not raped Arabella, but he had loved her passionately enough to consider taking what he had believed was his. And Arabella had meant to allow him. Thomas cringed now, remembering from that night how far a man could be driven in rivalry over a woman.

In reality, he and Henry VIII were not so different.

❖

Catherine sat across from the king as they returned to Greenwich in his private rolling litter alone together. It was a stifling enclosure papered in damask, the window openings hung and hooked closed with heavy silk. She had not known how to refuse the king's invitation to escort her home; nor was she certain she had wanted to. Her uncle had been watching her, and Henry had asked so sweetly and flatteringly. She could not refuse. And the night had actually been fun.

Henry had made her so comfortable that she almost thought of him as an ordinary man. But she was aware, all along, that he was not. The contrast between Henry the person and Henry the king, and the danger of being caught off guard by it, captivated her.

Yet as the carriage bobbed and swayed, the only person she could really think of was Thomas.

"I never loved the queen, you know. Not this one, anyway," Henry suddenly said, shocking her back into the moment. "I did not even know her before we married."

She struggled for the right thing to say to encourage his confession. She knew her uncle would want her to ingratiate herself into the king's confidence. "I understand how it is to be forced into things."

"I suppose you do, with Norfolk and all."

"My lord uncle means the best for me," she said, not entirely convinced by her own words.

"Anyone who knows you would wish that," Henry said gently. He searched her face for a reaction, but she humbly lowered her head.

"Thank you, Your Majesty."

"You must not call me that, not when we are alone like this."

She struggled not to fidget or move away from him. "What should I call you then?"

"My mother called me Hal."

"Your mother was a queen." She laughed, trying to sound light-hearted, though she was tired and her thoughts were with Thomas.

"Perhaps one day you will be one as well."

Catherine tried to look at him, but the expression in his eyes was of a hunter after the hunted. He struggled to reach for his lute on the seat next to Catherine with a deep, unflattering grunt. Henry took it just as the driver hit a rut in the road and the little conveyance shook.

"I have written a new tune," he announced.

The litter rocked and swayed even more, and Catherine felt a wave of nausea come over her from the unending swaying. "Do you mean to play it now?"

"Yes, and for no one but you."

"Your Majesty . . . Hal . . . I am flattered."

"You are meant to be," he said with a sly smile.

Catherine saw that same boyish spark she had noticed earlier that evening, and she thought again of the king in his youth. She wished she had known him then.

He sang the song for her as he played. His voice lingered on each note as he gazed at her deeply, as if each word came from his own heart. Catherine leaned back against the velvet-covered seat, more flattered than she had ever been before. She was just a girl, yet he, the king, was singing to her.

When he finished the song, Catherine had to catch her breath. "That was beautiful, Hal."

"I hoped you would think so," he said, as he put the lute down and took her hand in his. Very tenderly, he drew her fingers to his warm, wet lips. "What I mean to say, my dear Catherine, is that I would be honored if you would wait for me."

It was the first time he had ever spoken her given name, and he did so with such tenderness that it made her want to weep. What struck her now was how vulnerable he seemed and how different from the strong, invincible image she had come to know.

"What exactly would I be waiting for?"

"Much is about to change. I may be king, but I am also a man, Catherine. You mustn't tell anyone, because it would not do for a king to admit such things, but I have made far too many mistakes. I want to end that chapter of my life. I want peace." He looked intensely at her, and Catherine was moved. But she knew that those eyes had looked with love upon Catherine of Aragon, Anne Boleyn and Jane Seymour before their deaths. She felt a strange shiver of fear at the thought. Would her fate be similarly sealed if she were to bring Henry his peace?

"But can one have peace in life as well as excitement?" Catherine asked.

"It is certainly one combination I have yet to try." The king chuckled.

Hearing his laugh, Catherine struggled for the right thing to say without sounding uninterested or overeager, or displaying the fear she felt. She had gambled that she was smart enough to gain the love of her life and instead she was winning the King of England. She must account for everything she did and said to her uncle sooner or later. But before she could speak, the carriage hit another deep rut in the road, and Catherine was thrown against the king. She felt his excitement for her growing beneath his wide leather belt and the drape of his doublet. Embarrassed, she quickly pressed herself back against the tooled leather carriage seat. For a moment she was horrified, until she saw the king's pleasure.

"There are many things I have yet to try," Henry said suggestively, but Catherine did not dare ask him what he meant. She did not want to know.

❖

When Catherine returned to the queen's apartments just past midnight, the others had already retired. She tried to pass silently to her own small chamber up a small flight of stairs. She had gone only through the second-floor gallery when a guard stopped her silently with a hand to her forearm.

"The Duke of Norfolk has called for you upon your return. Follow me."

Catherine walked silently behind him, fearing the worst from the late-night summons. Her uncle was an intimidating, powerful man, and she had not grown to like him or understand what motivated his actions during her time at court, despite his gifts of dresses and jewels.

As she was shown into a chamber overlooking the knot garden, she saw Norfolk and her grandmother standing together like two sharp-faced stone statues carved into the exterior of Westminster Abbey.

"Tell me you were not going to Culpeper just now," said the duke in a deep, accusatory tone.

"I was not," she said, wondering, since she had been so careful, how her uncle knew about her late-night visits with Thomas.

"Things reached a critical juncture this evening," he said, as he began to pace the room.

"Critical, Your Grace?" she asked innocently, though she knew what he was going to say.

"You rode home in the company of His Majesty," he said, piercing her with his deep eyes.

"He specifically requested my presence."

"Yes, indeed. That, however you accomplished it, was splendid work on your part." Norfolk waved a hand covered in rings and turned toward the fireplace hearth, gazing at the gold and azure flames.

"Did the king take any liberties while you were alone?" the dowager asked, her lips pursed.

"No, Grandmother. He kissed my hand and played a song he had written for me, but those did not feel like liberties."

Norfolk looked away from the fire and met her gaze once again. "He told you the song was written specifically for you?"

"Yes, my lord uncle. It really was quite beautiful. I was surprised by the honor."

"That was just what he did for Anne when he began to court her. He has not done that since," Norfolk mused. "This is happening far more swiftly than we could have hoped. Through the Duke of Suffolk, the king has requested your company again tomorrow when he rides, which is why we waited here for you tonight. This is a critical moment for our family, and you must be prepared. See that you take special care with your grooming in the morning. He favors women who are clean and stylish. You will wear the new grass green satin gown to highlight your eyes."

Catherine nodded dutifully. "I shall have Lady Rochford and Mistress Basset attend me."

She watched her uncle and grandmother exchange a glance and their expressions grew tentative. "Someone else will attend to you from now on," Agnes Howard announced.

"Surely Jane and Anne are more than enough help for me."

"That is not the point," the dowager said, as the door behind Catherine clicked open.

Catherine turned in response and saw the last person she expected to see coming toward her out of the shadows.

"What an elegant dress, Mistress Howard," Mary Lassells said, barely hiding her contempt as she scanned Catherine up and down. "You certainly have changed since our days at Horsham."

"What is she doing here?" Catherine asked, forgetting her manners entirely, as her defenses rose.

"Oh, now, is that a proper way to greet an old friend?" Mary asked, stepping closer toward Catherine.

Catherine took a small, uneasy step back. "I heard through my dear Mistress Barwick at Horsham that you had gone to live with your brother, John, after I came to court."

"I did."

"Yet here you are . . ." Catherine said, clearly confused.

"Money does not come easily to most of us, so I was forced to seek employment once again. I thought attending my dear friend at court would be the best way to employ my skills," Mary said with an odd little laugh.

Catherine was surprised at Mary's audacity; for a girl in a plain dress and simple cloth hood, she was very certain of herself. But most of all, Catherine was surprised by the change in her grandmother. The dowager usually stood tall and proud, unafraid to voice her opinions, but now she had slipped into the shadows, saying absolutely nothing.

"You requested a position from my lady grandmother?" Catherine asked, still trying to make sense of everything.

"I did not need to ask twice. Her Grace is a generous woman," Mary said, casting a falsely sweet smile in the dowager's direction.

Catherine desperately wanted to know why Mary Lassells was really there. Judging from her grandmother's behavior, she knew she had not willingly acceded to Mary's request. There was only one thing in the world that Mary could have used to obtain her position, and that was her promise of silence regarding Catherine's past. Catherine looked at Mary, who knew the most damaging details possible, and she tried to gauge her motives, but Mary's expression gave nothing away.

She had no choice but to accept Mary's place at court. At least for now.

She nodded dutifully. "As Your Graces wish," she said, bowing to her uncle and grandmother as she tried not to choke on her words. "Welcome to court, Mistress Lassells."

❖

Catherine rose in the grainy, silent darkness of early dawn, having slept little. She hastily donned a costume and walked very swiftly down a tangle of dark corridors, up a flight of stairs, passing torches long ago extinguished, to the gallery that led to Thomas's small, private room. She was desperate to see him and make certain that he had understood about last night. She felt like things were spinning far beyond her control, and she needed the assurance of his gaze and touch to let her know that what they felt for each other was something real. Something far beyond passion.

The door was not locked when she reached it, so Catherine glanced around to be certain she had not been followed, then let herself in. She was stunned. Thomas's bed was strewn with withered rose petals, most going brown at the edges, and it had not been slept in.

"Sorry. Culpeper stayed in town last night, I'm afraid," said Gregory Cromwell from behind her. She spun around, startled. His blue eyes were wide, his costume was rich, and he did not look particularly sorry at all.

"That would seem the case," she said curtly. But she was not upset that Gregory was there, only that Thomas was not.

"Well." He tipped his head thoughtfully. "*I* am here, at least. There is something to be said for that."

"Really? And what would that be?" Catherine asked, wondering what Gregory was doing out of his bed at so early an hour.

He glanced around the corridor, then looked back at her. "You know, I'm not likely to be at court much longer. Your uncle is working hard to blame the king's failing marriage on my father, and when he succeeds, which I have no doubt he shall, I will be gone right along with him. So you may want to take advantage of my ample charms while you still can."

To both of their surprise, Catherine stepped toward Gregory and kissed him hard in the doorway of Thomas's room.

She did not want to think anymore. She was confused about her relationship with the king and angry about Mary Lassells, but most of all, she was disappointed at Thomas's absence. She had come early that morning hoping that Thomas would be there to say that he understood everything and knew how difficult it was to carry out the duties of the Howard name. But his absence proved that he did not understand. She could only imagine where he was, or with whom.

She was frustrated that nothing in her life was under her control. At this moment, she was everyone's pawn, including Henry, the duke, the dowager, Mary Lassells—perhaps even Thomas. Well, she would show them. She would throw everything in jeopardy.

Her emotions converged wildly as Gregory pressed her back against the doorframe and opened his mouth over hers. They stumbled into the room, crashing into furniture as they tore at each other's clothing. Catherine closed the door to Thomas's room with a defiant thud.

They did not reach the bed. He pressed her against the cool plaster wall, pulling her skirts above her waist. He could not take her swiftly enough. It was fast and full of base need, as their arms and legs splayed out against the wall. When it was over, Gregory collapsed against her as they both struggled to catch their breath.

They did not speak at first. Catherine smoothed her dress back down in the silence, and Gregory straightened his netherhose, raking a hand through his hair before he looked at her again.

"You are really quite beautiful, you know. You could entice anyone."

"So they tell me," Catherine said distractedly as she tidied her hair.

He opened the door and held on to the handle, lingering in the doorway, then glanced back at her. He gave a small, almost sincere smile. "For what it's worth, Mistress Howard, I really do wish I could be here to see what happens to you in these next months. I think I might have helped you."

"I believe I have had enough of your help," Catherine said, suddenly wanting to leave.

"There is no such thing as too much help when one is dealing with the king. Or with the Duke of Norfolk, for that matter."

"Thank you, Gregory," she replied, forcing a smile.

"I would wish you luck, but I suspect a charming girl like you will make your own. Oh, and I'll not be mentioning our little encounter to Culpeper. If the gossip I hear around here is any indication, that poor sot is about to face quite a lot more disappointment as it is. And there's no sense kicking a lad when he's down."

She had meant to feel as vindictively as she had behaved—if Thomas wanted to play the game of hurting each other, she could play it better. But as Gregory closed the door behind him, she had only one overwhelming sensation: remorse, for what she had just done to them both.

❖

When she returned to the queen's apartments this time, it was to a great deal of commotion and whispering in the outer rooms, as if something important had just happened. No one even noticed as Catherine walked through the archway into the privy chamber, knowing she was late, and just praying that no one would notice. It was only another instant before she saw why.

Standing near the leaded glass windows, through which the Greenwich morning sunlight streamed, were the Earl of Waldeck, the Duke of Suffolk, Mother Lowe, Jane and the queen.

"And where does the king wish me to go if I am to leave his court?" Anne asked in her heavily clotted English.

"The palace at Richmond is being prepared for Your Grace. It is a lovely dwelling in beautiful countryside," Suffolk explained.

"Is this about the divorce he seeks?" asked Mother Lowe.

"I believe so, madam, although nothing has been finalized yet."

Anne and Waldeck conversed rapidly in German as Catherine approached and made an unseen curtsy. Jane looked up first, followed by Mother Lowe and the earl.

"Perhaps Mistress Howard should not be here just now," Mother Lowe said in an accusatory tone, arching her brow. A deep silence descended upon those surrounding the queen, and all eyes in the room fell upon Catherine. Anne did not smile as she usually did when she saw the beautiful young girl who had tried to help her learn to play the lute, and in whom she had once attempted to confide.

"No, Mistress Howard is one of my own ladies," said Anne of Cleves. "She shall remain."

The glares of disapproval were like a weight upon her. She felt even Jane regard her suspiciously from the corner of her eye. Catherine knew what everyone was saying about her, and she knew she deserved it.

"His Majesty has made it clear to me that he has no desire to bring any humiliation upon Your Grace. It is simply his belief that a separation of space, for a time, would be beneficial to you both," said Suffolk.

There was another flurry of German between Anne and Waldeck, and an awkward silence among the others, before Waldeck could translate the queen's words.

"The queen desires a private word with Mistress Howard," Waldeck finally announced. The queen's ladies immediately departed to an adjoining chamber, leaving only the queen, Catherine, Mother Lowe and the earl.

Anne walked toward Catherine with a swish of her heavy skirts and spoke to her directly in English. Her words were low and carefully chosen.

"What would you do in my place, Mistress Howard?"

Catherine felt a lump of guilt growing in her throat, hard as a stone that she could not swallow.

"With respect, Your Grace," she managed to say, slowly and deliberately, ". . . perhaps I am not the best one to ask."

"I agree with *that* well enough," Mother Lowe quipped curtly beneath her breath, just loudly enough to be heard.

"Your own cousin came before me. You shall likely come after. I believe that more than qualifies you to speak." Her expression remained absolutely calm. "Would you go without a fight, Mistress Howard? Or would you risk losing your head by staying? What do you think?"

What did she think, indeed? Catherine simply could not believe that the kind, funny and gentle king she was beginning to know would sanction his own wife's execution without reason. She was only coming now to understand that there must have been many reasons for the fall of Anne Boleyn. Yet that did not mean the current queen had no reason to fear the king's wrath. She chose her words carefully and spoke them slowly.

"I do not believe he would ever harm you, but I was raised hearing that the king is of firm mind and strong stance. If His Majesty has made up his mind, I fear there is little else for you to do but go."

Anne considered Catherine's words. "That is what I told Waldeck, but he said, for the sake of Cleves's reputation, I should fight for my place, as the first queen did." Anne looked at Catherine with an unwavering gaze, as if she were prepared to follow the earl's advice.

The hit was direct. Catherine had not guessed that the quiet, soft-spoken queen was possessed of a talent for battle. Catherine felt a shiver, along with a heightened sense of respect. The queen suddenly linked her arm with Catherine's and walked her away from Mother Lowe and the earl.

"You are better suited to him; I can see that," Anne continued in her careful English. "The way he looks at you when you enter a room, he becomes like a little boy. When men behave that way, all hope is lost."

"Oh, Your Grace, I really do not think—"

Anne raised her hand in a gesture of surprising authority, another thing Catherine had not expected from the queen. "Let us not, shall we? I prefer easy honesty at this point. I am fond of you, Catherine."

"And I am fond of Your Grace," Catherine quickly replied.

"I cannot return to Cleves after this. I would feel so disgraced. And I do like it here in England."

She looked directly at Catherine again, the pockmarks on her face in stark contrast to Catherine's own smooth, young skin in the harsh glare of morning's light. Catherine could only imagine the pressure Anne must be under from Henry, Cleves and from her own sense of public failure. Yet she remained dignified.

"When the time is right, will you speak to him for me?" Anne asked.

"I will. If it comes to that," Catherine promised.

"It will come to that." Anne smiled sadly. "Many thanks." She released Catherine's arm and Catherine made a small curtsy. But before she could leave, Anne caught her hand again.

"Thank you for not lying to me. Lies are so much worse than the truth." She smiled sadly once again.

"I shall always try to remember that," Catherine replied with a heavy heart for the great truth she, and the rest of the court, was keeping from the queen who did not yet know she was gazing at her own successor.

❖

The Duke of Norfolk stared squarely at mousy Mary Lassells just long enough to ensure that she was sufficiently uncomfortable in his presence. He had not offered her a seat in the vast library of his apartments, which smelled heavily of leather-bound volumes by Cicero and Aristotle. The old warhorse was in no rush. He was accustomed to playing cat and mouse, and he was good at it.

"So, then, shall we speak plainly, or will you leave the task to me alone?" he finally asked.

"What would my lord of Norfolk like to know?"

"Oh, no, my dear, the question is, What would *I* like *you* to know." The duke steepled his wrinkled fingers, bejeweled with a single chunk of ruby set in silver. He regarded her so intensely that she was forced to flinch. While she looked away for only an instant, he caught the hesitation. *Splendid*, he thought. Even momentary weakness made the job so much easier.

"You are here because you have successfully blackmailed my niece. Not a very pretty reality for my family, yet there is a certain honor among thieves, so I can respect that about you. However, one must always know one's limitations."

He scratched his lightly stubbled chin, pausing for effect, then bore down on her with another lethal stare, reducing her to what she truly was: a little village urchin masquerading before him as a lady of power.

"You may have succeeded in frightening the dowager duchess into giving you a position at court. But make no mistake: Dealing with me shall be an entirely different experience. If you make so much as a move against my niece, if you do the slightest bit of harm to her, you shall not return to that thatched little hovel from whence you came, or any other godforsaken place, for that matter. They shall find you in unidentifiable pieces, long after they surrender me to my own holy grave. Now, have I made myself clear to you, my dear?"

"Crystal, Your Grace." Mary Lassells was completely self-possessed as she matched the duke's stare with her equally level one. She was not undone by him, as he had expected, which surprised him. And there were few things in life any longer that could surprise the man who meant to be the power behind the next Queen of England.

"So long as we understand each other," he said, settling for the last word.

❖

Later that day, as she sat alone in a room smaller than a dressing closet, Mary Lassells dipped her pen into a small pot of ink and placed it to the paper. Her scrawled handwriting was nearly illegible, but the words and meaning were there.

Mary felt triumphant as she wrote to her brother, John. It could not have gone any better, she thought. Unassuming little Mary Lassells from the house on the edge of the Horsham estate had made it all the way to the English court, and she had bested the powerful Duke of Norfolk. For the moment, anyway.

Her goal now was not to overplay her hand . . . until the time was right. "Wretched Catholics!" she cursed beneath her breath. They got what they deserved, the hypocritical lot of them, when they lost power in this court and the kingdom. The duke and his saucy little whore of a niece, who had stolen not one but two men about whom she had cared, would get their comeuppance once her work here was finished.

If she played her cards correctly, she could earn enough money so that she and her brother, John, could live comfortably for the rest of their days as well. Now, finally, she could move her plan forward.

Chapter Ten

July 1540
Nonsuch Palace, Surrey

$\mathcal{A}$s July came and a dry wind moved across England, the court moved to the lush, cooler environs of the partially constructed palace of Nonsuch in Surrey. The shift of a few miles for the massive ensemble of courtiers and servants changed everything. Such a production it was—luggage, furniture, servants: a parade of silk- and velvet-clad humanity.

With his wife out of sight and Cromwell in London, unable to object to Henry's plan for a new wife, Henry was now free to spend every hour he could with Catherine. For a jaded, aging man like the king, the promise of a girl like Catherine Howard was life's blood. He felt invigorated by her beauty, girlish humor and laughter, and the prospect of taking her virginity.

Henry craved her like air.

He watched her as she rode near him, winding through the forest, which was cool and thick with ferns, lacy trees and the sweet trill of birds among the branches, and he tried his best not to stare. He felt like a boy again, shy and uncertain with her beside him. He had never felt this way, not even in those early days with Anne. Anne Boleyn had bewitched him with her flirtations and by withholding the very thing he craved. But Catherine made him want to be better and do better. She made him want to begin again.

He felt his loins stir and swell against his saddle as he thought of her small, delicate body. Henry smiled to himself as he wondered what she would think if she knew what lay below his velvet, silver-threaded doublet. Ah, but there would be time for that. She was no bawd, and he did not desire her for that. Catherine Howard was different. He had noticed that from the beginning. He must tread softly with so innocent a beauty.

He glanced at her again, careful not to be caught staring. She was talking with Jane Boleyn. The two of them were thick as thieves, he thought. Having Jane back had brought a certain healing.

As casually as he could, Henry cantered his horse over beside them beneath a lacy canopy of trees. "So tell me, Mistress Howard, how do you find my forest?"

"*Your* forest, sire?" She smiled.

"Why, of course. These are my trees, my streams, my branches above us."

"Should we not say first that they are all possessions of God?"

"Gifts from God to his king." Henry chuckled.

"In that case, I think I like it all very well."

Henry decided to steer the conversation in a different direction. "Like your uncle, are you a Catholic, Mistress Howard?"

He saw Jane shoot her an anxious glance, then look away. Neither of them had expected the question.

"Yes, I am a Catholic. I follow my God and my king, most certainly."

"In that particular order, Mistress Howard?"

"God above all things, as the Bible commands."

"Well, under that circumstance, I could accept being second in your heart. But that is the only one."

Henry smiled at Catherine's sweet naïveté. No one else would dare speak to him that way, but from her, it was enticing. Suddenly he was aware of the look on Jane's face. She seemed uncomfortable and kept glancing around, as if she were trying to hide the expression on her face. Henry had the feeling that she was trying to hide something more than her expression. It bothered him, but he decided to dismiss it. Catherine had been brought to him from the countryside as an innocent and a virgin, so there could be nothing to hide.

They stopped near a rushing stream so the horses could drink and rest. Henry led Catherine away from the other courtiers, who sat idly among the trees or strolled as the tables were spread for the dinnertime feast.

"They are watching us, you know," he said with boyish delight.

Catherine smiled and lowered her eyes, which he guessed she did to impress him with her humility. He adored her innocence, but he would teach her all the ways of the world. In time. For now, he would give her just a small lesson.

"Shall we scandalize them the more?" he asked, intent on igniting things right there among his friends. Before she could answer, Henry reached over, cupped her small chin in his meaty hand and leaned in to kiss her. As he drew back, he saw a look of innocent surprise light up her face, which stirred him even more deeply.

"Tell me, my little Cat, is there some wish you have, some secret desire that only a king could fulfill? More dresses? Jewelry, perhaps? I would give anything to you."

He watched her lower her eyes, but he could see that she was actually considering the possibilities, as an eager child might. He bit back a smile. She was, after all, a Howard.

"If I am to receive a gift from the king, I would wish it to be of Your Majesty's choosing," she finally said with a sincerity he had not expected.

"A surprise?" he asked.

She nodded as he reached to gently run a finger along the line of her jaw. The feel of her smooth, porcelain skin against his fat, soft finger reminded him of how young she really was. Just then his leg began to throb, as if a spell had been broken by the harsh reality of their age difference. He knew he needed to sit, but he could not let her see his weakness. No, not ever that.

"Very well, then. I am up to the challenge. Now, will you do me the honor of joining me for a bit of dinner?"

"A pleasure, sire," she said with a smile.

As he led her back toward the others and the wonderfully rich aroma of cooked meats, he was already considering which of the royal jewels he might give her without seeming too ostentatious. Though he struggled to decide on the gift, of one thing he was certain: He was wildly, boyishly in love with Catherine, and nothing was going to change that. Jewels were just the beginning of everything he meant to give her.

❖

It was late that same afternoon, yet the king's party had taken a detour on their way to Nonsuch and had not yet arrived.

The king never rode for this long anymore, Thomas thought as he paced the length of the gallery outside the presence chamber, wringing his powerful hands. Now that Catherine was with the sick old goat, Henry thought he was young again. It would serve him right if he ended up in bed with a raging fever for a month, with that vile infected leg of his. So long as Catherine was not in bed with him.

Thomas glanced up at the carved French wall clock at the closed entrance. Could time actually pass this painfully slowly? Last night had been such a grand mistake. In an attempt to forget Catherine, he had drunk too much ale and slept with a pimple-spotted village girl, who turned out to be a vulgar replacement for Catherine. For the first time in his selfish, ambition-driven life, Thomas had actually felt real guilt. Catherine Howard was a rare jewel who deserved absolute loyalty from the man who truly loved her.

"You would be wise not to let the king see you pacing outside his door like a jealous rival," Edward Seymour said from behind, startling him.

Thomas stopped pacing and watched as a broad shaft of crimson late-afternoon sunlight filtered through the window and fell between them. Of all the men who served the king, Thomas liked Edward Seymour the least. Like himself, he had a lethal combination of ambition and dazzling looks, and he was not only Earl of Hertford, by the king's command, but a member of the trusted privy counsel.

"You have no idea what you are talking about, and even if you did, you would be better served by keeping your opinions to yourself," Thomas sharply replied.

"Well, you'll not win her now that the king desires her. Everyone knows she is next," Edward replied smoothly, brushing aside the irritated look on Thomas's face.

"Next?" Thomas asked, thrown off by the remark.

"To be queen, of course. There were two Queen Annes. In the world of irony, does it not follow that there would be two Queen Catherines to follow suit? Then, perhaps, a Queen Jane after poor Catherine is inevitably cast aside?"

Without thinking, only feeling the old violence of his youth rising up, Thomas seized Seymour by the collar, choking him until he could not breathe.

"I really ought to kill you!" Thomas growled bitterly just before he let go. "But then you would be at peace and I would be in the Tower."

"Might be worth it to see the fair son pay." He shrugged.

Suddenly there was a commotion in the gallery behind them, loud enough to stop their own argument. The king and his great coterie were returning from their ride. Both Seymour and Thomas straightened their doublets, smoothed their hair, adjusted their hats and cleared their throats, and with no quick means of escape, each prepared his most courtly bow. All evidence of their skirmish was gone in an instant.

A heartbeat later, a large assemblage of gentlemen and ladies and the king himself approached, laughing and chattering. Thomas had missed the main party, since he had not returned to his post early enough that morning, but it was just as well, he thought as he saw the king's arm linked very tightly with Catherine's.

Thomas felt his stomach seize, along with his heart.

When Henry caught sight of him, he stopped, as did the rest of the large ensemble gathered around him.

"Tom! Edward! Here you both are!" he said in a jovial tone, extending his free arm to them, the long sleeve belling out beneath it. "You both missed a marvelous ride today. I really should do that more often. Tom, whatever youthful indiscretion kept you from our little group, I hope she was well worth it."

Everyone but Catherine laughed at the king's sense of humor. Thomas knew he could hardly deny it, as there was no other acceptable excuse for not attending the sovereign.

Thomas bowed again deeply. "My apologies, Your Majesty."

"I shall want all of the most glorious details about her later," Henry quipped, winking.

Thomas felt ill. There was a vulgar quality to the whole exchange, and his guilt was made worse by Catherine's presence.

Thomas swept into a third bow, wanting the conversation to end, when, suddenly, it did. The king seemed to tire of the moment, so he turned to Catherine, pressed a light kiss onto her cheek, and began walking with her down the gallery, holding tightly to the one woman Thomas Culpeper would never get out of his heart.

❖

It had been physically painful.

As she sat next to the king at supper that evening, Catherine tried not to think about the expression on Thomas's blanched face, or the sick feeling in her stomach when the old king led her away with his thick, sweat-dampened arm.

She sat idly now while the king joked with Wil Somers about something she did not hear—or care to hear, for that matter. Instead, Catherine silently scanned the room for Thomas, knowing he must be present if he hoped to remain within the king's good graces. Wil Somers said something else, and Henry laughed so hard that he began to cough uncontrollably into a cloth held to his mouth, causing two groomsmen to come to his aid. When he had recovered, she felt his hand slip onto her knee beneath the table cover. She was repulsed, fully aware of what a sick old man he really was beneath the glittering trappings of royalty. At that moment, Jane slipped into the room, sat down on Catherine's other side, and lifted a goblet of wine. She leaned very casually toward Catherine, as if she were about to ask her to pass the saltcellar spoon.

"Master Culpeper desires a secret meeting. He bade me tell you that his heart depends upon it," Jane whispered.

She took a swallow of wine, then glanced around, smiling and nodding. Catherine sank back against her chair, her own gaze sliding to the king. He was still conversing with Wil Somers, and his soft, fat fingers were casually resting on her knee. Catherine was angry with Thomas. The implication of what he had done last night was clear. Yet both of them were victims of their circumstances, and she knew in her mind that she could not be too angry with him for that. Her heart was another matter.

"When does he wish it?" Catherine asked.

"Now. He has pleaded with me to converse with the king while you retire with a headache. He is waiting for you in his chamber."

Suddenly, Henry leaned toward her from the other side. "Are you enjoying yourself, my dear?" he asked, smiling. His fat face was glistening with perspiration, and there was a drop of spittle on his lower lip, hanging above his beard. "You look so serious. You should let good Wil here put a smile back on that pretty little face of yours. Wil, do tell her something amusing!"

Catherine pushed her chair back slightly, preparing to stand as she looked into the king's blue eyes. "I'm afraid, sire, that I have a rather dreadful headache, and I fear I shall need to lie down until it passes."

His hand slid away from her thigh and she could see him stiffen with concern. "I shall call my physician at once. You should be seen in case it is something serious. I could not bear it if you were ill."

Catherine smiled sweetly but wanly, calling up all of her old skills. "It is nothing, really, sire. I get them from time to time after a long day in the fresh air. It is a nuisance, I know, but I always need to lie down to let it pass. I shall be fine in the morning."

Henry's worried gaze hardened as he looked from Catherine to Jane, then back again. "Very well, but I shall expect to see you bright and early at matins, and then we shall have a good game of shuttlecock."

"It will be my honor, Your Majesty." She nodded and stood.

"Will you take Lady Rochford with you?"

"That is not necessary. She can remain here and catch up with you. I know my way," Catherine said sweetly.

"I shall not hear of it. A beautiful young girl like you should not go unescorted in my court. There is no telling what trouble might find you. Guard, see Mistress Howard to her chamber." Henry motioned to an attendant nearby.

Even as Henry spoke the command, Catherine was considering what route to take so that she might pass unseen to Thomas's chamber from her own.

❖

Across the vast table, Norfolk had watched the scene with great intensity. So then, Lady Rochford had fit herself seamlessly back into things here at court—powerful confidante, friend to a prospective queen, and likely go-between for her and her lover. If he could persuade Jane to report everything to him, she would be useful, and he would not object to her growing connection with his niece. This dalliance with the Culpeper lad had been one thing when Catherine first arrived—a way of preoccupying her free spirit until she was called to duty. But now that the divorce from Anne of Cleves was nearly complete, and the king seemed intent on making Catherine queen, she must forget the boy and focus on the final steps of the plan. Nothing and no one must threaten that.

Especially not a handsome, romantic sort like Thomas Culpeper.

Norfolk snapped his fingers over his shoulder in a commanding gesture without turning around, and was immediately answered by a young, freckle-faced page.

"Your Grace?" The page bent down to the duke.

"Take a message to Lady Rochford. Tell her we must speak privately. She is to come to my chamber alone the moment the banquet is over," the duke said.

❖

Thomas kissed Catherine desperately and pulled her against the broad expanse of his youthful chest. They stood alone in the shadows and swiftly descending darkness of the private quarters above the rest of the court.

"I know I should have told you before, but I was willful and stubborn, and for that I beg you to forgive me. I am in love with you, Catherine—hopelessly, eternally. My life begins now and ends only with you."

His declaration was a balm for her aching heart. Hope. Passion. She knew these things would be included in a future with Thomas. Yet it was too late. The king's whims and desires had set her destiny in motion, and Catherine knew enough from her grandmother's tales that once Henry desired something he could not be stopped. Still, when she and Thomas were alone like this, she could forget the obese, foul-smelling sovereign.

Trying to escape the inevitable, Catherine sank into the protection of Thomas's safe, warm chest as he kissed her. And she wanted nothing so much as to escape, as if she could, by coupling with his powerful body and melting into his very soul.

As always, the passion came first, followed by exquisite tenderness as they lay entwined in the bedding, their damp bodies still joined.

"I'll not let him have you," Thomas murmured defiantly into her unbound hair, which lay like a thick amber wave across his bare chest.

"I believe it is already too late for that," Catherine replied sadly.

"It will not be too late until the day he marries you, which we can prevent if I claim you first," Thomas said with determination.

Catherine rolled onto her side, propped herself on her elbow, and gazed down at him. "You would take your life in your hands, and mine as well, if you defied a king like Henry."

"I am not so certain. He likes me. He thinks I understand him, and he me. Perhaps if he were made to see that we are in love . . ." Thomas trailed off.

"You do not know my uncle very well. He would have us both killed before the king could send us to the Tower." She pressed a finger to his lips. "This is serious business, my love. Thomas Howard has spent his entire life becoming one of the most powerful men in England, second only to Cromwell and Henry himself, and he has done so by using the women in his family. I am the next rung in his ladder to ultimate power."

Thomas arched a brow, seizing on Catherine's use of the king's name. "Henry, is it now?"

Catherine smiled sheepishly, embarrassed that she had allowed that to slip. She knew he would not understand the enormous pressure being brought to bear upon her in this. "We both must do as our king bids. What other choice do we have? It makes no difference what we say or do, really. He is King of England, and we are all here for his pleasure."

"Well, you are mine, Catherine Howard. And I am yours. That is eternal."

"If only you had declared yourself a few days sooner. I would not have felt so free to accept his favor." She sighed.

"Well, what do you expect me to do, just give up without a fight? That, I'll not do." Thomas climbed out of bed and walked naked, with his elegant stride, to the window. Leaning on the wide wooden window frame, he gazed out into the vast darkness. Catherine could see the wheels of his mind turning, thinking of what to do next.

"I can reason with him. I know I can. He may be king, but he is a man first, and he respects the connection between us. I have seen it myself a dozen times when he asked my opinion or told me tales from his heart. I knew all about his feelings for Jane Seymour before

Anne Boleyn was even sent to the Tower. And later, after Jane had passed, I believe I was the only one to whom he admitted that he married Queen Jane too quickly after Anne's death."

She went to him and wrapped her arms around him from behind, pulling his back tightly against her chest. She laid her head on his broad, bare back and closed her eyes. "He may have confided in you, my love, but think of it. It was always selfishly. The topic, the focus, was always him. You were only telling him what he wished to hear, as everyone else at court does."

He turned to her and took her into his arms again, and there was a sense of desperation between them. Outrunning fate was something neither of them could do, and despite their brave faces, they both knew it.

"I have never been in love before, not truly," Thomas whispered into her hair.

"What about Arabella?"

"I was infatuated, yes. I'll not lie to you. But did you not ever play at love in your youth, only to realize, later, how it did not measure up to the real thing?"

An image of Francis Dereham came to mind. Though she had once promised him her love, she knew now that her feelings had been naive and childish. She was relieved that he had gone to Ireland to seek his fortune, and that he was not even in England anymore, much less a part of her life.

"I realize that now," Catherine said softly.

He looked down at her seriously. "He's just a man, Catherine. He might want you now, but he shall not want someone whose heart already belongs to another after all he has endured in love."

"That is a huge gamble, and we have no guarantees that he will not punish us." Catherine sighed. "Because he is not a man first, as you say. He was a prince all of his life, and then a powerful king accustomed to getting his way. My uncle says if Henry wants it, then it is his. After that, there is nothing."

❋

Near dawn, Catherine slipped unseen and weary back into her own little room. She had taken her life in her hands with this dangerous game, and she knew it. But there was no choice. She was doing it for Thomas, because she loved him. If there was even a chance that he was right, if he could make the king see that this was a true love match, if he could appeal to Henry's romantic heart and save her from a lifetime with a decaying old man, then she must let him try.

She sank onto the edge of her bed, crumpling like a rag doll. She was exhausted and confused by her choices. It was too much for a girl who had never had to make a single serious decision in her life before she came to court.

Suddenly Jane appeared in the doorway, with Mary Lassells standing behind her like a shadow. They had risen early to wait for her. "Where the devil have you been?" The poor thing has been crying like a baby all night." Jane gestured toward the foot of Catherine's bed.

Catherine glanced down to find a box decorated in crimson velvet sitting on the floor. Inside was a white, mewling kitten with a sparkling collar of bright green emeralds around its neck. The poor little thing was terrified and lonely, its wide eyes dark as opals.

A cat for Cat, she thought.

This must be Henry's promised gift. Suddenly she began to weep as she never had before. Tears of frustration and sorrow streamed down her cheeks, and she could do nothing to stop them.

This tiny kitten was a symbol that Henry wanted to be vulnerable with her and give her the deepest part of himself. In the seasons to come, Catherine Howard would remember this as the exact moment when all hope for her future with Thomas was lost.

In a show of friendship and gentle concern, Jane brought her a lace-edged handkerchief and a cup of Malmsey and waited for Catherine's tears to subside. When Catherine had collected herself, Jane sank onto the edge of the bed beside her. "We need to speak of something."

Catherine looked up, her nose pink and running. She wiped the last of her tears away as Mary lingered silently beside the door. "About what?"

"A threat to you, and what you must do about it."

"To me?"

"The greatest threat: the Lord High Chancellor."

Catherine sniffled, not understanding. "He has done nothing but be cordial and kind to me. I do not dislike Master Cromwell at all."

"Catherine, do you really see nothing? Think of it!" Jane whispered urgently so that no one would hear them. "Do you honestly suppose an ardent Protestant like Cromwell would allow *you*, a Catholic and the niece of his greatest rival, to move nearer to the king without a vicious fight? Just think of it. He set the wheels in motion for His Majesty to marry Anne of Cleves, which turned out to be a disaster of epic proportions. He is desperate to maintain what he can of his position and dignity while clinging to it all like a drowning rat to a sinking ship as your uncle works against him. Do you not suppose he would do everything in his power to sabotage his rivals?"

"I am not his rival. I am just a girl," Catherine said in disbelief.

"You are far more than that, Catherine. Everyone at court knows it but you, apparently."

"What is it you are asking me to do? I don't understand."

"I am asking you to be careful. Forgive me for saying so, but I am your friend, so I must. Your nightly activities are no longer a secret. There are rumors circulating about you and Master Culpeper, rumors not of a flirtation but of a passionate love affair. The rumors would be harmless if you were just two courtiers, but you are the love of the king, and Thomas is his favorite servant."

Catherine heard the words but could not make sense of them. She had been discreet. They both had. "Rumors are just that," she said stubbornly.

"Perhaps," Jane replied, "until they reach the king's ear. He is not a man who tolerates disloyalty. Trust me. I saw Henry's love for Anne turn to bitter hatred. He went riding with Jane Seymour, as if he had not a care in the world, the day she died on the block on Tower Green."

Catherine's heart began to pound. She knew the story, but it was another thing to hear it when she was so near the throne. "What does Cromwell have to do with Thomas and me?"

"He is a master, like the Duke of Norfolk, but more fearsome in his desperation. Mark my words: You are not safe at this court while Cromwell draws breath. There is nothing as important to him as the Reformation. When he hears of the situation with Master Culpeper, he will use it against you. He will do everything he can to prevent another Catholic from becoming queen."

Catherine tried to push back the rising tide of panic. "But what do you want me to do?"

"Protect yourself and Master Culpeper, if it is not already too late," Jane said ominously.

"But how? I have no power here!"

"You have the ingenuity of a woman and skills that you developed at Horsham. You told me so yourself."

"But that was with silly things! Silly men! They were games!"

Catherine cried, refusing to believe that her feminine wiles would be an effective weapon in a possible battle for her life.

Jane was calm and firm. "The Lord's training ground, believe me."

"I do not wish any harm to come to Thomas in this."

"And *I* do not wish any harm to come to *you*. So will you listen to my suggestion?"

Catherine considered that, knowing she had no other friend at court she could trust besides Thomas. The story of how Jane had betrayed her own husband and allowed him to go to the block on the rumor that he had bedded his own sister had always sent a shiver of fear through Catherine. But she had no other choice. She must rely on someone here at court, and Jane had proved trustworthy so far.

"Yes, please, Jane. Tell me what to do."

"Use well with the king what you learned of men. And realize you cannot risk your life for Thomas. After all, beneath the jewels and velvet, the king is just a man who wants to love and protect a woman. He must now become the only man in your life."

❖

The round of summer banquets, masques, endless games of shuttle-cock, hunts, and forest rides was exhausting, especially since Thomas had slept so little for the past few nights. Today was particularly bad, since his body ached from constantly besting all the others, but he was thankful the king's entertainments were mainly sedentary. Thomas still needed to be attentive and witty when spoken to, especially if he wanted to keep his standing with the increasingly moody and temperamental sovereign. He could not afford to anger or disappoint Henry until he gained his approval of the marriage between himself and Catherine Howard.

Thomas was encouraged by the story of Henry's sister, Mary

Tudor, who had married Charles Brandon, the Duke of Suffolk, without the king's approval. At first Henry had exiled them in France, but after time had healed his wounds, they were welcomed back to England with open arms. Brandon had said that he was fortunate to have kept his head during the bitter affair, which Henry called the worst betrayal of his life. Thomas could only hope for the same outcome.

Tonight there was another masque, and the king and his closest friends and aides would play parts. Everyone would be disguised but the king, whose steadily growing girth and hobbling gait made it impossible to conceal his identity.

Thomas wore a black strip across his eyes, and brightly colored beads were sewn onto the full sleeves of his doublet. Looking for Catherine, he feared he would not find her amid the courtiers and the distracting crowd of cheering townspeople who were invited to view the entertainment from the gallery above. He could make out the king, of course by his girth, and Lady Lisle's long copper hair, which was turning slightly gray, under a French hood. But the identity of nearly every other person around him was a mystery.

That was what usually made this event so interesting.

Thomas slipped easily through the crowd of masked courtiers and the magnificent display of colors and fabrics, glowing torches and glittering jewels. Perhaps tonight, after the masque, if all went according to plan and the king were in a jovial mood, Thomas would speak to him of the girl he loved, man to man, friend to friend, as he had done half a dozen times before. Only this time, once he had gained Henry's sympathy, he would identify the girl as Norfolk's niece. His heart raced at the thought of the gamble he was taking. Thomas knew he owed the king everything. But those who risked the most gained the greatest reward, and Catherine Howard was worth everything.

As Thomas Culpeper contemplated his next move, Catherine

walked toward the king and the group of important advisers and ladies who surrounded him. She had been well instructed that one of Henry's favorite games was to pretend he was anonymous, so she must play along until he chose to reveal himself. She could smell his sour breath as he turned to her, and she fought the reaction from her stomach.

The mask across her eyes was white, bordered in gold and studded with tiny diamonds. Since she wore the only white mask and a new silk gown in a distinctive shade of pale rose, given to her by Henry, she was certain he knew who she was. Catherine saw him smile beneath his intricately detailed mask and bow to her.

"My lady," he said, taking her hand and bringing it to his wet lips, as he liked to do.

"My lord." She dipped into a curtsy, making certain not to call him "Your Majesty," as part of their game.

She knew that the duke would be watching to make sure she played along. She looked around and recognized Lady Lisle, as well as Thomas Cromwell by the shape of his nose just beneath his mask. This man who had first been kind to her at court had come from his duties in London just for the event.

"My lady of the white mask," Cromwell said evenly, extending his hand to her. "I imagine we must remain ignorant of each other's true identities. What a delightful mystery our good king has created for us, wherever he may be."

It was now or never. Catherine knew what she must do.

After she made certain that the king was watching her, she gave a little shudder and withdrew her hand from Cromwell's. She looked away and rubbed her hands together, grimacing slightly, as though something had stung her. She saw the king look at her, then shift his gaze to Cromwell. Others had noticed her reaction as well, and they shot one another curious glances.

The king, who had been taken up temporarily with his other guests, approached her again. Even from behind a mask she could see his concern. "Would my lady grant your humble servant a walk?" he asked, remaining in character but letting a bit of his usual gruff, commanding tone come through.

"Indeed, my lord."

They moved together through the crowd to the other side of the room, where giant torches cast shadows on the plaster walls. "You know who I am, do you not?"

"Am I supposed to?" Catherine asked, not sure if they were still playing the game.

"I am the one who will give you the world if you shall allow it."

Catherine smiled at the king's boyish delivery. "Sire, I would not have known you."

"And yet you came away with me anyway."

"I was drawn to your spirit, of course. No mask can hide that."

Pleased with the innocent flattery she had cleverly woven into her reply, he held her hand down by his side, where her dress and his wide velvet coat met, so no one could see. They stopped near an open door, the cool summer night air pouring into the stifling room.

"I must ask you something," the king said in a grave tone.

"Ask anything, Your Majesty."

"Hal," he insisted. "I could not help but see your face when Cromwell spoke to you. You knew it was him, did you not?"

"I did," Catherine replied. She had successfully baited Henry with her bit of acting, but she had to remind herself what it was really for. She thought back to Jane's advice. *Use well with the king what you have learned of men.* Eliminating Cromwell as her adversary and gaining the king's sympathy were steps toward her ultimate goal of being with Thomas.

"And so?" he asked, trying to make sense of Catherine's reaction to Cromwell.

"You shall think me foolish," she demurred.

"Never."

"I had a dream."

"You dreamed of Cromwell?"

"Not of him. But of what his father might do to me, to all Catholics, if I remain at court." She lowered her head, as if she were troubled by her religious loyalty.

The king was taken aback. "If either of them ever harmed a hair on your head, I swear, by all that is holy—"

"He has not done a thing," she hurriedly replied, then paused for an instant and whispered, "Yet."

Catherine could see the king weighing her words. "But you fear him? You fear Master Cromwell?"

"Catholics fear all Reformists, Your Majesty. The chamberlain is committed to his beliefs, as am I. He has made no secret of that." She found it easy to dredge up true tears just then; all she had to do was imagine her life without Thomas. "Yet Master Cromwell is such a powerful man, and I . . . I am only—" She stopped, letting her tears speak for her.

She could see the strong effect they were having on Henry. He touched his hand to her cheek in a reassuring gesture.

"You will be adored and protected. At any cost."

Catherine could actually see the swell of romantic fervor in him as he stuck out his massive barrel chest and swelling gut with youthful bravado. Her heart lurched with guilt at his chivalric display. But she had no choice. Jane had made that clear. She must play the game she had learned at Horsham. Failure was not an option. Catherine turned away for a moment, feeling the cool air dry up her crocodile tears.

"I have said too much."

With a fat, bejeweled finger, Henry turned her face back toward him. "That is impossible."

"The last thing I want, truly, is to make trouble for anyone."

"You must leave that to me, my dear. Anything that frightens you shall not be tolerated as long as I draw breath," the king assured her with a gentle smile. It was impossible not to be drawn to his sweet side.

Her emotions were mixed, but she had to move forward with her plan.

"I still feel badly for saying anything about it," she demurred once more, prompting him to dry the last tears on her face with his ruby-bejeweled index finger.

"Nonsense. Cromwell has had too much power for far too long. But it is power that the trusting side of me granted him, to my own great detriment, since he advised me to take the wrong wife. Thus, it is power that I must take away. But you leave that to me, my beautiful Cat. Now," he said, smiling, "shall we go and see who will be the first to figure out who is behind my mask?"

"That may take a while," she said flatteringly, surprised when he puffed out his chest again, as if he seemed to believe that no one in the room knew his identity.

But that did not matter. She had done what she needed to do seamlessly, she thought as he led her among the dancers. As they made their way, they saw Anne Basset smiling at the king and Lady Lisle pushing her toward him.

"Excuse me for just one dance, would you?" he asked. "I promised her mother, and she will never let me hear the end of it if the girl is not first. But you shall be my last."

Across the room, Thomas watched the king take a partner by the hand and begin a lively tourdion, dancing as if he still had the vigor of youth. They twirled and turned together in perfect rhythm. Spectators in the gallery above cheered the king as he executed a modest version of one of the famous kicks of his youth. As the dance carried them closer to Thomas, he was surprised to see the king's partner was delicate and pretty Anne Basset. Thomas knew her by her coppery hair, though most of it was tucked beneath a fashionable hood like her mother's. *This is a very good sign*, he thought. The Basset girl was just Henry's type—petite, sweet, seemingly innocent—and he knew how long Lord and Lady Lisle had been trying to offer her up. He saw the king's hand on her waist slip down a little lower than it should have.

Thomas's plan to win Catherine just might be easier than he thought.

After the song ended, Norfolk moved to the king's side and said something casually into his ear. The king bowed to Anne, holding her hand a little longer than decorum called for. Then he and Norfolk strolled away from the other dancers in Thomas's direction. Thomas lowered his head slightly and looked away so they would not notice him as he listened to their conversation.

"How does it go?" the king asked.

"It moves slowly, sire. Cromwell has finally put the nullity suit before Parliament, yet it languishes there. He wrestles daily with the knowledge that, in pushing it through, he is accepting his own error of consigning you to a faulty marriage. But I am told that you shall be a single man in a month's time."

"Finally." The king sighed. "How long until I may remarry? She will not wait forever, Norfolk, whether she is your niece or not."

"She will wait, sire. You have my word. However, now that the antidote to your cancerous marriage has been found, we must rid ourselves of the vile contagion that caused it in the first place, before his beliefs contaminate the entire country."

"What do you suggest?" Henry asked.

"My lord Cromwell is following the teachings of Martin Luther quite boldly now. Bishop Gardiner heard him say as much. He also heard Cromwell say—forgive me for being blunt—that if Your Majesty were to reject Lutheran doctrine, he would take up his sword and fight you himself."

Thomas felt the frozen silence between them. "Are you certain?" the king finally asked.

"Very."

"Vile messenger of Satan! No one goes up against the king and wins. No one."

"What are we to do about the threat, Your Majesty?"

"Take him to the Tower," Henry grumbled with the voice of a bitter old man. "He was a friend, and now he is an enemy. Do what you will. If all you say is true, Norfolk, you can cut off his head, for all I care. Now, leave me to dance. This is supposed to be a pleasant evening." Henry looked about the room, ending all talk of Cromwell. "Where the devil is my little Cat? Find her for me, will you?" he asked, more of a command than a request.

Thomas sank against a stone column, his blood running cold. He was shaking. In all his years at court, he had never seen such a ruthless side of the king, who was often moody, but mainly nostalgic and kind. Cromwell's death sentence was a clear warning that for Thomas a life with Catherine Howard was impossible. Not only did the king want her as his next queen, but her uncle, the same calculating and powerful man who was behind Cromwell's ultimate destruction, would stop at nothing to make sure it happened.

As his thoughts crystallized, Thomas could feel the black bile of disappointment rushing up from the pit of his stomach. This was a war he could not win. All around him, the laughter, music and strong scents of food and spilled wine became an ugly blur, and the need to vomit was beyond his control. He pushed through the crowd and made it as far as the gallery, where he vomited into a stone urn, then collapsed onto the cold floor into the anonymous dark.

❧

Two days later, while a summer rainstorm pelted the stained-glass windows, Thomas Cromwell sat stiff-backed at the counsel table in London for what he believed would be a general meeting of the privy counsel. He was surrounded by Edward and Thomas Seymour, Charles Brandon, Thomas Wriothesley, Stephen Gardiner and the Duke of Norfolk, the latter two of whom had returned to London from Nonsuch specifically for the pleasure of watching the coming spectacle unfold before them. As Cromwell fingered a gold cup on the table, six of the king's stone-faced guards entered the chamber, led by the captain of the King's Guard. Two of them pulled Cromwell roughly to his feet.

"What is the meaning of this?" Cromwell growled, dredging forth a tone of hollow indignation.

Murmurs and remarks of surprise rose up from the others at the long, polished council table. Norfolk remained silent but stood slowly. While biting back a smile and mustering a stern expression, he placed a hand on Cromwell's shoulder, pinching it just slightly, and said, "It seems you are under arrest."

Bemused by what seemed an outlandish declaration, Cromwell scoffed, then gave a little half laugh. In the heavy silence that ensued, his smile fell, and he turned to each of the members of the counsel.

Norfolk relished his vengeance. His great rival's expression collapsed in fear as each of the men looked away.

"Arrested? What the devil for?"

"For treasonable heresy," Norfolk declared in a matter-of-fact, cold tone as he pulled the ceremonial garter, marking his vaunted title, from around Cromwell's neck.

"Oh, and for the abuse of power as well," he added with a cruel smile.

"If this is some sort of practical joke, I find no amusement in it, Norfolk. I intend to speak at once with the king about this—"

Norfolk cut Cromwell off. "His Majesty, Henry the Eighth, sanctioned the arrest himself."

Cromwell's dark eyes bulged in shock, then filled with fear as the guards began to lead him by force from the chamber. "Where am I to be taken? Is there even to be a trial so that I might defend myself against this travesty?"

"Oh, you shall be allowed to speak, my lord. Saying something in defense of the king's divorce might prove useful."

"Will it save me?" Cromwell asked in desperation.

"Only heaven and His Majesty know for certain."

"Then allow me to address him! I shall say anything he wishes!" he pleaded.

Bishop Gardiner arched a brow and rose from the table. His hands were steepled piously as he said, "Render unto Caesar what is Caesar's and unto God what is God's, my lord Cromwell. And who are we to go against gospel? We commit you to God. The king cannot save you now."

"Take him to the Tower, by order of His Majesty, the king," the Duke of Norfolk coldly commanded.

Chapter Eleven

The day after the masque, in the customary train of thousands, the court journeyed on royal progress to Hampton Court. The palace, on the north bank of the Thames, was vast, the lush, green grounds accessible by a grand stone bridge. Nobles, servants and cartloads of furnishings, clothing, huge tents, artwork, silver and dishware trailed behind Henry for miles. But he was oblivious to everything and everyone, save for the petite, sweet-faced girl who rode a gray palfrey at his side.

Now that there was no real impediment to his desire, as Anne was safely tucked away at Richmond Palace, Henry saw that his little Cat was clothed like a queen. She knew it delighted him to give her exquisite dresses of the finest velvet or Spanish silk, the most fashionable little French hoods and caps, and jewels to ornament her ears, smooth neck and fingers.

Catherine glanced down at the tiny white ball of fur in her arms, sound asleep and nestled in a green velvet satchel that perfectly matched the emerald bracelet around its neck. Catherine smiled. A kitten had been the most charming gift of all.

Henry was beside her, his girth concealed by a dashing cape of purple silk and matching cap, both edged with costly silver thread. His saddle was tooled in silver, as were the stirrups and reins. The buttons on his doublet were diamonds and pearls. She knew the costume was meant to impress her, and it did.

"How is our little friend?" he asked, glancing over as they entered a forest lane and wound their way beneath a grove of lichen-covered trees.

Catherine glanced down again at the sleeping kitten. "Precious enough to melt any heart, Your Majesty."

"I hope that includes your own, Mistress Howard."

"Your Majesty has hopes regarding my heart?" she flirtatiously asked.

"Since the moment I first saw you. But then, I believe you have known that for a while now."

She was expected to banter with him like this. Her uncle was not beside them, but his lackey, Bishop Gardiner, was, and she knew perfectly well that all of it was a test she dared not fail.

If only the very core of her soul did not belong to Thomas.

Catherine tried her best not to glance back too often, lest it be obvious that she was looking for the king's aide, who was, once again, mysteriously absent from His Majesty's side. Jane had told her that Thomas had spent most of last night dancing with pretty Anne Basset. While she knew it meant nothing, Catherine was certain that he had embraced the inevitable, along with the rest of the court, and had begun to console himself by looking elsewhere. It would explain why Thomas did not call for her after the masque, she decided.

As she had predicted, they could not outrun the king's desires.

Judging from his behavior, Thomas knew that as well.

"I am eager to show you my Hampton Court," Henry said. "It is an incredibly beautiful place, given to me many years ago by Cardinal Wolsey. Someday, perhaps, I shall be able to give it to you."

"Me, sire?" Catherine asked, genuinely surprised.

His small, wet mouth quirked into a smile, which made his fat, copper-bearded cheeks bulge. "Well, at least share it with you. Grand as it is, it could use a woman's touch."

Catherine knew perfectly well that he had married her cousin in the chapel at Hampton Court, since she had been told by her mother of the many changes and designs Anne had brought to the place, and she wondered if he had said that intentionally.

"I am eager to see it," she said sincerely.

"And there are two very special people I would like you to meet tonight."

"I shall be honored."

"It is convenient that we both desire the same things, Mistress Howard," he said with a smile and a tip of his head.

❖

Mary Lassells, who was riding beside Jane Boleyn and behind Catherine, listened with bitterness to the exchange between the king and the empty-headed Catholic.

"I pray he takes your head one day, as he did Mistress Anne's," she muttered cruelly beneath her breath. "May God have mercy on your foul soul."

But Jane did not hear her. Jane was also trying to eavesdrop on their conversation, maneuvering her horse closer to the girl who everyone knew would be the next Queen of England.

❖

Catherine had been given the most luxurious apartments within Hampton Court, save the king's. They included a suite of rooms facing the grand gardens, orchard and tiltyard beyond, and were the queen's rooms.

She twirled around, then collapsed on the grand mahogany bed with its tester of elegant blue silk. She was happy to be free of her horse so she could enjoy these continual indulgences to which she was so quickly growing accustomed, along with her lavish new lifestyle.

Mary Lassells appeared suddenly at her bedside, looming over her with a new green satin gown over one arm and a blue one over the other. "Which do you desire to wear to supper, Mistress Howard? I understand there will be a surprise this evening, so you should look your best."

Catherine caught something in Mary's tone, though she could take no umbrage at her words. She sat up, casually pulled her long hair free of her pearl-studded hood and draped it neatly across her shoulders. She saw that Mary was looking at her with a peculiar expression. Was it envy or something more? Whatever it was, she knew she had to be wary of Mary's every word, movement and expression. Catherine had not forgotten why she was here.

But then a new voice distracted her.

"I prefer the green. It will go best with your eyes."

The words from behind her were unmistakably Henry's. He stood in the doorway, hands on hips, legs wide apart, cradling in his meaty arms the tiny white kitten he had given to her.

"And we really do need to give this little thing a name." He chuckled.

"Would Putette do well enough?" she proposed, referring to the French word *peut-être,* meaning "perhaps" or "perchance." It was cleverly representative of their relationship, since Catherine had not yet committed to him or his romantic overtures. Henry tipped his head back with laughter.

"I believe it will do splendidly. Now that we have solved that, would you like to take a walk with me?" he asked tentatively.

Catherine, charmed by his seeming shyness, accepted the invitation.

They walked slowly, to accommodate Henry's painful leg, down a long, vaulted corridor with a high hammer-beam ceiling, down a twisted staircase with pillars supporting small statues of Welsh dragons, and out into the last of the afternoon light. A bloodred sunset played across Henry's face, and the strong scent of ambergris nearly masked the foul odor coming from the open ulcer on his leg. He was, in this moment, magnificent and normal. They strolled together without servants or aides, as if they were not the King of England and his soon-to-be queen. They stopped beside a long, neat hedge, and he took her hand.

"So tell me, my Cat, does Putette's collar please you?" he asked.

"It is extraordinary, sire."

"Dearest Catherine, when we are alone, please remember to call me Hal; otherwise I feel positively ancient and distant from you," he gently scolded her.

"But there is a great distance between us. You are the king, my lord," she said, smiling gently, "and I am merely a girl at your court."

"But I am also a man who has not felt loved for a very long time," he said huskily, growing emotional.

She tipped her head as a shadow crossed his face, which was fat and lined yet full of history and loss.

"Do you feel loved now, Hal?"

"I am not certain yet." He squeezed her hand, then changed the subject. "I see now that emeralds are the perfect complement to your flawless skin."

With his other hand, he withdrew a necklace of diamonds and

emeralds from a pocket in his doublet. "It is the companion piece to Putette's collar. It once belonged to Queen Cleopatra, who enslaved men with her beauty, just as you have enslaved me."

As he awkwardly held the necklace in his hand, Catherine felt a surge of warmth toward him. He was a powerful king, yet he stood before her like an adolescent boy, spouting hackneyed lines, desperate to please a young girl from the country who had owned only two proper dresses before she came to court.

Henry gently turned her around and clasped the piece of jewelry around her neck. "There. Perfect. Just as I knew it would be."

She fingered the unspeakably luxurious stones, cold against her throat, as she turned to face him. "Hal, they are too much."

"I want to give you the world, Catherine, and all I ask in return is that you go on making me feel as young and hopeful as you do when I look at your sweet face. If they make you happy, a few trifles are nothing compared to the joy you bring me."

She touched the necklace again, the jewels in it hard, smooth, reassuring and powerful. "They do."

"That is all I hoped to hear," Henry said, smiling. "At least for now."

❖

Framed by a blacked-out window and dressed in stiff black fabric, twenty-four-year-old Princess Mary fingered her rosary beads angrily. Her Spanish features betrayed her indignation.

"I am not going to see her, no matter how much you plead, my lord. Your future wife is younger than I am! It is an abomination." Mary voiced her disapproval with uncharacteristic bravery, reminding Henry of her steel-tempered mother, Catherine of Aragon, and her grandmother Queen Isabella. "I know I shall despise her, so why should I bother?"

"Nonsense, nothing has been decided upon yet, and your opinion of her matters to me," the king pleaded.

"That vile Boleyn woman caused my mother's early death and her own, and I expect no less from her cousin. And, forgive me, Father, but you failed to consult me about your other three wives, so why does my opinion matter here?" Mary demanded, crossing her arms, with her long bell sleeves over her chest like a punctuation mark. She boldly turned her back to him, a gesture so reminiscent of her mother that it sent a chill up Henry's spine.

There were few in the world who could get away with such flagrant acts of disrespect. Before his daughter, he had been most lenient with his beloved sister Mary Tudor, but she was dead now. Ah, how he missed her. Though she had caused him some trouble in the past, their candid interactions had made him feel like a regular man. His courtiers bowed and scraped and praised his name, but he had no idea whether any of them truly loved him for himself.

But his sister Mary had always loved him just for being Hal.

His daughter was fortunate to have her name, which reminded him of those lost days and endeared the girl to him. "I still want you to come to dinner," he coaxed. "There is a visiting troop of acrobats from Spain to entertain you and Elizabeth, and musicians from Venice who are incredibly skilled on the recorder. I remember how much you love the recorder."

"I'll not be nice," she warned.

He tipped his head, smiling. "Elizabeth will be nice."

"My half sister is six. She knows no other way to act when she sees you."

Of his three children, Elizabeth, who had suffered greatly from his wild anger toward her mother, was most like him—not Mary, not even his precious only son. With her copper Tudor tresses, pale blue eyes and stalwart heart, Elizabeth was just like him.

"Elizabeth knows her place," he said.

"My place was beside my mother, the true queen, and in the true faith."

"I thought you and I had worked through this years ago, Mary." The king sighed.

"So did I. But that was before you decided to propose to another Howard girl."

"Mary, look. I want you to like Catherine. It is important to me, not as your king but as your father. Will you at least try?"

Mary carefully considered his words. "I cannot promise anything. She is too young. I do not trust her already."

Henry left his daughter, hoping she would relent, or at least try to see Catherine's positive qualities. It did not help that his future bride had the same name as Mary's mother. He understood that. It would be difficult for any child.

With a ring of nobles surrounding him, Henry limped down a long, wide corridor lined with tapestries and flaming torches to his presence chamber. He passed guards in scarlet livery, their tunics embroidered with the Tudor rose, and more nobles, who bowed and tried to flatter him. In the banquet hall he was received with even more tiresome, solicitous bows. Their pretensions could be wearisome, particularly when his leg pained him. He sat beneath the huge canopy of state on a raised platform, breathed a great sigh, and waited, yet again, for the evening's festivities to commence around him.

After he drank half a cup of spiced wine, Henry found himself searching the room in almost humiliatingly adolescent anticipation for the bright, pretty eyes of Catherine. He was uncomfortable and weary after a day on horseback, and his leg was more painful than he dared to admit. But neither his age, ill health, nor steadily decaying body mattered a whit at that moment. He would be a free man soon,

God willing, and everything would change once Catherine accepted his offer of marriage.

A moment later, little Elizabeth was escorted into the room by one of His Majesty's most important aides as a show of her stature, the perpetually elegant Thomas Seymour, who was dressed in a doublet of silver satin with black slashings. Henry's little copper-haired daughter walked proudly, he thought, amid gossipy whispers and polite applause. She wore a gray silk dress studded with pearls, and her hair was drawn back and crowned with a matching circlet of pearls. She was completely self-possessed for what was not yet even her seven years. It was quite remarkable, for he had not seen her for several months and was struck anew by her demeanor. Perhaps it was his age or his new hope for the future, but Henry suddenly wanted to spend time with all three of his children. Their circumstances were not their fault, particularly in the case of Elizabeth. The little girl had suffered the most, knowing as she did that she was the only one of the three royal children whose mother had lost her life by execution.

Elizabeth approached him and dipped into a full and proper curtsy. "Your Majesty," she said with impeccable diction.

Henry smiled and held open his arms, relieved to see nothing of Anne Boleyn's bewitching sparkle in his daughter's young eyes. It felt good to embrace the child, he thought, taking in the fragrance of her sweet young self and relishing her genuinely loving grasp around his neck.

"Sit beside me," he said, directing her to the empty gold-and-velvet-covered chair on the raised platform to his left. Above them, the ceiling was still decorated with red, blue and gold badges displaying Anne Boleyn's and Henry's intertwined initials. "Tell me all about Hatfield. Does it still suit you?"

Elizabeth hesitated for only a moment before sinking into the chair, her young back straight as the blade of a knife. "Well, they still call me Lady Elizabeth because of what happened with my mother, not Princess, though everyone knows I am. But otherwise, it is not horrible."

Henry bit back a smile. He knew how grand and lovely the estates were in Hertfordshire, where Hatfield was situated. "I am pleased to hear that."

"Is my sister coming? They told me she was."

Henry did not want to disappoint the child, but neither did he wish to lie to her. "I hope she joins us. It would please me if we were all together."

"But we are not all together. There is still Edward," Elizabeth reminded him.

"I was informed by aides at Windsor that your brother has caught a summer cold, unfortunately, and his attendants thought it wise for him to remain there for now."

"Yes, a king must protect his heir first and foremost."

She was clever, he thought, with another burst of pride. Whatever she made of her life, he was certain of one thing: Elizabeth would never suffer fools gladly. At that moment, he wished he might live long enough to see her grow up.

There was so much promise in her.

Henry and Elizabeth turned their attentions to the festivities as acrobats began to perform on the bare, torchlit floor. Rousing cheers drowned out all conversation, but it did not stop Henry from noticing when Catherine finally entered the room. She was wearing the green gown and the magnificent emerald necklace he had given her. Dainty, sensual, with a hint of the devil about her. How glorious it would be when he bedded her at last!

With a wave of his hand over his shoulder, Henry summoned a nearby page.

"Bring her," he said, nodding toward Catherine.

An instant later, Catherine stood before him on the raised platform. She gave a polite curtsy, emerald silk pooling at her ankles. As she rose, she looked directly and familiarly at Henry. As it always did when she was near, Henry felt his body stir.

"Your Majesty has provided fine entertainment," Catherine said.

"Come and sit beside me," Henry said, indicating the empty chair on his other side. "There is someone I would like you to meet."

Catherine dutifully sat, flounced out her emerald skirts, and took a fresh cup of wine before Henry eased back into his own chair. No matter how much he wanted Mary to be there, he knew it was better that his more judgmental older daughter had not yet arrived. Elizabeth was the one who would give Catherine a real chance anyway.

Without being prompted, Catherine caught the little girl's eye. Just as she had done with Edward, she leaned forward with her bright, genuine smile and introduced herself.

"Hello, I am Catherine Howard."

"I am His Majesty's daughter Elizabeth."

Henry crossed his arms over his barrel chest and pretended to watch the acrobats, but he eagerly listened to every syllable.

"Your Grace's dress is incredibly lovely. Is it French?" Catherine addressed Elizabeth as a princess, a daring move, since she had been removed from the line of succession. Henry appreciated her sensitivity, as he knew she would do so only if she realized that he had not made the situation regarding the succession clear to his young daughter.

"It is Italian, and it is too tight," she replied, turning her little lower lip out in a pout.

"Mine are always too tight as well." Catherine softly laughed.

"Yet they say we must never show our discomfort. We must either smile or have our stays cinched even tighter."

Elizabeth giggled in response. Henry bit back a contented smile and signaled for more wine from a liveried servant with a large silver ewer at the ready. He wanted to get very drunk to celebrate the moment. Elizabeth liked Catherine, and the rest of the world would like her as well.

But just as the acrobats were finished performing and as the music was to start, and before Henry could bring his goblet to his lips, he saw his elder daughter, Mary, approaching. As usual, she was dressed in severe black and her spine was stiff. She was not smiling. This would either be interesting or very awkward. Yes, more wine, Henry thought. On evenings like these, there could not be enough wine in the world.

Across the room, Mary Lassells was watching the scene play out. Watching and waiting.

❊

As the brightly costumed Venetian musicians began to sing, Catherine noticed a young woman in black approaching the king. Her stony expression was framed by an older-style gable hood, and she wore a simple gold cross around her neck. There was a striking difference between this young woman and the other ladies of the court, who were ornamented boldly in beads, stones and pearls. Catherine was wary of her.

When the king greeted her, Catherine realized who she was. A chair was brought and placed between Catherine's and the king's, forcing Catherine to the side. The severe-looking young woman sank onto the proffered chair with an air of entitlement.

"Ah, here you are at last," Henry said, his smile wide and welcoming. "I had begun to think you were not coming."

"I had begun to think I wasn't coming either," Mary replied crisply.

She looked to the other side of the king and smiled and nodded to Elizabeth. But she did not acknowledge Catherine before she turned her attention back to the king.

"Ah, dancing! I would fancy a bit of that this evening," Henry exclaimed. He held out his fat, bejeweled hand to Mary as the Venetian musicians struck up his favorite tune and the guests began to rise from their seats. "Mary, would you do me the honor?"

She nodded and rose stiffly as the king's ornate chair was drawn back for him. He smiled despite his daughter's formal demeanor.

Left to her own devices, Catherine seized the opportunity to speak to Elizabeth again. She seemed lonely without another young person to speak with in the room. Catherine knew it would please her uncle and grandmother if she made an effort with the royal little girl. But more than that, Catherine actually wanted to get to know her.

"Do you like dancing?" Catherine asked.

"I only dance with my governess, and she is not a proper partner, so I am not certain if I like it yet. She says I step on her feet a little too often."

Catherine was surprised by the girl's self-possession and charmed by her refreshing candor. "They did not allow me to dance at Horsham until I was much older than you are now. I still cannot dance as well as the other ladies here, and I especially cannot keep up with the king."

Elizabeth studied her, tipping her little head. "Truly?"

"Very truly." Catherine smiled.

Elizabeth put a finger to her lips as if she were about to share a great secret. "I do not like being raised in the country," Elizabeth whispered.

Catherine could sympathize. "Nor did I. It was frightfully dull, and the temptation to fill my time with foolish activities was too great. I always knew there was more to be had, and my suspicions were confirmed only when I came to court."

She smiled and glanced at the king and his elder daughter as they danced—two tall, lumbering royals both draped in too much velvet.

"Are you going to marry my father?"

Catherine was surprised by the question. The young princess was shrewd for a girl of seven. "I have not been asked."

Fortunately, she thought. Her heart ached at the possibility that she would marry someone other than Thomas Culpeper. She had not seen Thomas for days, and it had become clear that he was avoiding her. She understood why, but still, the reality wounded her. Even though she knew in her heart the outcome she wanted was impossible, Catherine still wanted Thomas to fight for her. She wanted a fairy-tale romance and a man to whisk her away.

But do you really want that, Catherine, or do you want the power and glory of being queen?

The question sprang into her mind, sudden and jarring.

In the darkest parts of herself, she was lured by the idea of marrying the king. She had waited all of her life for excitement, riches, love, passion and power—things she had only heard or dreamed about while growing up at Horsham.

And then it occurred to her that perhaps there was a way to have it all. It was a dangerous gamble, certainly, but would juggling Henry and Thomas be all that different from juggling Francis Dereham and Henry Manox? It was not exactly the fairy-tale romance she had hoped for, but it would have to do if she meant to keep Thomas in her life.

She was smiling as the dance drew to a close. Mary sat back

down beside her, and Elizabeth joined her father for the next dance. Mary, with her tightly pursed lips, stiffened spine and clasped hands, cast a pall over Catherine's happy mood. She shifted in her seat and gave the princess a cautious sidelong glance.

"You do not fool me," Mary remarked without looking at her.

"Your Grace?"

"I have seen your type in and out of my father's life before."

Catherine's jaw dropped. She waited for a moment, searching her mind for the right thing to say. Mary's words were difficult to respond to or refute, because Catherine was keenly aware that she had lived a frivolous life, where her beauty had helped most of her indiscretions to be forgiven or, at the very least, overlooked.

"I am in His Majesty's life only by his command, Your Grace."

"My father's commands, or more properly his whims, are powered by lust, Mistress Howard. To know this, we need only look at his decision to convert the nation from the true faith for the sake of Anne Boleyn." Mary did not deign to glance at Catherine. "I do not like you," she said, her voice tinged with spite.

"I gather that, Your Grace."

"At least you understand that much. A pity your own cousin did not show such prudence."

Catherine was tired of these endless comparisons between her and her ill-fated cousin, but before she could respond, Mary turned her head sharply and bored into Catherine with her dark and glistening Spanish eyes. It was a gripping sensation, akin to demonic possession. Catherine suppressed a little shiver and sat up straight.

"I do not want to defy your wishes by marrying the king," she replied to Mary, thinking of Thomas. "I would be happy to retire to the country."

Mary arched a black brow. "Would you now?"

"I would," Catherine said firmly.

"You are as transparent as Anne Boleyn. She never could hide her true colors from me or my mother, which was why we were both sent as far away from court as possible, no doubt. If I speak my mind about you, it could happen again, but believe me, I have no wish for exile. So I shall sit here and smile at my father and pretend that I actually like his fifth wife-to-be, who is seven years younger than I, his elder daughter."

"But we understand each other," Catherine said.

"Indeed we do," Mary acknowledged.

The king and Elizabeth returned to the platform then in a swirl of velvet and a swish of satin, their faces flushed and happy. They both nodded to the courtly applause and the baser shouts from the gallery above. Every dinner was a spectacle, and the crowds expected to be entertained. Catherine watched Mary's terse expression melt into a smile as she watched her father, and she saw pride on the king's fat, drink-reddened face as he reveled in the reunion with his daughters. The royal family occupied themselves with lively chatter then, giving Catherine an opportunity to slip away from the table. She found Jane talking with starched and proper Wriothesley across the room. Catherine asked Wriothesley to excuse them as she pulled Jane to the side.

"Have you seen Master Culpeper?" she whispered into Jane's ear.

Jane gestured with her eyes to a pillar across the room. Thomas was leaning against it, cloaked in shadows, watching the festivities from a distance.

"Take care, Catherine," Jane whispered. "This has become more than a game to you."

"It has never been a game with Thomas."

"You have known him for only two months' time," Jane argued.

Catherine turned away. "I feel as if I have known him for a

lifetime." She left Jane to Wriothesley then and walked toward Thomas.

When he saw her approaching, Thomas tried to turn and leave, but she caught up with him, clamping a hand on his arm. The connection was instantly a strong one.

"I haven't much time. We must speak privately," Catherine urged.

"The risk is too great," he said, not daring to look at her. "Everyone knows you are about to become the king's wife."

"You know my heart will never be his. Please come away and speak with me, Thomas; I beg you. We have only a moment as it is," she pleaded.

Thomas relented. Down the corridor from the great hall, they found a small, dark alcove that smelled of beeswax and urine. The moment they were inside, he swept her up and she wrapped her arms around his neck, pressing herself against him desperately. She began to kiss his cheeks, neck and chin.

"I have missed you! Why have you been avoiding me?"

"You know why, Catherine. I love you, but I value both of our lives. The king regards you as his property, and he does not suffer thieves."

He pushed her away, but she pressed into him even more tightly.

"There must be something we can do to fight this," she whispered urgently as her fingers snaked down to his codpiece, searching for reassurance of his passion for her.

Thomas tipped his head back as she touched him, his eyes closing, but he tried to regain his senses. "This will solve nothing, Catherine," he warned in an agonized whisper as she pushed her hand past the waistband of his trunk hose, latching onto him with a tender, experienced hand.

Catherine kissed his neck, then his mouth as she touched him. "I am only taking what is mine, what I want more than anything in this life to be mine."

It was dangerous, with courtiers and guards passing by just beyond the shadows, but that only heightened Catherine's pleasure. As they kissed more urgently, mouths open, tongues entwined, Thomas covered her hand with his and began to guide it in a rhythm that quickly brought him to the brink.

When it was over, Thomas sank against the paneled wall, his face half-hidden in shadow. "Marry me," he bade her in a deep whisper. "Run away with me at first light. I have enough money saved to last us at least a year and—"

"And then what will we do?"

"We will find a way. We are smart and resourceful."

"But neither of us is resourceful enough to outrun the king, much less my uncle. No, let's not lose hope. There are so many beautiful and willing girls at court. Perhaps the king will grow weary of me before his divorce is finalized."

Thomas was not swayed by her optimism. "That would be impossible. No one else at court possesses your rare combination of beauty, youth, vigor and charm."

Catherine was flattered, but not fooled. "The king simply desires someone who could make him feel young again, which any determined girl could really do."

"I am not willing to risk it, Catherine," Thomas said firmly.

"And I am not willing to risk our lives," Catherine said, trying to make Thomas see reason.

Thomas straightened the pleats of his doublet, tugging them hard in frustration. "You won't marry me, will you?"

Catherine sighed. "You have to give me time. If we are very fortunate and he grows weary of me or finds someone new, he might sanction a marriage and settle an estate on us. He favors you so much, Thomas, and I have seen his gaze upon Anne Basset more than once. If we are strong enough to wait it out, we just might win."

Thomas framed her face with his hands and kissed her again. "I never knew you were such an optimist."

"I never had anything I truly wanted until now," Catherine said with a smile.

Five minutes later, she rejoined the king, who, it appeared, had not stopped laughing and talking with his two daughters for an instant. Nor had he stopped drinking. She could see that his cheeks were flushed, his eyes were bloodshot and his words were slurred.

"Ah, there you are, Mistress Howard! I thought someone might have stolen you away."

"Of course not, Your Majesty. I only needed a breath of air after such a sumptuous meal."

"Not one of your headaches again, was it?" he asked, too drunk to be truly concerned.

"No, sire," she replied.

"Ah, good, good. Because if a rival had stolen you away, I would have to kill him," he declared with a laugh. She felt an odd little shiver but shook it off with a gentle smile.

"My father says you play cards well," Elizabeth interjected.

"Better than I dance," Catherine replied, grateful for the change of subject.

"Nonsense, you are a delightful dancer," Henry declared as he took a large bite of the meat pie before him. The juice dribbled down his chin and glistened on the whiskers of his copper beard. Catherine forced herself to look away to hide her repulsion.

"Your Majesty flatters me."

"I hope so," he said with a grin.

"Will you play with us tomorrow after prayers?" Elizabeth asked.

"I shall not be joining you, I am afraid," Mary said quickly before Catherine could respond. "I must read Saint Thomas Aquinas with my ladies after prayer and discuss it. They are all planning on it."

"How frightfully dull." Elizabeth giggled.

"Now, now. Only good can come by reading godly works," Henry said.

"But my lord Seymour says those are the works of the Papists," Elizabeth countered.

"My lord Seymour seems not to be the best influence on our Elizabeth when the two of them are brought together," Mary remarked in a clipped tone.

Catherine knew that her ardent belief in the true religion could bring her closer to the king's elder daughter, but she chose to remain silent for now. The king, after all, had initiated the reformed Church of England. She did not want to approach that hornet's nest.

As she looked away to avoid the tension, she caught a glimpse of Thomas watching her from across the room. His expression was one somewhere between sadness and pity.

She was trapped, and they both knew it.

When she returned to her room later that night, she sank onto the edge of her bed and kicked off her shoes. As they clattered to the floor, she saw, on her bedside table, a large silver brooch in the shape of a rose. Such an exquisite piece of jewelry could have come only from the king. The girls, other maids of honor, in her doorway tittered and whispered as she picked it up, confirming her suspicions. Catherine looked more closely at the costly gift. The petals had been painted pink and the stem was encrusted with diamonds. It struck her that it had been fashioned with absolutely no thorns.

What a unique flower, she thought, yet how utterly unrealistic.

❖

The next morning, after matins, Catherine was shown to the king's great private gallery. The vaulted space was carpeted, and had a row of floor-to-ceiling windows with a view of the garden, and walls that were lined with tapestries, mirrors and maps. She was there by the king's command to play cards with His Majesty and his youngest daughter. She was surprised then to see Norfolk's son, Henry, Edward and Thomas Seymour, the king's two nieces, and Lady Lisle and Anne Basset seated at a large marble-topped Venetian table. Having another young beauty there such as Anne would put a new and interesting spin on things, Catherine thought. With talk of the divorce between the king and queen at a crescendo in the halls of court, many, besides her uncle, were intent on offering a replacement for Anne of Cleves.

Lady Lisle was foremost among them.

For just an instant, as Catherine watched the king's eyes drop to Anne Basset's cleavage and linger a moment too long, she allowed herself a spark of hope. After all, if His Majesty chose someone other than her as his next queen, how could anyone blame her for healing her broken heart by moving on?

"Do sit beside me, Mistress Howard," Elizabeth said excitedly.

The sound of the little girl's voice drew Catherine back from her thoughts and made her smile. Elizabeth seemed so eager to be friends with her that it was slightly shocking, especially in the face of Mary's open contempt for her. When she glanced at the king, he nodded for her to sit in the chair between him and Elizabeth. She heard a light scoff at the gesture from Lady Lisle, who quickly pretended to clear her throat. When she had recovered herself, she pierced Catherine with her gaze.

"That is a lovely brooch, Mistress Howard," Lady Lisle said, drawing everyone's attention. Catherine touched the rose at her breast and caught the king's preening expression.

"Thank you. It was a gift."

"Quite an extravagant one," Lady Lisle said with a hint of scorn in her voice.

"I was honored to accept it."

"It was from the king!" Elizabeth excitedly interjected. "I helped him choose it from the royal collection."

"What a delight." Lady Lisle sniffed as she picked up her cards.

"So tell me, Mistress Howard," said Edward Seymour as he began to deal the cards quickly, sending them in a spray across the glossy inlaid table. "Where has my lord Duke of Norfolk gone? I've not seen him since we were at Nonsuch."

"He is in London on business for the Crown," the king quickly replied in a gruff tone, exchanging a glance with Catherine. His brows merged into a frown as he studied the hand of cards he had been dealt. "It is my most ardent wish to see him return as soon as possible. I want the whole business over with, believe me."

"It is my wish as well, Your Majesty. He is a good friend to us all," Edward replied.

"Do stop, Edward. Envy is such a difficult thing to mask, even with flattery," the king retorted, not in the mood for the usual games.

Just then, a page appeared bearing a dispatch for Henry. He bowed and handed the folded vellum to the king, who broke the wax seal with his fat thumb. Silence fell around them as Henry read and began to scowl. Catherine glimpsed the bold and scrawling handwriting, though she tried to avert her eyes.

When he finished reading, he laughed, then crumpled the inked vellum. He cast it to the floor and, with a huff, struggled to his feet.

Everyone else quickly rose with him. Their smiles and expressions of ease gave way to worried looks. Henry grunted as he hobbled across the room to the open doors. A page dutifully followed.

"Is there to be a response, Your Majesty?" the page asked.

"None. My silence will say it all." He drew in a deep, rheumy breath, and Catherine watched as he tried to collect himself. His face was red, but his expression was frighteningly blank. Catherine hoped the letter had nothing to do with her. She did not want to be the cause of the cold, dead look in his eyes.

Chapter Twelve

*I*t was not the scene that Norfolk expected when he was shown into Cromwell's vast chamber cell, which faced the barge-dotted, briny Thames. Cromwell's eyes were glazed, and his once impeccably shaved chin was now covered with a scruffy white beard. Still, the duke refused to yield to even the slightest tug of pity. He had waited too long not to relish fully the great chief minister's final destruction.

But Norfolk knew that Cromwell would not go down without a fight. "You lied to the king!" Cromwell cried, lunging at his elegantly dressed rival as Norfolk tossed his gray kid gloves onto a table.

"Come now, Thomas, you made your own bed with him when you showed antipathy for the true religion, which first set these wheels in motion. You have become a dangerous heretic, and that cannot be allowed to prevail."

"I follow the faith of our sovereign, for the love of God!" Cromwell shouted, his face red with anger.

"Now, that *is* a pity, choosing ambition over your faith," Norfolk said coolly.

"You have never chosen anything *but* ambition!"

"Yes, but Howards are more judicious in exercising their ambition." Norfolk began to pace the room. "Shall I tell you your first mistake? You did not realize that the king's devotion to the false religion follows his desire. When it served Henry to go against Rome to win Anne Boleyn to his bed, he did it. In time, his desire for another will bring him back to the true faith." He casually ran a finger over the surface of a bureau thick with dust. Wrinkling his nose, he rubbed his hands together before he continued. "You have heard, of course, that His Majesty will soon take another queen. A devoted Catholic queen."

"Your niece."

"Who else?" Norfolk paused as his gaze fully descended upon his defeated rival.

"I am to be executed, am I not?"

"It would seem so."

"But I just testified on His Majesty's behalf in the divorce suit. I took the blame for everything, and he is a free man now! Can you not speak to him for me, at the very least? Tell him I am ever his humble servant and I have learned from my errors. I will retire to the country if he prefers. I have family, Norfolk. You know my Gregory. For the love of God, to whom you say you are so devoted, can you not show me a bit of mercy?"

"Dear Thomas. Groveling does not become you."

Norfolk strode purposefully to the door and gave it one sound rap. A moment later, the clatter of huge keys in the iron lock filled the strained silence as a hot and dry summer wind rattled the leaded windows.

"Then what the devil did you come here for?" Cromwell raged.

Norfolk glanced back, his lined, drooping face full of disdain. "Why, to bid you farewell, of course. And now I have done that," Norfolk replied coldly.

✦

The next afternoon, at Hampton Court, the dowager duchess and the duke appeared unannounced in Catherine's apartments. The duke was still wearing his riding clothes. His boots were mud-caked, his ruddy, veined cheeks were flushed, and his long, gray kid gloves were bunched in his hand. The scents of wool and leather swirled around him.

As they entered the room, Catherine rose from her embroidering hoop, surprised by the unexpected visit. Jane rose beside her. Mary Lassells was folding linen across the room, but available to hear every word should there be some interesting exchange.

"We must speak privately," Agnes announced with an uncharacteristically broad, beaming smile, revealing gray, uneven teeth that people rarely saw because she so infrequently smiled.

Catherine glanced at Jane. *Oh, Lord, no*, she thought, feeling a sudden, cold rush of panic. Both of them coming together to speak with her could not be good. She cleared her throat, then straightened the folds of her dress, trying to prepare herself, but the room began to spin and her legs went weak. Catherine was quite certain, as the duke rubbed his hands together, that she would not survive this.

"Lady Rochford has my complete confidence. Can she not remain? Her presence has become a comfort to me."

"Catherine, this is not a time for childishness," said the dowager. "Did we not leave that behind at Horsham?"

"Oh, now, Agnes, the girl is right. Lady Rochford may actually be of assistance to us, with her broader female perspective," said Norfolk, casting his gloves onto a table with Catherine's Bible, bound in worn red leather. There was a glass flagon of wine beside it. He poured himself a silver cupful and swallowed the entire contents before he turned to Catherine.

"It has happened at last. Glory be to God. I have just come from Parliament. The last of the testimony has been given and the details finalized. His Majesty is officially a single man, and I myself delivered a petition from Parliament to the king begging him . . . Let me remember . . . ah, yes: 'For the good of your people, we implore you to enter into a fifth and final union with a new queen, so that God may bestow upon His Glorious Majesty many fine, strong sons.' That last bit, of course, was my own elegant turn of phrase."

"Saints be blessed," Agnes murmured, steepling her hands and pressing them to her lips with a dramatic flourish.

"What of the poor queen?" Catherine dared to ask, not certain she even wanted to hear the response.

Norfolk chuckled. "You are not to worry about her. The princess of Cleves will want for nothing, since she had the good sense to comply throughout the divorce proceedings. The details have been worked out." He poured himself another cup of wine, then held the silver cup to the sunlight as if looking for flaws. "She is to remain in England as the king's 'dear sister,' which is how she shall be formally known henceforth. She will be given Richmond Palace and Hever Castle, Anne Boleyn's family home."

He feigned a little expression of regret before he continued.

"She will also be given precedence over every other lady at court, after the king's daughters and the future queen, of course. Thus, I arrive at our purpose for this visit." The duke drank the wine in one gulp, then set the cup back down with a flourish. He was smiling. But it was nothing mirthful. Rather, it was a cool, calculated grin.

"Naturally, as we spoke of his being free, and even obligated to remarry, the subject between His Majesty and myself shifted away from Anne of Cleves."

Catherine sighed audibly, causing the dowager to shoot her an angry glare. She tried to maintain her composure, but the room was stifling and unbearably hot, made worse by the tension in the air. Catherine felt the sweat pool in the space between her breasts beneath her heavy silk gown, and the hard boning of the stomacher pinched so tightly it made it impossible to catch her breath. She hated summer.

"He asked me if he would meet with an objection if he pursued your hand, my dear."

Catherine was in a panic. *Did you tell him yes, most definitely yes?* She longed to throw herself at the duke and cry out these words. *Did you tell him he is old and decaying, that he smells worse than death? Did you tell him that I would object and shriek Thomas's name?*

"Of course, I said His Majesty's consideration of so unworthy a girl as my niece is an honor to all Howards."

The dowager was beaming. Jane shifted beside her.

I shall not survive this, Catherine thought, her heart thumping wildly against her chest. *I know I shall not!*

"He wishes to speak privately with you during a walk beside the river in an hour's time."

Catherine's heart was in her throat. She had known all along it might come to this, yet now that it was here, it felt more like a sentence of death than a great honor.

Save me, she thought. . . . But no one could.

She was on her own.

❖

Henry preened before a full-length, gold-trimmed mirror while a group of his gentlemen-of-the-chamber, including Thomas Culpeper, stood behind him. As he studied his reflection, the king allowed Wriothesley to douse him liberally with musk-scented oil. He lifted his chin, straightened his bell-shaped sleeves and turned sideways before the mirror, trying to catch a glimpse of the man he once had been—a man who could actually make Catherine Howard fall in love with him.

Henry Grey, Marquess of Dorset and husband to Henry's niece, took a smoothing comb to the king's clipped copper beard. As his courtiers fussed over him, the king caught a glimpse of Culpeper in the mirror. He was a damnable god of perfection, Henry thought with an uncharitable burst of envy. Thomas reminded him of what he once was. Women of the court had flocked to him, not because he was their king, but because he was as gorgeous as Thomas Culpeper. He had been thought the most handsome man in England, and he knew it.

How much he had taken for granted in his youth. He had given only scant attention to the women who adored him. Now he saw them grimace when he touched them, even the grateful and most ambitious ones. Life had made him many things. A fool was not one of them. But ardor never vanished, nor the needs of a man—even a royal one.

"So tell me, Tom," he said, turning around and feeling a sharp pain shoot up his ulcerated leg. "How do I look?"

"Perfection, as always, sire," Thomas said with skilled aplomb, which irritated Henry.

"Ah, Tom, you disappoint me, when it is your honesty that I most favor."

"I desire only to please Your Majesty."

"You may desire that, my boy, but you should also strive for honesty. As with Wil Somers, it is the main reason I keep you around." Henry smiled at the thought of his favorite fool, but it faded when he saw Culpeper's smile. Those perfectly straight, white teeth, so like the keys of a virginal. Henry tried not to scowl.

"So tell me, Tom, what news have you of the fair sex these days? It is odd that I have heard no tales of your exploits recently, and with poor Wil ill, I fancy a good tale to lighten my mood. I am nervous as a cat right now, and uncertainty is not a state I favor."

"Nervous, Your Majesty?"

Henry turned back to the mirror while Thomas waited for an answer. Dorset laid a thick gold baldric over the king's neck and arranged it over the shoulders of his sleek, thin, lynx brown coat. The adornment glistened with rubies and pearls and a diamond pendant in the center.

"I am going to take a wife," the king confided in a gentler voice than usual. "That is, if she will have me. I am no fool, despite what people may say—'There goes the king, married four times. Who would want to take him on?' I hear gossip, just as the rest of you do. But she is different. She can make me different, if she will take me into her heart, not just her bed. Though I cannot resist the thought of her perfect body beneath my bedcovers."

To Henry's surprise, Culpeper grimaced and paled. He looked as if he might be ill. They had spoken many times of women and their exploits. It was the thing Henry valued most about their relationship, so Thomas's reaction was odd, to say the least.

"May I say how pleased I am for you, sire?" Thomas managed to say.

"You may say what is in your mind, Tom."

Thomas hesitated before going on. "If that is true, sire, then it would please me if you would grant me leave to retire from court for a time."

Henry had been adjusting the feather hat that the Earl of Southampton had placed on his head, but he froze and stared at Thomas's reflection in shock. "What the devil?"

Culpeper turned away from the mirror, his discomfort palpable. Suddenly Henry leaned back and gave a boisterous laugh.

"A jest like that was not what I had in mind when I asked you to lighten my heart, Tom. Of course you cannot leave me. I've grown accustomed to you. I need you here, especially if she accepts me.

After all, it has been a long while since I have sought a young beauty like Catherine, and I know you cannot say the same."

Henry saw a blanched, uncharacteristically panicked expression transform the young man's perfect face.

"Do relax, Culpeper," he directed affably, giving himself one more approving glance in the long mirror. "I am not calling you a knave, or trying to insult you. I merely mean you have experience and can offer me guidance as I proceed."

Thomas interjected, "But I had planned to retire to the country and—"

"Silence!" Henry cut him off with a flick of his jeweled hand. He was growing irritable indulging such petulance, when all he wanted to think about was the beautiful girl who waited for him outside. *Fool boy, he thinks his desires are more important than my needs*, Henry silently grumbled as he hobbled toward the door, putting Culpeper out of his mind.

❖

Was this how Anne Boleyn felt when she walked to her death on Tower Green? Catherine thought dramatically, as two palace guards led her to the place where she would meet Henry.

The king had not arrived yet, so she paced nervously along the grassy banks of the river and watched ducks cut across the water, which sparkled like jewels in the late-morning sun. Long willow branches hung heavily and dipped into the water where they met the spongy shore.

She looked far more exquisite than she felt in another new gown, her auburn hair swept back and covered with a gold mesh coronet. Soft, wispy tendrils at her forehead and temples prevented the style from appearing too severe. At her throat was the emerald necklace that the king had given her, although it felt more like a hangman's noose.

Catherine now knew that this day, this moment, had been her

uncle's goal all along and the reason she had been brought to court in the first place. Yet still, the thought of what she was losing by accepting her royal destiny caused Catherine's eyes to fill with tears.

Suddenly she caught sight of a shadowy figure beneath one of the willows. She recognized the figure and sprang back with a gasp. It was the last person in the world she expected to see. Leaning cavalierly against the trunk of the willow was Francis Dereham.

It was like looking at a ghost, and in a way she was. The specter of her past, in the form of Mary Lassells, and now Francis Dereham, was rising up to haunt her and destroy her family's well-laid plans.

"What are you doing here?" Catherine managed to sputter.

Francis gave her a mocking bow. "Now, is that any way to greet the man you are going to marry?"

He was still handsome, but in a noticeably countrified way, she realized. He was not urbane and elegant like the men she knew at court . . . like Thomas.

Catherine was annoyed by the reminder of their marriage pact. "Those were childhood games, and you know it!"

Francis laughed bitterly. "Alas, it was never a game to me. Besides, you were sixteen, sweeting, well past a babe's age. Remember the sarcenet scarf you made for me?" He drew it from a pocket in his beige jerkin and held it up to her. "I still have it, just like every memory of what happened between us. Look at our initials stitched into the fabric, so prominently entwined together, which anyone would take as proof of our great love for each other."

She did not take the bait, but she was growing anxious. She had been told that the king would be there any moment. Catherine glanced nervously at the path that led from the palace to the riverbank. She knew the king's infatuation with her was based on his belief in her innocence, and that was an illusion Francis could easily shatter, so everything in the world, especially her uncle's ambitious goals, was riding on how she conducted herself in the next few minutes. If she did not handle this absolutely perfectly she feared not only being sent away from court, but from Thomas as well. And not being able to at least see him was a circumstance she simply could not bear.

Catherine steeled herself against Francis's words and feigned a look of indifference. "What do you want, Francis?"

"To bring my wife home, of course."

"I am not your wife," she replied, trying to sound unconcerned.

"Ah, but we were trothplighted, which is nearly the same thing," Francis pressed on, unconvinced by her performance.

She began to feel desperation well up inside of her like a hot rush. But she could not afford to have Francis know it. She must focus on self-preservation.

"When last I heard, you had gone to Ireland to seek your fortune. How did you find me here, anyway?" she asked with a hint of boredom in her voice, as if she could care less.

"Such news travels swiftly, my love, even as far as Kilkenny." Francis took a step nearer, and instinctively she took a step back, betraying her anxiety. Francis tipped his head in amusement. "Oh, now, I merely wished to greet my wife properly."

Now she was certain he was here because he wanted something from her. "Do stop calling me that. You know perfectly well that I am not your wife."

"Let us not cavil with the details, hmm?" Francis said with a bitter smile.

There was a commotion across the sprawling lawn that drew her attention just then. As she had expected, a group of gentlemen, with the king at the center, walked toward her in a great swirl of velvets, satins, feathered hats, jewels and hearty male laughter. Catherine's heart began to race, and she fought a swell of panic.

She turned to Francis and said in a low voice, "I haven't much money of my own, but I shall give you what I can. How much do you require?"

"Oh, I do not want something as simple as money, you silly little mite," Francis replied, advancing toward her.

"What is it that you want, then?" Catherine asked.

"Find a way for me to remain near you and be a part of your world to advance my own." While the request was sincere, the way he spoke the words did not speak of love for her.

"Would you rather not have jewels? I have a rare emerald bracelet worth a fortune that my pet kitten wears. The king would believe that the little animal lost it. You could sell it and live not like a servant here but like a king yourself." She desperately tried to convince him.

Catherine glanced again at Henry, who had paused a few yards away to speak with one of his gentlemen. She was relieved to discover that for the moment she and Francis were obscured from the king's view by the trunk of the tree yet she could still see him through the heavy willow branches. When she looked back at Francis, she saw that his expression had gone stony.

"I want a position at court. I shall be your secretary once you are queen."

"How on earth would I ever explain that?" Catherine replied in astonishment.

"Why, you could say that I am a trusted old friend from Horsham, and it is your wish to have someone near you upon whom you can depend."

Trusted friend—how ironic, she thought in a full, raging panic as she stared into the face of a man who wanted to profit for himself from her position at court. Her only saving grace was that he would be ruining his own life as well if he pushed too hard. She had to gamble on the fact that he was smart enough to know that.

"I will speak to my lady grandmother."

"When?" Francis pressed.

"I am not yet queen! There is only so much I can do, Francis. Now you must leave before he arrives. You can see for yourself that he is coming!"

"Hmm, I don't know. I have always wanted to meet the king," he said, clearly stalling to toy with her.

"Very well. I promise I will see you made my secretary *if* I do become queen," she replied hurriedly.

"And I should take your word for that after you disavowed our own marriage?"

"An old country ritual does not constitute a marriage, Master Dereham. But very well, go to the duchess yourself. Tell her we have spoken. She will grant you what you desire and see that it comes to pass."

"Very well, I shall go. But you have promised. And this is a promise I fully intend for you to keep. One way or another."

Catherine glanced away in panic to see if the king was nearby, and when she turned back, Francis Dereham had disappeared. She took a deep breath to steady herself just as the king took leave of his men and approached her. She could not still her racing heart. She was overwhelmed by her confrontation with Francis, and upset that yet another person had power over her.

"Ah, there you are!" Henry exclaimed as he came upon her. Despite her turbulent emotions beneath the surface, she knew she must look lovely against the picturesque broad, blue sky and emerald grass. "I looked for you on the pathway. This wet earth makes it difficult to walk."

"Forgive me, Your Majesty. I was drawn down here. It is just so beautiful." Catherine curtsied and lowered her head respectfully. "I was not thinking."

He took her hand in his and lifted her chin up to face him. "Well, you will certainly need to work on that. A king must be able to rely upon the counsel of his queen."

She had known it was coming, yet now that it was here, Catherine could not quite wrap her mind around the enormity of it all. As she looked at his fleshy face, wet rosebud mouth and small, pale eyes, she began to feel sick rather than honored.

"Shall we walk for a bit?" he suggested.

"It would be a pleasure, sire."

"Hal," he corrected.

"Forgive me, Hal."

"I hope I will not have to forgive so much in the future. I am not the world's most tolerant man," he said with a smile, although there was a strangely ominous quality in his voice as he led her back to the brick pathway up the embankment.

"I shall always do my best. I am a quick learner."

"I can ask for little else. Except, perhaps, for your love in return."

After a small, awkward silence, Henry stopped and turned to her with a little grunt. A flock of geese flew past them overhead. Catherine felt her face flush. It was the moment for which she should have been prepared.

"I trust your uncle has spoken with you of my intention, Cat," Henry began.

"He did say that Your Majesty might feel an inclination toward me," she said slowly.

"I am madly, childishly in love with you, Catherine, and if you will have me, in spite of my many obvious and unsettling flaws, it is not only my inclination but my fondest wish that you become my wife."

Catherine must have grimaced or flinched, because she saw the king scowl.

"The notion of becoming Queen of England is not a pleasing one to you?"

Catherine recovered quickly. "It is an honor, the magnitude of which I cannot fully comprehend."

"But is it *your* desire, Catherine? Might I be fool enough to hope that one day such a young, beautiful and energetic girl might love me in return?"

He was surprisingly vulnerable. His eyes were wide with hope, and he was baring his heart to her. Everything a girl could ever dream of was before her, cloaked in exquisite brown velvet and glittering gold. Unfortunately, the man beneath the dream was limping, decaying and unappealingly obese. But this was not about Catherine or what she wanted. She reminded herself that this was about family, loyalty and a dynasty that had taken decades to build and then rebuild again. Everything was riding on what she said next.

"Hope is never foolish, Hal," she finally replied in a tone so sincere that she surprised even herself.

The king leaned over and placed a chaste kiss onto her lips. His breath was a noxious combination of food and stale ale, and she fought with all her strength not to recoil. When she opened her eyes and looked at him, she saw that he was smiling.

"Then we are agreed?"

She felt a sudden shiver. *Your fifth wife . . . but for how long? How long until I, like the others, displease you?*

"Yes." She forced the word from her lips because she knew she must.

"You have made me a happy man, my innocent little Cat. And I know I shall be even happier on our wedding night. But until the formal announcement is made to the people, for propriety's sake, I am sending you away from court to your uncle's home at Lambeth."

Catherine was taken aback. "When?"

"This afternoon. I do not wish to test myself. Your ladies are packing for you presently."

Catherine's mind raced. She needed desperately to see Thomas before she left. She needed to tell him the news herself. She owed that to him.

Henry leaned forward and kissed her again. It was less chaste this time. Inwardly, she cringed again at the taste of his sour breath, but she forced herself to smile sweetly and serenely, as she was trained to do. Satisfying the king was now her sole purpose.

"I will do my best to make you happy, sire."

"Hal," the king gently corrected her again, just as he belched loudly and put a hand to his mouth.

❖

Thomas balanced both arms on the casement of a large oriel window that faced the garden and the great river shining beyond. He did not want to watch, but he needed to see it. The king and Catherine. His Catherine. The proposal. The kiss. Everyone at court knew, but like reading the last page of a book, he needed to finish it himself, no matter how much he did not like the ending. Catherine belonged to the king now. *Keep her safe, Lord,* he whispered in silent prayer. *She will need Your gracious protection now more than ever. You are really the only one she has.*

❖

From the height of the gallery in the redbrick Clock Tower, feeble Thomas Cranmer, Archbishop of Canterbury, and close ally of the imprisoned Thomas Cromwell, had watched what he knew to be the king's proposal to the Howard girl, his dark, ambitious eyes shining. He had also seen a mysterious young man in a beige jerkin approach the young woman, then, moments later, the king. The archbishop had fingered the cross around his neck as he watched the king and the waif until they were nearly out of sight. He had then seen the mysterious man with the scarf in his hand watching the pair as well, concealed by the trees.

Apparently, the Culpeper lad was not the only one to garner private time with the little beauty who had turned the king's head . . . for now. What would great, bluff King Hal, as the people called him, think of his little conquest if he actually knew about not one, but two competitors? Cranmer bit back a clever smile.

Ah, but he would make use of those details another time. Not quite yet.

If only poor Cromwell could be here to see this. They both loved the thrill of the battle almost as much as their righteous cause. Cranmer hated Norfolk with a bitter violence that no clergyman should ever permit himself to feel, but he could not help it when the man he had fought beside for years now faced execution at the hands of that Catholic zealot.

But even without Cromwell's help, he would vanquish the Howards. And he would do it more methodically and more diabolically than they had ever managed. The destruction of a powerful dynasty would be Cranmer's gift to Cromwell's memory.

But Cranmer needed to wait for the right moment. Fortunately, the Lord Great Chamberlain had taught the archbishop the art of patience. It was indeed a virtue that the prelate now possessed in spades.

Chapter Thirteen

July 26, 1540
Lambeth House, London

*A*s the ghostly figure approached her, Catherine could just make out the face of the king. The apparition's expression was hardened by rage, and his eyes were wild and red, rather than green, like a wolf on the hunt.

She tried to cry out but no sound came. Distracted by a far-off sound, the apparition turned away. She ran and hid, cowering behind a huge stone urn, and watched the black-clad figure stalk through the dark room, cape flying behind him, a jeweled dagger in his hand. This cannot be Henry, she thought. This man, this specter, was wild and frightening, like some unleashed evil. Suddenly Catherine saw the other girl. Her hair was the same amber shade as her own. She was small and even more startlingly beautiful.

Run. It is not safe! Catherine tried to warn the girl. Yet no words would come. This cannot be happening, she thought. As Henry stalked toward the girl, she turned and looked directly at Catherine, as if she sensed her hiding there. Their eyes met at the very moment that the king slashed her throat with the jeweled dagger. Blood sprayed out like a crimson fountain as the girl's eyes widened with shock.

There could be no mistake. The face. The eyes. It was Anne Boleyn. A moment later, as if she were looking into a mirror, the face became her own.

Catherine bolted upright in her bed, her white muslin night-dress wet with sweat, her heart pounding like a drum. She'd had wild, violent nightmares before, yet nothing that had felt so like a premonition as this.

Jane Boleyn and Mary Lassells, who had both been sent to Lambeth to attend her, came running into her bedchamber, and Catherine realized that she must have called out. She was shaking violently, her mind still filled with the images from her dream, and she began to weep. Jane sank onto the edge of the bed with Mary behind her and took tight hold of her shoulders.

"You are all right. Breathe deeply," Jane commanded.

"I cannot."

"You can. Just breathe."

"But it was so real. It was like a vision of my future. He was killing my cousin . . . but it was also me!"

"Hush now." Jane tried to soothe her. "It was only a dream."

"Can you be so certain? I saw his eyes. There was murder in them, and not for the first time!"

"It's only natural that you would be afraid. The idea of becoming queen must be overwhelming. You are bound to be unsettled."

"It is more than that, Jane. He had her executed. He could just as easily do that to me!"

"There, now." Jane tried to smile as she pressed the matted, wet hair back from Catherine's face. "He loves you."

"He loved her once, until she made a mistake. What if I err as well? I cannot go through with it, Jane. Please, I beg you, help me find a way out of it. I cannot live my life in fear. You must help me!"

Panic rose wildly within her, like a living thing. The vision of

Henry's cold, dead eyes, full of brutal hatred, would not leave her thoughts. Jane turned to Mary.

"Bring Mistress Howard a cup of warm ale; then leave us," she commanded.

Mary hesitated for a moment, not wanting to miss the conversation, but then she honored Lady Rochford's status and did as she was told. After Mary closed the door behind her with a little click, Jane spoke again.

"Listen to me now," she said in a firm whisper. "Unlike Anne Boleyn, you have not only history, but me as your guide, and you can be smarter in your choices. Right now, the king is entirely besotted with you, and there is nothing in the world he will not do for you. It was just the same with Anne, but her mistake was in taking his love for granted and letting her ambition rule the day."

"But I do not want Henry to rule me. My heart and soul belong to Thomas!"

Jane shook her head firmly. "You must never, ever let anyone else but me hear you say that again."

"But who else would I tell but you, Jane? You alone know my heart in this."

"And I am the more in danger for it. You must never slip up or mention aloud your love for Master Culpeper, or all three of our lives will be in grave danger. Everyone must believe that you belong to the king now, for you will be Catherine Howard, Queen of England."

"But how can I live without the man I love? I am young and vital. Henry is old and fat. He is a decaying wreck of the man he once was!"

"A man who has the power to make your nightmare a reality," Jane declared with a strange, frosty realism that settled into her like a winter chill. She waited a moment as Catherine stared into her eyes, uncertain now where to turn, whom to trust, or even what to do next. As if sensing the question, Jane said, "Look, you are right to trust me, and you can. I am in this far too deeply already to abandon you. Once you are back at court, I will find you a way to meet with Master Culpeper. I have no idea how, so that it will not endanger us all, but I will think of something. Only speak no more of it to him or to anyone else until I do. No one can be trusted in something like this. Everywhere you turn, there are spies who would rather see all three of us dead than another Catholic as queen."

Feeling the pull of sleep, led by the weight of desperation, Catherine lay back down on the crisp, white bed linen and let Jane pull the bedspread over her. She wanted to sleep forever.

"Try to get some rest. The king will come for a visit tomorrow and you must look your best."

The image of the ghostly king and the dagger dripping with blood came to her again. She tried to push it aside with thoughts of Thomas, but she realized that she had no physical object to remind her of the man she would always love, or their precious time together. Perhaps it was just as well, though. It would only remind her of all she had forever lost by agreeing to marry the king.

❖

Mary had let the door click to a close, but after a moment she opened it again. Catherine was, as usual, too self-absorbed to notice. Katherine Tilney and Joan Acworth had accused her at Horsham of being envious. But Mary knew better. What motivated her, and her brother, was not envy but rather commitment to the true path toward God, which, if those Howards rose again to power, England would be stripped of as they were misled again by the Catholics.

That could not be allowed to happen.

Mary strained to hear every word. The dream. Thomas Culpeper. Catherine's fear of making a mistake.

When Catherine Howard eventually did make that mistake, and she would, Mary Lassells would be there. And when she returned to court, she knew God would lead her to the proper partner to help her use that mistake to the Reformation's advantage. She might be just one woman, but like everyone else who had found a way to court, she too was driven by ruthless ambition. The rest she would leave to God, she thought, making the sign of the cross as she slipped, unheard, into the darkness of the great corridor.

❖

"The king comes!"

There was a quality of panic in the announcement, which set the entire Lambeth household in motion as dogs yelped at the king's arrival in the courtyard. Catherine stood stone still as Jane clasped the king's necklace around her throat. The air was permeated with the aroma of cooked meat from the kitchens below and fresh wood polish on the elegant linen-fold paneled walls. The Duke of Norfolk's staff had been preparing for days for the king's private visit.

"Do I look proper for the king?" Mary Lassells asked, as she glanced at her own image in a free corner of the mirror.

The question surprised Catherine as she prepared to greet Henry. "You look fine," she replied quickly, then put the moment out of her head.

As she descended the staircase, followed by the dowager duchess, Jane and the king's niece Lady Douglas, she saw the king waiting for her in the entry hall. He was costumed in a wide, dove gray doublet trimmed in silver and slashed to reveal white satin underneath. When he saw her, he smiled broadly and held up his hand to her. Everyone else fell into deep bows and curtsies.

Catherine took his hand as she reached the last step.

"Leave us," Henry commanded.

She heard her grandmother give a little huff as she left with the others. When they were alone, Henry held her out at arm's length to admire her.

"Well worth a summer ride back into the city. Worth anything, actually," Henry flattered her. Without warning, he pressed a kiss onto her lips with the sensual familiarity of a lover. She was prepared this time, and she successfully steeled herself against his foul breath.

"These days have seemed an eternity," he said huskily.

"It is a pleasure to see you, Hal," she replied softly, using the king's nickname without prompting for the first time.

He touched the jewel at her throat and smiled. "I see you are wearing my gift."

"I wear it every day, as it is my most exquisite possession."

"So far," he corrected. "Which reminds me . . ."

Henry led her into the library to the left of the entry hall. The grand room was made intimate by large upholstered chairs, tables and a tapestry. Once they were inside, he withdrew a ring from his doublet that literally took her breath away as it glittered in his meaty palm. The stone was the size of an almond, surrounded by pearls.

"It is a pink diamond, the rarest in the world. I could think of nothing more appropriate to mark our formal betrothal." Without waiting for her response, the king held up her hand and slipped the ring onto her finger, where it sparkled in the late-afternoon sunlight.

"Does it please you then?"

"How could it not?" Catherine asked, smiling more sincerely than she had meant to. She felt as if she were betraying Thomas, but she could not afford to feel that way anymore. More than just being awed by his power, or even appreciating his moments of tenderness, Catherine must allow herself to care for the king. It was the only way to survive.

"Shall you say it then?" he asked, seeking a more solid confirmation of her pleasure.

"It pleases me greatly . . . Hal."

At her words, Henry smiled like a little boy who had gotten his way. "There, now, see how easy that was? You needn't be timid with me, my little Cat. When we are alone together, I shall always be your Hal to whom you can say anything. Speaking of which . . ." He glanced around. "Where is our little kitten? I've not see her since Nonsuch. She must be growing into a sleek and gorgeous little creature by now. I suspect she shall soon outgrow her collar and shall need another. Do have her brought to us," he happily instructed Catherine as he took her hand.

She dutifully obliged by ringing a little silver bell the duke kept on the fireplace mantel. Appearing before the king was a privilege, and since Jane outranked Mary, she had the pleasure of responding to the summons. She dropped into a deep and proper curtsy.

"Please have Putette brought down from the basket in my bedchamber, Lady Rochford. The king would like to see her."

"Of course, mistress." Jane nodded dutifully, but just as she turned to leave, the king spoke to her.

"My lady Rochford, how are you? It seems a long time since we have exchanged more than a perfunctory word or two."

Catherine could see that Jane was surprised by the familiar tone in his voice. "I am well, Your Majesty. Yes, it does seem a lifetime."

"You are looking quite healthy. Is your position with my future bride to your liking?" he affably asked.

"It pleases me greatly, sire."

"Splendid. Mistress Howard shall need a trusted friend in the coming days, one who knows all of the small details required to be queen. You do remember the details, Jane, do you not?"

"I believe I do, sire."

Catherine looked at them each in turn. She was touched by Henry's apparent desire to make a fresh start with the one woman she thought of as a friend. As Jane went upstairs, an awkward silence fell between them. Henry was staring at her, and as they sat down together on a tapestry-covered settee, she realized that he had not let go of her hand.

"I've chosen Oatlands Palace," he announced.

"Your Majesty?"

"For our marriage ceremony. It is in Weybridge, which is in the most picturesque little forest, like a fairy-tale land. Since I cannot bear to let you sleep alone any longer than I must, we shall wed in two days' time . . . if it pleases you, my dear."

His deep green eyes were so wide tucked into the full folds of his cheeks, their expression so childlike, that Catherine forgot for an instant that he had the power to see someone executed in a heartbeat, even his own wife.

Before she could reply, Jane returned, and the gloomy thought vanished. But Jane stood in the doorway, her face white as a sheet as she made a feeble curtsy.

"What is the matter, Jane?" Catherine asked.

She paused for a moment, averting her eyes. "It is the kitten, Mistress Howard."

Catherine bolted to her feet. The little thing had become quite dear to her. "What is wrong with her?"

"She is . . . well, she . . ."

"Out with it!" Henry bellowed, as he struggled to his feet beside Catherine.

"I beg you pardon me, sire, but it looks as if the poor thing has been poisoned," Jane said, trembling.

Catherine ran to the doorway. "That is impossible! She was fine just before the king arrived."

Jane blocked her path. "Do not go up, mistress, I bid you. It is not a pleasant sight. I shall have one of the servants—"

"No, I mean to see for myself," Catherine said firmly.

She was halfway up the staircase, the king lumbering after her, when he bellowed, "Heads will roll if this is true!"

As they entered Catherine's bedchamber, they found two servants kneeling beside the little basket next to her bed, talking in low tones about how they should dispose of the little body.

Catherine charged forward indignantly, tears in her eyes. "Leave her! I shall bury her myself."

Henry struggled with great effort to kneel beside the dead kitten as the servants curtsied and backed out of the room. Catherine saw, to her horror, foam seeping from Putette's little mouth, the priceless bracelet gone. Who could be so cruel as to harm a tiny creature, and who would dare to take such a priceless piece of jewelry from the soon-to-be queen? Her wild thoughts were interrupted by the king, who, to her absolute shock, was weeping like a child as he picked up the still-warm body.

"Dear one . . ." He sobbed as he stroked her head with his thumb.

There was much evil in the world, and Catherine knew her country upbringing had prevented her from knowing the half of it. But she could see that someone in her uncle's house meant to do her harm. She could not be naive about that.

"We shall give her a proper burial together," Henry announced, cradling the kitten like a baby.

The sight of his big, meaty arms wrapped around the small thing, the tender display of his heart, and the tears in his eyes overwhelmed Catherine.

"I shall find out who did this and cut out his heart myself!" He sniffed, trying to compose himself.

"Now, you do not mean that," Catherine gently countered with a hand on his shoulder as she sat back on her heels beside him. "Perhaps it was just an accident."

"Murder is never an accident." He sobbed, angry all over again.

She was certain that no one in the world had ever seen this side of England's sovereign. The thought softened her toward him all the more. Though she had been away from Thomas for only two days, she wanted to take everything this gentle giant offered her: riches, power, tenderness, devotion . . . nothing short of the moon and stars. She wanted it badly enough that she stopped wondering what had happened to the priceless missing bracelet.

She parted her lips then to let Henry kiss her, their eyes brimming with tears.

❖

Behind a velvet curtain with gold tassels in Catherine's bedchamber, Mary Lassells listened to every word between the king and that vile Howard girl. It had been easy to poison the cat without anyone suspecting her. How easy it would prove to sell priceless jewels was another story. She fondled the little bracelet, safe inside the deep pocket of her skirt, knowing it was worth a small fortune. She knew it would help the cause of the Reformation. Hopefully, her brother, John, would know how to find a buyer for the vulgar and ostentatious bracelet without getting caught.

For now, she had her hands full trying to single-handedly topple a dynasty.

Chapter Fourteen

July 27, 1540
Oatlands Palace, Surrey

$\mathscr{A}$t the close of July, a plague raged through London. Warned of its severity, Henry sought to keep the royal court in the cool Surrey countryside, far from danger. In the meantime, it was announced that His Majesty would marry Mistress Howard, niece of the great Duke of Norfolk, at Oatlands Palace, nestled among the bucolic safety of trees, lawns, streams and clear skies. It was to be a small, private ceremony, the complete antithesis of the king's most recent marriage ceremony, from which his coffers had still not recovered.

Henry had been told that he would need a papal dispensation to marry Catherine, since she was Catholic and a first cousin to his deceased wife Anne Boleyn. Henry knew that would delay the wedding by months, but he had no intention of waiting that long to marry and bed his sweet, innocent beauty. So, as the ecclesiastical authority of the Church of England, he informed the stunned privy counsel that he would grant a dispensation to himself.

"And I want all three of my children there. When will Edward arrive?"

"He remains at Windsor, Your Majesty," Archbishop Cranmer

explained as they surveyed the chapel site. "They say His Grace is fatigued by the heat, but he is regaining his strength with the aid of cool baths."

"Very well. Send word back that he should rest. I have waited this long." Henry shrugged. "We shall wait one day more for my son."

Though Henry had convinced himself that he could be flexible in his arrangements, an ominous feeling had been gnawing at him since the day he proposed to Catherine. He felt oddly pressed to marry her, not just because he was eager to consecrate their union, but because he sensed that she needed protection from something. He wanted their marriage to be a safe harbor for Catherine.

There was a time when he would have asked for Cromwell's advice. Though he had been ambitious and underhanded at times, Cromwell had always been a trustworthy friend to the king. Until the very end, Henry had always been assured of his honesty. Cromwell had been the only check against the raging ambition of the Howards and Seymours, but by tomorrow, he would be gone and the two warring families would have free rein. Thank God for Cranmer. He might not be the most eloquent or socially adept man—in fact, the archbishop was a frightful bore—but he would help Henry maintain order.

Henry's thoughts returned to his children. "Well, at least Mary and Elizabeth are here."

"They are, Your Majesty." Cranmer nodded as he piously steepled his hands.

"And the medal has been struck?" Henry asked, inquiring about Catherine's secret wedding gift.

"I am told that the first one shall arrive tomorrow," Cranmer confirmed. "I am certain the queen will be honored by your gift."

Henry paused at the altar and turned to the prelate. "So,

Cranmer, since you are here to advise me on the matrimonial road ahead—"

"I should hope to serve Your Majesty in any and all ways you find pleasing."

Henry flicked a wrist at him dismissively as colored light from the stained-glass window fell upon them both. "Yes, yes, then serve me in this way: Tell me if there are any reasons why I should not marry Catherine Howard. This is, after all, my fifth attempt, and I would very much like it to be my last."

He watched Cranmer's face carefully as he made his request. He had learned at an early age that the truth always lay in the eyes, even with the best liars. Wolsey had been a prime example of that, God rest his soul.

"I know of nothing against the lady, sire," Cranmer said firmly. But he had hesitated for a moment too long. Henry caught it and held his breath, waiting for the archbishop's next words.

Cranmer carefully continued. "Surely there is talk of the lady's great beauty . . . and there are, doubtless, men of your court who envy you greatly for having won her."

"Anyone in particular?"

"None that I know of, sire."

"I could not survive being made a cuckold again. It was unbearable the first time," Henry said, referring to Anne Boleyn.

"The lady seems a different sort, sire."

"She does at that." Henry scratched his beard thoughtfully. "So then you have no gossip against her at all?"

"I do not. But if that were to change, then of course my loyalty would be to Your Majesty." Cranmer bowed respectfully.

Henry smiled. "Good. See that it is."

❖

A small reprieve. It was all Catherine thought of as the page stood before her, having made the king's announcement. For one day more she would not be queen. For one day more she would not belong to Henry. While she had resigned herself to the life that now lay ahead of her, and was even excited by aspects of it, for one day more she might hope for the dream of Thomas. She did not even know if he was here with them or if he had stayed behind with the bulk of the court who had not been invited to be present at her wedding.

Catherine had not seen Francis Dereham for days. He remained in London, which she gratefully saw as her grandmother's wedding gift to her.

She could finally relax and enjoy herself now, and she looked forward to the evening's festivities. She knew the guest list for supper included Elizabeth, whom she was excited to see, and Mary, with whom she was less thrilled. But as queen, Catherine knew she must learn to take the bad with the good and handle it all with grace. And she must remember that all three children were motherless. She certainly could sympathize with them, and thus make the most of her relationships with them.

Followed by a growing group of court ladies, Catherine walked slowly along the flagstone path to the place beyond the little terrace where she had been directed to wait for the king. She pressed thoughts of Thomas from her mind. Wherever he was, it was better he was not here. Looking into his eyes tomorrow, seeing him hurt when she married someone else, would have been unbearable.

The great, girthy king hobbled toward her, struggling not to grimace. Catherine thought it absurd that he attempted to mask his illnesses and obesity with sparkling jewels and a swath of priceless Spanish velvet. But Henry was her life now, and she must hide her true thoughts behind a smile.

"You look beautiful," Henry said, a shaft of sunlight picking up the copper tones in his shaggy beard. The white plume of his hat fluttered in the warm summer breeze as he gave her a courtly little nod.

"I am sorry about the postponement, but I want to assure you that the Archbishop of Canterbury is here to officiate the wedding and everything is prepared for tomorrow."

"Your son's presence is important."

"It is everything. I want you to know him, Cat, as you know my daughters. I want you to be a second mother to each of them. I want you to be a part of everything in my life," Henry said earnestly.

"By God's grace, I will," she dutifully replied. Catherine knew she must respect any request regarding the king's only son, for he would be her king one day.

He drew her hand up and gently kissed her knuckles. His pudgy, ring-covered fingers were clammy, as always, and his face was perspiring from his walk down the path. But she did not withdraw in disgust. His courtiers, dressed in elegant silk and velvet, and gold chains, left the king's side and began to speak quietly amongst themselves.

After they were alone, Henry turned to her and said, "I have something for you." Without waiting for a reply, he brought forth from his doublet a single, real pink rose on a long, bare stem. The fragrance of it hit her immediately. "It is a perfect rose. You will see that there are no thorns. This variety grows only at Oatlands, which is why I decided we should be married here." He smiled shyly. "For luck."

Catherine took the flower and brought it to her nose. "It is exquisite," she said, sincerely moved by the gift.

"It is as you are to me: beautiful, flawless, without the power to wound anyone. You are my rose with no thorns, and you shall be unrivaled as the true queen—the one who should have reigned beside me all along. But now I have the rest of our lives to make that up to you, and I mean for the world to know it." Henry ran a hand along the line of her jaw and stopped just above her chin. The motion was surprisingly gentle, she thought, for such a big man. "You will help me be tender. You will make me young again. I want that hope returned to me, that optimism, that trust. I want *you* for all of these reasons and more."

"And so you have me, Hal," she reassured him. Though he had endeared himself to her over time, she knew that she could never actually fall in love with him. At least, not the way he wished. Whether she ever saw him again or not, her love would forever belong to Thomas Culpeper.

❖

Late the following morning, as a bold burst of summer sunlight streamed through the stained-glass windows of the Oatlands chapel and the sound of bells pealed loudly above them, Catherine walked down the aisle toward a broken, bloated and smiling Henry. She tried hard not to tremble. Her head was high with feigned confidence, but seeing his smile gave her real strength.

The only attendees were her uncle, Bishop Gardiner and Lady Rochford, who was there to help her if she fell or vomited, both of which at this moment she felt like doing.

This will be simple and quick, she told herself with determination as she put one foot before the other, heading toward the altar in the small, hollow, ancient-smelling chapel. *You will say your vow and it will be over*. It was odd, she thought, how these last days had changed her. She was more willing to embrace her responsibilities, which was helped by Henry's sweet, gentle devotion and complete adoration. He was smiling at her as he tipped back on his heels, draped in a massive coat of ermine-trimmed velvet. His face was bright and his deep green eyes were twinkling.

The strong aromas of incense and candle wax made her dizzy as she walked toward the candlelit altar, and the jewels on her shoes bit into her heels. She could even feel blood begin to squish between her toes. No one could see the shoes beneath her gown, but Henry insisted that she wear them. They were elegant. Rare. Expensive. It was what a proper queen wore to her wedding. Only the finest of everything. Catherine only hoped that the blood was not an omen of things to come, since it reminded her of her dream.

The actual ceremony seemed brief after the long walk down the aisle. When she was required to speak, she did. She nodded, exchanged a brief smiling glance with the king, and then it was over. Quick and painless. The hard part was what awaited her that night.

After the banquet, the overflowing platters of food, the decanters of wine, the smiles and the mind-numbing round of congratulations, Catherine would have to give herself to Henry. She would do it mechanically, as she had given herself to men at Horsham, and she would pretend that it was pleasurable, though she had only ever truly made love with one man. But she could not think of that any longer. Thomas and their precious days together were far behind her.

⁂

In a back corner of the royal chapel, concealed by shadows and a grand column, Thomas had watched every syllable, word and gesture of the ceremony. He had needed to see it for himself, as he had the proposal. Irrevocably, she was Henry's now. Catherine was Queen of England. And he was a man with a broken heart.

"Culpeper, what are you doing here?"

The censorious voice belonged to Stephen Gardiner, Norfolk's ally. Thomas turned slowly toward him.

"You're not to be here. The king was most specific. Only those he personally invited were allowed to attend. Besides, as a gentleman of the chamber, you are needed upstairs to prepare for the king's wedding night."

Thomas nodded to the bishop and walked away, too heartbroken to make excuses for his presence at the ceremony. He could not fight against any of this.

He was sure that Catherine did not even know he was at Oatlands, since he had decided to keep a low profile. No need to upset her. It was enough for him to be near her, to see her from a distance or to catch the slightest scent of her perfume as she passed along a corridor and he lingered in an alcove. It was the only thing that enabled him to rise from the cold comfort of his small bed every single morning to don the costumes of a gentleman.

Right before he left the chapel, he saw the new royal couple make their way back down the aisle as the invited few gave their congratulations. He waited, watching her until the last possible moment, when, fearing she would see him, he turned and slipped silently out a side door. Today was a day to get very drunk indeed. He would need some liquid courage to prepare the king's private bedchamber for the wedding night. He could not allow himself to think of his one true love lying naked on the bed for the pleasure of another man.

❖

Three hours later, the banquet hall was swollen with a crowd of celebrating courtiers, and the air was stiflingly hot. Amid the musky sweat and the aroma of cooked food, Catherine sat beside Henry, whose porcine face was flushed crimson with wine. He was holding her hand in his sweaty palm beneath the table linen, running his thumb with a sickening, seductive rhythm along her forefinger.

Suddenly, he stood and raised his gold goblet high, and the

courtiers, musicians and servants fell to a hush. Catherine glanced up at her new husband, who tried to focus his drunken gaze on the crowd.

"My guests, my friends, today we celebrate my new queen and yours—Catherine, the epitome of beauty, grace and innocence."

Someone near her muffled an unmistakable snicker. Catherine glanced up at Henry, who appeared not to have heard it. He was still smiling with a silly, besotted expression on his face.

"To that end, a new ceremonial medal has been struck to mark this very important day, bearing a new motto for the best, the brightest and final chapter of my reign. I present it here, before all of you."

He held it up and everyone gasped with appropriate drama, although no one knew what it said yet. Henry continued, "It reads '*Rosa Sine Spina.*' A rose without thorns. That is my wife, and your queen."

Everyone applauded, but the glacial smiles around her only echoed what she already felt. Would she be able to live up to the king's flawless vision of her?

He had set her on an impossibly high pedestal, and from that it would certainly be a long way to fall.

❖

At the precise moment that the new Queen of England lifted a third cup of Malmsey to her lips in celebration of her marriage, Thomas Cromwell, formerly the second-most-powerful man in England, was led shackled and trembling to Tower Green.

A proud man, he tried, at first, not to weep. Such a display would not befit the Lord Great Chamberlain, even as he strode toward his death. A crowd had worked its way past the walls, anxious for a good show. It was scandalous and "right fun," they gossiped, that the king should wed his fifth wife on the very day that his once most trusted aide and friend was to be beheaded.

When Cromwell saw the block before him and the sickening smiles of the blood-hungry citizens, terror took the place of dignity and he lost his resolve. "Oh, God, I cry for mercy! I have been a true servant!" he wailed. "Most gracious king, I am calling! Have mercy on my soul, which has never betrayed you or the true religion!"

The stone-faced guardsman, who would have bowed to him at one time, stiffened and spoke as he turned away. "His Majesty cannot hear ye. And if he could, your pleas'd mean nothin' to 'im. I'm to tell ye our king tossed your letters into the fire and laughed as he did. Now lay down your head there, just so, on the block. 'Twill be faster for you that way. Right's right. Ye don't go betrayin' a king, my man. Not this king, anyway," he added with a hollow laugh as the hooded executioner advanced.

❖

As Cromwell laid his head on the block, Catherine stood still as a stone. Anne Basset and Margaret washed her thoroughly with scented cloths. She must be pleasant for His Majesty.

The king despises uncleanliness in his women, one of the ladies in the room whispered with a dark chuckle. *If she shows up unclean, it could even prove fatal*, she added.

But Catherine's heart was beating so loudly that she could not identify the voice. That mattered little anyway. She knew she had no real friends here other than Jane. She glanced over at Mary Lassells, lurking, as always, in the corner of the room as if to underscore that fact.

Catherine allowed Anne Basset to lift her arms, one at a time, and run a warm, wet cloth along each of them, from her shoulder, past the elbow and slowly to her fingertips. Silently, Catherine's elder sister Margaret followed the same path along her body with the king's favorite scented oil. Catherine tried to slow her heart, but each moment was more difficult than the last. She was sorry that she knew what lay ahead. Catherine closed her eyes, refusing to think of Thomas and trying not to imagine Henry hulking and sweating over her.

Jane came to her then with a delicate linen-and-lace shift and slipped it over her head. The bell sleeves whispered down as she lowered her arms. Catherine felt the cool, new, too-tight band on her finger, her blood pulsing around the ring as if it were cutting off her circulation. Lady Lisle advanced and began to brush her long hair over her shoulders and arrange the curls around her face.

"It is time, Your Grace," Jane announced.

Catherine silently followed her ladies to the king's rooms, where she found silver moonlight filtering in through the windows, casting shadows across the floor. There were long, lit tapers, their flames shimmering above gold sconces along the walls, but there was no fire. It was too warm for that.

Catherine moved toward the bed as the door clicked to a close behind her. He had not arrived yet, so she had some time to collect herself. Though the room was full of incense, romantic candlelight and soft shadows, it felt like a prison cell, this evening the beginning of her sentence. From now on, everything would be determined for her.

Just as Thomas Cromwell had met his end this day, Catherine would as well, though in some ways her fate was worse than death.

But before she could dwell on her thoughts, the door opened again, admitting a long shaft of light into the bedchamber. She could not breathe. She could feel nothing but the slamming of her heart against her rib cage. Catherine heard a flurry of activity in the corridor beyond. Voices. Muffled laughter. The door closed, and Henry stood in the doorway, lingering for a moment, looking strangely unsure of himself as he gazed at her. The candles flickered. There was more male laughter beyond the closed door. The sound made her feel tawdry, for she knew how public a king's wedding night was. She knew she was lucky the act between them would not be witnessed, as it was in some courts in Europe. She tried very hard not to think about her first time with Thomas.

"Lie down," Henry directed her.

The guttural tone of his voice surprised her. There was something primal and powerful about it. She did as he instructed, slipping quickly beneath the heavy damask bedcovers.

He moved across the sweetly scented bedchamber, extinguishing all of the candles until the only light in the room came from the moon. He stood beside the bed, obscured by the half-drawn tapestry bed curtain.

"Close your eyes," he instructed her in the same low, deep tone. This time she caught a note of trepidation.

He does not want me to see him naked, she thought, remembering Thomas's long, lean torso when she saw him unclothed for the first time. Even the memory took her breath away.

Suddenly she was struck by a thought. Perhaps she should think of Thomas. It could make her more receptive to the distasteful duty that lay ahead.

Catherine heard Henry's dressing gown slip across his skin and pool onto the floor before he sank heavily onto the edge of the bed beside her. The entire bed shifted under his weight. He smelled of freshly applied musk, which she did not find wholly unpleasant, but his breath was still sour as he moved closer toward her. A heartbeat later, his fingers were in her hair and his bare leg was warm against hers. *God, please do not let it be his leg with the festering sore*, she thought frantically. He would surely sense it if she recoiled in disgust, even in the slightest.

"This is going to hurt, I'm afraid. Forgive me for that," he whispered, his lips very close to her ear, just before he pressed a kiss onto her cheek, then another onto her earlobe.

She felt his desire for her against her leg just before he settled himself over her with a huff of effort. It was the heavy, animalistic sounds he made, more than anything else, that made it difficult to keep picturing Thomas. *Breathe*, she told herself. *Just breathe and it will soon be over.*

His manhood was big enough that her small body resisted it instinctively at first, which she knew was a blessing in maintaining the ruse of her virginity. Catherine put the back of her hand to her mouth, then made a little gasp as he worked himself over her with great effort and perspiration. She closed her eyes and did not touch him or wrap her arms around his broad, square back. She could not hold on to an inkling of the Thomas fantasy if she did.

Mercifully, he groaned one last time and it was finally over. Her chest and belly were covered with his perfumed sweat as he rolled off of her with another grunt of effort. Catherine drew in a breath, willing the vomit in her throat back down. Henry took her hand and held it to his lips as he lay beside her. His chest was heaving as if he had just run a race.

"Are you all right?" he asked, seeming unaware or unconcerned with the absence of blood, so great was his trust in her. His genuinely gentle tone eased her sickness. "I hope it was not too painful this first time."

"I am fine," she managed to whisper in reply as he hoisted himself onto an elbow and pushed the hair back from her face.

"I'm glad. And it will become more pleasant each time; I promise you that. I have many things to show you, many ways for us to pleasure each other, which I will teach you in time."

He seemed to forget his previous reserve, allowing her to see his fleshy, pale breasts beneath patchy coils of copper chest hair now that they had been intimate.

"Does the medal as well please you?" he asked, his face bright with a hopeful smile.

"It is glorious, sire, a great honor to my entire family," Catherine replied truthfully, though she still worried about living up to the inscription.

"Ah, it is Hal, sweetheart, remember?" He took her hand and pressed it to his moist lips. A wave of nausea passed over her again, but she pushed it back with a smile. "It is but the beginning, Cat. There is so much I want to show you, to share with you, besides this, of course, which I must warn you will be every night. I know I will never be able to get enough of you." His eyes twinkled in the luminescent moonlight. "And you shall need a motto of your own."

"A motto?"

"Every queen must have a phrase that marks them, one by which they live."

Catherine thought of the four queens before her, each of whom surely had a motto, and three of whom were dead. Clearly, she would need to choose a motto that not only fulfilled the tradition of emphasizing the values and traditions one held dear, but in her case, one that would keep her alive.

"I shall send Wriothesley to aid you in your search. He is quite poetic. But in the end, the choice must be yours alone or it will mean little."

"As you selected yours about me?" Catherine asked.

"Yes, I did it entirely on my own. I would not have had it any other way."

"I shall speak with him tomorrow then. I want to be a good wife and a good queen," she said sweetly.

"You shall be spectacular at both," he replied, running a thumb along her chin and down the column of her throat. "Have you any idea what you do to me? How my heart, and the rest of me, burns for you already, and it is but our first night?"

Before she could answer, Henry took her hand and pushed it down beneath the bedcover, where she could feel him growing hard again. "I warn you, there'll not be much sleep for either of us to-night," he playfully declared, forcing her to hold him.

She watched his eyes roll to a close.

"God above. How can you be an innocent when you make my blood boil as if you had done this a thousand times before?" he asked with a guttural growl.

❖

Near dawn, Henry sent for food. He was ravenous, as always, and so, surprisingly, was Catherine. Sitting cross-legged atop the bedcovers in her delicate lacy shift, which she had once again donned, she ate gingerbread and sweet figs with her fingers as Henry gazed at her, his bare arms crossed behind his head as he reclined against the headboard.

"How could God have made such a lovely creature for me after the long, complicated life I have lived? I kept asking myself that all night last night, even while you slept."

"I slept?" She was surprised.

"Only for a little while. But it's all right. It is a pleasure watching you sleep." His expression was earnest, surprisingly so. His thumb grazed her cheek and moved once again down to her throat. "You looked like such a child, so innocent. It has been an eternity since I have been with a beautiful woman."

"Queen Jane was very pretty," she risked saying. She looked at the portrait on the wall beside them, which was haunting, even in the darkness. Jane Seymour gazed down upon them as if in judgment. Catherine saw his jaw tighten.

"Her portrait does not do her justice. Holbein is usually a splendid painter, but he does not capture Jane's goodness here. . . ." He trailed off wistfully. "Well, perhaps I am not being objective. She gave me a son, so she is very dear to me. Her memory shall live in a corner of my heart forever."

She could not quite believe there were tears in his eyes as he spoke the words. He straightened to be rid of them, as if he sensed they were not manly.

"I am sorry you lost Jane. It must have been hard for you to lose a wife and for Edward to lose his mother."

Henry looked at her gratefully. "But he has you now. All three of my children do."

"I think Mary would rather have anyone but me," Catherine said softly.

"Give her time, Cat. I know that she wants to care for you," he reassured her.

"She has quite an odd way of showing it."

"We Tudors all do." He smiled at her. "She has been through a great deal, most of which is my fault."

Catherine leaned closer to Henry, her amber hair falling onto his pale, bare chest. She was emboldened by their candid conversation. "May I ask you something?"

"Anything," he replied.

"Did you ever love Mary's mother?"

Henry drew in an audible, raspy breath. He rolled onto his back and gazed up at the canopy for a long time before he answered. "Passionately, once. But that was another lifetime."

He ran a hand along the line of her jaw. "Let's put this talk aside.

You are the only one in my life now," Henry declared. "You will be different from all the others."

"I believe you," Catherine said in response.

And just then, she did believe everything Henry told her.

❖

Three days later, in the dirty, cobbled, dung-covered streets of West Smithfield, just outside of London, the bloody executions began. Henry kept Catherine tucked safely away in the verdant surroundings of Oatlands, blissfully unaware of the resurgence of the battle over religion. He wanted to maintain his bride's blithe innocence for as long as he could.

"Is it done?" Henry asked Norfolk in a strangely hollow voice one afternoon while Catherine and her ladies played shuttlecock. He looked down at her from the wide window in his study, watching her giggle as she played and danced around.

"They are all dead. Reverend Gerard, Reverend Jerome, Dr. Powell, Dr. Abel, Dr. Barnes." Norfolk reported their names blandly.

"Featherstone, as well?" the king asked.

"Hanged, drawn and quartered, as ordered, Your Majesty."

Henry took a deep breath and slowly exhaled, the only noise in the otherwise silent privy chamber. "A good many lives were lost for speaking out."

"The country must be taught a lesson, sire," Norfolk said firmly. "We cannot have the clergy denying your supremacy. That sort of rebellion could spread like wildfire, and then how would you lead?"

"And Your Majesty must remember," Stephen Gardiner chimed in, "some of them insisted that you were still married to the princess of Aragon, making your son—"

"I know what it means, Gardiner!" the king snarled.

Catherine was twirling and skipping in the courtyard by the

fountain below, while her ladies laughed in encouragement. A group of young courtiers, led by Cromwell's son, Gregory, advanced to watch the women play. The young and handsome Cromwell was looking far too familiarly at the queen. No one on this earth dared do that. Henry leaned heavily against the window frame, suddenly angry at everything and everyone. Norfolk watched him clench and unclench the jeweled fingers of his hand into a tight ball.

"I have been generous to Cromwell's son, have I not? I allowed him to remain at my court, despite the fact that his father was a vile traitor."

"Your Majesty has shown incredible grace and forbearance under the circumstances," Norfolk said, flattering while he waited to see what the king was about.

Norfolk stood beside Gardiner, cautious of his every word. He had heard this particular tone in the king's voice only twice in their long association: the night Henry sanctioned the execution of his own wife, and the day he signed the death warrant against one of his dearest friends, Thomas Cromwell.

"I have, haven't I?" Henry responded, still looking down at the courtyard below. His sights were locked on Cromwell's son, as though he were a stag to be hunted. Gardiner and Norfolk exchanged the slightest glance. "Have someone follow the boy, but make certain he is not discovered. I shall find it of enormous interest if the Cromwell lad advances upon my wife. Catherine is too young, too innocent to know how to deal with the charms of a handsome and well-schooled young man. Fortunately for her, her powerful husband most certainly does."

Norfolk was pleased to hear that the king was willing to deal with any threat to his marriage, real or perceived. He took a step closer. "There is another young man who should be made an example of. The rest of England will surely take notice, and it will quiet the malcontents."

"The bishop of London says the boy speaks out regularly against the sacraments to anyone who will listen," Gardiner added.

Both men saw Henry stiffen. "If that is the case, have the bishop condemn him to burning."

The king's pronouncement was so sudden and cold that even Norfolk shivered.

"He is fourteen, sire. Do you not wish even to know his name?"

"His name matters not. But tell the bishop to behead him first then," Henry amended without turning around. "After all, I am not without mercy. Now, one of you take care of the Cromwell lad as well. The other, see the queen brought to me at once. I've suddenly a mind to see my wife privately," he said, needing the reassurance that only Catherine could give him.

Chapter Fifteen

August 8, 1540
Hampton Court, Richmond

*H*enry and Catherine rode together by barge down the river through the winding green hills, returning to the haven of Hampton Court following their wedding trip to Oatlands Palace.

Catherine had surprisingly enjoyed the eight days of spoiling and pampering by her husband, and all of the activity surrounding their marriage, so much so that both had forgotten poor little Putette and who might have killed her. Every bad moment of the past seemed very far behind them.

Though he did not appear to be a sensual lover, Henry was ardent and eager to please. Her distaste at seeing his bare, pink, waxy and rotund body was easily masked with a dozen different games and by the forgiving glow of candlelight. It was also diverted by the gifts he showered upon her each time she succumbed. In those first days, there were so many dresses, furs and jewels that her dressing room and closet literally sparkled with pearl-dotted silks, satins and velvet, all sewn with rubies and diamonds as well.

The only thing she still lacked was true friends.

In that regard, she missed Thomas and even fun-loving Gregory since her royal marriage. Now her company consisted mainly of

Jane, her elder sister Margaret, and Lady Isabel Baynton, the wife of the new chamberlain. She also had to keep her guard up in the silent yet constant presence of Mary Lassells and her new secretary, Francis Dereham, both of whom she did not trust in the least.

Only after Henry fell asleep late each night was she able to be alone with her thoughts. Henry's glorious palaces had swiftly come to feel like prisons, and her well-dressed, noble attendants were now like her jailers. A shrewd look from Francis or an artful smile from Mary only reinforced her feelings.

It was in those moments that her longing for Thomas was at its greatest. She hoped he would walk gracefully into the king's privy chamber, just as wonderfully nonchalant as when they first had met. Or that he would be at the king's side when she joined His Majesty for dinner.

But that day never came.

He was still at court, Jane told her. She had seen him herself. "He is busy with his duties," she would say. But Catherine knew it was just an excuse.

On their second day back at Hampton Court, as her ladies prepared Catherine for the banquet where Henry would officially introduce her as queen, Catherine gazed blankly across the vast, paneled room. She felt apart from the activity as they dressed her in an elegant French-cut burgundy gown, with a stylish matching pearl-dotted hood revealing her long flowing hair as it fell to her shoulders.

She'd had a dream last night that Thomas had come to her and they had told Henry everything. In a blind rage of jealousy, Henry had chased her through the corridors, his face wild with fury. He had been wielding the same jewel-handled dagger from her last dream.

She did not even notice when Jane came dancing into the room, her face lit with a smile. Her friend leaned close to whisper to her, "I have brought you someone to cheer you up. You have not seemed yourself these past days."

Catherine's heart raced and blood flooded her face. Could it possibly be? It had been twelve days since her last desperate meeting with Thomas in the alcove, twelve days since she had been spirited away to Lambeth and then on to Oatlands to become queen. Twelve days since she had given up all hope.

Until now.

Jane took her by the hand and led her away from the others. Catherine's own hand trembled in anticipation.

They passed through one chamber, then another, the hems of their wide gowns sweeping against the paneled walls. Catherine felt as if her heart were going to burst right through her very tight stomacher and the elegant burgundy silk gown over it. But when Jane opened the door to the chamber where her mystery guest waited, it was not Thomas's face she saw.

First Mary Lassells, then Francis Dereham. Now, before her stood her two Horsham cohorts in everything bad and wrong she had ever done. Was this some sort of bad jest orchestrated by Wil Somers for the king's pleasure—or her torment?

"Your Grace," Katherine Tilney was the first to say with a false, unnatural smile as she curtsied.

"Your Grace," Joan Acworth repeated with a clumsy curtsy.

How on earth had her grandmother, powerful doyenne of the ambitious Howards, and her uncle allowed Mary, Francis and these two empty-headed country girls to come to court? Catherine stared at Jane with a pale, panicked expression. She seemed genuinely surprised that the queen was not smiling.

"You do remember them, don't you?" Jane asked. "They lived at Horsham with you."

"I remember them well," Catherine replied, her tongue feeling as dry as desert sand. "It seems like only yesterday."

"I thought it might cheer you to have familiar faces among your servants."

"This was your idea?" Catherine gasped in astonishment.

"Not entirely. But they had already written to the Dowager Duchess of Norfolk, and I merely encouraged her to bring them," Jane said, sensing that she had made the wrong decision.

"Do I not already have Mistress Lassells and Master Dereham if I feel overcome with nostalgia?" she snapped.

Jane looked at the two pretty girls, with their seemingly angelic expressions.

"What, precisely, are they to do for me?" Catherine asked angrily.

"Attend their queen, of course. Like the rest of us."

Catherine caught a glimpse of Mary Lassells lurking, as she often did, near a tapestry curtain and scowling at the new arrivals. Perhaps rivalry between them would keep this new threat at bay. Catherine knew there was little she could say to object anyway. She did not want to arouse the king's suspicions by protesting against the presence of her "friends." She felt surrounded on all sides. *I am a prisoner of my past and my future . . . I have no choice.*

"You shall see them settled?" she finally asked Jane, feigning a smile with every ounce of determination she had.

"Of course." Jane smiled in return. "It is done, Your Grace."

❖

"You are to attend the banquet tonight and sit near His Majesty at the table. It is as simple as that," portly, silver-haired Charles Brandon announced to Thomas. His tone, as always, had an air of impatient frustration.

"I was planning on going to London tonight for a bit of amusement," Thomas protested.

"And deny the king in the process? That would be most unwise."

Thomas had just returned from a brisk ride in the country in an attempt to get as far from Catherine as he could, which he did each morning after performing his required duties for the king. By calling in favors, he had managed to find hours of service early in the morning, when Henry was returning from bedding the love of Thomas's life—not in the evenings as His Majesty went to her. Both posts were a nightmare to a man desperately in love, but this one made him feel just slightly less like choking the life out of His Majesty in angry jealousy. Now he would be forced to sit and watch the king as he fondled Catherine with his greasy hands at the table. At least he would be with Gregory. The two of them could drink great volumes of wine and commiserate over their respective losses.

"Am I at least to be seated near Cromwell's son? I suspect he shall need the good cheer tonight as much as do I."

Brandon tipped his head and peered at him curiously with his dark eyes. "You do not know?"

"Know what?" Thomas asked.

"Young Cromwell has left court. He was not invited by the king to Hampton Court."

Thomas was stunned. It was widely believed that the king meant to demonstrate his own grace and forgiveness by keeping the boy at court, especially since he had played no part in the Cromwell scandal.

"That makes no sense," Thomas muttered.

"It does if he desires something that belongs to the king."

Thomas felt a chill move down the length of his spine and meet the revulsion that moved through him at the same speed.

"Gregory Cromwell and the queen?" Thomas gasped. "Is . . . Was there something between them?"

"It is unclear. I, and many others, heard rumors of their possible misdeeds before the marriage, but I suspect the king does not know of such stories, or else Gregory's punishment would have been far graver. No, I believe he merely sensed something . . . *inappropriate* in Gregory's manner toward the queen, and that was enough for him. He can be a vicious man when he feels threatened, Tom."

Thomas thought of Cromwell and the group of recently executed clerics who had fallen victim to the very viciousness Brandon described.

"But were she and Gregory . . . were they . . . ?" He could not force himself to say the word, but he had to know if the rumors were true.

Brandon, like an old uncle, wrapped his arm around Culpeper's shoulder. "Well, no one knows for certain. But there was a plentiful bit of corridor gossip about the queen when she first arrived, stories that she was less of a maiden and more of a strumpet, stories that obviously never made it to the king's ears. Foolish as they seem now, there were even stories involving you."

Thomas closed his eyes tightly to push away the image of Catherine with Gregory Cromwell.

"She is a beautiful girl, though," Brandon amended as he studied Thomas. "Almost makes me wish I had been a younger man when she first arrived. It seems as if I, too, might have had a chance with her, along with everyone else."

Thomas was tense enough to snap the neck of the venerable duke right then and there. It was not that he had believed her an innocent when they met. He had known she was not, and in the beginning, that had made it all the more interesting.

Yes, in the beginning. Before he had loved her.

Thomas forced himself to calm down and walk with Brandon down a long, window-lined corridor, where they were joined by Edward Seymour and Thomas Wriothesley, on their way to the banquet.

It would be a sumptuous feast, Edward Seymour said, and it would have to suffice, since the king had spent such an exorbitant amount of money on his last queen's coronation. There was not enough left now to have one for Catherine.

As they walked, Thomas found himself uncertain of how he would survive the evening, let alone the coming days. Seeing Catherine, watching her with him . . . knowing what newly married couples did privately . . . He squeezed his eyes shut and stubbornly chased away the images of them together. Catherine belonged to the king now. Thomas accepted that. Understood it. But he did not have to torment himself by watching every single second between them if he could help it. That would only lead to madness.

The banquet hall was suitably grand, as he had expected it to be, the walls covered in gold arras. There were so many torches and candles burning against the bright fabric that it looked ablaze. Fortunately it was crowded already, Thomas thought, so he could slip effortlessly into the throng unseen. Brandon, Seymour and Wriothesley were already speaking with others, and all three had goblets of wine in hand. Thomas would need to catch up, he thought irritably, taking two goblets at once from a servant's silver tray.

On the other hand, there was not enough wine in the world to face a night like the one ahead.

He had a reprieve of only a few moments before he saw her. But it was enough time for the palliative qualities of the wine to take full effect. He eyed her critically as she stood beside the king in an elegant blue velvet gown. There were more powerful people assembled in the room than he had ever seen, and each noble, ambassador and dignitary greeted the new queen, bowing deeply and reverently to her, his former lover. *Stop!* he told himself, consuming the next goblet of wine in a single swallow. *Never*, argued a dark voice inside of his head, *because you will never be able to stop loving her.*

He looked away, disgusted with her. With Henry. The king was pawing Catherine openly and kissing her cheek before everyone, not caring a whit about the display. Most of all, Thomas was disgusted with himself for having fallen so painfully in love with a Howard. How had he ever let that happen? Like everyone else, he had known why she had been brought to court. She was not allowed feelings and desires of her own. She was a pawn.

The crowd of well-wishers swelled, and Thomas was thrust ever closer to the king and his new queen. Henry kissed Catherine's cheek yet again and gazed at her in adoration.

It was a moment more before she even noticed Thomas.

He saw her smile fall. Their eyes met for only an instant, and her face paled. It was as if he heard her pain, and she his. There was a silent language between them beneath the music and laughter. Henry was still touching her. He seemed unable to pull himself away. Thomas's head was spinning from the wine. His heart had shattered already.

"Ah, there you are, Tom! Come greet your new queen."

Henry's voice was light and full of cheer. Thomas struggled to conjure a believable smile.

"Your Grace." He bowed deeply before Catherine, yet he did not bother to hide the little spark of contempt behind his gaze. He knew none of this was her fault, but she had that much coming. She had changed so much already, from the tip of her impossibly fashionable new hood, bejeweled in diamonds and rubies, to the sweep of her gown, more daringly ornate than the gowns of any of the last three queens. Her appearance was beyond ostentatious . . . and nothing at all like the Catherine Howard he knew.

"Master Culpeper." She acknowledged him with a polite nod but she did not smile. It was as if they had met in only a cursory way, and even then a long time ago. It chilled him to see her like this, so different from the wanton, smiling girl who had come to his bedchamber and made him love her. He struggled for something clever to say.

"You make a very convincing queen."

That most certainly was not it. He had to will himself not to bite out his own tongue. Fortunately, the king seemed not to have heard him as Charles Brandon approached from the other side and muttered something in the king's ear behind a raised hand.

Catherine flushed and lowered her eyes.

"There is much effort behind my appearance," she softly countered, gambling on the fact that Henry was not listening.

He struggled against the sensation of pity. Henry kissed her on the cheek again, and in response, Thomas forced himself to turn away. The evening had only begun, but he knew he was not nearly drunk enough to face what would likely happen next: more public displays and an eventual abandonment of the evening for the bedchamber.

As he turned around, he was shocked to see the face of a girl he had not seen for months.

Katherine Basset had changed a great deal. She had almost matured into the beauty her elder sister, Anne, was. He marveled at how Lady Lisle had managed to raise two such beautiful daughters, but he stopped when he realized that she was just like the Dowager Duchess of Norfolk or the Seymour matrons, who raised the women in their family as pawns.

"Mistress Basset," he said, acknowledging her with his most

charming smile. "This is, indeed, a surprise. I had heard you had not been admitted to a place here."

"Things change swiftly at court, do they not, Master Culpeper?" She laughed a soft, tinkling laugh. "For now, I am only a guest. After that, we shall see."

❖

The beginning of the evening was a whirlwind of food, wine and congratulations. After Henry and Catherine had settled into their seats on the raised dais, they were entertained by mummers, acrobats, madrigals from Venice, which Henry fancied, and songs written to celebrate Catherine as the new queen.

The king and queen sat in front of a rich gold cloth with the letters H and C boldly entwined in gold thread. At her throat, Catherine wore yet another new gift from Henry, this one given on the eve of her formal presentation as queen.

The ruby pendant was unbelievably elegant, as were the king's previous gifts. Yet none of it meant anything as she watched Thomas speak with one of the prettiest girls Catherine had ever seen. She looked just like her older sister, only her hair was paler, her cheeks slightly rounder and rosier. The turn of her nose was undeniably a Basset family trait. Clearly, the Howards and Seymours were not the only two dynasties intent on using their beautiful daughters to their advantage. The fact that Lady Lisle's second husband was currently in the Tower for political failures in Calais had not so far blocked her daughters' paths to success.

Catherine gave in to the swell of jealousy as she watched Thomas dance with Katherine Basset. She had no right to be angry, but that mattered little to her heart.

They were laughing, and she could see Thomas lean in to whisper to her during the turns. She should be happy for him. But love was too irrational for that. Did he not know that this was not the life she would have chosen if there had been any other way?

Would you really have chosen another way if you could?

It was that same obstinate voice that haunted her mind and dreams. She angrily pushed it aside as she watched Thomas pair a second time with Katherine Basset in a slower, sultrier court dance. She felt her anger rise along with her heart rate. Katherine was touching him, gazing into his eyes. . . .

Eyes that had shown her his soul.

"Are you all right, sweetheart? Do you need a breath of air again?" It was Henry's rheumy voice, Henry's clammy hand grasping hers beneath the table cover, Henry's foot against hers. "I know these evenings can be overwhelming."

"No, I am fine. It's all very lovely." Catherine smiled.

"I had hoped you would think so. Norfolk assured me you were up to it, but sometimes the old buzzard is far more interested in how things make him appear than how they make others feel."

Catherine bit back a smile. "You describe my uncle perfectly."

"Time brings a certain understanding."

"And does my uncle of Norfolk understand you?"

"Parts of me quite well, I should think."

"And the other parts?"

"Safely locked away for only a certain few to see. My precious sister Mary was one of them. She could always see right to the core of me, no matter what I tried to hide."

He glanced at Charles Brandon, her widower, older, more stout and graying now, yet still an incorrigible rake, and Catherine followed his gaze. "Not unlike Tom. Those two are cut from the same cloth. Just look at Culpeper over there with Lady Lisle's daughter. He has had the elder and the mother before her. They are like bees to honey with him. Personally, I fail to see the attraction, unless you favor devastating good looks, great wit and sensuality," he quipped.

Catherine bit her lower lip until she nearly broke the skin.

"A pity that even with all of his admirable qualities, he still cannot compete with my husband," she said smoothly. She then gave him a seductive look so loaded with suggestion that Henry shifted his wide body in his chair and squeezed her hand even more tightly.

"If not for the fact that this evening is entirely for you, I would scoop you into my arms this very moment and haul you off to bed."

Catherine fought a sudden wave of nausea as he whispered the words into her ear and pressed his wet lips to her neck in full view of the court.

She had caught sight of Thomas watching her, which had momentarily shaken her belief that she could ignore Henry's physical traits and focus on his skills as a lover. To her horror, Thomas nodded to her alone, smiled ever so slightly and wrapped his arm over Katherine Basset's smooth, beautiful shoulders as he led her out of the banquet hall. It was clear to Catherine what they were going to do.

Yet the pain of betrayal must be endured. Just like one's duty, she silently told herself.

❖

Mary Lassells stood in the doorway of Catherine's little paneled writing closet, watching Francis Dereham. On the carved French writing table were an ivory pen, a crystal pot of ink, a dish of sand and a miniature of the king poised on an easel. It was likely painted well before the queen's birth, Mary thought ruefully as she gazed at the image of a tall, slim and smiling Henry. If he knew the real woman he had married, would he smile so broadly now? Or would she end up like Anne Boleyn? Now, there was a delicious thought! Mary would need to say a prayer later to redress her impure desire.

She walked into the room as Francis sorted through letters of congratulations and separated them by importance into two piles.

"I suppose I should say I am surprised to see you here, but I actually am not," Mary said accusatorily.

"I could easily say the same," Francis Dereham replied, nonplussed by her critical tone. He set a collection of letters down and leaned back in the queen's elegant, embroidered chair. "So, what do you desire exactly?"

"I do not want us to get in each other's way. That's all," Mary replied casually.

"Simple enough, though I doubt our goals are the same."

She arched a brow. "You believe *I* have an ulterior motive for being here?"

Francis chuckled. "Do you not? I knew well enough of your brother's Reformist convictions when we were at Horsham. I think you are waiting for her to slip up."

"What about you? You do not actually believe you are going to win her back, do you?"

"She is my wife," Francis replied simply.

"A silly country trothplight is not a marriage," she said with a hint of scorn in her voice.

"Still, a commitment is a commitment."

"If that meant anything, she would be with Thomas Culpeper."

"That arrogant bastard?" Francis asked in genuine surprise.

"The very same." She smiled victoriously, happy that she had told him something he did not already know. "Gossip about them was all over court when I arrived, but apparently the king did not hear the whispers of his servants," she said bitterly. "But do you actually believe you can challenge the king and get her back in your bed?"

"I would assume that is just what your man Culpeper is doing. Why not me? I knew her first, after all. If I do not win her, I am certain there will be just compensation."

"More than you have already received in your appointment here?"

"Will you be settling for your position?" He smirked.

"You know me well, Francis. Let us call ourselves unlikely partners, shall we? We each want something different from the queen, so neither of us will be a threat to the other."

"Well, if you send the golden goose to the Tower, that would prevent me from marrying her."

"She is a papist!" Mary retorted in frustration.

"We cannot choose whom we love, though, can we? I seem to recall your interest in a certain music teacher. Besides, if you are not too overzealous in your plan, we can both achieve our desire. You will be rewarded for ridding our king of another woman who has betrayed him, and I shall gain a bride with a stipend as large as the last queen's, on which we can both live smartly," Francis fantasized.

"Even you are not crazy enough to entertain such a fantasy. Only someone who was quite deluded would think such things possible," Mary growled. "You have lost your sense over a pretty face and a willing smile."

Dereham quirked a smile of his own. "Oh, and I thought your entire motivation was religious. Now you sound jealous that no one admires you so much as to fantasize on your behalf."

"I always despised you," Mary lied, refusing to recall the moments when she had cared for him after Manox.

"I did not find you a particular temptation either."

Mary decided to change the subject. "Katherine Tilney and Joan Acworth are here as well, you know. They could ruin everything."

Francis rubbed his chin thoughtfully. "Then we will need to be careful. As I said before, let us be partners of a sort."

She scowled as if she had tasted something foul. "That really is a vile thought."

"Not any more spectacular for me," he agreed.

"If we both gain what we came here for, it will be worth it, though."

"Remind yourself of that," Francis said dryly. "And try not to get either of us killed in the bargain, would you?"

❖

They lay together in the massive carved bed, the heavy curtains drawn around them. Henry seemed content just to lie still, propped on an elbow, watching her.

"Are you not bored yet by the view?" she asked, as the candle burned low in a silver sconce on the table beside them.

"Would that such a thing were possible."

"I think you are biased." Catherine smiled.

"No, just in love." He ran his hand along the side of her face, a hand that, for once, was not moist and sweaty. There was a long silence before he said, "I will be even more in love when you can say it in return."

Henry looked at her squarely with an unblinking gaze. She knew what he wanted, but she had given him so much already: her body, her fidelity and her compassion. She simply could not surrender her heart to him as well.

And yet, what was one small lie?

More of a distortion, really, she thought. She cared for him, and if uttering three simple words would make him content, why would she deny her husband that illusion?

As she looked at him, her sense of guilt began to grow.

"I've finally chosen my motto," Catherine said, changing the subject when she could not summon the words.

"Oh?" Henry said, a look of interest in his eyes.

"Do you want to hear it?"

"Of course I do, if you chose it yourself."

"You told me I must, and I always honor my king," she parried in a light tone.

"I would rather have you honor your husband."

"I shall always do that, of course."

"A charming reply." He smiled, pressing his mouth fully onto hers.

"My motto is 'No other will but His,'" she announced in a soft voice, pulling back to see his face as she told him.

Henry was silent, and for a moment she was afraid he did not approve. She had chosen it herself, but she had asked Charles Brandon's and her uncle's opinions. Though she and Henry were closer than ever, she still could not afford to make a misstep with him.

Suddenly, tears brightened Henry's aging green eyes, and he pulled her on top of his muslin-covered chest, comfortable and relaxed beneath the bedcovers.

"You are an unparalleled blessing to me, Cat. I see now that I was only a foolish boy playing at love before. I am almost ashamed at how I let them wound me and rule my heart, but I had no idea that you were out there, waiting."

He closed his eyes, and Catherine wondered if he was referring to a specific person, but she did not press him. Henry's heart was a complex thing.

"I did not know you were there either," she said sincerely.

He chuckled, breaking the emotional tension. "Truly? I thought all Howard and Seymour girls were raised to prepare for the possibility."

"Prepare for the attention of the king, perhaps, but never of Henry, the man."

She could see that her words struck him. He was gazing at her as if he were trying to see straight into her heart.

"So, I am a surprise?" he asked with a slight smile.

"An enigma, as well."

"Ah, but that is where you are wrong, my love. I have only ever been one man with you."

She considered his words. "It is how you are with the rest of the world that creates the mystery."

"So long as I am always the same in your arms, why should you concern yourself with anything else?"

"Your point is well-taken," she replied, unable to suppress the soft giggle that passed across her lips, or the words that flew suddenly from her mouth.

"I love you, Hal," Catherine said.

❖

Thomas walked heavy-footed into the king's privy dressing chamber the next morning. Mercifully, all signs of Catherine were gone. The grand bed in the room beyond was covered neatly with a tapestry quilt. He could not deal with Catherine and Henry this morning with his head throbbing from too much wine and far too little sleep.

As he suspected, the wine had not helped, and neither had the girl.

Noble or not, wealthy or not, she simply was not Catherine.

"Oh, Tom, there you are," Henry called out. He caught Thomas's reflection in the long mirror as dressers clothed him for matins. "My, you look a bit worse for wear this fine morning."

"My apologies." Thomas bowed.

"Hazard of our strong will toward passion, I suppose." Henry laughed. "It is a blessing that I no longer need to hunt like a wolf in the forest for the sweet lamb, for she is already mine. You should take a hint from me and find a lamb of your own."

It was not only the words, but the cavalier laughter with which they were delivered that caused Thomas's jaw to close like a vise. He suppressed the retort rising at the back of his throat: *I found a lamb . . . and you took her.*

Instead, Thomas chose to bow again. He had been at court long enough to know how to play the game.

Even against the master, who held all of the cards.

Henry walked in an irritating strut away from the mirror in a gray velvet doublet and matching hat, which was jauntily tipped to an angle in the French style. A white plume bobbed on top. The ensemble was ornate enough to nearly hide the massive bulk of his body. He draped an arm over Thomas's shoulder in the brotherly way he had done a dozen times before.

"So tell me about her, whoever she was," Henry bade. "Was she grand?"

"She was of no consequence," he answered evasively.

Henry caught his gaze. "I will not tell her mother you said that. She is a vindictive woman, but then, you are as familiar with Lady Lisle as I am," he said with a wink.

"Yes," Thomas answered carefully.

"In truth, I did not want the other daughter here at court. They are a strangely seductive family of women, and I have not been im- mune to their charms. Keeping Anne around out of guilt is bad enough. You, on the other hand, are free to experiment with all three of them, as it pleases you," Henry said, as if granting Thomas permission.

But it did not please him. Random sexual exploits had ceased to please him the day he had fallen in love with Catherine. He would play the part only because it was expected of him.

They walked together a few paces toward the privacy of a window seat. "So, old friend . . ." Henry began.

This was not going to be good. Thomas could tell that the king wanted to have one of their manly chats about women, and he simply was not in the mood.

"With the young ones, is it your stamina that pleases them? Or can one hope to conquer with style over longevity?" Henry asked earnestly.

The small amount of porridge that Thomas had eaten earlier threatened to reappear at the continual thought of the king with Catherine. "Respectfully, sire, I believe it is I who should be asking you."

"You know perfectly well I have tired of the chase, Tom. The young ones fancy you. The old ones as well, for that matter. But though I am settled, I have a startlingly young wife, and I am not quite as young or energetic as I once was. Do not misunderstand me. It is not that I do not desire her. She is an exciting, exhausting temptress, denying me nothing. I can scarcely get my mind or my prick, for that matter, to consider much else."

Thomas was overcome with anger and wild jealousy. *My urge to crush your skull right now is stronger than any sense of loyalty I have left for you! I would die happily for my crime, knowing that you would not be able to lie with her again!*

"Not having had a wife, perhaps I am not the best judge." Thomas struggled to sidestep his rage.

"Nonsense. What I am speaking of has nothing to do with marriage, Tom." He chuckled, and the sound was low and base, as if they were speaking of a Bankside whore.

"I will advise Your Majesty any way that I can," he forced himself to say.

"Very well. Do you find that intimate stroking and tenderness can be enough for the young ones?"

Of course not. Especially not one so fiery as Catherine, Thomas thought. "Yes, of course," he said instead. "Especially when the tenderness is schooled and elegant."

Henry smiled in relief. It seemed that the king believed him. Perhaps that would mark the end to this horrifying conversation.

"Join me at prayer this morning. I shall be meeting the queen, whom you may observe in order to further advise me. Then you shall join us at dinner later so you may judge how schooled I am beyond the bed. You will be like a teacher watching his finest pupil."

Or a fool, powerlessly watching his greatest rival, Thomas silently amended.

"It would be my pleasure, Your Majesty," Thomas replied with a courtly nod, nearly choking on the lie.

Chapter Sixteen

September 1540
Richmond Palace, Surrey

The next day, the king's court continued their royal progress, this time floating serenely toward Richmond. Catherine and Henry led the way on a huge, majestic barge strewn with scented rushes, followed by twenty-six others. September marked a need for a return to reality from the country idles of summer, but a prolonged drought and a plague continued to rage in England, and Henry feared being too near London.

Between the distractions of banquets, hunting, dancing, singing, new gowns and jewels, the end of two months as queen had come quickly for Catherine. So had an unexpected sense of devotion, if not love, for the complex, generous and tender man she had married. She found herself truly enjoying his company.

But the one thing she truly did love was being Queen of England. She was denied nothing. In fact, her life would have been quite perfect if she were not so irrevocably bound to another man.

For the most part, Thomas kept his distance, which she knew was not difficult to do, as there were many others willing to edge their way forward to smile, nod and compliment the royal couple. Catherine was sure that onlookers were revolted by the shameless displays of flattery, but they were her security. She would never end up like Cromwell, the poor clerics or Anne Boleyn. She had made all of her foolish mistakes in her youth. The past was behind her. She would learn how to be a good wife and a good queen, and perhaps, over time, she would even learn how to love Henry VIII.

Richmond Palace belonged to Anne of Cleves and was her permanent residence now. Henry was fully prepared to honor his "good sister" with kind affection during his visit. He felt compelled to maintain friendly relations with his former queen, of whom he had always thought kindly despite their unsuccessful marriage.

Catherine's heart skipped a beat as she walked with Henry and a small entourage up the wide stone steps to be received by the former queen.

Catherine suddenly clung like a child to Henry's arm. "I am so nervous."

"You need not be." He smiled indulgently and kissed the top of her head.

"Are you certain she'll not be angry that I took you away from her?"

"I never believed she wanted me anyway."

"Foolish woman." Catherine giggled, nestling her head against his velvet-clad shoulder because she knew it would flatter him. He smiled more broadly and bent down to kiss her cheek.

"Just follow my lead. It shall be awkward for only a moment or two."

"All right, I trust you, Hal."

"And I trust you." He winked as he said it, but she knew it was true. She suppressed a little spark of guilt when she thought of her past indiscretions and the white lies she had told him from time to time.

Anne stood at the open double doors inside the foyer with

a group of dignified Germans. She greeted the king and his new wife with the most genuine smile Catherine had ever seen, and she shocked everyone when she, the woman who had worn England's crown less than three months ago, fell into a deep and reverent curtsy before the new queen. Anne lowered her head, which was covered in a traditional gabled hood, to her successor for what felt like an awkwardly long time. When Catherine glanced over, she saw Henry smiling.

After Anne rose, he embraced her warmly.

"It is so good to see you, Anna," he said sincerely, using the name she preferred, though he had never used it during their marriage.

"And you as well, sire," Anne said humbly.

"Your English is improving," he said, pleased to hear her speak with more ease.

"Thank you. I work on it with my tutor every day." She smiled. "Please do come in."

They advanced into the grand foyer, from which a traditional wooden staircase, lit by stained-glass windows imprinted with shields and stars, led to the other floors.

"You are comfortable here?" he asked as he took Catherine's hand, limping noticeably as they walked.

"Very comfortable. I wish never to leave England," Anne replied.

"Richmond is yours, so that is one wish I can grant."

"Your Majesty has granted me many."

They went into a small paneled dining hall, where a table had been laid with food and wine. Anne's liveried servants stood like stone statues at the ready to tend to their royal guests.

"I thought you might be hungry after your journey. Or would you rather rest first?" she asked in her thickly accented yet clear English.

"Are you all right?" Catherine quietly asked Henry.

He grimaced a little, his leg obviously paining him. "Just rather warm. It was a long ride. Perhaps I will rest for a while. But you two stay here and reacquaint yourselves. I am sure you have much to speak about."

Catherine chose not to argue, uncertain whether he needed the rest or if he was unselfishly allowing her to spend time alone in Anne's company, which she had always enjoyed. Catherine kissed his cheek and smiled as he left them.

"His Majesty looks well," Anne said as they sat at the table beside a lovely, polished buffet gleaming with costly pewter pieces. "Marriage to you agrees with him far more than when he was married to me," she said kindly.

Catherine felt a little twinge of guilt. There was not a single note of envy in the former queen's voice.

"He is a surprisingly wonderful husband, more misunderstood than I ever guessed."

"And yet Cromwell and the others are dead by his command." She said it so softly that Catherine almost did not hear it.

"Others?" Catherine asked.

"The king has been incredibly good to me. I should say no more."

"I know you refute the papacy and my family's beliefs," Catherine gently reminded her. "So it is fine if you speak your mind with me."

Anne paused for a moment, as if she were considering. "I love Henry like a brother. But there is another side to him than the one he shows you."

Catherine felt herself bristle in defense, though she did not want to offend Anne when she desperately needed allies. The religious question in England was a big and volatile one, and she would have to tread lightly.

"If there were other traitors who lost their lives, I can say only that they must have deserved their fate," Catherine replied, repeating the official stance of the court.

"Do you not think there might have been recourse other than death?" Anne asked.

It was not a question Catherine could answer without defying the king, and her entire life thus coming unraveled. She knew that well enough.

They spoke of many other things after that and the time passed quickly. Henry joined them just as the sun was setting, and the evening became a blur of laughter, singing and far more Gascony wine than any of them required. As the evening progressed and Henry and Anne conversed easily, Catherine felt free to glance around the room, hoping to see Thomas. He had joined their entourage, along with Brandon and Jane, but she knew he was doing his best to remain in the shadows. Still, just to catch a glimpse of him now and then would bring her more pleasure than any of the riches Henry could ever give her.

Predictably, Henry ran a hand along her leg beneath the tablecloth and nuzzled her neck as they ate, drank, talked and laughed about light, harmless things. Even with this annoying distraction, Catherine relished the conversation between herself and Anne, particularly about how frightening and overwhelming it was to be Queen of England. After all, there was no one else in the world who had been admitted to their small, exclusive group.

It was an odd yet wonderful camaraderie, Catherine thought, as Henry corrected Anne's English, causing them all to laugh. Anne seemed not to harbor the slightest bit of malice against them, though she had been replaced by one of her own attendants.

As Henry patiently explained the history of Richmond to his former wife, Catherine finally saw him. Thomas was in the corridor beyond the dining hall, whispering with two of the royal guardsmen. The tremor she felt at seeing him rocked her completely, as it always did. Henry's gravelly voice gradually faded into a muffled, incomprehensible sound. She tried not to fantasize about Thomas as she watched him standing magnificently, and smiling that velvety, dazzling smile she knew so well.

She squeezed her eyes shut, but when she opened them he was still there, still smiling. He turned slightly and their eyes met from across the room. Everything seemed to go completely still, as if the moment were caught in a painting, rich with details and meaning. Catherine tried to drink it in, memorizing it all for later, when she would be in Henry's huge, fleshy arms, wishing fate would give her the same freedom Anne of Cleves had so effortlessly found.

A moment later, Catherine sensed that Henry's droning had ceased. Anne had fallen silent as well. To her horror, she felt Henry's hulking body tense, and his moist hand loosened in hers beneath the table. Instantly she redirected her gaze to Henry and leaned her head against his shoulder, fearing that she had been caught gazing at another man.

"Is that Master Culpeper there?" Anne asked, oblivious to the moment. "I have not seen his handsome smile forever."

Henry scowled slightly, just enough for Catherine to see it. "He looks slightly ill to me. A bit pale," he observed. "I pray it is not the ague. I want to avoid whatever could harm those dearest to me."

Catherine thought better of saying that Thomas appeared as healthy and magnificent as ever. She knew there was something more behind his words. Henry had been more explosive than normal these past two days, and she tried to tread softly in all things. Before their honeymoon was even over, he had been forced to consult with his privy counsel on complex matters of state. France was pushing its borders into English territory. A more direct act of aggression could not be far off.

It was not difficult for Catherine to see how swiftly and randomly those around Henry paid the price when he was under pressure. She squeezed his hand tightly and leaned nearer until she felt the tension in his body begin slowly once again to fade.

❖

Later that evening, Henry's entourage met again in his former privy counsel rooms, decorated now with the banner of Cleves. Norfolk, his son Surrey, Seymour, the new member Cranmer, Southampton, Brandon and Wriothesley sat at the long, polished oak table with the king at its head. Catherine sat beside Henry, though it was the sort of meeting that was never attended by the queen. But Catherine was different. Everyone could see that Henry meant to make her a different sort of partner.

"We have no choice but to act against such a blatant act of hostility," Norfolk calmly advised him.

"Have we the manpower to quell the French threat?" Henry asked, rubbing his bearded chin with his thumb and forefinger in a contemplative gesture.

"I do not believe it shall come to that," the younger Howard replied. "Because of Lord Lisle's weak performance in the region and his consignment to the Tower, I believe they are only pressing to see how far they can get."

Norfolk turned away as the king began to nuzzle Catherine's earlobe.

Brandon bit back a groan.

"Considering all that is at stake, I would advise Your Majesty to send a contingent to Calais for a bit of English saber rattling. I believe my lord of Surrey here is more than up to the task," Norfolk said.

There were only slight grumblings of surprise that Norfolk would propose his own son for the honor. Seymour shot Henry Howard a jealous glare, then looked away.

The king kissed Catherine's cheek for the dozenth time. "Very well. The lot of you go. Southampton and Surrey, give the French a good scare. I've dealt with them before, and they do not frighten me."

"Indeed you have, sire." Norfolk nodded just as he caught another angry glare of disapproval, this time from Cranmer, his new rival. Cranmer had been at court for years, but only now, after Cromwell's demise, had he made himself a much greater force and threat.

"And, Norfolk, when we leave for Greenwich tomorrow morning, see that Master Culpeper is not among us. It seems he might have a touch of the ague. I cannot allow anyone, no matter how fond of them I might be, to inflict that risk upon my court, or my queen."

Culpeper, Norfolk thought in surprise, rolling the name around in his mind. It was a name he had not contemplated for weeks. There were enough complications ahead without looking backward to the old ones. *Catherine is not foolish enough to dally with Culpeper now that she is queen*, he thought. *She would be risking not only her own life, but the entire Howard family, and Culpeper as well*. If only he had a niece with beauty and half a brain. But no one got everything in life. No one, that was, but him.

"I shall see to it myself, Your Majesty," Norfolk promised without looking at Cranmer or Seymour.

Cromwell was dead, and his minions were no threat to Norfolk now.

❖

Well, well, well. Master Culpeper, is it? So perhaps the great Howard family has an Achilles' heel after all, Cranmer thought. So taken was he by the revelation that he was the last to leave the counsel table. He steepled his hands and watched as every man stood, acknowledged the king and queen, and backed out of the room. His thin lips were stretched tightly into a sneer as he digested the new information. He saw it as a final message from Cromwell. Or God. Or both. Such must be the glorious perspective from heaven.

The only question was what to do with the gift. Time, he was quite certain, would tell him that. But he would be on the watch, just like all the other Protestants at court, to unseat the little Catholic queen when the time was right. They had all come too far to let the king's lust, and thus his poor judgment, trump the true path for England.

Thomas Cranmer silently swore that oath to himself.

❖

It was ten days before Catherine dared to write a letter to Thomas, who had been sent to London amid a drought and a plague. She sat alone beneath a trellis heavy with musk roses and honeysuckle vines just beyond the timber-framed tennis courts, reading her words one final time and missing him all the more.

Master Culpeper,

I was told you are sick, which troubles me very much, and will until I hear from you. I pray that you send me word on how you are, for I never longed so much for anything as I do to see you and speak with you, which I trust will happen shortly. The thought comforts me very much, and when I think of you departing from me, it makes my heart die.

I pray that you will come to me through Lady Rochford, for then I shall thank you for that which you have promised me. I take my leave of you now, trusting that I will see you shortly. I would you were with me now that you might see what pain I take in writing to you.

Yours as long as life endures,
Catherine

"Are you certain you want to do this?" Jane asked as she came up and stood before Catherine under the trellis. She had enlisted Jane's help in securing a messenger who would hold his tongue for the right price. To that end, Catherine held up the necklace that her mother had given her. The small, precious ruby at its center glistened in the soft sunlight.

"No, I am not certain. But there is no other way. I need to know that he is all right. I saw the way Henry looked at him. You did as well. We both know his temper."

With a heavy, anxious heart, Catherine folded the missive and handed it to Jane, along with the last connection she had to her mother. She was giving away a part of herself to ensure that another part was safe, she told herself.

"You are certain, Jane, that your messenger will wait for Thomas's reply?"

"He agreed to, yes," Jane confirmed.

Catherine let out a small sigh. "Then go now, please. I will not be able to breathe until your man returns."

AUTUMN

The Third Season

"No Other Will But His."
—Motto of Catherine Howard

Chapter Seventeen

The English victory over the French at Calais was swift and thorough. Indeed, winning had taken no more time than it had for the French to deliver the threat in the first place. The French ambassador, the Duke of Vendôme, gave Henry Francis I's assurance that no aggression had been intended. Surrey and Southampton returned victoriously to England, just in time for Christmas.

Catherine busied herself with the organization of the Yuletide festivities. Two of the king's three children, Elizabeth and Edward, as well as the princess of Cleves, had just arrived at Greenwich for the holiday celebrations. Only Mary had declined the queen's invitation with a polite but cold explanation that her physicians believed it unwise for her to risk travel during the harsh months of winter.

Catherine put a brave face on for her husband's sake, but bringing everyone together for the new year had been intended as a wedding gift for Henry. Catherine knew how much it would have pleased him.

Mary had known it as well.

At the end of November, Thomas had been admitted back to court, but he and Catherine rarely saw each other and did not interact beyond the occasional polite nod or glance. The king's arm was always tightly linked with hers as she and Thomas passed in the corridor. She knew Henry was sending a message for the entire world to see—particularly Thomas.

But she was glad he had returned. A painful glimpse of the man she still loved was better than no glimpse at all, she reasoned, trying her best to be happy and see the good in life.

She remembered even now how her anxiety about him, during his absence, had tortured her, and it was painful still to recall his response. He had sent an impersonal note assuring her only of his safety. That had been so much worse, she thought, than even a glimpse of him at a distance.

As Christmastide approached, Catherine decided to turn her failure with Henry's daughter into a victory with another relative.

She could never get over the idea that an old woman like the poor Countess of Salisbury, cold, alone and frightened for her life, had been consigned indefinitely to the Tower. Margaret Pole was Henry's nearest blood relative and the last of the Plantagenet line. She was a frail woman of sixty-seven and had been in the Tower for nearly two years. Catherine did not understand how a venerable relation and the last tie to his much-adored mother could be treated with such cruelty. Treason was a term that was easily bandied about and used to dispose of anyone objectionable. It was the charge that had brought down Anne Boleyn and Cromwell. Now the same fate loomed for the countess. Catherine shook off a little shiver of fear, seeing a pattern to her husband's anger.

But perhaps she could change the pattern.

Catherine needed to prove to herself that she could bring out Henry's gentleness for all the world to see. She wanted to be a positive force in his life and mend his reputation for cruelty. Accomplishing that, she believed, would give her the reason her heart craved to make peace with this marriage.

Those thoughts weighed heavily on her mind and heart, even as she let him chase her naked around their bedchamber early one evening before Christmas. She used a large chair as a barricade between them, her hair long and wild around her shoulders.

"Come on, Hal," she said, giggling. "Don't be slow." They were playing a seductive version of blindman's buff, and Henry could barely walk straight with the blindfold on.

"If you catch me, I shall give up the notion," she said, though she was serious at heart. "And if you surrender, then you shall allow me to send a Christmas parcel to the Tower for the countess. Only a few warm clothes for the winter."

Henry laughed with a great bellow, barely able to catch his breath. His breathing was as heavy as his laughter. "If we are going to play rough, I shall demand a great deal more than your surrender of a notion, my little Cat."

"It is a deal. I shall surrender anything you like, if there is anything left of me you wish to have."

"All of you! You are deep in my blood, woman!" he declared, dodging and weaving around the furniture. "I can never get enough!"

She tipped over the chair, and he finally capitulated, sinking down, flushed and out of breath, onto the edge of the great feather bed. As he tore off the blindfold, her smile was open and genuine.

"So, will you allow me to send some things to the countess?"

He slumped, then sighed, his smile fading. "Why must you press me so, Catherine, on things you know nothing about?"

"I know an old woman will be cold this winter, and we have the power to change that."

"Why do you concern yourself? She is a traitor to England, to me, and thereby a traitor to you."

"She is your blood relation, Hal. It just seems wrong. The poor woman has been locked up there for two years already."

For a moment he seemed angry, until he saw the tears in her eyes. They were genuine tears, not just for the prisoner, but for the notion that the gentle man she had come to care for was capable of brutality against his own family. She wanted desperately to prove the world was wrong. Finally, Henry pulled her into his arms and pressed a kiss onto her forehead.

"You have a heart too tender for your own good, dearest one," he said.

"Oh, I am not finished. I plan to ask you to spare her life as well in a grand show of mercy from a great and beneficent king."

"Do not press me too far, Catherine. You may not like what you see." A dark, ominous look passed over his face as he spoke the warning, but in spite of the shiver she felt, Catherine remained composed. Henry had already yielded more than she had expected. And that was when she realized that she really could use her status as queen for more than her family's advancement.

She tried to understand things from Henry's point of view. Perhaps murder was like a Pandora's box: Once one opened it to solve one's problem, one could not close the lid. But Catherine refused to let Henry succumb to it. She was his wife now, and under her influence those days would be over. She could lead her husband. She could guide him back to what was right and good. She would no longer be a pawn, but a true queen, she told herself. Her newfound ambition gave her a strange sense of peace. This, she believed, was the era of Catherine Howard.

❖

After Christmas Day, Catherine found Francis in her cozy little study one afternoon, sitting, as usual, at her desk. She paused in the doorway, still angry that she had been forced to adopt him as her private secretary. The entitled manner with which he riffled through her private papers did not help.

"What do you think you are doing in my chair?" she asked with a note of irritation.

Francis did not miss a beat. His smile was suggestive. "Waiting for Your Grace, of course, as always."

He meant the double entendre, and she knew it. When they were forced to work together, Francis's words were always laden with innuendo. Though she was disgusted by him, she had to tolerate it. Queen or not, she knew she could not trust Francis, because, like the three women from Horsham, he still held the power to destroy her. She did not know if he was vengeful enough to do such a thing, even though ruining her would certainly spoil his own position at court, if not jeopardize his life.

"Your Grace wishes to send a letter?" he asked. He had been called by her servants early New Year's Day to meet her.

She advanced and stood over him haughtily until he was forced to surrender her chair. She sat down and gave her instructions as he moved into one opposite her. "You are to craft a letter to Princess Mary asking after her health during this cold spell of weather and telling her she was missed here at Christmas."

"Were not both of the king's daughters stripped of that title?" Francis challenged her.

She glared at him. "They are both princesses as far as your queen is concerned, and that is all you need worry yourself about."

"And if you bear the old king a child? Will you worry about it then?"

"If I am blessed by God to bear His Majesty a son, the child shall be his second heir, after Prince Edward. My son will have no bearing on the role of the king's daughters in his life or this country."

"My, but Your Grace has matured much in a year's time. You are scarcely the girl I chased around the attic at Horsham." He smiled wickedly.

"Master Dereham, you know me not at all. You knew a simple, bored country girl, but she is gone forever."

"The one who made me this?" He drew forth the lace-edged scarf she had stitched with their initials, with which he enjoyed taunting her from time to time. Unfortunately, the girl she had left behind had the same initials as the woman she had become. The FD and CH would be damning evidence with a jealous husband, and she knew it.

Her eyes widened as he pressed the fabric to the tip of his nose dramatically. "Your scent lingers still."

She scowled at him. "What do you really want, Francis, to keep you quiet?"

"Only what, and who, was promised to me."

"Is this post not enough?"

"It is a respectable beginning," he admitted.

"Do you want more money than what you currently earn here? Is that not truly it?"

His smile twisted as he met her eyes. "It is enough to know you remember what was between us when we—"

Before he could finish the words, Catherine saw a lily white hand clamp down on the nape of his neck and draw him from his chair with little effort. The element of surprise had worked in Agnes Howard's favor.

Her voice was as cold as her hand. "Listen to me very carefully, Master Dereham. You are here at court because I desire a smooth transition for the queen. But do not press me too far, sir. This is a powerful family, and we know how to devour vermin like you and spit out your bones without a single thought."

He arched a brow at her. "And what of the things I might reveal before you do?"

"It is possible you could create a problem for us, but any damage you could cause would be on the way to your own demise," the dowager reminded him.

He shrugged. "That might prove worth the sacrifice."

"I do not believe you will decide that in the end. You were always too selfish to be a martyr."

"Are any of you Howards really different?"

Her onyx eyes hardened in contempt as Catherine sat in stunned silence, watching them. The dynamic between them was beyond master and servant.

"You certainly could push any one of us and see. But do remember that we have been at this court game for decades, and we have promoted two of our own blood to Queen of England. The only power you have is some gossip about the king's beloved wife. Also, while you are contemplating your next move against the lot of us, do consider the recent fall of Lord Great Chamberlain Cromwell. It would be far simpler, albeit less gratifying, to destroy a country boy for threatening my granddaughter." She smoothed out the front of her dress. "Have I made myself clear?"

"Quite," Francis said sulkily.

"Splendid. Now get out of my sight. I cannot tarry with guttersnipes on an empty stomach."

Once he was gone, Agnes raised Catherine from her chair and, for the first time in Catherine's life, drew her tenderly against her bony chest. Unaccustomed to such familial shows of affection, Catherine's body tensed, but her grandmother did not release her. She patted her back gently and whispered a "Hush." It was only then that Catherine realized she herself was weeping.

"I don't know why I am . . ." Catherine sobbed, unable to explain her tears.

"Shhh. It is to be expected, my dear. You have lasted longer as queen than our Anne did before she had her moment of weakness and cried to me like this."

"But I thought Anne was in control of everything until the end."

"She was a complicated girl, quite good at presenting the image people expected. But that takes effort and skill. And as you now know, that can be exhausting."

Catherine looked up with tearstained cheeks, still unable to fathom being embraced by her grandmother, wrapped in the same arms that had held a cane against her too many times to remember. "What if he speaks to the king?"

"That is a possibility if we anger him too much, so we must walk a fine line. But as the great Julius Caesar once said, one must keep one's friends close and one's enemies closer. That is what your uncle and I are doing for you."

"Forgive me, Grandmother, but you have never spoken to me with such kindness before," Catherine said, her eyes filling anew with tears.

"You have never been my queen before," the dowager duchess explained.

❖

As spring came, Catherine thought she might be with child.

All of the signs were certainly there, and Henry had barely let her alone a single night since they had married nine months ago. She was young, strong and healthy, the royal physician had told her yesterday. Perfect for bearing children.

Henry had laughed and said it was about time.

They decided to keep her pregnancy a secret until they were certain, but Henry could not keep the joy and contentment from his face as they rode down the river amid a parade of barges, each ornamented festively with bunting and flags fluttering in the cool April wind off the water. The azure sky was cloudless. A young boy in a rust-colored costume played a gentle tune on his flute to entertain them. Catherine squeezed Henry's hand, taken by the sun on her face and the sweet music surrounding them.

"So, have you considered my request?" she sweetly asked.

"Is it not enough to content yourself with redecorating my privy chamber at Hampton Court, which is so in need of a woman's touch?"

"Not when a poor old woman languishes in the Tower, Hal," she firmly replied.

She felt him tense and loosen his grip on her hand, as he always did when she brought the subject up, but she would not back down. There had been too much bloodshed since she became queen, and the idea of adding to the number of deaths was unthinkable as long as she could prevent it.

"Sweetheart," he said, smiling suddenly, then turning to kiss her cheek. "I will not let you be troubled by political matters, no matter how well-meaning your intentions. It would not be good for our unborn son."

Her heart swelled, and a part of Catherine hoped she was carrying his child. She knew what it would mean to her entire family if she were to bear a son. The Seymour family still benefited from Jane's legacy, her sickly boy.

"I do not want to be troubled either, Hal; I just want to help you see what is right."

"What the devil would you know about any of it?" he snapped

so harshly that she felt almost as if she had been struck. The music continued, concealing their argument.

"Forgive me," he finally said, smiling again, calmed by her silence. "I did not mean to be so harsh with you."

"I only wish to help," Catherine said, still stung by his words.

Henry pulled her closer, pressing a kiss onto her lips, as he did so frequently that she was made dizzy by it. "You will help me most by choosing a new fabric for the bed, along with some window coverings, as soon as we arrive. Wolsey chose the current ones himself, so you have some idea of how old they are. Now they are riddled with moth holes."

She did not know she was frowning until he rubbed his forefinger teasingly between her brows and smiled more broadly.

"I know it is not easy for one so young to be queen," he said. "But it is even more difficult to be king at every age. There are decisions to be made each waking hour of every day, difficult decisions, and I need you to support me, not battle against me."

"Will you at least consider a pardon for the old countess, Hal . . . for me? Over two years in that drafty, stone tower seems more than enough for any woman to suffer as penance."

"There is no one who can get to me quite as you do," Henry said begrudgingly.

"May I take that as a yes?"

"Decorate our bedchamber very prettily, and we shall see."

Catherine had never felt so proud and empowered in her life. She was not just a silly, mindless girl, no matter what her uncle said. No matter what the entire court believed. She could do this; she could make a difference in England.

"I love you," she said, meaning it at last.

❖

Jane Boleyn stood, hands on her hips, in the queen's oak-paneled private dressing closet, surveying the scene before her.

"Just what do you think you are doing there?" she said accusatorily.

Mary Lassells was on her knees over an open casket of jewels, her pale skirts fanned out around her. She turned with a start. Around her throat was a necklace of emeralds and pearls, and Catherine's rings were on each of her fingers. Mary reminded Jane of a little girl caught playing dress-up with her mother's best things. Mary stood uneasily, though her face did not bear signs of contrition.

"I was only polishing everything for Her Grace."

"By wearing them?"

She glanced down at her small hands and began calmly to remove the rings. "I meant no harm, my Lady Rochford."

"The queen is always at risk. It is my job to determine if you meant any harm," Jane snapped.

"I thought you were her companion," Mary challenged.

"I am here to protect her, and that is all you need to know," Jane said severely.

Mary Lassells replaced each of the rings into the casket, then closed the lid as Jane continued to glare at her.

"I will always be nearby, Mistress Lassells. I not only have the confidence of the queen, but the ear of the king, so you would be wise to consider your actions in the future. And do remove Her Grace's necklace before you return to your duties. His Majesty has been known to cut off heads for far less than stealing jewelry from the queen."

"I did not intend to steal anything," Mary countered, which was the truth. At least this time. The small fortune her brother had collected on the little cat's collar would finance their Reform work for a long time to come. The foolish queen hardly seemed to care that it was gone. Or wonder who might actually have taken it, and why.

❖

The Spanish ambassador sat beside Catherine at the banquet that evening in the great hall at Hampton Court, full of flowery solicitations. She smiled and nodded at a dignitary in black and gray with a ruby-studded baldric across his broad chest whose name she did not care to remember. She was already feeling the encroaching boredom of another long night of food, wine, music and endless banter.

A fleeting memory came to her as her mind drifted off. It was a night at Horsham when all the girls had escaped their dormitory prison and gone out into the starry night in their bedclothes, whispering, laughing and dancing. It was that feeling of freedom she remembered most—something she would never feel again.

"You look like you need rescuing. Dance with me, sweetheart," Henry said cavalierly, leaning over to whisper to her as the ambassador continued to drone on.

Catherine was relieved as he helped her to her feet and led her, limping noticeably as he did, toward the dancing area. "You needn't do this for me if your leg is bothering you."

"When I look at your lovely face, I feel no discomfort at all," Henry replied gallantly.

He bravely attempted to lead her through a tourdion as the court looked on. Catherine was so concerned about Henry's leg and the pain his pride concealed that at first she heard only a word or two uttered by two courtiers who stood nearby.

"It was horrendous, they say. The bloodiest murder yet. Everyone is talking about it," one courtier said.

"The executioner was no more than a boy. I heard it took him five blows to cut off her head, poor old thing," the other one added.

The breath was literally knocked out of her in one painful rush. Everything around her began to spin. Unaware of what she had just heard, Henry continued smiling. The music was loud and the overwhelming stench was not of food any longer, but of death.

"What is it, sweetheart? You've gone pale as a ghost."

She had stopped dancing and was standing stiffly. She was stunned. "You lied to me yesterday, Hal, right to my face. You told me you would consider pardoning her. Was that before you sent the poor old countess to her death, or was it afterward?"

Catherine did not wait for a reply, or even consider what harm might come to her for angering a man who could sign his own relative's death warrant, then dance and smile before her body was even cold in the grave. She spun around, her dress sailing out behind her as she ran from the room.

To her surprise, the king was right behind her.

"How dare you turn your back on me? I am your king and your husband," Henry growled in her ear, clamping a hand onto her arm as the whispers and murmurs of the courtiers filled the great hall.

Just as they passed out of the main doors and into the privacy of the corridor, Catherine spun around, her dress a whirl of ice blue silk. She saw his face was blazing with as much anger as her own.

"You will not humiliate me like that before my people, madam, do you hear me?" he growled at her again.

It was the most frightening voice she had ever heard, yet it did not move her as much as the horrendous lie he had told.

"What if I do? Will Your Majesty execute me, as well? Or will you send me to the Tower to languish away? God knows you are capable of treating even your queens that way."

The blow against her cheek was swift and hard. His hand felt like a brick, and there was an audible crack of flesh. Instantly, the crimson expression of fury on his fat face fell to white shock.

"I did not mean that; I did not mean to hurt you. You know I . . ."

His words fell away as she reached up to touch the flaming wound on her cheek and felt a wet trickle of blood from where one of his rings had caught her delicate skin.

"I shall call the physician. That needs tending."

Catherine was not distracted from her anger for a moment. "Why, Hal? She was only an old woman. You let me believe you might spare her."

"I never intended to spare her, only your feelings on the matter, for as long as I could," he admitted.

"By lying to me?"

"Do not question my authority ever again, Catherine. I love you desperately, but thinking you can change me is something you shall live to regret." His words were cold. His tone held a warning she had never heard before.

But in that moment, her regrets were already too numerous to count. She could not believe that she had thought she could truly love a butcher, no matter how elegantly he dressed or what costly gifts he gave her. The crown upon her head was worse than an albatross around her neck. At least she still had her neck, she thought with a mix of horror and fury.

For now.

"I am leaving for London at first light," he said with a deadly calm. "I have business to attend to there. Considering your delicate condition, it would be best if you remain here until I return."

My condition? she thought, the sudden revelation slamming into her with more force than his palm. *Jésu! Pray God I am not pregnant. Pray God I do not carry a monster's child!*

❖

She had run from him and he had not gone after her.

That was all she remembered. Catherine had no idea, as she lay on the damp earth, how she had gotten into the maze on the castle grounds and found the protection of its tall, clipped ivy walls. Racked by convulsive sobs, her chest heaved and her tears blinded her. But the arms so tightly wrapped around her were familiar, warm and comforting. Thomas Culpeper said not a word, only held her tight in the self-protective coil in which he had found her, and let her weep. His calm strength was the greatest balm to her shattered heart. While she wanted to ask how he had found her, she was afraid to speak.

If he was a dream, she knew it would destroy her.

Tenderly, he stroked her temple with his thumb as he held her like a child on his lap. The only sound was the crickets' rhythmic chirp nearby.

"Why did you come?" The four words were more of a croak of syllables than a question.

"I have always been here," he answered in his deep, beautiful voice, which made her want to cry even more.

"If the king were to find us—"

"He'll not find us. I happen to know that His Majesty has retired for the evening."

The mention of Henry was a harsh, cold blow. But Henry had not come after her. He did not know where she was, nor care. God forgive her the sin, but she was glad of it.

Catherine inhaled deeply before she opened her eyes. She could not bear to think she had conjured Thomas at a desperate moment like this. But he was real. She could see that in every elegant turn of his perfect face, highlighted by a silver quarter moon above.

"Why did he have to do it?" she asked.

"The Countess of Salisbury? It is complicated, my love, and the king is a complicated man, driven by the past more than anyone likes to admit. Her sons betrayed him. She did not rise up against them when she had the chance."

"But she was old, a harmless woman."

"Our king does not abide betrayal in anyone, least of all from women he once trusted."

Catherine knew his words were all too true. And now she too would have to focus on surviving.

Thomas was still stroking her face with one gentle hand, the other wrapped protectively around her.

"I could kill him for striking you."

"Then you would be no better than he is, and your fate would be that of the poor countess."

"It would be well worth it to me, other than the fact that I would be leaving you unprotected."

"You cannot protect me. No one can."

"It helps me to believe I can, though," Thomas said huskily.

The pressure of his thumb against her temple was no longer soothing, but sending a wave of desire coursing through her trembling, weakened body. The sensation was one she thought she would never feel again.

"You are leaving for London in the morning. He told me he has business there," she warned him.

"I am not accompanying the king."

Catherine struggled to sit up and face him. She was dizzy and slightly nauseated. There was hair hanging in her face, and her dress was covered with dirt, but she cared nothing for any of that. Staring into Thomas's eyes gave Catherine a sense of renewed strength. "How can you avoid it?"

"I shall be deathly ill in the morning, unable even to rise from my bed. You know how the king is about anyone with anything remotely contagious."

Her weak smile was full of surprise. "You are very devious."

"I prefer to think of myself as resourceful."

"And do you see yourself as charming as well?"

"Committed," he countered.

Her smile faded then. "I am not free to be committed, Thomas; you know that."

"Oh, I was committed to you, body and soul, long before you were not free, if I remember it correctly."

"It is pointless."

She looked away, but he brought her face back with a single, powerful finger. "Love is pointless?"

"Your commitment to me is pointless. The king is a dangerous man."

"That is not a surprise to anyone, Catherine."

She loved the silky way he said her name.

"It was to me, which I suppose makes me the stupid, empty-headed child everyone believes me to be," she said sadly.

"Loyalty is not stupidity."

"Apparently it is in my case."

They were facing each other, and he was near enough to kiss her. The current between them was powerful. But she could feel him keeping his distance. Kind, gorgeous and noble as well, he was still the only man who ever really had her heart, or ever would.

"Are you ready to go back now?" he asked.

"No. I would like to stay here like this forever," she said honestly. "But perhaps I should return before the servants begin to wonder. Where do the rest of the king's gentlemen believe you are?"

Thomas helped her to her feet and linked his arms around her, as he had done so many times a lifetime ago. "No one wonders where I am. I am a single man at court with a rather notorious reputation."

"Oh." She looked away, feeling an unwarranted shiver of jealousy, until he brought her face back around.

"It isn't true, you know."

"Isn't it?" she asked, thinking of Katherine Basset.

"At court, gossip is always much more interesting than the truth," he said, echoing the words he had told her long ago.

"Not in our case," she countered.

"Meet me back here in the maze tomorrow?" He pressed a tender kiss on her mouth and she melted into it, feeling her own passion flare just as he pulled himself away.

"Come at sunset."

Catherine considered the invitation. "My ladies usually like to rest at that hour."

"Excellent." He smiled that same dazzling smile that she loved but that told her it was a grand mistake to agree. Yet she was absolutely powerless to deny him.

"My sweet fool," she said with a sad smile. "We are going to get ourselves killed. But I still love you so."

"I adore when you call me that. . . . And you know I have never stopped loving you."

❖

Henry did not join Catherine in her bedchamber that night as he ordinarily would have, and when Catherine inquired about him the next morning, Lady Douglas told her that His Majesty, the privy counsel and much of the court had left at dawn for London. The overwhelming feeling of freedom she felt at the news far outweighed the fear she felt for having angered him. Since she had first come to court, they had never so much as quarreled, and he certainly had never left her behind. Henry could scarcely bear to be in a room without her, so this was bound to incite gossip and bring a new flurry of rumors about her and Thomas. All she cared about now, though, as she stood before her long, gilt dressing room mirror and saw the thin, bloodred wound on her cheekbone and the raging purple bruise forming around it, was seeing Thomas again.

Jane stood behind her in a deep blue velvet gown and a rope of heavy pearls, offering silent support as Catherine touched her wound, feeling the sharp effect of the bruise.

"The Duke of Norfolk is here. I held him off as long as I could."

"Does he appear angry?" Catherine asked, aware of the ire she might have provoked in those other than the king.

"Very."

At Jane's confirmation, the tall oak door was thrown back on its hinges and crashed into the wall. The grand, intimidating figure of Thomas Howard swept into the room in a long black surcoat with a silver baldric across his chest.

"How could you be so foolish!" It was not a question.

"Do you have any idea what this could cost us, how Cranmer and others work against you, even as we speak? You have given them a golden opportunity," he bellowed, his face mottled in fury.

"He killed her in cold blood," Catherine said defiantly.

"That was none of your concern," Norfolk volleyed, waving his hand in the air dismissively.

"I am his queen!"

"Catherine, you are meant to satisfy his needs in the bedchamber and bear him sons. Your attempt at anything more jeopardizes us all."

He was standing close enough that she could feel his hot breath on her face as he spit the angry words at her.

"I was told he was furious with you for that scene you caused before running away. You made him look like a fool."

"*I* was furious with *him* for murdering an old woman!" she countered.

"Do not make the mistake of overestimating your own impor-tance, Catherine. Remember you are the fifth in a line of replaceable queens. He has proven that much!"

They were both shouting. Catherine could see from the corner of her eye that her ladies and the royal guards flanking the door were listening intently.

"Where were you last night?" he asked, changing the subject.

"Here," she said, half truthfully.

"And before that?" He pressed. "Mistress Lassells told me you returned alone to your chamber after midnight. Your dress had to be burned to hide the layer of dirt before any untoward story could be spun about it."

"I fell," she said simply.

He arched a brow. His lips were pursed so tightly that they ap-peared bloodless. "Then you rolled around in the dirt afterward for good measure? I may look old to you, but do not assume I am a fool, Catherine. And do not gamble with Henry on that score either. He has given you his heart and made you his queen. For that, he expects full fidelity. Cuckold him and you shall not live long enough to regret it," he warned.

"I have been faithful, my lord."

He paused, scanning the room, presumably seeking guilty faces. "Good. See that you remain that way in His Majesty's absence. I will go to London and speak on your behalf. I am told you may finally be with child, so that should help our case. When he sends for you, go to him repentantly, and never again let me hear that you have questioned his supreme authority."

"Even against murder?" Catherine asked, refusing to drop the point.

"Especially that, or the next time it may well mean your head, or even my own."

❖

Archbishop Cranmer had remained behind at Hampton Court to keep an eye on the Duke of Norfolk and to find out precisely why the king had gone off to London without his nubile young queen.

Mary Lassells stood before him. She had spared no detail about the events of the previous night. He had heard the servants gossiping that morning about the scene at the banquet, but Mary was a more practiced storyteller, telling him not only about the fight but also about the meeting with Thomas, which she had seen herself by her habit of lurking.

The foolish, zealous woman was worth every penny he paid her.

He handed over the small leather pouch stuffed with coins and watched her greedily secret it in the voluminous folds of her modest skirts. In war, one searched for weaknesses. Cromwell had taught him that. Though he was dead, his anger would live on until the Howard girl was gone and forgotten.

Cranmer was as committed to that as ever.

And he was getting closer.

Chapter Eighteen

Freedom is not treasured until it is lost.

Catherine did not fully realize that until ten days following Henry's departure for London. With Jane's help, she and Thomas met each day deep within the twists and turns of the maze. Two right turns, a left, then another right. Thomas brought wine, cups and whatever food he could take from the kitchens without being noticed. Jane always lent them a well-prepared alibi after admonishing them to adhere rigidly to it.

Catherine worried about being discovered, but there was a familiar, guilty pleasure in it as well, like the old days at Horsham. They met and had long talks about everything. He held her hand and touched her face, but never anything more.

"I believe I am finally with child," she confessed on the day after the king had sent for her. He wanted to reunite with her at Whitehall Palace for the May Day celebrations and had called for her to join him on the morrow.

"I hope it is the king's child," Thomas teased.

"I wish it were yours," she said sincerely.

"Fortunately, we know that is not possible."

"That would be a blessing to me, not a mistake."

"I am guessing His Majesty would feel differently about that."

"Bessie Blount's bastard child did well enough before he died."

"Ah, but that was the king's mistake, not the queen's," he corrected.

She traced a line along his smooth jaw, where just a gentle stubble of a beard remained. It was a rare physical connection between them, both of them mindful of the limits imposed by her marriage.

"Would you have wanted a child with me?"

"I would have wanted everything with you," he said softly.

"I hope it's not true. I do not want his child. I do not love him."

"You mustn't say that. It is your duty. The country depends on an heir in case Prince Edward does not survive."

The truth of his words wounded her. He sounded like the Duke of Norfolk. She shot to her feet in response, tipping over her cup of wine. "Duty be damned."

"Henry controls it all."

"Not my heart," she declared.

They were close and he was perfection as he stood before her. Close. Unattainable. Forbidden. Nothing had changed between them, nor could it. When she kissed him, with the high walls of ivy protecting them, she fully realized that. Their mouths met, the kiss chaste at first; then, sweetened by the past, it deepened as she wrapped her arms tightly around his neck. After a moment, he pulled away, yet his gaze was locked on her.

"We cannot do more," he murmured.

"I know. I bid you not to hate me for wanting to, though."

Thomas grabbed her by the waist. "How could I when I crave you like a drug, even in my sleep, when my mind and soul are filled with the taste of you, the memories of every curve and angle of your sweet, smooth body."

The words had been spoken softly, but so intensely and full of truth that her eyes filled with tears. Thomas reached up to brush them away with his thumbs, then gently held her trembling jaw.

When he kissed her this time, he did not hold back. She could feel his longing for her. But as the kiss deepened, something moved near the corner of the hedge, and Catherine jumped back with a start, her senses piqued.

"Did you hear that?"

"I did." Thomas's body instantly tensed in alarm as he scanned the corners of the tall hedges.

"Who would follow us?"

"A dozen people that I can think of, and then some. Fortunately, everyone of influence has gone to London."

"True." She tried to breathe.

But influence came in many forms and wore many disguises, her uncle had said. Unfortunately, Catherine was too preoccupied with thoughts of Thomas, whom she would not see alone again after that day, to care about anything else.

She was not sorry, no matter who might have seen.

❖

Catherine hated London, with its dirty, clotted waterways, filthy cobbled streets and the constant threat of disease. Yet she was relieved that the king had finally sent for her. Their quarrel was over. He would be angry when he found out that no child was growing inside of her, since her flux had begun just as she left that morning, but she was secretly relieved. She did not want Henry's child when her heart was so full of Thomas. Perhaps that would change with her return to Whitehall, and she would be able to make peace with her duty once again.

Henry was waiting for her alone on the water landing in an elegant, dove gray doublet trimmed with silver lace and a smart hat. A group of servants stood far behind as he helped her to the shore. Without hesitation, Catherine curtsied to her husband. She knew her duty to him, and to her marriage, no matter what her true feelings were about the night she had witnessed his dark side.

Henry took her hands and drew her to him with a smile. "Welcome home, sweetheart," he said, and she knew for certain that their quarrel really was over, if not in her heart, then at least in his.

They watched a bearbaiting match on the grounds of the palace, holding hands tentatively as they sat next to each other in the gallery. Catherine was surprised how quickly the tension faded between them, in spite of all she still secretly felt.

After supper, she prepared herself, as always, and waited for Henry to visit her bedchamber. They had been apart for eleven days. But he did not come. The next morning, when she arrived in the chapel for prayer, Henry was already kneeling beside an unexpected guest. Anne of Cleves lowered her head beside him on a prie-dieu at the altar. Catherine had not even been told that the former queen was invited to London, and now here she was in the royal chapel, as if she still bore her title.

Catherine advanced beside a Yeoman of the Guard and was seated just as Henry and Anne stood and turned toward her in the pew. Anne was clearly pleased to see her. Henry was more reserved.

He had never loved Anne; in fact, he had called her the Flanders mare when they were married. Everyone at court knew that. But Catherine was still uneasy, even after their successful public outing yesterday. Perhaps the quarrel was not over. Perhaps they could never reclaim their former happiness together. Would Norfolk believe that she had come to London ready to comply with the king's wishes, if Henry were to replace her with a more predictable queen?

So many thoughts flowed through her mind that she heard not a single word the cleric said from his pulpit. She watched Anne and Henry exchange knowing little smiles throughout the sermon. Was it something more than friendship now? Was that even possible? Why had no one informed her that the former queen had come for a visit?

"It is so good to see you again," Anne proclaimed in her Teutonic accent, linking her arm with Catherine's as they finally left the chapel. The king, Norfolk and Norfolk's ambitious son Henry strolled a pace ahead along a walkway facing the river.

"I wish I had known you were coming. Yet still it is a lovely surprise," Catherine said, trying to conjure a smile.

Anne tipped her head slightly, as though she had not understood. "Are you certain?"

"Of course." Catherine's smile was genuine now.

"Henry speaks only good words of you."

"I wish I could be certain of that. Has he told you that I angered him, and he left me alone at Hampton Court?"

"I did hear, but not from Henry," Anne admitted.

Catherine shook her head. "Everything is so confusing just now."

"He loves you. That much is very clear."

If only I loved him in return, she thought as they walked out into the inner courtyard. How much easier everything would be then. Life here, she thought, was like balancing on the head of a pin. Catherine knew she could not keep up this dangerous game forever. One wrong move and she would fall, losing everything.

❖

As they left the chapel, Archbishop Cranmer, Thomas Seymour and Thomas Wriothesley walked together a few paces behind the current and former queens. It was quite a sight to behold. The women's arms were linked, their heads lowered in some private conversation only the two of them could share.

The king walked with a pronounced limp, well ahead of the women, beside Norfolk and his son Henry. The Howard men were trying to do damage control, since the king and queen were still obviously estranged. The current state of things pleased Cranmer enormously. He had been prepared to do battle with the Catholics for the sake of the Reformation, but this young, foolish girl was taking care of it for him. To top it all off, the Lassells wench was an extraordinary find, as motivated by envy as she was by her faith.

Cranmer bit his lower lip to hide a smile and steepled his hands piously as Thomas Seymour droned on about the hunt that would take place later that afternoon. *Poor, proud Henry*, Cranmer thought, as the king waddled like a velvet-clad Christmas goose. The "hunt" that Seymour spoke of was a bastardized version of the sport that Henry had loved in his youth and barely required any physical activity. But it was fitting, he thought, since Henry did not work hard for anything anymore. He waited for everything to be brought to him. Food. Wives. The heads of his enemies.

And, less welcome, perhaps, some damning information about the queen, which Cranmer intended to personally deliver.

He pushed away a nagging sensation of guilt. Later, he would pray for forgiveness from Almighty God, but right now, he was convinced that, in some things, the ends did well justify the means.

❖

The king had not called for Anne Basset for a long time, yet she could not resist going to the royal bedchamber after prayer when he did. She knew that the potential benefit outweighed any insult to the queen if the infidelity were discovered. Her ambitious mother reminded her daily that she was first a subject of His Majesty and then a maid of honor to the queen, an appointment that she had sought from Anne of Cleves but at last received when Catherine became queen. Besides, did not all kings have lovers? The pressures upon a sovereign were vast and many. How could the queen be expected to soothe all of them by herself?

Had Catherine not, in essence, done the very same thing to poor Anne of Cleves?

Anne lingered at the foot of the king's carved poster bed as he lay watching her like a massive creature beneath the bedcovers, his bare leg propped on a velvet tasseled pillow. Everyone at court knew that the ulcer on his calf must be kept open and draining to prevent further swelling and infection, so no one remarked at the sight or the horrendous stench, which not even liberal doses of musk and ambergris could mask.

A small fire blazed in the hearth beside her as Anne dropped her white muslin dressing gown seductively to the floor, then advanced toward the king, as she had done before.

❖

Later that afternoon, everyone sat tightly packed in the little timber-framed gallery above the brick building with the open gallery for observing the hunt, constructed in the vast, lush park. The yard below, enclosed by nets, was strewn with hay, and the air was full of the sour, stifling stench of perspiration and noxious perfume.

Catherine wanted to be anywhere but here. Yet Henry finally looked happy, and the angry glares from her uncle had ceased after the king had taken Catherine's hand and dotted her cheek with kisses.

She must tolerate everything to win back his favor.

The king's requested companion for today was Thomas Culpeper, and he stood beside him at the ready. Both had gilded crossbows in hand, stamped with the royal arms. Thomas was relieved to have been asked to hunt with Henry, even in this sham of the sport. There was danger in the king's waning interest in anyone, especially the queen and himself.

As the unsuspecting deer were driven into the pen below, Catherine turned away. She was sickened by the sport, which amounted to little more than a slaughter with refreshments. Henry shot an arrow, then another. The first deer fell, then another and another. The crowd of courtiers applauded. Henry turned to acknowledge them with a proud smile and a regal little wave.

Catherine saw his gaze linger just an instant too long on Anne Basset.

So that was why she had not had a conjugal visit from her husband. Of course. She glanced again at Thomas, whose weapon was trained on one of the larger animals below. Catherine was surprised when she saw him adjust his bow before he released his arrow. It was a slight movement, but it was enough so that the arrow missed its target. While she knew how much he enjoyed the challenge of hunting, Thomas was never one to take advantage of unfair circumstances.

It was a fact that made her love him all the more.

Suddenly Henry faltered. His bow clattered to the ground and he staggered back. Thomas cast his own bow to the ground and caught the king in a powerful hold. Murmurs and whispers rose as Thomas helped the king back to his seat, and Catherine knelt before him, concern in her eyes. When she touched his face, it was blazing hot. He was clearly burning with fever.

"Hal, what is it? Are you all right?"

"I am perfectly fine. Stop fussing over me, you witless girl, just because you know no other way to make amends!" he growled, his temper flaring as he swatted her hand until she drew it away and sank back.

"Forgive me; I was only trying to—"

"We must call for your physician, sire," Thomas interjected as he pressed a gentle hand onto the king's shoulder.

Henry's angry gaze descended full force on Thomas, his eyes glazed with sudden rage. "And what the devil are *you* droning on about, Culpeper? Is there truly no one with more than half a brain whom I can rely upon around here? Unhand me, boy! I am perfectly fine."

The concerned whispers around them fell away, and no one dared utter another sound.

"Perhaps you should lie down, at least. It is so warm out," Catherine tried to suggest in a soft, wifely tone of concern.

"And why is that? So everyone can say that King Henry is too old and fat even to hunt penned prey? Laugh at me, will you? I think not!"

His voice boomed and his fists were curled tightly with pent-up anger. Then, before Catherine could speak another word, Henry slumped back in his grand carved chair and his eyes rolled to a close.

When everyone lunged toward the king, it was unclear whether or not Henry VIII was dead.

Not long afterward, Catherine listened to the king's physician, her arms wrapped tightly around herself, in the privy chamber. She tried desperately to make sense of all the information as a contingent of the king's guard blocked her entry to the bedchamber. His Majesty was gravely ill, owing to the ulcer on his leg, the physician calmly explained. In spite of their medical interventions, the wound was clogged. They were attempting, once again, to drain the buildup of fluid in order to spare his life, but the king's condition was very weak. He had developed a fever that would likely kill him if it did not break soon.

Thomas stood beside Catherine, careful not to touch her, but having him there with her as a silent support was a great comfort. A group of courtiers stood around them.

"I must go to him," Catherine insisted.

"His Majesty does not wish for Your Grace's company just now," the physician gently informed her.

"But I am his wife—his queen!"

"He is well aware of who you are. However, the king wishes you not to see him in his condition."

"But he should not be alone!" Catherine felt surprisingly panicked. Even after their quarrel, she still cared about him.

"His Majesty is not alone. The princess of Cleves is with him," the physician explained.

His words were a blow to her pride. Cranmer stood behind the physician, gazing at her with contempt. Her uncle was nowhere to be seen, and there were no other Howards nearby to support her. Once again, she was on her own.

"His current queen should be with him when he is ill, not his former one," Catherine countered stubbornly.

"Perhaps there is more between them than any of us have guessed," Cranmer commented. The strange tone in his voice brought Catherine a shiver, and she wrapped her arms more tightly around herself.

"His Majesty shall send for you when he is ready to receive you," the physician promised, his gaze sliding back and forth between the archbishop and the queen.

Catherine had no choice but to relent. She turned away and the king's two nieces followed her. She did not want their company, but that mattered little. Nothing she wanted had ever mattered.

Catherine did not go to dinner with the rest of the court. She could not bear to see Anne Basset or Anne of Cleves and force herself to be pleasant to either of them. Nor could she imagine her uncle's fury at how she had driven the king to publicly humiliate her at the hunt when she was supposed to be securing his heart once again for the sake of the family.

Everything seemed off somehow, as if the balance of power had shifted. Catherine felt like one of those poor penned deer now, her senses heightened, though she knew there was no way out. She was so preoccupied by her thoughts that she did not see Francis Dereham waiting for her in the small alcove beside her bedchamber as she swept through, skirts rustling. His hand clamped onto her arm over her puffed velvet sleeve.

"We must speak privately," he urged in a cool tone.

She met his expression head-on. "Privately, we have nothing to speak about."

"I am told the king's end is drawing very near."

"You were told wrong, sir. He will recover."

"And if he does not?"

"I'll not think of that."

"Yet *I* think of it every waking moment. I think of us being man and wife, as we should have been all along." He released his tight grip and ran his fingers up the line of her arm to the curve of her neck, where they stilled.

"The same warm, silken flesh that I remember," he whispered into her ear.

Suddenly, Francis was jerked from behind and thrown against the wall with such tremendous force that Catherine heard the wood paneling crack. She looked up with a start to see Thomas Culpeper looming, taut and angry, over Francis like a raging bull. His face was bloodred, his nostrils flaring, and his fists were wound tight as he pummeled him. Francis coiled against him in self-defense, but Thomas was too powerful, too full of rage. He drew the stunned secretary up by the collar and struck him again with such force that Catherine heard a crack as she saw a ribbon of blood spout from his nose.

Mary Lassells and Jane Boleyn dashed forward to help Catherine draw Culpeper off.

"Thomas, stop! Please, I bid you, stop!" Catherine pleaded, horrified by the sight of so much blood.

Even the three of them together could not tear him away from Dereham, who slumped like a rag doll in Thomas's viselike grip.

"Thomas, stop. For me," Catherine urged again.

Thomas's fist was halted by her plea, inches from Dereham's blood-streaked face. A moment later, his tense body slackened. He released his grip and Francis crumpled to the floor. Thomas's chest was still heaving as he growled, low and menacingly,

"And if you *ever* touch her again, trust me, next time I will finish the job."

Mary and Jane helped Francis struggle to his feet as Catherine went to Thomas. She sank against his chest and he wrapped her tightly in his arms, her judgement abandoned in the moment.

"I would have killed him."

"I know," she murmured, feeling the crash of his heart against her temple.

"I am not just talking about that silly country fool. I am also talking about the king, who publicly humiliated the woman I love."

Catherine's heart skipped a beat. "I am his wife. He can speak to me as he chooses," she acknowledged sadly, nestling deeper into the fleeting protection of Thomas's powerful arms.

"That does not matter. I would kill anyone who ever harmed you," he declared.

❖

As she hovered over a wounded, quivering Dereham, Mary Lassells watched the others clean his face with cool water. *Finally*, she thought. Yes, it was time. Patience truly yielded the sweetest rewards. At last, there were enough witnesses to support the allegations she was about to make. It was time to write to her brother, John, to implement their plan. This was her moment. There would be no turning back from what she was about to do. There would be no stopping her from what the Lord would have her do.

❖

In a fever-induced kaleidoscope of sounds, images and excruciating pain, Henry lay motionless in his grand bed, dreaming. Faces were dancing across his mind as in a puppet show. Arthur . . . Nan . . . sweet Jane . . . Wolsey . . . Catherine . . . even Cromwell. So many, many losses. *Poor, dear Cromwell. What a fool I was*, he thought, as the ghostly images hauntingly smiled. A hand reached out through time and beyond his dream. He knew it was Cromwell's hand. *How did I ever allow it? Why did I ever believe Norfolk and Gardiner . . . How did I allow Catherine's uncle to convince me with accusations that could only ever have been false?* The same Catherine who argued against his decisions and tried to change his mind, filling his head with twisted facts, just as Norfolk had done. Cromwell had only ever been a faithful servant and a trusted friend, a man who would be here now if only . . .

Opening his eyes was a struggle, like trying to rise up through miles of mossy water.

"Your Majesty . . . sire . . . can you hear me?"

The sound of his physician's voice, deep and filled with concern, called to Henry through the water, and he tried again to move toward the surface. With great effort, he opened his eyes. Physicians and his gentlemen-of-the-bedchamber formed a ring at the base of his grand bed in the deep, amber candlelight.

"Your Majesty has been very ill, but there is improvement."

"How long have I been asleep?" he rasped.

"Two days, sire. The queen waits for you in your outer chamber. She has been there nearly this entire time. May I call her in?"

Cromwell's sad face floated in his mind.

"No, I do not wish to see her."

"What shall I tell her?"

"I care not what you tell her. Now leave me to my dreams and my memories," Henry growled.

The malaise, like the infection, lasted a fortnight.

Henry wallowed in his nostalgia, guilt and regret, refusing to let go of any of it, or to see Catherine. He could not bear to let her see him like this, or allow her to try to cheer him. He did not want to be rescued.

There were no banquets, masques, music or dancing in the days that followed. There was only the quiet desperation of the king's heart. He knew that once he returned from the past, he would have to deal with the silent movement of religious factions, whores, a queen and a former queen, so many of whom were preparing for someone else's downfall. The only question was, Whose downfall would come next?

Chapter Nineteen

*W*ith the crispness of autumn came a great renewal. Henry's health crisis had been averted. He had returned to Catherine's bed and accepted her affection, effectively ending their estrangement. When her flux did not come, she announced to Henry, with relief, that she might be pregnant at last. Norfolk was pleased with her, Francis avoided her, and Jane sympathized with Catherine enough to pass notes between her and Thomas and arrange fleeting meetings for them. Jane had been assured that their friendship was chaste and that his occasional company had cheered and strengthened her through Henry's rather frightening alteration.

Jane watched them from a distance. She saw them embrace and murmur a few words of greeting in the safe harbor of the orchard before they slipped away to be alone together. She lingered a moment beside the splashing fountain and a sentry line of emerald topiary trees. She was right to help them, whatever it would mean. She wanted to make amends for her bitter implication of her own husband in Anne Boleyn's infidelities and help the new queen by being a loyal friend.

Poor Catherine was so naive, Jane thought. Everywhere she

turned there was a threat to the queen. Cranmer, who was still associated with her family's enemy, Cromwell; Wriothesley, who was allied with Cranmer; even Anne Basset, who would take her place in a heartbeat. Catherine trusted too easily and forgave too quickly. But, oddly enough, Jane trusted Thomas Culpeper because Catherine trusted him. She saw his pain and longing for her, which might have driven other men to jealous acts of betrayal. But not Thomas. She was not certain whether she was courting disaster by allowing Catherine to meet with him, but if she could make amends this way for her own sins, it would be worth it.

As she turned to leave the fountain, full of renewed conviction, Jane ran headlong into stony-faced Archbishop Cranmer.

"Why, my lady Rochford, what a pleasant surprise to see you. Whatever brought you to such a distant spot, alone, today?" he coldly asked, intent, she could see, upon waiting for a reply.

✼

They walked together deep within the orchard amid the sweet fragrance of apple blossoms and the safety of lush trees. Thomas took Catherine's hand, so warm and reassuring against his own fingers. She felt her breathing slow, and warmth spread through her at his touch. The connection between them was everything.

"So then," he finally asked. "Is it true this time?"

She knew what he meant without elaboration, and she looked away. "No. But, God help me, I wish it were now. Henry is so unhappy with me." Once again, her pregnancy had proven to be a false alarm.

"How can that be? You are his perfect queen."

"I used to be. But I have made too many mistakes."

"Were those not all before you married?" he asked, trying to ease her guilt.

She paused and touched a tree branch. "That will matter little to him once he discovers them. And the funny thing is, I do care for him. I worry about his health. He has such problems with his leg, and he insists upon pretending he does not. He dwells too much on his youth, I fear."

Thomas was looking at her intensely. "I understand a man's longing for something he cherished but can no longer have. Give him time, my love. He will have no choice but to grow accustomed to how things are, as I have done."

Thomas raised her hand to his lips and kissed the knuckles just above her wedding band. "He is fortunate that you remain true to him."

"That is not true of my heart," she said, surprising him with her personal revelation.

They walked with their hands linked as far as the aviary, which they did each time they stole a few private moments together. That and a few kisses were the only physical connection either of them allowed since she had become another man's wife. Catherine claimed that so long as they were not lovers, she was remaining faithful to Henry. She said it with such conviction that he had even convinced himself of it, though he knew he was dangerously indulging in her naïveté.

Thomas fell silent as they walked back toward the grand brick palace, which slowly slipped into view before them. Luckily, the path seemed to be free of other courtiers.

So it was a shock when they turned a corner to the aviary and saw the king, Charles Brandon and Edward Seymour strolling directly toward them.

❖

Henry smiled broadly as he saw Thomas Culpeper walking alone toward him, Catherine having escaped only a moment before. "You are always so elusive lately, Tom," he said. "I have not seen you anywhere since yesterday. No doubt you have some great tale with which to regale your king."

Henry wrapped an arm around Thomas's broad shoulders and, as always, tried not to look too closely at his perfect face. Instead, he tried to coax some fun out of the boy, who was more like a brooding poet now than the lighthearted womanizer he once had been.

"Come walk with us. My physician says a bit of exercise and a dose of sunshine will do me good."

Henry watched Thomas glance behind his shoulder as something moved near the aviary. He heard the sound himself but saw nothing. He smelled a strikingly familiar scent then, something wholly female, but he could not place it.

"Come along, and spare not a single detail." He kept his arm across Thomas's shoulders. "So, how do you find the little Basset wench these days?"

"Anne?" Thomas asked in surprise.

Henry chuckled. "I've been done with her for days. No, I meant the younger one, Katherine. Is that not her name?"

"Is she at court as well?" Thomas asked, seeming to sidestep the question.

"Lurking about. I was thinking of taking her with us when we leave for York tomorrow."

Henry was surprised at Thomas's hesitation. Culpeper had always encouraged a good time.

"What of the queen?" Thomas asked.

"My wife will not accompany me this time. She may be with child at last, and since she is not quite the fertile mare I had hoped, no chances can be taken."

"I see," Thomas said thoughtfully.

Henry narrowed his eyes in suspicion, his expression devoid

of his customary, carefree smile. "You disapprove of me with the younger Mistress Basset?"

They were strolling a pace beyond the others, and as they reached one of the many grand splashing stone fountains, Henry sank onto the curved edge and motioned for Thomas to join him.

"Such a thing is not for me to say," Thomas replied evasively.

"That is true, unless I ask you, and I have asked. Your hesitation these past few months during our more frank discourses troubles me, Thomas. You know I value honesty in you."

Henry saw Thomas grimace, as if he had been struck by something sharp. He knew the boy was keeping something from his king. Henry had already asked Brandon and Seymour for details, but only Wriothesley's response suggested something untoward. Perhaps there was a forbidden dalliance. *Someone's mother? Someone's wife?* Henry thought with a twisted smile. Ah, well, nothing he had not enjoyed in his own active youth. Whoever it was, he would hear about it sooner or later. He always did.

"Never mind for now. Let us go to dinner. That, at least, is one pleasure we can still enjoy together," Henry good-naturedly teased. "Besides, I have not seen the queen yet today, and after last night, I should inquire after her health. I used her pretty well for a woman carrying a royal child. I am thankful she is young and strong enough to take the full weight of her king."

Culpeper shrank back, which surprised Henry. Could this handsome youth who had such a way with women have been tamed by one who had finally reached his heart? Henry wondered.

※

The queen's household gathered in velvet cloaks and hats on the brick-lined courtyard as a cool autumn wind blew to bid the king farewell. Henry's courtiers were already assembled on horseback or in litters, while the king, who had privately used a stepladder to mount his horse, advanced on a silver-studded saddle on his elegant Spanish jennet. He held the reins tight with black kid gloves. When he nodded to her, Catherine moved nearer and held up her hand. Henry extended his own.

"I will miss you," she said.

She knew he still was not entirely well. But he tried hard to maintain a front, ruled by pride rather than sense.

"Take care of your health," he replied, smiling down at her. "Give me a fine, strong son this time."

"I shall do my best," she replied, knowing that she was not with child. She had not been able to bring herself to tell him.

She caught sight of Thomas then on a large black bay, a few paces behind the king. She could tell, as he looked away, that he was trying very hard not to be a part of their royal farewell. But she maintained her gaze and he turned irresistibly toward her, their eyes meeting. The pain that shot through her was all too familiar now. As her eyes misted over with tears she looked quickly away, and Henry chuckled at her.

"Dear sweetheart," Henry said gently, leaning down slightly. "You are ever my rose with no thorns, aren't you?"

Without saying more, he raised his gloved hand and signaled, with kingly authority, to the trumpeters, who let loose a fanfare of music. The courtiers were gone then in a blaze of horses, flying banners and ribald male laughter.

Chapter Twenty

November 1, 1541
York, England

 he course of the royal journey took the king's entourage from Doncaster to Pontefract, and to York for All Saints' Day. Meanwhile, Catherine remained at Hampton Court. By the end of the monthlong separation, the king was anxious to return to his wife. Henry missed her and longed for her, despite the fact that there was no royal child. But he had decided that she was young and strong enough to invest hope in, so long as he returned speedily to her bed.

The memory of her sweet, warm and willing body played across his mind as he strode toward the great stone cathedral on a hilltop in York in a costume of luxurious gold and silver. He was surrounded by an elegantly clad group of his courtiers, including Charles Brandon and Thomas Culpeper. Trumpeters, drummers, the peal of bells and the cheers from the surging crowd of townspeople marked their arrival with great fanfare.

Moments later, inside the vaulted chapel that smelled heavily of beeswax and incense, Henry sank into a pew with the others behind him. It was then that he saw the letter addressed to "Your Majesty," sealed with a stamp of red wax, tucked into the corner of the pew.

He would have disregarded it, but then he saw that the seal belonged to Cranmer.

As the Archbishop of York moved toward the altar, Henry pushed his thumb beneath the wax and cracked the seal. In his mind, Cranmer was indelibly linked with Cromwell, whom he desperately missed. Whatever Cranmer had to say, he would listen. Henry scanned the page as the archbishop began to speak.

The words, printed in a bold, black script, were a confusing jumble at first: *warning . . . the queen . . . promiscuous past . . . proof . . . evidence . . . account given to the privy counsel.*

Henry squeezed his eyes shut, trying to make sense of the slander. He opened them again, struggling to push back the bile and anger rushing up his throat as he finished reading the indictment. Someone had come forward, Cranmer wrote, with grave concern for the king. A man named John Lassells had brought proof to the counsel that the queen had not been pure when they married and had actually been betrothed to another. Norfolk and Lady Rochford had a hand in maintaining the ruse since her arrival at court.

Not Catherine . . . not my rose . . .

Henry could not catch his breath. There was a lump of fury and pure disbelief in his throat. There must be some mistake. People came to the privy counsel every month to slander someone in his court for personal gain. But why would Cranmer want to implicate his wife . . . his love? Henry's anger spun far beyond his control, and dark thoughts swirled like a tempest as a rich, sobering chant echoed from the gallery above and through the chapel nave.

Henry sat motionless, stunned.

Catherine . . . Jésu! Not another Howard wife to betray me.

By the time the service was over and he went back into the street, his shock had become full-blown rage. Today his leg was aching. Now so, too, was his heart. He had not trusted Cromwell and Cranmer before, and he regretted it every single day. But he had been given a chance to make amends. He would not make the mistake of doubting them again. For Catherine to have lied to him about her past, after he had so willingly trusted her, was unforgivable. Norfolk had presented her to him as a virgin, and she had perfected the ruse on their wedding night. Lady Rochford had obviously assisted her, since the two of them were always thick as thieves. As he had feared, Catherine had made of him a cuckold and a fool.

One thing Henry could not abide was being deceived. Especially by a woman he loved.

He wanted to kill the vile bastard who had defiled his wife. His eyes darted among the faces of his courtiers and friends. He was relieved when he realized that the culprit was not likely among them, since he had married her so soon after she had come to court.

. . . Or was he?

After the service, once he was safe within the confines of his privy chamber, he faced Charles Brandon, Thomas Wriothesley, Edward Seymour and Thomas Culpeper, some of his greatest intimates. Henry's heart was shattered, as well as his senses. In his mind, their concerned expressions became condescending sneers, mocking him for taking a fifth wife. And another Howard.

"Did you all know about this?" He waved Cranmer's letter at them. The sound of his deep voice rolled like thunder through the cavernous hall. "Which of you knew the queen had made a fool of me before we married? Who? You, Brandon? My oldest and closest friend, my brother? Did you know she'd had a lover?"

"No, sire. I did not know," he lied.

"Wriothesley?" He polled them one at a time, his bejeweled hands on his wide hips in tight, bloodless fists, his porcine face crimson with fury.

"I did not," Wriothesley replied, wisely avoiding the truth as well.

"Seymour?"

Edward Seymour hesitated before answering. "In truth, there was the odd rumor, Your Majesty, but no one knew for certain."

"And no one thought to tell *me* of a damning rumor?" His voice boomed again. "Culpeper, you have always been forthright with me. Did you not think to tell me about this?"

"Spreading a rumor about your queen would have been treasonous at best, Your Majesty."

"Yet it is more than a rumor. Proof was brought before you and the rest of the privy counsel! So then, who is the vile dog who dared deflower a maiden intended for the King of England?" he demanded as he limped the length of the room. Everyone else remained absolutely motionless. Only when the king's back was turned did they dare to exchange quick glances.

"Whoever he was, I swear by all that is holy, I shall tear off his head and stick it on a pike myself on Tower Bridge!"

Henry grunted as he limped back and forth, hands still on his hips. "Give me his name, Brandon! I need a name. I will know everything, by God!"

"The informer, Master Lassells, is the brother of one of the queen's companions from Horsham. I believe the gentleman was a page in the employ of the dowager duchess," Brandon replied.

"His name, Brandon! Give me a name!"

"Francis Dereham, sire."

"The queen's private secretary?"

"The same, sire."

Henry slapped his forehead and turned away. He felt his lip quiver as he pressed back tears of shock. The betrayal was like a dagger.

"We were recently told that their acts of intercourse were witnessed by several others besides Mistress Lassells at Horsham, Your Majesty," Brandon added.

"Send word to Hampton Court that Dereham is to be taken to the Tower at once."

"Your Majesty, if I may . . ." said Thomas Culpeper. "As I understand it, no one claims the queen betrayed you once you were married."

"She was betrothed to Dereham before the marriage, Thomas," Wriothesley pointed out, "which is actually worse."

Henry turned around very slowly. He was unable to see through his furious tears, though he did not care. "There was a-a-an," he sputtered in disbelief, "an actual contract between them?"

"That is what Master Lassells has stated to the counsel, sire," Brandon cautiously confirmed.

"All the saints in heaven!" Henry sobbed as openly as a child, surrendering his face to his hands. "How is it possible that I could have such great misfortune with every one of my wives?"

"Perhaps, sire—" Seymour cautiously dared, hoping to calm him.

"Silence! All of you! You all encouraged the marriage, except for Cranmer and my poor friend Cromwell! There is blood on all of your hands! Bring me a sword, Thomas, and I will ride to Hampton Court right now. Bring me a sword, I say!"

Each of the men exchanged worried glances, then averted their eyes, knowing only too well to what this mood could swiftly lead.

"Your Majesty," Brandon tried, stepping forward. "Surely you understand that you cannot kill her yourself."

"Why not, when she has already killed me?" the king bellowed in anger.

"Perhaps you should hear her out once you have regained your composure."

"To what end?" He was incredulous. "So she can convince me of more lies? No. If I go to Hampton Court, it will be to cut out her heart with that dagger at your hip, just the way mine has been taken from me!"

Henry reached for the jeweled dagger in the hilt at Brandon's waist, but Brandon was quicker, covering it with his hand. "Sire, no, I urge you to wait. The truth will come out eventually, and she will be punished without your raising your own hand. Please, Henry," he added in a lower, more intimate tone. "Mary would say the same. You know that is true."

The reference to his most beloved sister was Henry's undoing, and a new wellspring of tears flooded his swollen cheeks as he collapsed onto an upholstered chair. He surrendered his face to his hands once again and began to shake his head.

"Why? I gave her everything. I gave her my heart, my life . . . I gave her England!"

None of the men dared to answer him; though Henry did not expect them to, because there was no answer he would ever accept.

This was Catherine's fault. His rose was a choking weed. She did not deserve Hal's love or forgiveness. The devil could decide what to do with her, because Henry VIII no longer cared.

❖

Catherine.

Thomas was filled with fear for her. She had been so noble and so strong. But he had been a part of this complex court long enough to know what would come next if he did not find some way to stop it. Catherine was in grave danger, and she would have no way of knowing until it was too late. For now, Henry still did not know about them, and Thomas would be able to use that to their advantage.

But time was of the essence.

Thomas thought quickly of whom he might trust to get a word

of warning to her so she would not be forced to make a confession. He had seen Henry's face, and he knew he would not forgive her if she confessed to sleeping with Francis Dereham . . . or anyone else, for that matter.

Hampton Court was at least a full day's ride away, and anyone of low stature who left for the queen's court would be suspected, since there was no innocent reason they would ever journey alone. Thomas paced his room. Much of this was his fault. Perhaps he should admit that to Henry in order to deflect some of the punishment from Catherine. But admitting his guilt now could only make things worse for her, because Henry had trusted Thomas as well.

He knew there was only one way to get word to the queen. He would be risking her life and his own. Everything hinged on his decision, but there was no turning back now for either of them.

WINTER

The Final Season

"Short is the joy that guilty pleasure brings."
—Euripides

Chapter Twenty-one

December 5, 1541
Hampton Court, Richmond

*T*homas Wriothesley was shown into the queen's privy chamber as Catherine sat among her ladies, embroidering the image of a thornless rose onto a new cambric nightshirt for Henry. In the corner, near the fire, a young boy played a tune on the flute as the women talked softly amongst themselves.

Seeing stern-faced Wriothesley, Jane glanced over at Catherine with an expression of concern. There was no solicitous smile of greeting on his face. He was an intimidating figure, big and barrel-chested, dressed in black velvet with a rich ermine collar. The hat he wore accentuated his long, thin nose and high, glistening forehead. It was not Wriothesley's custom to pay a sudden call upon the queen, most certainly not unannounced like this, surrounded by a contingent of stone-faced yeomen of the king's guard.

"Your Grace," he said with perfunctory courtesy as he swept into a polite but controlled bow.

Catherine laid down her embroidery. "Sir?"

"Alas, there is no more time for music," he dryly announced.

One of the guards seized the boy, whose flute clattered to the floor as he was led by the arm out of the room. The whispers from her ladies rose around them.

"What is the meaning of this?" Catherine asked, feeling a mix of panic and indignation.

"I am afraid Your Grace is being placed under house arrest," Wriothesley confirmed.

"Arrest?" Jane croaked as she sprang to her feet. "By whose command?"

"The king's command, as are you, my lady Rochford."

"But why? What has Her Grace done but be a good wife to His Majesty?" Jane asked with as much indignation as Catherine felt.

Catherine slowly came to her feet, although her legs were trembling. Her mouth had gone very dry. Anne Boleyn. Cromwell. The clerics . . . The old Countess of Salisbury.

"You have disgraced His Majesty with your behavior, and you conspired to keep him ignorant of it in order that he might marry you," he announced, before adding with a sneer, "Your Grace should have known better from your cousin's example."

"But how am I involved?" Jane asked.

Catherine saw the panic on Jane's face, but she was not angry that Jane was trying to save herself. She knew how deeply her friend had been caught up in the last scandal with a queen, and she could not now begrudge Jane her life.

"You have been the queen's greatest confidante at court, have you not?" Wriothesley said. The tone of his question was glacial and his eyes held no emotion.

Jane lifted her chin defiantly in response. "I have."

Catherine quickly came to her aid. "My lady Rochford knew nothing. You cannot blame her for my indiscretion."

"It has been testified to that those words are inaccurate. Perhaps she cannot be blamed for your indiscretion, but she shall pay a harsh penalty for facilitating it."

Catherine began to sob now, the tight rein she had held on her life and her heart, everything her family had planned for—all of the expectation and pressure—unraveled in that moment like a skein of yarn.

"Leave her out of this, I beg you! My mistakes and decisions were totally my own!"

"Did you know of her youthful affair with Master Dereham, who was brought by her own grandmother to serve in the king's household, right under his nose?"

Jane bravely responded, "I was unaware, in the beginning, of the extent of their relationship, sir, until I overheard Mistress Lassells speaking with Mistress Tilney about Master Dereham's successful plan to blackmail the queen in order to have her affection returned to him."

"There is one more complication," Wriothesley said, thrusting a letter toward Jane. "Apparently, Master Culpeper gambled that I would be a trustworthy messenger, since we served the king side by side for so long. We shared a wench or two in our time, and he knew I was coming this way. The words, while rather obtuse, urge Her Grace to maintain her silence. You must have drawn Culpeper into your web of deception as well. How deeply remains to be seen. But the truth does have a way, like cream, of rising to the top."

Dear God, no, she thought wildly, racked with sobs. Catherine could not bear to think of Thomas implicated in this scandal. She remembered how those around Anne Boleyn had fallen with her. She felt the darkness of the past rising, uniting her destiny with Queen Anne's. Her dreams really had been premonitions.

If only she could see Henry, make him look into her eyes so he could see that, while she had made a foolish, adolescent mistake with Francis, and perhaps kissed Thomas after their marriage, she had never done anything more. She had never been unfaithful to him. She was so overwrought and fearful, she failed to attend to the warning in Thomas's desperately sent message, the one that would now cost him so much.

"It was a youthful folly, a horrid mistake!" Catherine confessed, weeping as she gazed up at Wriothesley with doleful, pleading eyes. "There must be something I can do! Please tell me, my lord, what am I to do?"

"Dereham has been arrested, so I know not what you may do now. The wheels are in motion already. Perhaps be thankful that, for the time being, you are only under house arrest." He turned to leave, then paused and turned back. The silver baldric across his shoulders glittered in the sunshine through the paned windows. The glacial stare had not left his face. "Ah, there is one thing."

"Anything," Catherine said desperately.

"Pray that His Majesty has developed a more forgiving heart over the last years when it comes to the fidelity of his queen," he said.

❖

Thomas found a broken hulk of a man hunched over a polished oak table as he walked into the king's drafty bedchamber the next morning. At first, Henry had not acknowledged any of his gentlemen, and the light meal before him had gone untouched. The ewer of wine beside it was still full. But suddenly, as if sensing a friendly soul, Henry glanced up. His eyes were glazed, bloodshot and unfocused, and his face was blotched red.

"Ah, Tom, my old friend. Please."

Thomas advanced cautiously as Henry turned to gaze out the window at the cold winter landscape. "You, of all the men at my court, know about women. Once, I might have asked Brandon what to do, but he is too old now to be of help to me in a matter like this."

Thomas felt guilty for his role in the king's pain. But he kept his demeanor calm.

"I shall do what I can, sire."

"Can you make lies into truths for me, Tom? Or make the past insignificant to a man's heart?"

"Would that I could," he answered honestly. "It does seem to me, though, that no one is ever completely what they seem. Not even the two of us."

Henry looked back up at him again, and it took all of Thomas's strength not to look away. "You knew about the queen?"

"Only the court gossip. Not the story."

Henry's eyes brightened with another flurry of tears. "She was not what she seemed. Not an innocent. She had a lover."

Thomas could sympathize with the king. He had felt the same way when he had found out about Dereham. "I would like to believe we all have the power to change, that a great love can alter each of us, that none of us arc the sum total of our past. I know that, in my life, I have been permanently changed by the love of a woman."

Tears ran down Henry's bloated cheeks in a steady stream, catching in his beard as his chin quivered. "But I am the King of England."

"Are you not a man first, sire? Will you not regret it for the rest of your days if you do not give Her Grace the opportunity to prove that the boy who came into her life before you ceased to matter once she met you?"

Their eyes locked and Thomas felt a shiver of guilt, but he shoved it aside and maintained his confident exterior. Everything in the world depended on it.

"You risk a great deal speaking to me this way," the king warned.

"Have you not always urged me to do so?" Thomas countered.

"I have."

"Then I urge you to give Her Grace a chance to prove she is the woman you believed her to be. You had planned to reunite with your wife at Hampton Court. Go ahead with your plan. See her, speak with her. Then decide. That, at least, is what I would do—if she were my wife."

He was tormented by his last words, which only reminded him of what Catherine could never be. But if he could save her through his unlikely and enduring friendship with the king, he would do it.

Henry ran a hand behind his neck and let out a great sigh. "You're right, as always, Tom. I will see her once the anger in my heart fades." He looked up now, tears still in his blue eyes. "She really is my rose with no thorns. Perhaps a childish indiscretion long ago is not so horrendous. Perhaps allowances could be made for that. Since there was a betrothal, it is likely that my marriage to her will be declared null after Dereham confirms the story. But things with the princess of Cleves ended well enough. Perhaps this, too, will be the case for Catherine and me."

Finally, a smile turned up the corners of Henry's small mouth. And, for the first time in a long while, Thomas dared to allow himself a spark of hope that, by some miracle, they might be together after all.

"Your Majesty is a benevolent man," Thomas said, bowing to the king.

"You know very well that I am nothing of the sort. They call me a butcher now, wild and unpredictable in my old age."

"Your Majesty is still full of enough youth and vigor to prove them all wrong."

"If that is what I decide to do about her," the king added.

"Of course, sire," Thomas said. "If that is what you decide to do."

❖

For five long days after he arrived at Hampton Court, Henry did not see Catherine nor speak to her. She was, however, given a daily report on the parade of women he invited to dine with him or stroll with him in the gardens. She was being advised by his counselors to acknowledge her precontract with Francis Dereham and allow an annulment to move forward. Several members suggested that the queen be sent quietly to a convent. It could be much worse, Jane observed, reminding her of how things had ended for Anne Boleyn.

As if Catherine needed the reminder.

Perhaps, after a time, once things had died down and Henry had replaced her, she could petition him for a situation like Anne of Cleves's, and even seek out a second marriage. But she must be patient, Jane said, and they both must pray.

As much as Catherine longed to go and plead for his understanding and mercy, her greatest hope was in remaining silent and out of sight to allow his rage to cool.

As light snowflakes fluttered past her leaded windowpanes, she at last received a visitor. Hearing Jane go to the door, Catherine sprang from her chair, full of renewed hope. *At last*, she thought. *At last, I am saved!*

Her visitor, however, was not the king. . . .

Chapter Twenty-two

✣

December 6, 1541
Hampton Court, Richmond

*I*n his severe black cape and hat with lappets over his ears, his craggy face devoid of emotion, Archbishop Cranmer stalked forward, pushing past Catherine as if she were of little consequence. Behind him was his personal secretary, who sat down at the queen's writing desk. He drew forth a sheet of vellum, a pen and a pot of ink from the walnut-and-leather writing box he had brought along.

"Master Dereham has confessed to everything, madam. Now it is your turn, so you might as well take a seat. It is going to be a long afternoon."

Panic coursed through Catherine like a white-hot wave, and for a moment she could not move. She knew instantly that whatever she said could be used against her.

"I said sit down, Lady Catherine," Cranmer demanded.

The alteration in title was a direct hit. Still, as a new flurry of bitter tears flooded her face, she could not prevent a show of pride. "I am your queen, my lord archbishop."

"That is incorrect. You forfeited your honor, so you have surrendered your rights as queen."

His tone was cruel, exacting. She felt Jane hovering behind her, and if she had turned around to look at her, she would have seen her panic mirrored in her friend's expression. The secretary at the desk lowered his head and began to scratch swirls of ink onto the open sheet of vellum.

"During his questioning, my lady, Master Dereham confessed many interesting things," Cranmer began.

"Perhaps he made them up under duress," Catherine said quickly.

"There was proof shown of your marital precontract—a scarf you made for him with your initials entwined. The only hope you have is to confess the truth."

"Do not do it," Jane urged in a whisper from behind her, suddenly overwhelmed by fear. "I am not certain that we can trust in the king's mercy. His fury and wounded heart could overtake everything else, as it did with your cousin Anne Boleyn."

"Confess everything, my lady Catherine, and there may be mercy for you. Say nothing, and there is a well-worn block on Tower Green at the ready."

She gasped, fingers splayed across her mouth. "Hal would not dare. He loves me."

"A man betrayed is not a man to be trusted," Cranmer said with a sneer.

"I have been a loyal wife," she cried, hearing her own frantic tone rise.

"And what were you before?"

"A foolish girl!"

"You told him you were a maiden."

"I said no such thing."

"Then you allowed him to believe it, at least. Your guilt is the same."

"Omission is the same as lying?"

"His Majesty believes so. And not a soul in your family did anything to alter the perception, so great was the ambition of the Howards."

"I love the king!" Catherine wailed.

"You bedded your secretary."

"Before I was queen!"

There was a small silence. Cranmer bit his lip to stifle his victorious smile. "Thank you, my lady, for confirming what we already knew."

"You do not understand." She lurched forward, tumbling out of her chair, eyes shining with desperate tears. "Let me speak with the king! Please let me make him understand!"

He shook his head slowly in a show of feigned pity. "I am sorry, my lady. The king was most specific when I came here. He does not wish to see you."

She stiffened. "What does he wish?"

"Only for the truth. All of it."

The truth. That was a hornet's nest she could never explain, and one Henry would never understand. Frustration welled within her, choking her until she could not breathe. This was all a horrendous mistake. She had been a good wife. A faithful queen. She had never rebuffed him, never made him feel like anything but the youthful prince he had been once. Catherine needed to see him. If she could look into his eyes, she could make him understand, and he would forgive her.

But she needed a chance, a moment only.

Suddenly Catherine bolted for the door, her chair clattering behind her. Skirts gathered up in her hands, she sprinted out into the open gallery. One chance. That was all she had.

"Hal! Hal, please! Where are you?"

The cadence of footsteps behind her was heavy. Ominous. The

king's guard and the archbishop were advancing. She stopped, spun around, her eyes wide with panic. Tears slid down her face as she cried out in pure terror.

The hand on her shoulder was icy through the velvet.

"He is hunting, my lady. He cannot hear you. Alas, there is much more for us to speak of," said Cranmer. "By His Majesty's order, you have already lost your title, your money has been sealed, your jewels confiscated, and your household is to be disbanded. You would be wise to confess the full truth in your own words if you have any hope of saving your life or Lady Rochford's."

"Tell him!" Jane begged suddenly. "There is no other choice left to us!"

❖

As Henry limped through the gallery with Anne Basset beside him, he heard the whispers. He had not been meant to hear them, nor had he wished to. He had spent the day in the forest to escape them, but there would be no escape. *She is no better than Anne Boleyn*, they said.

Those ancient wounds had been cut open and were raw again.

But as Henry hobbled across the gallery, he heard something else. It was the unmistakable echo of Catherine's pleading cry. At first it surprised him, but anger, not sympathy, swelled in his heart. Catherine Howard was not his wife. She never had been, after all. He turned away from her call, taking Anne Basset's hand stubbornly in response.

After Cranmer had finished interrogating Catherine and Dereham, he came to Henry with Southampton, Wriothesley, Brandon and Seymour. There was not a hint of mirth on their faces. Henry knew what they wanted without asking.

"I went to the Tower to see Dereham this morning, Your Majesty," Cranmer announced dryly. "May we speak privately?"

Henry released Anne's grasp, leaving her behind as they continued on.

"How bad is it?"

Cranmer dared to touch his shoulder in a gesture of support as they walked. "I beg you, allow me to speak entirely alone with Your Majesty."

They went together into the small, private oratory inside the chapel within the palace walls. It was quiet and full of soft shadows. Cranmer closed the door.

"I know not how to tell you this, sire."

"Straight out, man. That is always the best way," he replied irritably. What more could there possibly be; what worse news than that the woman he had loved so dearly had lived a lie? "Have we proof for the annulment?"

"We do."

"So, he confessed?"

"To more, I am afraid, than we ever expected."

Henry lowered his gaze for a moment and said a small prayer for strength. He was not certain he could bear to hear that there were even more thorns on his precious rose.

"Out with it, Cranmer," he snarled.

"After I saw Dereham at the Tower, I went straight to Lady Catherine for confirmation. But alas, I did not need it, as the information had already been confirmed by several of her ladies."

Henry did not look up, and his tone was very low. His body knew instinctively how to protect itself from heartbreaking attack when he sensed its approach. He'd had a lifetime of it already.

"There was a reason Master Dereham was never a threat to Your Majesty here at court."

"Did their affair end before he arrived?" Henry asked.

"It did, sire, because there was someone else here, among your courtiers, who had succeeded Dereham in the queen's affections before he arrived from Horsham."

Henry drew in a labored breath, then exhaled. "Very well, Cranmer, tell me who it is."

❖

It was over. Everything Catherine had tried to balance for so long was taken from her. Cranmer had badgered her for hours upon hours, questioning her about every word she spoke. And the secretary scratched away on his vellum, recording it all.

She had not meant to involve Thomas, but Francis Dereham had already done so. Mary Lassells and Katherine Tilney had confirmed it. She knew there had been no point in the lie, so she had tried to explain. Her only hope had been to make the archbishop understand that she had never once dishonored her husband by having intercourse with another man during their marriage.

Her explanation had not been well received.

Shortly before her interrogation began, Jane was removed by guardsmen from the royal apartments. Catherine knew they wanted to see if her friend would corroborate her story.

Jane never returned.

Near midnight, Wriothesley had entered the privy chamber, where Catherine sat in the window embrasure, arms wrapped tightly around her knees, trying to hold in what was left of her sanity. She had listened with closed eyes as he had announced that, since she was no longer queen and would be removed from court, there was no longer need of her servants. The charge, he said blandly, would be treason. Only her sister Margaret and Lady Baynton were allowed to remain.

Cranmer had painted her as an adulteress, and she had tried desperately to deny it, but the archbishop layered the sordid details of her past like paint, which steadily covered her own version of the truth.

"Was Culpeper your lover or not?" he pressed for the third time, his voice brittle and threatening.

"My lord, I was *never* unfaithful to the king."

He arched a brow. "You did not meet him clandestinely on the back stairs?"

"We only spoke!"

"Did you not exchange glances while in the king's presence?"

She tried to press the panic back, but it was too powerful. "He was often in the presence of the king. I would acknowledge him, but that is all!"

"You did not refer to His Majesty's dear, trusted friend as your 'sweet fool'?"

Catherine's blood went absolutely cold. There was no one else in the world who knew her pet name for him besides Thomas. At that moment, she knew there was no escape. They knew everything. The opportunists, the Reformists, the vultures had won.

Dear Thomas, my heart, did they torture you to get you to tell them my name for you? she asked herself. *What have they done to you to make you betray me?* But she could not bear an answer. Cranmer had driven her, cleverly and methodically, to the very edge of sanity, from which she would fall if she knew the truth.

But, even so, her undoing came when Cranmer held a letter out to her. She saw her own writing, her own passionate plea, and her signature beneath the words:

Yours as long as life endures.

And so it was true. They had everything. She, Thomas and Lady Rochford were under arrest. And their fate was sealed.

She thought of him as she lay on the floor beneath the window, curled in a protective cocoon. He deserved so much better from this life.

Short is the joy that guilty pleasure brings.

The ancient quote, which had often fallen from her grandmother's lips, was strangely prophetic in hindsight.

Now that they had broken her, it was Wriothesley's turn to drive the first nail into her coffin. He loomed over her.

"You will leave by morning's light, my lady Catherine."

He did not expect a response and did not receive one, but her mind raced through a host of questions anyway.

Was she to be taken to the Tower?

Would she be sentenced to death?

Could Henry, an old, fat, bitter wreck of a man, whom she had nevertheless cared for, be so cruel as to refuse her side of the story?

Had Anne Boleyn felt this way on her swift journey to the block?

Had Anne tried to reason with the tyrant?

What had been her plea?

"You will take only your sister and Lord and Lady Baynton with you," Wriothesley added, breaking through her thoughts. There were too many things to weep for, and Catherine was certain she did not even know all of them yet. If Cranmer had his way, however, she would know them soon enough.

Take care, my greatest love, she thought. *Forgive me for loving you . . . and save yourself if you can.*

❖

Before Cranmer's final visit with Catherine, Thomas was brought into the king's presence, not in velvet or silks this time, but in a white muslin shirt and rough, gray wool pants, his hands bound by heavy chains. His wrists and hands had gone numb several hours ago.

Not so his heart, or his conscience.

He was responsible for all of this.

Despite the look of utter devastation on the king's face, Thomas did his best to bow to Henry.

"Spare me your false show of fidelity," Henry said with a voice so hollow and thin that Thomas was stunned.

The king's expression was blank, yet the advancing age and despair behind it were as clear as a cold moon in the winter sky. He sat hunched, his usually broad shoulders weak and rounded. His costume was gray and unadorned, like mourning attire. A single large candle burned on the table beside him, as if it were a last monument to something or someone. Perhaps it was, Thomas thought.

"I'll not ask you if it is true. There is too much evidence for you to deny. I do, though, want to hear you say how you could have betrayed not your king, but your friend. I trusted you, Tom."

Thomas felt the sting of Henry's words. Yet no matter what he said, Thomas knew he had already been tried and convicted. His sin was unforgivable.

"All of those months when I spoke with you about her . . . asked your advice . . . when I confided in you . . ." The words barely escaped the king's lips.

"It was over by then," Thomas reassured him.

"But you loved her."

"Yes."

It was all Henry needed to hear. "Take him."

Thomas did not look back as he was led away, chains cutting into his wrists. But when he came to the door, he paused for a moment. His soul would have found no rest if he had not.

"Have mercy on her, Henry, I bid you. She did love you."

He was not certain if the king had heard him over Henry's own sobs as the door slammed shut behind him.

❖

Syon Abbey, a building of ancient stone and ivy, stood in the massive shadow of Richmond Palace, the home of Anne of Cleves. Both were grand, imposing structures set along the same stretch of silvery, snaking river. But while one former queen thrived in one building, another waited in the other to face her end. Catherine saw the great difference in their fates, but also saw how their paths nearly touched.

Catherine rode on horseback, weak and defeated. Margaret, Lady Arundel, Lord Baynton and his wife, Isabel, rode silently and stoically beside her, along with a contingent of royal guards thick enough to prevent any thought of escape. But she had no desire to run. Her will was sapped, since she knew that Thomas had been taken to the Tower, as had Jane. Even the dowager duchess had been detained for her crimes, though the old woman's fate seemed uncertain. Catherine was to remain at Syon Abbey until her case could be heard. That was more consideration than Thomas, Jane or the duchess had received.

Catherine did not realize, at first, that the train had stopped until she saw the commotion. She could see one of the king's guards speaking with another who had ridden out from Richmond Palace. His tunic bore the emblem of Cleves. Catherine waited silently as the two men spoke back and forth. Finally, the guard went to Lord Baynton.

Catherine was completely ignored in their exchange.

"The princess of Cleves craves a word with the lady," the guard blandly announced. "Our orders were to see her directly to the abbey, but considering the lady's position as the king's good sister, we risk insulting her, and thereby His Majesty, if we do not pay our respects."

Catherine glanced at Isabel, but her long, slim face betrayed nothing. "They say you may have five minutes," she said evenly.

They advanced down a treelined causeway as the majestic palace, with its massive stables and outbuildings, blossomed into full view. There was a great deal of activity in the courtyard, horses being led by grooms and gardeners carrying flowers and greenery, as if it were any other day. Catherine was helped from her horse by someone in a cloak and hat whom she recognized as the Earl of Waldeck, Anne's aide.

"Her Grace knows you haven't much time," he said in his deep, thickly accented English. "She will meet with you in there." He pointed to the rounded, open side door to the stables. "You will have only a moment. It is all Her Grace dares risk."

A guardsman left Catherine at the door, and she was alone as she entered the small side room of the stables, which smelled strongly of horses and hay. A great shaft of sunlight filtered in from a small window near the roof. A moment later, Catherine heard soft footsteps.

She turned and completely lost what was left of her heart.

Catherine almost did not recognize him. Gone was the gorgeous courtier with the dazzling smile, the perfectly tousled hair and the costly wardrobe. The man who stood before her was beaten, his wrists chained. She went to him, a low, anguished sob tearing up her throat.

"Oh, look at you. . . ." She wept, wrapping her arms around Thomas as he bent for a moment to nestle his face against her hair.

"Look at us both. Yet you still smell of flowers."

His square, perfect jaw was bruised, and there was an open wound near his eye. She had known that his confession would not have been extracted from him with ease. But she did not want to waste a moment on details that did not matter now.

"How is this even possible?" she murmured.

"You were good to Her Grace. She never forgot," Thomas said gently.

"She told you that?"

"Her man, the one distracting the others, told me."

Catherine shook her head, unable to see through her tears. "But how did she even know? We were only ever discreet."

"Apparently the only one who did not know was the king."

"I was never unfaithful. You know that. I never meant to hurt him."

"Nor did I. I believe, somewhere in that wounded heart, he knows it. But Cranmer and the others have convinced him otherwise."

Tenderly, yet with all the love she had ever felt, Catherine pressed her lips to his. Bittersweet. Fateful. A final moment. "I love you," she whispered.

"And I will love you for all eternity."

She gently kissed his cheek, then his chin, where sweat and dried blood mingled.

"Only a moment more," a deep Teutonic accent warned from beyond the door.

Catherine tried to stop her sobbing, but it was impossible.

"I want you to know," Thomas said brokenly, "I do not regret anything, not a moment, even if it brings me death."

"Nor do I." She wept.

"Do you not believe in our Lord's heaven?"

"I do. Even now."

He tipped his head and tried his best to conjure that familiar smile. "Then we will meet there, all right? I shall be the one waiting for you to come and mend my broken heart."

He was doing his best to look brave, to be, as always, what she needed.

"I cannot bear this!"

"Be brave. It is not lost for you yet. You are going to the abbey, not the Tower. He still has time to reconsider."

"No!" she cried. "I have no wish to live in a world without you in it!"

Catherine was clinging to him when she felt a hand clamp on her shoulder. "I'm afraid it is time," the earl said.

Thomas pressed a kiss onto her cheek. "Don't cry. Please don't let that be my last vision of you."

"I cannot help it." She choked on a sob.

"We both can help it. Because we both know you did not actually betray him. Neither of us did."

"I did in my heart." Catherine wept. "I only truly loved *you*."

"But you were faithful to the king with your body. Go to your death bravely, if that is where the road leads you, as I shall go to mine."

The Earl of Waldeck began gently to pull her. "You must return to the courtyard. You have risked too much time here already."

"When do you leave?" she foolishly asked, knowing that the answer would torture her for as long as she lived.

"I am at Richmond only as long as you are. The princess of Cleves cannot risk detaining us any longer than that. Since it falls on the road to London, I do not think the king will question her if she says that one of the horses fell lame and needed to be changed."

Catherine pressed a final kiss onto his mouth, and Thomas kissed her back with all his passion.

"I adore you," she said, weeping.

"Meet me," he urged her with that same knowing smile. "I shall be first, so I will be waiting. Come to me in heaven, my love."

She felt hollow as they parted from each other, but she could not help but think to herself, *I regret nothing. I would not change a thing.*

These last moments were a gift. She would have thanked Anne, but she knew everything and everyone she touched from now on was at risk.

As the former queen rode on, Syon Abbey grew before her, a great, monolithic prison, and the palace of Richmond faded behind her. She had made her share of youthful mistakes, but she had also tried to be what everyone wanted her to be. For a single, shining moment, she believed she had been a glorious queen, and that everyone else's wishes were her own.

But her heart had remained true. She knew that God would see them together, for He knew that, of all the mistakes she had made, Thomas could never be counted among them.

History might judge her differently.

She held her head up to the sunlight, feeling its warmth through the wind as she rode toward the abbey. She refused to cry anymore. She refused defeat.

As she thought of Thomas and how soon they would meet again, she smiled.

Author's Note

$\mathcal{T}$homas Culpeper and Francis Dereham were tried for treason and were executed at Tyburn on December 10, 1541. Catherine Howard was subsequently tried and found guilty of adultery and high treason against the king. Owing to Henry VIII's affection for his youthful companion, Thomas was not drawn, quartered and disemboweled, as he might have been. Rather, for the crime of loving the king's wife, he was shown leniency and simply beheaded. Dereham was not shown the same mercy. Both of their heads were later put on display at London Bridge. Thomas Culpeper was subsequently buried in St. Sepulchre-Without-Newgate in London.

On February 13, 1542, Catherine was executed at Tower Green as Anne Boleyn had been just six years earlier. Just as her husband had been also six years before, Lady Rochford was beheaded, as well, having been found guilty of assisting the queen and Culpeper. Catherine Howard was buried near her cousin within the walls of the Tower beneath the altar pavement in the chapel royal.

As in each of my novels, I have taken great care in *The Queen's Mistake* to recount historical events as they occurred. Various subplots and the motivations of some secondary characters, where necessary, are fictionally enhanced. In this book the historical character Mary Lassells's story was combined with that of Joan Bulmer, another of the Horsham servants, for the sake of brevity. I have also modernized Catherine's single surviving letter to Thomas for clarity, and I have repeated the rumor that Henry VIII was the composer of the English folk song "Greensleeves," although this is disputed by scholars and it is believed to be Elizabethan in origin.

As she went to her death on the block at Tower Green, Catherine Howard staunchly maintained that she had never been unfaithful to Henry VIII during the time of their marriage. Her fervent pleas to meet privately with him went unanswered, and ghostly sightings have existed for centuries of Henry's fifth queen haunting the halls of Hampton Court, crying out, unanswered, for her husband's mercy.

On July 12, 1543, Henry married Katherine Parr, his sixth and final queen. Their marriage lasted four years, until his death on January 28, 1547, at the age of fifty-six.

—DH

Diane Haeger is the author of several novels of historical and women's fiction. She has a degree in English literature and an advanced degree in clinical psychology, which she credits with helping her bring to life complicated characters and their relationships. She lives in Newport Beach with her husband and children.

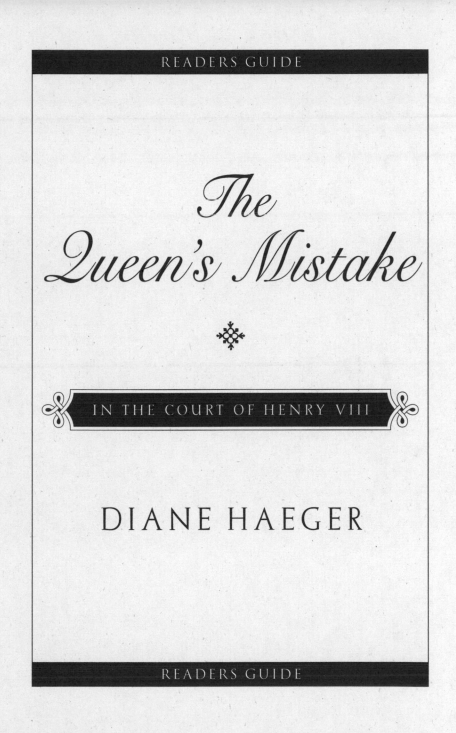

The Queen's Mistake

✣

IN THE COURT OF HENRY VIII

DIANE HAEGER

QUESTIONS
FOR DISCUSSION

1. Prior to reading *The Queen's Mistake*, what, if anything, did you know about Catherine Howard? Were there any aspects of her life that surprised you?

2. Discuss Catherine's relationships with Henry VIII and Thomas Culpepper. What attracted her to each man? How do you think she was able to juggle her feelings for both men simultaneously? Do you think that Catherine truly loved Henry?

3. At a young age, Catherine has consensual sexual relationships with several men, including Henry Manox, Francis Dereham, Gregory Cromwell, and Thomas Culpeper. Do you think her promiscuity was unique for that time period and a young girl of her class? What are the negative and positive effects of her sexual experience on her relationship with Henry VIII?

4. The Duke of Norfolk and Dowager Duchess Agnes Howard make many morally questionable choices throughout the novel, but they both claim that they have the best interests of their family at heart. Do you think this is true? If so, do you think their choices are justified by this claim? If not, what do you think their true motivations are?

5. Henry has deep misgivings about ordering the execution of Thomas Cromwell, especially after he discovers Catherine's indiscretions. Do you think his regret and his anger at the Duke of Norfolk and Stephen Gardiner contributed to his decision to execute Catherine?

6. In English history, it was not unheard of for future queens to serve in the households of the then-current queen, particularly in the court of Henry VIII. However, it was quite rare for these queens to have the friendly relationship of Anne of Cleves and Catherine Howard. (After all, Catherine of Aragon never warmed to Anne Boleyn when Anne was in her service.) What factors do you think made Anne of Cleves and Catherine Howard's relationship so unique?

7. Religion is one of the greatest forces in this story. What did you know about Catholic-Protestant relations in the Tudor era before you read this book? What role did religion play in Catherine's ascension to the throne and her downfall? What does each character have to gain by allying him/herself with a particular religion?

8. Mary Lassells and Francis Dereham start out as lowly country servants but both manage to rise from their humble roots and obtain positions at court. Although they are clearly portrayed as villains and play a role in Catherine's downfall, do you find their actions underhanded, or do you sympathize with their desire to better their situations? Do you think their ambitions are any dif-

ferent from Catherine's desire to help her family at the expense of Anne of Cleves and Thomas Cromwell?

9. Henry VIII has complicated feelings for each of his past wives and children. For instance, Henry continues to feel betrayed by Anne Boleyn long after her death, but several characters still refer to her as his greatest love. How do you imagine Henry would remember Catherine after her execution?

10. What do you think is the biggest mistake that Catherine made over the course of the novel? Do you think her mistake truly led to her downfall, or do you think the outcome of her story was inevitable?